D1435401

SLEEP

SLEEP

StoRiES

stephen
Dixon

COFFEE HOUSE PRESS
MINNEAPOLIS

The stories in this collection first appeared in the following periodicals, to which the author and the publisher extend their thanks: *Agni Review, Appearances, Boulevard, boundary 2, Carolina Quarterly, City Paper* (Baltimore), *Confrontation, Florida Review, Glimmer Train, Harper's, Iowa City Magazine, Literal Latté, Literary Review, Lowlands Review, Michigan Quarterly Review, Pequod, The Journal, Thin Air, Trafika, Transatlantic Review, Triquarterly,* and *Western Humanities Review.* "Sleep" also appeared in *The Best American Stories of 1996* (Houghton Mifflin).

Coffee House Press is supported in part by a grant provided by the Minnesota State Arts Board, through an appropriation by the Minnesota State Legislature, and in part by a grant from the National Endowment for the Arts. Significant support has also been provided by The McKnight Foundation; Lannan Foundation; Target Stores, Dayton's, and Mervyn's by the Dayton Hudson Foundation; General Mills Foundation; St. Paul Companies; Butler Family Foundation; Honeywell Foundation; Star Tribune Foundation; James R. Thorpe Foundation; Dain Bosworth Foundation; Pentair, Inc.; the law firm of Schwegman, Lundberg, Woessner & Kluth, P.A.; and many individual donors. To you and our many readers across the country, we send our thanks for your continuing support.

Coffee House Press books are available to the trade through our primary distributor, Consortium Book Sales & Distribution, 1045 Westgate Drive, Saint Paul, MN 55114. For personal orders, catalogs, or other information, write to: Coffee House Press, 27 North Fourth Street, Suite 400, Minneapolis, MN 55401. Good books are brewing at www.coffeehousepress.org.

LIBRARY OF CONGRESS CIP INFORMATION

Dixon, Stephen, 1936 –

    Sleep: stories / Stephen Dixon

      p.   cm.

     ISBN 1-56889-081-0 (alk. paper)

    1. United States—Social life and customs—20th century—Fiction.

I. Title.

PS3554.I92S59   1999

813'.54—dc21

98-56280

CIP

10 9 8 7 6 5 4 3 2 1

contents

To My Mother

the rehearsal

Red stops in the park to watch an opera rehearsal. A concert version of the opera will be given tonight on the acoustical shell stage where the rehearsal's taking place. Forty thousand people are expected to attend. The size and conduct of the audience will be compared favorably in the reviews with those of previous years. Most people will bring blankets and sit on the grass. A few hundred will bring chaise longues and collapsible chairs and put up with the complaints and groans of the people on blankets directly behind them. About half the crowd will have picnics before the opera begins. It will still be light then. Many champagne and wine bottles will be uncorked. Several groups will cook on hibachis. One group will have a six-foot-long hero sandwich delivered to it. The crowd surrounding this group will applaud the sandwich's two delivery boys. The sunset will illuminate the outlines of the westerly clouds. Someone will pump up and suspend above his party an orange weather balloon and during the performance blink a flashlight off it to indicate applause. An announcement will direct parents of lost children to the bowling green permit building in back of the audience. It will get dark. A little cool. Several of the infants brought along will begin to cry. Stray dogs will weave through the crowd scavenging for food. The orchestra and chorus will begin assembling on stage. All planes will have been rerouted around this section of the park. Only an occasional police helicopter will pass overhead. The conductor and cast will enter the stage and take their positions to an intensification of applause. The city's Recreational and Cultural Affairs administrator will address the audience. He'll thank the generous benefactors who make these free performances possible. He'll say the trailerized shell created especially for these concerts will henceforth be named the Sally in honor of the recently deceased woman who donated the funds to buy the trailer and build the shell. He'll urge everyone to fight the increasing whittling away of recreational and bucolic park space by commercial and uncivic-minded municipal interests and to pick up all litter as they leave. He'll say "Now let the city's third annual opera-in-the-park summer season begin." The National Anthem will be played. Then everybody on stage will sit and rise again and bow to the audience. All of them except the lead soprano will be dressed in white. The woman who plays Lucia will wear a salmon-colored gown designed for her for this performance by a noted couturier. She'll receive an ovation after her Mad Scene tonight that will oblige her to curtsy from five to seven times. Almost the entire audience will enjoy the opera and have a good time. Many will comment how lucky they are it didn't rain, as was forecast, and that the midafternoon thunderstorm didn't last long enough to make the ground too wet to sit on.

Now the cast sits at the front of the stage for the rehearsal. The tenor who plays Edgardo is dressed in an undershirt and blue dungarees. The baritone who plays Enrico wears Bermuda shorts and a fishnet polo shirt. The lead soprano wears a brown chino shorts and short-sleeved blouse outfit designed by the man who designed tonight's gown. She has a lot of makeup on her face. Perhaps to prevent a burn, as some sun has streaked across the stage near her feet. The conductor is dressed in a white shirt with French cuffs and unloosened tie and has on tinted glasses. He raises his baton. "Quiet, everyone," a voice over the loudspeaker says. The orchestra plays. "No, no, no," the conductor says. "Excuse me again, please, but I'm very sorry." The chorus stands behind the orchestra in a single row that extends the entire length of the back of the shell. Some hold librettos. Many unstick their blouses and skirts from their skins and wipe their faces, necks, and arms with hand- kerchiefs and towels. The conductor signals. The cast rises. They share three microphones: Lucia and Edgardo on one, Enrico has one for himself, Alisa and the three male soloists on the third. Edgardo and the chorus sing. Lucia looks out to the meadow. For a few seconds during her slow semicircling stare she settles her eyes on Red standing about thirty feet away in the sun. He's one of around fifty people watching the rehearsal on the grass. He was walking through the park to the library when he heard the music. He knew an opera was scheduled here for 8:30 tonight if it didn't rain. He's familiar with this opera and was planning to go alone to it at eight with a rub- ber poncho to sit on and a bottle of chilled white Bordeaux or at seven with a married couple and a half gallon of chilled rosé. The couple hadn't decided yet. The wife was a little ill this morning and the husband might be too tired after work, but if they go they'll bring the blanket, picnic service, and food. When Red heard the music he redirected his walk to the shell a quarter mile away where he knew the music must be coming from. He'd seen the shell being detached from its trailer the day before and some of its wiring installed. He thought he'd watch the rehearsal a few minutes, continue his walk to the library and later return home along a shadier park route and work and read till around six when he'd call his friends to see if they'd made up their minds to go. What he didn't know was that there'd be an opera rehearsal in the park today. He did know that on this same day next week this opera company will perform Pagliacci and two Rossini overtures to fill out the program, if it doesn't rain. If it does rain the performance will be given two days later. The tenor, after his famous aria about a clown who must make people laugh while his own heart is breaking, will bow and thank the audience from three to five times for its prolonged applause. Then the opera will resume. But that's next week. Now the soprano and her flute accompanist rehearse the Mad Scene aria. The conductor cuts them off halfway through and says "Save for tonight." The audience applauds the soprano. The flutist shakes the spit out of his flute. The soprano looks at Red, who's not applauding, and then at her wristwatch. Red looks at the temperature-time indicator at the top of an office building facing the park. It's 1:10. It's 89 degrees. In the shade or sun? Red's been here for twenty minutes. His back's getting soaked with sweat. The conductor points his baton at a man standing near Red who's holding a walkie-talkie. The man says into the speaker "How goes?" The voice that comes out of the walkie-talkie from a man who's waving a white cloth at the end of the meadow where the washrooms and main refreshment stand are and where most of the last thousand people will sit tonight, says "Sounds dandy back here, Chris, how goes it down middle and below?"

"Perfect," Chris says to the walkie-talkie. "A-one, everybody," to the conductor, flutist, soprano. She smiles, sits, glances at Red. Why? She's very pretty. He didn't think so at first. She bunches back her black hair and lets it drop to her shoulders. She slaps at a bug on the arm of the first violinist who's seated a little behind her. The violinist says something that makes her throw her head back and laugh. Edgardo says "What gives?" She tells him while patting the violinist's hand consolingly. Edgardo nods but doesn't smile. While Enrico asks Edgardo what everybody's getting so amused about, the conductor alerts the orchestra and chorus and the soprano looks at Red. He meets her look for the first time, just to see what she'll do. She turns away. He would have liked her to hold her look on him a second or two longer. A signal so to speak, not that he'd know what to do with it. But her immediately looking away from him was a signal also. Does it mean she'll avoid looking at him from now on? She might not want to give anyone the wrong impression or put false leads in his head. Does she think she recognizes him from some place? Or he looks so much like someone she knew or knows that she still can't believe her eyes. It would be nice to be somebody she knows. To be standing where he is and knowing he's the man she cares very much about or at least is beginning to. To sit on the grass tonight and know that that voice in the air's coming from that mouth way over there that very often meets his mouth or very often will. And after the opera to wait around for her while she changes her clothes. To have a sandwich and beer with her at an outdoor deli or café. To go home with her where she could say "Well, how do you think it went tonight?" Not at his home, which is small, dark, poorly furnished, depressing. Where he could reply "I thought your singing divine but your acting imperfect. For example the way you bumbled around the stage trying to pull your sword from your sheaf." "I don't have a sword. And it's a sheath, not a sheaf. And you're pitiful. Come here." He'd come here. "Now what's this about someone's sword in a sheath?" "Cymbals, cymbals, cymbals," he could say and gesture to show the homonymic difference. "Mouth organ, mouth organ, mouth organ," she looks like she could say. "Oh, I am very tired tonight. And two more Lucias in two more parks this week. But I thought my dress dramatic, didn't you? Contrasting against everyone's white, swept back by the wind. But how do I get out of tonight's performance? By saying I'm no longer Lucia, that's how. 'I'm no longer Lucia, that's how.' Let's see, I'm Gia Lardo and I'm with Red writer and he's got a sword in his sheath I'm now going to speak symbolically of and even trumpet and drum on about till he dares step into the next room with me before I flop asleep right here." It could go on like that. He could step into the next room with her. She could have several nice rooms in a clean attractive building as she's done very well in opera these past few years. Lead roles since she won this company's annual audition contest. He recently read that. Also: several opera recordings and she's signed up for more. And she was once a champion intercollegiate swimmer who almost got a place on the Olympic team and her apartment has a terrace overlooking one of the city's two rivers and this long narrow park. There could be trees and shrubbery and a round glass-top table on the terrace they could eat dinner on two to four times a week. She's looking at him. She's planning to sing Salome in Europe this summer and remove all seven veils. To wear only a bikini bottom underneath and maybe for one performance to wear nothing as the role was written to be played. It would be the first, the writer of last Sunday's newspaper interview said. "Maybe a second," she said, "our researcher on the subject's unsure." She's looking at him. How could he get to meet her? Chance encounter on the street. "Uh . . . how do you do?" It'll never take place. The two books he had under his arm he sets on the grass between his feet. The manuscript he held in his hand he tucks under his arm. The conductor taps the podium with his stick. She stands with the rest of the cast. She wears sandals. The rest of the cast wear sneakers or shoes. Her feet are small. "Quiet, please," the loudspeaker voice says. Her legs are lean but well-made. The orchestra plays. It's the sextet they're about to sing. They're not stopping halfway through. The crowd has about doubled since he came. He once knew someone in her company who might have known her well enough to ask her to meet a good friend. She isn't married. She told the interviewer she's waiting for the right fellow to come along. He's here. Someone not in opera, she said, as those marriages usually end up as great battles of ego or arrangements to further one another's careers. And then most male singers, helpful, talented, and sweet as they are, too often because of the concentration of operatic roles all their adult life, tend to become loud, melodramatic, and vague. If he were her fellow he'd

STEPHEN DIXON / SLEEP

somehow arrange to go to Europe with her this summer. They'd stay in a hotel in Salzburg where she's scheduled to sing for a week. He'd take his typewriter along. They'd drink unfamiliar wines, take cool mountain walks, visit Beethoven's birthplace or is it Mozart's? Beethoven's is in Bonn. People would recognize her name, maybe her face. Someone would call him Mr. Lardo. She'd hold his hand under a restaurant table when strangers asked for her autograph in languages he doesn't understand. She would. She's looking at him. Private jokes between them while eating about symbols and cymbals and sheaths and sheafs. He'd of course have to say what a better time he'd be having if he was able to pay for his whole trip by himself. She could say her talent is no more estimable than his. "It's just that I'm making more of a splash right now or there's a shortage of young coloraturas these days. One day you might be better paid for your work and I can be getting peanuts for mine. Voices can go. I can give you many examples, while your talent can't do anything but improve. But why worry about my spending for us if I don't? I really don't. Another fine talent you have is for ruining good things and one which I wish you'd quickly lose. Because no soprano who sings the roles I do for the company I sing for gets any less money than I. I don't much like making recordings but maybe in ten years I'll be glad I had. And bedridden people and oldsters are able to listen to opera that way. But don't let me get soap-opery. I can't even work in the park for nothing as there's something called minimum union scale. That's the way it is. Drink some more wine. And my salary's way above the scale. If you want I'll give it all away and for a while we'll both be poor. Won't that be fun? But it'll only be for a short time as I love learning new roles and lieder and singing before huge audiences and that brings in lots of bread. I think our food's getting cold. I love feeding a man sometimes. No more thoughts about filthy money tonight, all right? May I feed you with my fork? Nobody's looking. Even so. This restaurant's particularly uncrowded for one so good. Now open wide. Now isn't this more fun? Have some of the sausage also. Try removing the food without scratching your teeth on the prongs this time. You know how I am about such sounds. Is it still warm? Now we've eaten from the same fork. What does that symbolize do you think? Take another bite. A little sauerkraut and potatoes on my schnitzel this time. Wide again. Like a good little boy. You still have some sausage on your tongue. Pass it from your mouth to mine as we must always share."

She's looking at him again. Usually only gay men look at him as interested and often as that. If he saw her looking at him at a party that way he'd walk over to her despite knowing who she is. And say something, though what? Not "How do you do?" again, but why not? But he must find some way he can actually meet her. Maybe when the rehearsal's done. But how long will that be? It's very hot. So it isn't just a question of time. The sextet's over. The cast speak to each other about the fantastic acoustics for a field so large and with so few enclosing trees. They seem especially friendly to one another. Alisa asks whether it could be the tall buildings that surround the park. They totally ignored the people applauding them from the grass. Some from already established blanket positions for tonight. On top of these blankets near the fence which is a few feet from the stage are thermoses, baskets, ice chests, reading material, sweaters, radios, portable record players, adult board games, and playing cards. The unrolled picket fence defines the grounds around the shell. Inside the compound are three Mr. John portable outhouses, two house trailers, a canopied picnic table where some men are drinking canned soda or beer and playing checkers or chess. He could meet her at this side entrance where a guard sits on a high stool under a tree checking the people coming in. He could say as she leaves "Excuse me, Miss Lardo, but I was just thinking . . . I mean the truth is that before . . . in front . . . I was standing there . . . perhaps you saw me . . . holding some books and a manila envelope . . . a little to your right and about thirty feet out . . . next to the walkie-talkie man for a while . . . that you have a very . . . pretty . . . remarkable . . . voice." Oh god. No good. Give up. Tongue-tied mind. Think what the actual presentation would be like. "Excuse, Miss, I Lardo and . . ." She and Edgardo are singing. The conductor cuts them off near the end of the duet. "Sufficient," he says. The loud applause trickles off. A thin old man sitting on a newspaper, his back burned and cracked by the sun, continues to clap alone. She looks at him and then at Red with one eyebrow raised. As if questioning this man's reason for applauding so much or maybe Red's in some kind of comparison for not applauding at all. He feels it's too hot to applaud. And then he generally doesn't applaud at concerts, shows, operas when the performers enter the stage, after arias, between scenes, after acts and when the opera's over and the cast and then the conductor with the cast and then when the conductor points to the orchestra, stand, curtsy, and bow. Maybe she thinks he's being aloof or disdainful in withholding his applause. After all, she could be thinking, it isn't easy singing in this stifling heat. Though it's he who's in the sun and she in the shade. Maybe he's trying to make a statement that he's different from the herd, more discriminating with his applause. Acting for her on the grass as she in a sense has been singing for him on stage. But why? And if she is, then how come she always looks away from him each time he returns her stare? He might not be applauding simply because he's too bushed from the heat. Or still tired from some past physical work he's done. Not that he looks much like a laborer, though he is wearing what could be considered workman's shoes and clothes. Casual, a bit grubby, so unmodlike, not put on at all. But that's such a silly thing to say about someone's clothes because of course they're put on. Either by him or someone else for him if he can't dress himself, and he has no physical disabilities as far as she can see. Just the opposite in fact. And his face is pleasant and intelligent looking, though not far out with the hair or glasses like so many people these days. The words she uses. Far out. Put on. Too much! Too much is just another example of her child's vocabulary. Teenager's, rather, if she wants to get even closer in her . . . what? The word is what? Analogy's the word. And he's about thirty-two to four. An age she likes her male companions to be about, as they usually have the same identifying factors in life as she. Similar, she means. She means . . . what? Oh to be good with words. Someone with a similar frame of reference is what she means. Brought up during the last world war. Not radical or revolutionary in politics or social and moral beliefs. Raised on radio shows, Saturday afternoon movie shows, the great show of shows of family, public schools, church, and flag. God Bless America . . . the first song she can remember learning by heart. Belting it out solo before the school assembly the first recital she had. She wonders if he likes her voice. She hopes he's not an opera singer himself. That envelope. Does it contain composites, resumés, scores? His chest. Doesn't look like a singer's, though that's not saying he's not built well. She especially likes his arms. Long and strong. And his neck. As solid and thick as her thigh. And that cute rear end that time he turned. High and small like a dancer's, though he's too heavy and bulky on top to actually be one. And his hair which has receded like an extended widow's peak and probably makes him better looking than if it hadn't receded at all. But that beaten-up fat envelope. What mysteries does it enclose? Spoiled sandwiches, newspaper, more books, material swatches? But he doesn't smile. And never any applause. Part of his strength does he think? Don't delve into that again. Some people just don't applaud. Some very quiet and self-conscious people especially don't. And he looks like he'd be quiet and self-conscious with lots of people though lots of fun and very open with someone he particularly likes. Though how can she tell? These daydreams. These acoustical shell park dreams. Easier to pass the time with, perhaps, though so silly to think she knows what's in his head. But saying he was her man or something like that. Like that. Why not? Just her own moony game again. Standing where he's standing and admiring the people admiring her for the way she sings. Well, after the rehearsal she'd meet him at the gate for lunch. She'd bring the food and even the wine which she'd first chill in the trailer refrigerator used by the conductor and the cast. They'd have it under a wide spreading tree. On thick big grass. Where there was no garbage around. Few people around. And she'd drink mostly iced tea since she wants her head extra clear for tonight. One sandwich for her, two for him. Cole slaw or macaroni salad she'd have made the previous night. And they'd lie on the blanket after she put everything away. She'd play with his hair. Bust up the peak. Run her finger around his lips, something she likes to do. And stick one finger in his mouth between the times he sips from his glass. A good wine glass with a long stem on it though one she wouldn't miss if it broke. He'd suck her finger. Something she likes done. And kiss her lips. Their mouths wide open. His tasting from wine. Tongues touching. What's she saying? Hers from iced mint tea. He looks like he'd like picnics with wine and fooling around some on the grass. Like he'd want to see her every day for months. Maybe marry her in a year. Who'd object to the tons of money she makes and high standard of living she keeps but who'd eventually know there's no escaping the way she lives. And have a child by her. Does he also think it's about time he had one? Such a fine looking boy it'd be. The rapturous parents with baby girl. Picnics with iced tea, formulas and wine. Now with the infant crawling off nowhere fast on the grass. And especially nonworking days when she could get as wine-woozy as she wants and where they'd return to her flat and put the child in the crib to nap and open the windows to get more of a breeze or lower it so they wouldn't start to sneeze and they'd settle down on her giant bed. How do people really meet? The men at parties of late have all been such frauds or drags. She hates even going out with them. She'd just like to stay home with her gentle intelligent man. It's been so long. Where'd he go? Gone like that. Most likely back to work or home. There he is. Getting an ice cream from the ice cream cart. It looks like the Red, White, and Blueberry flavor he's unwrapping, in honor of the upcoming Independence Day. He sticks the wrapper in his pocket. Bites into the pop. It's still too cold and hard. What a cute disgruntled face he made. He looks at her. She gives him a straight stare back. In honor of the upcoming Independence Day? How else to give a quiet self-conscious man courage? He looks away. He's not very brave. That's all right. It means he probably won't hurt anyone. Should she smile at him next time he looks? But that might just be enough to scare him away. And why's she so sure he's even interested in her? Maybe he's just curious why she keeps looking his way. She should really have more class. He's probably married. Three kids and a sublime adoring wife. What the hell ever got into her? Just another fantasy she's coasted onto some rocks. Though maybe with enough subtle encouragement from her he'll come to the gate when rehearsal's over, which shouldn't be too long from now. And say something such as how difficult introductions are under these circumstances, which might take more courage than she thinks he has. But it's up to him. Though it could be up to her. She could easily. Not easily, but she could, after the rehearsal, go up to him where he is, or around the side where he might go, and say something obvious though bendable enough to get out of, such as "I've been looking at you from the stage . . . I'm sure you noticed that . . . and I hope I haven't made you feel uncomfortable with my looks, I mean my stares . . . but I swear I know you from some place . . . ridiculous as that sentence must sound to you in its reversed gender state . . . but I swear . . . from maybe fifteen to twenty years ago . . . it's not that I never forget a face . . . I in fact forget most . . . but yours? . . . even the way you stand . . . I grew up downtown, you see . . . ." And what would be the difference if he said he was brought up uptown, out of town, halfway around the world, that this is his first visit to the city and he's only been here a day? Because if he acted in any way irrational or effeminate or intimated he's married, then she'd say "Then I guess I was wrong." That's all. "Wrong." And excuse herself and return to the compound. He'd never suspect. She'd be safe there once past the guard. If he did suspect then he'd just have to be honest to himself and think "She was interested in me till I opened my mouth, but that's the way things go." She could do all that. He's biting the ice cream. It doesn't always have to be up to the man. It's soft enough now. And if her words worked to the point where they got something going for themselves, then this whole embarrassing first meeting would only seem funny and harmless to them later on. He's smiling. At a child crying as it tries climbing out of its stroller. For the first time since she took notice of him. At the nurse having so much trouble trying to get the child back in. Then at her. She smiles back. They can both smile very easily when it comes to kids. She looks away. The ice's been broken. Nothing irrational or effeminate about him that she can see. If he's still around after rehearsal she's definitely going up to him if he doesn't approach her. She hopes he doesn't think it'll go on till tonight. If he does he'll probably leave. Everything is so much a matter of chance.

"Is everything all right?" the conductor says to the man with the walkie-talkie. The man says "All right by me." "And what about the little man inside your machine there?" the conductor says, waving his baton at the walkie-talkie. "He says everything's all right too." "Then we are ended with the rehearsal, okay?" "Okay by me, maestro," the man says. The conductor leaves the stage. The chorus begins filing out of the two exits in back. The musicians start packing their instruments and covering up the larger ones and leaving the stage through the shell's middle exit. The soloists are standing. Enrico adjusts his mike. Edgardo is tying his sneakers. The workmen walk across the stage dragging thick wires attached to the generator on the grass. Miss Lardo talks to the violinist who made her laugh before. She throws her head back and laughs out loud at something he says. She has a habit of running her hand across her forehead to brush away stray hairs from her eyes. She looks at Red. She smiles at him, pats the arm of the violinist and makes her way around the abandoned music stands and chairs to the middle exit. Red walks to the side she's coming out of. He waits near the gate where the guard sits. He'll start off with a compliment if she does walk past this gate. The words will come. Her smiles before were sure signs. All he can do is try. All she can be is polite and say thanks. And then, if nobody else is around. But of course other people will be around. She's the lead. She might walk out with an entourage. Even if there are other people around, though not if she's on the arm of a man or with a man she obviously cares for very much, he'll say "I realize, Miss Lardo,"—this will be after his opening compliment about her singing—"you must be extremely busy and all . . . and maybe what I'm about to say will sound presumptuous if not even improper to you . . . but I was wondering if you wouldn't like to have an iced tea with me or even a hot tea or coffee or some cold sangria at the park's fountain café which is barely a five minute walk from here." All she can do is say yes or no or she'd like to but no thanks or thanks for the invitation but she's quite tired or busy or not feeling so well or has a previous engagement or has to see her designer about tonight's dress or go to a hall to rehearse next week's opera or to her agent's about her European tour or she really must go, run, hurry, sorry, but thanks nevertheless. She might even say "Maybe some other time." He could then say "That'll be tough arranging unless we make it a specific time. How about tomorrow around now or perhaps for lunch at the café if you'd like?" She's talking to Alisa as they walk down the shell's exit steps some hundred feet away. She looks at the gate. He turns away. She's going to change her mind. He's getting cold feet. She's

STEPHEN DIXON / SLEEP

going to think he's standing there too conspicuously for her. He doesn't know what to do. She's walking along the path between the grass that leads to the gate. Does she really have to leave the compound or is she walking to the exit just for him? Maybe she'll stop along the path to make a right or left to some other place. Maybe she's walking on the path because it's easier on her sandals than the grass. Though he'd think the grass would be easier to walk on. Less springy and dirty and no wood chips to get lodged between her toes and between her foot and the sandal sole. The iced tea or sangria might be just what she wants. Will he soon find out? She's still walking along the path. His stomach aches. Getting the proverbial hemmed-in flapping wings again as he did with girls when he was a boy. His back faces the path. Is it just the stance she needs to put her in reverse? Listen, she could be thinking, if she can walk to the entrance so he can say what she thinks he wants to say, then he can stay and wait for her. That's what he hopes she's thinking. It's rough on both of us but we'll know soon enough, she could be thinking, he's thinking. Don't fall to pieces and fly out of here at the last moment, she could be thinking, he's thinking. Besides, she could be thinking, he's thinking, skipping off like that might embarrass me or worry me or do something to me and then I'm sure for the next few days you'll regret not having carried your plan through. He turns around. She's standing ten feet away. The guard's paring his nails. She's talking to the acoustician from before. She smiles. The acoustician laughs. The walkie-talkie voice says "I'm coming in now, Chris, all right?" Chris says into it "Right." She kisses Chris's cheek while the walkie-talkie's still by his lips. "No hanky-panky on the job now, Chris," the walkie-talkie voice say. Chris breaks up. She squeezes his fingers and winks good-bye. She continues to the exit alone. She looks at Red. Chris starts back to the shell. The guard's clipping his nails. Chris is stopped by the flute accompanist. Both look at Miss Lardo from the rear. "Don't I know," Chris says, fanning his face with his hands. She's at the exit. Red approaches her. What will he say? What will she say to what he says? Now's no time for such thoughts. But she'll think him so dumb. "Miss Lardo," he wants to say, "I feel I want to faint." Does she want him to be honest? Then "Miss Lardo," he whispers very low to her through a whistle hole, "I feel like I just might faint." The whole thing's too risky. She might say "Excuse me?" in a way to make him appear menacing to whoever's around. The guard might say "Is this man bothering you, Miss Lardo?" just to show he's on the ball and doing his job. Passersby might look at him disparagingly, threateningly, say something also. "Very nice," the guard says to her. "I was listening from my seat here and you sang prettily like a bird." "Miss Lardo?" Red says. She's past the gate. "Thank you, Jeff," she says to the guard. "Miss Lardo?" Red says. She looks at him as if for the first time. Why is this unfamiliar face saying this her face seems to say. "Pardon me?" she says. The guard looks at them. The flutist runs past saying "See you tonight, Gia." She waves at the flutist while looking at Red. "Pardon me?"

"I . . . well this might sound absurd to you, even extraordinary. Well, not extraordinary. Maybe not even absurd. But first off, I thought your singing before was very beautiful."

"Thank you."

"You've of course heard inane compliments like that hundreds of times before."

"Inane or not, they're always nice to hear. I don't knock them."

"I don't sing myself, you understand."

"You're much better off."

"Except maybe when I'm alone and walking through the park at nights. Not that I spend all my time walking through the park singing, mind you, though I do do it sometimes."

"This is beginning to sound a little bewildering to me."

"What I meant was that I don't want to give the impression I stalk around parks at night. That's not what I do. Neither did I want to give the impression that I don't walk through the park singing at night, which I sometimes do. But sometimes when I walk through the park—let's say, to the opera you're in tonight—well then, if nobody's around, within earshot I mean, I'll often sing to myself, though aloud, and very often melodies from opera, like the sextet aria just before, though with my own meaningless improvised words instead of the actual Italian ones. But this is getting equally confusing to me, which must be evident to you."

"Don't worry so much about impressions then."

"It was very hot out there watching you from the grass."

"I'm sure. I don't see how you people could stand the heat. And the ones who'll be waiting till tonight. But it is kind of hot standing even here."

They're in the sun. The guard's in the shade. The guard was listening to their conversation but resumes clipping his nails. A few people linger around them. Some of them watched the end of the rehearsal. All of them seem eager to get close to Miss Lardo to see what she's like offstage. One woman holds a pen and the libretto for Lucia di Lammermoor. She seems to be waiting for a chance to ask Miss Lardo to sign it. Miss Lardo bunches back her hair and lets it drop to her shoulders. The man's smiling and pointing to his throat. The woman asks Miss Lardo if she would please sign the libretto. Miss Lardo takes the pen and begins to sign her name on the back of the libretto. The woman says "Could you please sign it here, above the name Lucia, on the front?" Miss Lardo signs her name where the woman's finger was. The woman says "Thank you very much, Miss Lardo. I think you have one of the finer voices in the world, bar none." Miss Lardo says "Thank you." The woman walks away. Miss Lardo seems to point out the man's nervous foot movements to him. He lifts his shoulders as if to say there's nothing he can do about it and points to his belly. They speak. Most of their conversation can't be overheard. Just parts of it such as both of them saying "Why not?" She first. He second. She goes past the gate. The guard says

"Forget something, Miss Lardo?" She says "Yes." She heads for the trailer. "I hope it wasn't anything important," the guard says. For a few feet she runs to the trailer. While she's inside it the man seems to study the ground around him. He kicks a stone which bounces past the gate entrance. The guard looks at the stone till it stops and then at the man. The man's reading from one of his books. Then he closes the book, his finger between the pages he was reading from. She comes out of the trailer. She's wearing a skirt over her shorts. The skirt is the same material as the shorts and blouse. She walks quickly to the gate. The man's looking up at the tree the guard sits under. The guard's filing his nails. A bird's in the tree singing. The man's looking at the bird flying away when she comes up behind him and says "Surprise." Her hair is bound in back with a rubber band. She's removed all her makeup. She's carrying a tote bag. "That didn't take long," he says. He points to the limb the bird was on. "All birds are——" something, he says. "All birds?" she says. "Well certainly not every single one of them, but I'd say just about most." "Even there." "You still don't agree?" She shakes her head. He shrugs his shoulders. She looks at her watch. He looks at his feet, her feet. "You see when you said all birds I immediately though of magpies, grackles, crows, hawks and I don't know how many else." "I wasn't even thinking of them as birds," he says. "They're birds." "I stand corrected." "I didn't mean it like that." "Anyway I do." "Then if you do you do." She looks back at the stage. "I don't know if you still want to," he says. She says "What?" He points to the area where the park fountain café is. They walk in that direction together.

on a windy night

He's at the dinner table talking to his wife, their daughter's sitting between them and says to him "May I be excused?" and he says "How come you always ask me?" and she says "I don't always; I just did this time and some times before. May I?" and he says "Well, I don't know," glancing at her plate, "this is a pretty big decision and not so easy for one person to decide," and looks at his wife and she indicates Irene's done well enough with her dinner, and says to Irene "Okay, Mommy and I think you did all right, not too much spread around your plate to make it appear you ate almost everything," and she stands and he says "Please bring your plate and stuff into the kitchen?" and she does and goes to the piano at the far end of the next room and sits at it and he wants to resume the conversation with his wife, the subject was the mortar shelling two days ago of an elementary school in a large city in Central America, there hadn't been classes in it for months but children were playing in the school playground and some ten of them were killed, he said the national forces should go in and bomb the shit out of the bastards that shelled the city, she said that'll only lead to more shelling and bombing and killing of kids and soldiers who are just kids and who knows what else,

"Then what are they going to do about it," he said, "nothing?" which was when Irene asked if she could leave the table, now he says to his wife "What were we talking of before . . . you know, just before she—" and she says "Better we drop it, it was much too depressing, as things always are when the subject's suffering and there are no answers to it except more of the same and possibly even worse, though I don't know what could be worse than the incident we were talking about," and he says "Oh yeah, now I remember, you think it's what drove her away from the table?—maybe it was, and my cursing; she hates it, particularly the word 'shit,'" time's around 7:30, month's January, the end of it and it's very cold outside, approaching zero degrees and it'll probably be minus ten by morning, record of Hadyn piano sonatas and variations that was playing in the next room just ended, he thinks of getting up and turning it over even if he played the other side during the first part of dinner, though he missed most of it because of their conversation, when Irene starts playing the piano. Of course, he thinks, she sat down at it so why wouldn't he think she was going to play? Well, because she knows they don't like her playing while they're still eating. Either she sits at the table till all three of them are done, they've told her, or she does something quiet in the living room, like reading or drawing, or whatever she wants to do in any other place in the house so long as it's not something noisy or doesn't involve a lot of running around after she just had her dinner. Should he tell her to stop? Did she wait till the record was over before she started playing? It's a nice piece, though, mostly on the high keys but with occasional notes in the middle and bottom octaves and seems to be the most advanced and complicated one she's played, and he says "What's that you're playing, Irene? Irene?" and his wife says "Shh," smiling, finger over her lips and he mouths "Of course." The piece ends. It took about a minute, maybe a minute and a half, and she immediately starts playing it again. The piano's an upright, one his wife's grandfather gave

her when she was Irene's age, or a few years older: twelve, he
thinks she said, and less than a year later she stopped taking
piano lessons and took up ballet. "Maybe because you suddenly had this big responsibility of owning your own new
piano and you felt you could never live up to using it—that
happened to me with an expensive paint set my mother
bought me," and she said "Maybe that was it." Irene continues
to play and he looks at her and listens and doesn't know what
but something happens to him, he gets lost in it, thinks she has
such a lovely light touch, he's never heard her play better, but
more than that, there's something much more than that, what
is it? This has got to be one of the most beautiful moments in
his life, he thinks, he doesn't know why that is. Maybe the
calmness of the whole thing or something, her serious look
and way she's sitting so erect, studious way she looks at the
music book, certainly because it's his daughter playing and so
well and that it seems like a difficult piece, especially for someone so young with only a couple years of lessons, and that she's
reading the music rather than playing it from memory, he forgot that she could, and the piece is a slow sweet one and all
those high keys and she seems to love playing it and that she's
doing it only for herself, now a third or fourth time and each
time as delicately and where the piece seems as pretty and
sweet. And other things: soft light from the side table lamp
beside her lighting up her hair, that he's sitting here so comfortable after dinner, wine in his hand, and he sets the glass
down, lifts and sips it and sets it down again, his wife across
from him and both silently agreeing not to spoil the moment,
that it is—he can tell by the way she's staring at Irene, elbow
on the table and hand holding up her chin, eyes never off her
and with this wistful pensive look—something special for her
too, and that it's so cold out, treacherous, even, with all the ice
around the house, couldn't get his car out of the port now if he
tried, so they're sort of stuck here for the night, not that they'd
be going anyplace unless there was an emergency, yet warm

inside, the room what? 65? 66?, anyway, an ideal temperature, not too warm or cool, fire in the living room fireplace out but that's all right, nice glow from it gone but the crackle of the fire might interfere with the sound of Irene's playing, but his thoughts are interfering with his just taking in the whole thing, so he'll stop. He listens till she's finished. Then she gets up, turns around and bows in their direction but without noticing them it seems, so she's probably been rehearsing for a music school recital coming up, and goes back to the table, seemingly oblivious she's been watched. "Sweetheart, what was the name of that piece?" he asks after she sits, his wife resuming eating her salad, Irene picking a roll crumb off her place mat and about to put it in her mouth and she says "'On a Windy Night.'" "'A Windy Night'? But it was so slow and sad-like and tinkly. You'd think it'd have some title like 'Falling Leaves' or 'Distant Chimes' or something." "No, 'On a Windy Night.' That's because the wind, it's moving things back and forth, the trees swinging with it—I mean, pushed by the wind. Oh, I can't explain it. Here," and she runs to the piano, gets the music book and runs back and opens it to "On a Windy Night." "See—the words down here; it's a song as well as music," and she sings "'Over and over I hear a soft crying, down by the river the wind is sighing.' So there's the wind, pushing the willows and stuff. I thought so first too what you said, but Miss Rose told me," and he says "So you're playing that piece for a recital pretty soon, right?" and she says "Friday. You didn't see the paper they gave me for it? It's on the refrigerator. And 'Old Abe Lincoln.'" "How's that go?" and she says "Faster and louder, like logs being chopped by a tall strong man." "You played very well—didn't she, Bea?" he says to his wife and she says "Gloriously. I've never heard you play so well, dear," and he says "Same here. It was beautiful. I was very moved," and Irene says "Moved?" and he says "You know, touched, *here,* the heart," jabbing his chest. "And almost to tears—I mean, my eyes. Your playing and the music did it but especially your playing. And to see you doing it so well, hearing you, watching you, I'm telling you, my darling, it was one of the most beautiful moments in my life. I'm sure I'll remember it always," and she says "Oh no you won't," and Bea says "You're supposed to say 'thank you' or simply nod modestly or say nothing and look away. That was quite the compliment, and I feel the same as Daddy," and he says "Nah, she doesn't have to respond in any way to what I said. I'm saying thanks to her for the experience. I don't know what it means to me," to Irene, "so you can't know what it means, and that's the way it should be. You're a real pianist and you're playing real music—music that touches us with its sounds and whatever the rest of what music gives," and she says "No I'm not, and it's a kid's piece. I'm not even playing two years now," and he says "So?"

She takes a music book out of the piano bench, sits at the piano and plays a Brahms intermezzo she learned about twenty years ago. She's out of practice and the piece doesn't come out right. She has this piano and she should use it more. She used to get so much enjoyment from playing. No one had to force her to practice or play or even remind her. One, two hours a day she was usually at it. A half-hour, maybe, and on weekends, at the most one. In fact, that was her parents' approach: She didn't want to practice or play, so be it; she never wanted to take another lesson or even sit down at the piano again, that was her choice. She loved her two piano teachers when she was young, Miss Rose and Miss Beth. Such nice people and they loved children and were never strict or critical or anything like it and they gave her presents on her birthday and Christmas and after recitals and every so often stuck candy in her coat pocket as she was leaving and she always liked talking to them about different things if they had time. Her son doesn't want to have anything to do with the piano. She's tried to get him to take lessons but he says he hates the piano, all instruments that look serious, but the piano, upright or baby grand, he thinks is a particularly ugly one and he also hates the sound of it and that it takes up so much space in their little living room. "I like to listen to the guitar and drums sometimes," he's said, "but I'm definitely not a music person." Too bad, for when he sings he shows he has a good ear, besides a lovely voice, so why doesn't he give the piano or any kind of instrument, even the voice, a chance? She plays part of a Chopin mazurka from memory and it sounds better than the Brahms piece but it isn't one-fifth as good as she once played it. And up till a few years ago she was playing Chopin ballades, scherzos, an etude or two of Debussy's and some of the more difficult pieces by Satie. Suddenly she has a memory of her father. He was at the dinner table with her mother. It's her fondest memory of him, she's had it a dozen times at least, but not for years. She has many fond memories of her mother but this one is of her father. He was drinking beer or wine, maybe he was a little high from it, now that she realizes, but he didn't speak as if he were, or the way she remembers it, and he didn't look it either—the picture in her head she has—and it was too early in the evening for him to be high, at the end of dinner, and what's she talking about for she can't remember ever seeing him even a bit tipsy except at her grandparents' fiftieth wedding anniversary. Then he got plastered and had to be driven home and put to bed. Anyway, her parents were having dessert, she thinks—that part she really forgets, though she once remembered it. She was playing the piano in the living room, practicing for her lesson in a day or two, probably. She remembers the name of the piece: "On a Wintry Night." And it might have been winter also, for she remembers a fire in the fireplace and he only started one on his own when it was very cold in the house, so, freezing outside, and he wanted to save on the heat. He didn't much light them for aesthetic reasons, he said a number of times, except when her mother asked him to. Her mother loved fires, and for any reason. In Maine where they went for a few summers she liked them first thing in the morning in the cook stove and early evening in the fireplace when it wasn't even cold out, just cool. But he was never as nice to her as on that night when she was playing the piano, which is probably why the incident stuck and memory of it stayed. At least she can't remember him ever being so nice, complimentary and polite all at the same time. He said she looked beautiful and that she played very well. Usually he ignored saying what he thought she looked like unless she asked. He didn't like complimenting her too much because he thought it would go to her head and wouldn't really do anything for her but make her feel good for the moment. He used to say good looks can be useful but aren't important, it's what's under the pects and skull that count. Not an original or clever thought or even an inventive turn of phrase, except for the pects, but what he said. But she's getting away from it. The wintry night, her playing. He left the table and quietly sat beside her on the bench and when she looked up at him, while she was between pieces or just during a momentary lull in her playing, he looked, how should she call it? uncustomarily gently at her and said in this servile soft voice, she's almost sure that was it, "I'm sorry, do you mind my sitting next to you? Will it disturb your playing? If it does or you do mind for whatever reason, I'll go"—something like that, and just as something-like-that she said "No, you can stay if you want, I don't care." So she played some more, practicing for her lesson the next day—had to be that, for she rarely practiced much except on the day before her lesson and sometimes only on that lesson day, at least when she was that age, which was eight, two years after she'd started piano lessons. So she played and forgot he was there and it was "On a Wintry Night," or maybe "On a Winter's Night," or "wintery," which was a strong piece, she remembers, evoking a blustery winter's night, probably—stormy, even—and after she finished she realized he was still beside her and she turned to him, wanting some sort of response to her playing,

STEPHEN DIXON / SLEEP

probably, and he was crying. She said "What's wrong, something hurt?" and he said "No, it's you, my darling. You looked so beautiful playing, I couldn't take my eyes off you. Of course I always knew you were a doll, but I never saw before just how beautiful you are." She said something like "Thank you" or "Oh please"—anyway, something modest and short, which is what her parents told her to do when she got a big compliment, and then to look away so the person wouldn't think she wanted more and also that was a way of ending the subject or just getting the attention off her, and he said, and this she remembers distinctly, "Believe me, sweetie, the pleasure's all mine." A little while later, both still on the bench, she said "How about my playing, was it at least a little okay?" and he said "It was good, very good. In fact, very very good. I don't see how you could've been better. You play so well and have such poise at the piano, like a real budding concert artist. But what was the name of the thing you played? I want to remember it and this moment, and also in case I want to ask you to play it again." "'On a Wintry Night,'" and he said "Good, appropriate, it sounds like what it says it is, wintry, with lots of ice on the trees and heavy falling snow." Then he kissed her forehead and with her eyes closed, she remembers, she thought she had never loved him more than she was loving him now. And now she thinks that hasn't changed: she loved him a lot in her life but never so much as that moment, nor does she think he ever loved her as much, or showed it to her, as that one time. Then, which had to be just a short time later, she said "Want me to play some more songs I learned in piano class?" and he said "Sure, play them, I'll sit back at the table and listen." Or did he say "Play as many as you want, dear, but I'm going back to the table to talk with Mommy again"? Or maybe—she suddenly thinks this is it—she didn't ask if he wanted to hear her play more; she just played, and he got up, maybe said something like "Excuse me, sweetie," and went back to the table or somewhere else in the house. Anyway, that

STEPHEN DIXON / SLEEP

was some moment for her. She wishes there had been a lot more as deep and binding or something like that between them, or one that just combined his look with what he said and voice he said it in that time and where he was sitting or standing so close.

When his daughter asks him "What's the one memory of yours that stands out more than any other, or maybe you don't have one?" he says "No, there's one, I'm sure I've told you it, but the funny thing about it is that it's only half mine in a way, or whatever percentage you want to give it. Not 'percentage'; that's for percentages. But 'part, slice, cut.' Anyway, it's the memory of my mother telling me of the deepest one she had. I can sort of understand why it's her most vivid memory, or one of, though she said 'most,' but I don't know why her telling me it is the most vivid one I've had. But it is and it's stayed that way it seems forever, and I'm sure I've thought of it a good hundred times." "So what is it?" she says and he says "Gosh, I forget. No, only kidding. She's at the piano and her parents are at the dinner table. She's ten or so, maybe eleven, she said, and she's been playing the piano for three to four years, so by that time, and because she loved the instrument, she was pretty good. She said she didn't know why but when she was in the middle of dinner with them she all of a sudden had an urge to play. She thought it might have been because she'd been bad a little earlier that day, or her parents thought she had—you know, disobedient, that's all, for she was usually a very good child—and she wanted to entertain them somehow with her playing. Entertain? Amuse—you know; make them feel good. So she got up and went to the piano, no 'excuse me,' nothing like that—to play, she said, a very slow sweet piece for them. To sort of mollify them toward her with the sweetness and softness of the piece and . . . or what she thought was. . . . Not 'mollify.' Calm them, let's say; lighten the evening for them with her piano entertainment, but in the end—as a result of her playing—toward her and for themselves. Oh, I'm getting mixed up on this . . . but for her to just make things sweet for them, everything. But her father yelled out 'Where do you think you're going, young lady?'—I threw in the 'young lady,' for I don't know how he addressed her, then or anytime. And she said 'I only want to play for a minute,' and sat down on the piano bench—stool?—bench, and took out her composition book—whatever they call those music books with the pieces of music in them, the music pieces." "Music book," his daughter says; "that's what I call mine." "Okay, music book, and opened it to a composition called 'On a Winter's Night,' I believe, and started playing. Yes, definitely, I remember: 'On a Winter's Night.' You wouldn't have come across that same piece in one of yours, huh?" "I don't remember it," she says. "Just, if you did have it . . . Anyway, her father said 'Now listen, you, come back, you're not done with dinner. And your hands are dirty from the food—greasy—and you'll get grease on the keys and you're disobeying me besides. Play all you want, so long as it's not banging, after you finish dinner, but not now.' But she continued to play. He must've been saying 'Do you hear me, do you hear me!' You know how fathers are. But she said it was a situation where either she couldn't win if she returned to the table, for by now they'd be even angrier at her, at least her father, but she might win if she stayed and played and the music appeased him and—pacified him, I mean, calmed him down. Her mother said nothing. You never met her, she was a wonderful person, but her philosophy was that if two people have a dispute, let them work it out together till fireworks erupt; that before then, a third party should only butt in if asked. So . . . so, well, she continued playing and he got up and she could hear him throwing his chair back and she thought 'Oh my God, he's really angry,' but she kept playing this sweet piece, still hoping to win him over with the music while also calming him with it." "What do you mean?" his daughter says and he says "Why, wasn't that clear? Anyway, not important, because the music must've done what she thought it would. For after this very short piece was over—it might've taken three minutes, she said—she looked around, half expecting him to tear her off the piano bench, but he was back sitting at the table, smiling at her with this adoring smile she'd almost never seen on him before and then applauding quietly. 'That was beautiful,' he said. 'As beautiful a playing of a piano piece as I think I've ever heard. Sure, some of that feeling from me comes because you're my daughter, so I wanted to think those things. But I didn't know you had such talent. Even better, such love for the piano and music. Better than that, even, that you had such a gift for playing. For that's what you have, I swear to you and without exaggeration: a gift. If your intention was to calm me somewhat, you succeeded beyond everything. If it was also to get me to say what a beautiful child I have, you succeeded there too. I was deeply moved. Would you play the same piece for me again and then once more?' She couldn't believe it, she told me. She'd never seen such a quick change in him, at least from the bad to the good. And at first she really didn't believe it. She thought he might be setting her up—you know, tricking her; getting her to feel great about herself with these compliments and then after she played the piece a couple more times, saying 'And you thought that was good? What a laugh! It stunk to high heaven. You'd believe anything I'd say if it made you feel good. Boy, what power a father has over his kid.' But he didn't. She played it twice more and when she turned around to what she thought would be her parents at the table, he was standing right behind her and kissed the top of her head and said 'That was beautiful. As beautiful as the first time, and it left me with the same feeling. If you ever told me your goal in life was to become a concert pianist, I'd say that's not an unlikely thing for you to want to become.' Not 'unlikely.' What's the word?" "'Unreasonable'?" his daughter says and he says "No, but something like that, and good word, your 'unreasonable.' Anyway, he said to her that she played beautifully or divinely or one of those. And that he loved her—'I love you, sweet-heart'—and she said 'And I love you too, Daddy,' and that's all she remembered of her deepest memory and that she'd had it dozens and dozens of times. And for some reason it's also become—I must've been around eight when she told me it— my deepest memory too." "That's odd," she says, "that some-one else's deepest memory could become yours, but not improbable." "'Improbable,'" he says. "Good word too. Jesus, where you getting them from? But it's also the word her father said about her if professional or concert piano-playing was to become her goal. That 'That's not an improbable prospect at all,' I think she said were his exact words, or close. Anyway, there's my most vivid memory. Big deal, right?"

the school bus

He takes her out there every school day morning. "Maureen,
it's almost time, get your coat and backpack; I already got your
lunch and snack in it," and looks at his watch, they have five
minutes before the bus comes and it takes a minute or so to get
to the pickup spot. Usually she's not around; had her breakfast
and is gone. He yells again "Maureen, come on, we only got a
couple of minutes—a couple is two, two, so come on, get with
it," though they have about four minutes now and the bus is
usually a couple of minutes late. If it's early it waits till the
time she's supposed to be there: 8:40. If it gets there exactly on
time, it waits about forty-five seconds—he's seen it from their
dining room window and raced outside and yelled "Wait, hey,
bus, we'll be right there; bus, wait, wait," and once the driver
heard him and waited and once she did or didn't hear him but
left. Maureen comes into the kitchen. "I was in the bathroom,"
"I was saying good-bye to Mommy," "I had to clean up the cat
poop in my room and then wash my hands," "I had to brush
my hair," "I was looking for a hairbrush," "a hair tie,"
"Mommy said I should wear a long-sleeved shirt instead of a
short-sleeved, so I had to change," and so on: "I couldn't find
my sneakers," "the library books I have to return to school

today," "the science project I did last night," and he usually hands her her coat, having taken it off a coat peg in the kitchen and saying about some of the things she couldn't find: "You look okay," "You can bring them in tomorrow," "We haven't the time, so wear your shoes, even if it's for gym, unless you can find them in one minute," his coat or jacket or sweater or raincoat is on, and he picks up her backpack or takes it from her if she has it—that way they can get to the stop faster—and says "Quick, did we forget anything important—you have your homework folder in the backpack and your supply case and stuff? and your glasses—"Oh, my glasses, I'm sorry," she says if she doesn't have them and runs to get them from her room or off the dining room table where she set them when she sat down for breakfast—"Because I don't want you calling home later for me to drive to school with anything you left behind," and usually she has everything and they go. He's said a number of times as they walked to the stop "We should really get a plan going where the night before we check off everything you need and get them into your pack, except of course your lunch and snack," and she says "I know, it'd be so much easier," but they never have.

To jump ahead, though, they're at the stop. It's down the driveway and across the road from their house, maybe a hundred-fifty feet away. So it takes them, except when it snows or the driveway's icy or there's been a recent heavy snow, and if there has, school's usually called off, at the most forty seconds to get there, and he takes his watch from his pants pocket and sees they have two minutes till the bus is scheduled to come. He never puts the watch on because he'd just have to take it off in ten minutes when he showers. A couple of cars pass, one going maybe twenty miles over the posted speed limit, maybe thirty, and he often says something to the car when it passes or makes some hand motion but this time doesn't. He's in fact yelled several times at cars—"Hey, you're doing fifty in a twenty-five zone, and there are kids going to school now, you idiot," and shaken his fist sometimes and sometimes just yelled "Slow down, goddamnit," and she's said "What's wrong?" and he's said "Didn't you see it?—that car's going way too fast," and once she said "Don't, Daddy, you shouldn't scream on the street, people will see or get mad," and he said "Don't tell me what to do." Today she looks at the car disappearing down the road and says "That driver should slow down, right?" and he says "Yeah, but what can you do?" and she says "Me? What do you mean?" and he says "You know, you yell your head off 'Don't speed, you bloody moron,' and it doesn't mean anything. They'll do it next time anyway if they don't live on this road a couple of houses away, so know you know them, or know you don't recognize them from the market or someplace, but even there I could be wrong," and she says "I don't get it, what?" and says "Really, forget it, nothing." Usually he starts the conversation while they wait. About her school, teachers, friends, Mommy, what she might want to do this weekend, and once a week they'll go over the more difficult spelling words they went over last night for the spelling test today, and so on. He often reminds her that her lunch is in the backpack and her classroom snack, which she'll have in an hour and a half, is in the zippered pouch in the pack. If she's buying lunch that day, which she only does if the month's menu on their refrigerator door says "lasagna" or "tuna salad plate," he'll tell her her lunch money is in a wax paper bag, or wrapped in aluminum foil, and in the zippered pouch under the snack. Snow on the ground, they usually talk about it or make some snowballs and throw it at a bridge weight limit sign nearby. Raining, he'll hold an umbrella over her while they wait or ask if she wants to hold it over herself, for when it's raining he always comes out in a raincoat and hat. If there's only a little snow left at the stop, she'll kick it, he will too sometimes and step on it, both will, trying to smash it, and doing that often reminds him when he was a boy in New York City and walking to school and how he thought if everyone in the city kicked just a little bit of the remaining dirty snow off the sidewalks into the streets . . . but the last two times he told her that she said "You told me it already about the little dirty snow," and he said "Did I? My mind doesn't work well so early in the morning," and the last time he said that she said "You told me that the last time too, but that time you said it doesn't 'function well so early.'" Mud, he tells her to stay out of it, she'll get her shoes caked, and when she has boots on, he says "It probably isn't a good idea to get your boots muddy, but go ahead, walk in it, they're rubber or some plastic that feels like rubber, and what the heck are boots for?" She wanders off sometimes, while he holds her pack, to toss a rock at a tree, inspect something on the ground, climb on a big mound of frozen snow and stamp around on it, if she has her boots on, or only with shoes if he thinks the snow's solid enough where the shoes won't go through. While she's off he usually looks at their house and grounds across the road, at the windows to see if he can see any sign of his wife, at Maureen to make sure she's okay, passing cars on the two-lane road, road turn where the bus can first be seen, though they can hear it a good fifteen seconds before they see it. About ten seconds after it rounds the turn, it pulls up to them, big red STOP sign on its left side swings out, and door opens.

But get ahead. Bus comes. When he first heard it he said "Bus, bus darling, get ready," and she dropped the stick she was outlining her sneakers with on the ground and grabbed his extended hand, which he usually does since he usually extends it, and waited on the grass with him for the bus to stop. Right after the door opens he usually says good morning to the driver and she usually says "Morning," and "Hiya, Maureen," and Maureen usually just smiles or says hi and gets inside the bus. But just before she climbs up he kisses her cheek or top of her head and usually she puts her lips out for him to kiss and he always kisses them when she does that. If he's still holding her pack he hands it to her, though most

STEPHEN DIXON / SLEEP

times he gives her it the moment he sees the bus and often when he first hears it, since once, maybe two months ago, he started back to the house and the bus honked from a few hundred feet away where it had stopped and the driver yelled out her window "Mr. Foreman, Maureen's school bag," and he saw he was still holding it and ran to the bus. Week or so before that he only noticed he still had it when he got home and he immediately drove to her school and was there before her bus and waited for her, though he could have left it with her teacher in her classroom. But what he's saying is that after they kiss and she gets on the bus, and they always kiss, always, even when she's angry at him for something earlier that morning or just got angry at him at the stop—it's happened if, let's say, she wants to slide on some ice and he doesn't want her to because he says she can slip and maybe break a leg and "that's all we need," and so on—she sits in the first row on the right side. She has her pick where to sit since she's the first kid on the bus, but she usually sits there, right across from the driver, or in the window seat behind it. He's never asked why she chooses one window seat over the other and never any other seat on the bus and the first row the most. And as the bus starts up—actually, it's already started up, the engine's never turned off—so as the bus pulls away he blows a kiss to her and she kisses both hands and blows him a kiss and smiles, a smile so broad and wonderful—those aren't the right words, there are no right words for it, it's just a big, open, loving, beaming smile but one in addition to saying all that about it is impossible to describe, at least to him—and she keeps blowing him kisses with two hands and he to her with one hand and sometimes he yells between kisses as the bus pulls away "Good-bye, dear," or "dearest," "good-bye," not that she can hear him with all the windows closed except the driver's sometimes, so maybe she can hear him through that one when it's open. So? So it's the best moment of the day, a simple fact. The best minute or two, in fact, one could say. She looks so happy. It makes him feel so happy. The event's so simple: kiss kiss, smile, wave, good-bye, dearest, good-bye, his darling child gone till late that afternoon when she gets off the bus and walks home alone. Her smile so big and wide and full and just for him, like no smile's ever been, or one he can remember, at least from day to day. She doesn't smile like that for anyone else that he's aware of or for anything else he does for her any other time of the day. He doesn't know why this is or what makes it but there it is and it makes him feel so good during it and right after that he often runs back to the house slapping his fist into his palm and smiling, his whole body feeling lighter somehow—he's not kidding—and the same thing happens just about every weekday.

He's tried to figure it out a few times. She's the only kid on the bus when she gets on, so she doesn't feel self-conscious blowing kisses and smiling at him like that. She has no other distractions—kids to talk to, a friend she's eager to sit next to or someone she wants to avoid. Not the driver either: she's involved with her job, closing the door, seeing that her passenger's seated, getting the stop sign flush against the side of the bus, and driving off, and for some reason Maureen doesn't feel self-conscious doing these things so close to her. Substitute driver: same thing; Maureen will usually say as the bus pulls up or as she gets on "Someone else today" or "Another driver" but Mrs. Orr," and then go to her window seat in one of the first two rows and do all the same things to him once he's initiated it. So it's just the two of them, really, and that's why he thinks she feels free to blow kisses and the rest of it, and every day, probably because like most kids she likes to repeat things, maybe to make them memorable, though on that score he's not that sure. And he? First of all, as he said that feeling during but particularly after, and it makes her happy so that also makes him happy, and she sees how happy it makes him so she's even happier, and so on. And he wouldn't mind doing it if other people were around. It's she who'd mind, he thinks,

STEPHEN DIXON / SLEEP

and who'd call it off, and if she had said something about it before, with or without people around, he would have gone along with it instantly and maybe unquestioningly, which leads to the next part of this: why it all stopped.

There are other kids on the bus one day. Ten, fifteen, maybe. It's spring, snow's all gone, weather's warmer. "Good-bye, Daddy," but back up a bit: bus pulls up. "Good-bye, Daddy," he kisses her cheek, she puts her lips out, he's already given her her pack, reminded her that her snack's in the pouch, but then she pulls her face back before he can kiss her lips and steps away from him. "What?" he thinks and looks up at where she's looking and sees several kids staring out the bus windows at them. "Other children," she says; "I wonder why," and gets on the bus, first few window seats on the right are taken and she walks further back. "How come all the passengers today?" he says to Mrs. Orr after they exchanged good mornings and she says "They altered my route. Maureen isn't my first pickup any longer. She's in fact the last part of the first half, whichis why I was late." "You were late? I guess you were; I didn't think of it. Day so nice, we were just talking." "Five minutes late. Had to start out fifteen minutes earlier to get here at even this time. This is when I'll be picking her up from now on, give or take a couple of minutes. Eight forty-five, so have her here tomorrow at that time. Coming back, also add on five to seven minutes." "I'm at work when she's dropped off." "They eliminated one bus, I'm told—I haven't got the whole story—and distributed the kids from that one to three other buses. Ones you see in here are from the canceled bus's route. But from this point on I'll be picking up the same kids I usually do, minus a few at the end who another bus will pick up. It's complicated to explain but it saves money for the county, so I suppose it makes sense. You'll get used to it quick enough," and she pulls the stop sign in and door shut, looks in the rearview and side mirrors, nods to him and drives off. He looks for Maureen in the bus, has his hand on his lips ready to blow a kiss. She's near the back, in an aisle seat on his side—the window one's taken—and she looks at him and he blows a kiss at her and she just continues looking at him, no smile, he yells "Good-bye, my darling, have a great day," and she makes some mouth motions, he doesn't think she's saying words, and still no smile. He goes home unhappily. His best moment, he thinks, the absolute best moments of his day. Well, he had it more than half a school year. Maybe some parents will complain or for whatever reason the county will bring the other bus back before the school year's over or maybe next September she'll again be the first one on the bus.

But move on. When he gets back from work that night— he'd forgotten to tell his wife about the new bus schedule when he got back to the house that morning so called her from work to expect Maureen home five or ten minutes earlier, he'd figure, or even later, "I forgot to speak to the driver about what time Maureen would be dropped off," and she said "How come they didn't tell us about this before?" and he said "What's the difference, five minutes, ten?" and she said "But suppose it was Maureen who was being picked up five minutes earlier? Maybe that happened to some children from the canceled bus and they weren't there on time and the bus came, didn't see them, and left, which is what you tell me it does with Maureen if she's even a minute late," and he said "I'm sure their parents were notified beforehand, or Mrs. Orr got there at the right time or even a few minutes early but waited, but nothing worse that that," and she said "Who's she?" and he said "Maureen's bus driver. I've told you about her. Pleasant woman, around middle-age, with long ringlet-like blonde hair and always very sweet to Maureen. Anyway, it didn't happen to us, so why fret about it?"—he tells Maureen he missed their blowing kisses this morning and waving good-bye and such and her smile especially. "I never told you but your smile, as the bus drives away, is the nicest I've ever seen in my life and the highlight of my day, and it's just as nice every single time. It's so open and outgoing and warm, or something; I just love it," and she says "Thank you, but I hate the new bus trip. I had to sit way in back and I bet I have to from now on. All the front seats by the window were filled—those are the best places. It's the more smooth ride there and it's the fastest place to get off. It's not comfortable in back. It's bumpier and stuffy and I smelled gas smells there and I couldn't get a window seat except for the last row and that's the worst one on the bus. No one takes it. The motor's under it so the seat's always hot. I did get to school about the same time as usual but it took me much longer to get home. I used to be the first stop going home too." "How's that?" he says. "I can't see someone being both picked up and let off first. Didn't the bus on the old route retrace its ride back? Meaning, if you're the first one picked up going, I'd think you'd be the last one dropped off coming back." "No. And now, going home, I'm on the bus a lot longer than before because of all the other kids or something." "Mrs. Orr didn't tell me that. In fact I just assumed you'd be home a little earlier even." She says "She said she forgot to tell you and some other parents about the different times with the bus coming back, so I should. But also that you're not at the stop anyway when the bus takes me back. And all I do then is cross the road, which I've been doing, and I can do that by myself." "She said that?" "No, I am. She said she waits in her bus every time till we're all across, so it's probably all right the way it is now, even if we are home a little later, for those who do it alone. She has these big red stop signs—" "Yeah, I know those. Cars front and behind are supposed to stop when they see them and wait till you're across, but sometimes some bozos don't." "So far all the cars have. But that's how I always get home. Mommy doesn't have to come out to meet me. She thinks I can do it on my own because it's safe. Though she says she does, when she hears the bus stop, go to the window to watch me. Maybe from tomorrow on I can get to the bus by myself in the morning." "No, I like taking you. And morning's not the afternoon. Traffic's heavier then, not that it's ever a lot on our road—but people going to work and driving their kids to private schools and things like that. The garbage trucks come early. I just wish you were still the first kid picked up. After you get on tomorrow couldn't you just quickly get a seat, even if it's an aisle one but on my side, and throw me a kiss as I'll do to you? I love it when you do. And some days I'm sure there'll be empty window seats near the front somewhere where you can do it." "Not with people watching. It's embarrassing. Let's only say good-bye when the bus comes, if you won't let me get it alone. And no kisses except maybe a little one on the cheek from you if you want to only give me that." "Okay. I can understand. I don't much like it but that's the way it has to be. Of course I could, if I let you go to the bus yourself, give you at home the same kinds of good-byes we got used to at the bus stop. But it wouldn't be the same for me, I think—no bus pulling away with your big smile and right after that me racing back to the house as happy as can be. Anyway, that won't be till at least next school year."

So he continues taking her to the bus. She often says he doesn't have to and he says next year, next year, maybe. He says he likes to make sure she gets across the road all right. She says doesn't he trust her by now? She can do it by herself. She knows how to cross—you look both ways and don't take any chances—and there aren't that many cars in the morning, or not as much as he said. He says he knows she knows how to cross the road, but some drivers, few cars as there are in the morning—though he feels there are more than she thinks—speed to work when they're late, and most high school kids who drive cars, and there are plenty of them around here, speed anytime of the day whether they're late or not. And she's still just a small kid—smart but small, and by small he doesn't mean small for her age—so not a large visible object, if she gets what he means. So because of all these things and other things he hasn't even spoken about he just doesn't feel right yet about letting her walk to the stop alone, and he waits with her, gives her the backpack which he still carries for her to the stop, usually tells her that her lunch bag is in the pack, if she's not buying lunch in school that day, and if she is, then that the lunch money is in a wax paper bag in the backpack pouch along with her midmorning snack. She doesn't let him kiss her anymore at the stop. Kids are looking at them through the bus windows. He continues to say good morning to the driver and occasionally say something about the weather to her and get a good morning back. Every so often he sneaks a kiss onto the back of Maureen's head when she steps into the bus. She doesn't react to it in any way; nor does she usually look at him anytime when the bus leaves. She's in her seat—she has to be, it's the state law; school buses—maybe all public buses—can't go till every passenger is seated. When she does look at him he always waves hard and a couple of times she waved back. Flap of her hand; that's it. But no smile, or maybe no smile nine times out of ten, and certainly no smile like the big ones she used to give. Usually when the bus leaves she's looking at her lap or staring out the window at anything but him or she's talking with the kid she sat next to, an acquaintance she's made since the new route started or someone from her class or grade. He blew her a kiss a couple of times when she was looking at him but she turned away so fast that he stopped blowing them. One thing he hasn't given up—instinct, habit, reflex, but something—and whether she's looking at him or not, is waving at the bus as it drives away. A few times some kid on the bus, and a different one each time, mocked him with fake waves and smiles back. Once, a boy put his finger up at him when he was waving; just like that, out of nowhere, the finger. He just shrugged. What else could he do? He's asked her if the new kids on the bus are okay. "Sure, same as when I used to ride it before they came on." And coming back? Same thing? No horsing around or rough stuff from them, or worse? "Never. The driver wouldn't let it. Worse they do is throw candy and gum wrappers on the floor or leave them on their seats, and mostly the older boys in back. The driver gets very mad when she sees it and says she'll let the bus stand there forever if they continue doing it and also don't clean the mess up, and sometimes that she's going to tell their parents what sloppy kids they are, but I don't know if she has."

After the bus goes down the road and makes a turn and disappears, though he can still hear it for a half-minute after, he walks back to the house, has another coffee and reads the paper for about ten minutes before dressing for work. Same things he used to do when she was the first rider picked up, but his mood's different now. Then, he'd remember her smile and way she blew kisses at him. He'd tell his wife. He'd say "I don't know how it happens or why it is but every single school morning, or just about, Maureen gives me the happiest moments of my day." "I know, you've told me, a few times," she once said. "I mean," he said, "you give me happy moments too, plenty of them, but there's something about those happy moments she gives me. The bus, her kissing, that smile—you know, especially that big broad absolutely adoring smile—loving, adoring, whatever—that just does something to me that nothing else does, or possibly even can." "I know, and I'm glad for you. It must be wonderful, and for it to happen every day or almost, doubly wonderful, almost miraculous, I'd say." "How so?" and she said "That something so wonderful and fulfilling and the like could be so easily attainable and repeated each time." "That's true. That's probably the reason too. I hope it never ends." "Consider yourself lucky that it's gone on this long and is still even happening." "You're right, but enough about it. Sometimes if I think too much about things I like, the pleasure of them, somehow, goes away. Better it just happen every day without my thinking about it, right?" "I guess," she said.

comparing

A man says something and the woman answers. He answers her and she says what she says she's always wanted to say to him but up till now . . . Well, she says it, he hears it and gets rabid, but really hysterical. What would be the best word or at least a better word than those two for what he gets? "Rabid" 's okay for now, so's "hysterical," and he says what he says he's been aching to tell her since the third or maybe even the first . . . She cuts him off a little way through what he starts telling her and answers him and it goes too far, "Way too far," he says, "Not far enough," she says, with him answering that but even more vehemently and her shrieking something incomprehensible at him or just to get it out of herself but at the top of her lungs and then she's alone in the apartment, he's somewhere outside it. On the other side of the front door, past the hallway, down the stairs, any of those places—bottom floor landing, building's vestibule, the street perhaps, standing on it in front of the building or somewhere near or walking along it in one direction or another. Or he's in a shop or store by now—could be. Sitting having coffee at one of the coffee bars that recently opened up a couple blocks away, right across the street from each other. Or standing up in one, since both only have a few

stools, having coffee or ordering one or checking the menu
board above the servers behind the counter for today's special
coffees and the different kinds of coffee drinks they always
have and looking at the pastries in the display cases. Both bars
have great pastries and coffee but one has an even wider variety of coffee blends, so chances are, also because he thinks it's
quieter and more attractive than the other and he always
prefers a quieter place, he's in that one if he's in one. Or by
now he could be in a coffee bar a few blocks away—he loves
coffee and a coffee bar or just a more ordinary or typical or
standard place for coffee like a luncheonette or café is often
where he'll go when he's tired or irritable or needs to do a little thinking, which is what he might think he needs to do now.
Or he could be in a different kind of shop or store a few blocks
away or waiting in a bus shelter or on a subway platform for a
bus or train or already in a bus or subway car, with or without coffee. Probably without. Much as he loves coffee and
might now think he needs it, he doesn't like walking around
or taking a subway or bus with a container of coffee, especially
a hot one, which is what his would be since he only takes his
black. So definitely without coffee, if he's on the street or in a
subway or bus or waiting for one, and if he only wanted to go
one or two stops on the subway and it wasn't delayed or about
twenty blocks on the bus, he could by now be at the station
he wanted to get off at or halfway to his stop on the bus. But
that's about as far as he could be now from the apartment
unless he got a taxi in front of the building moment he stepped
outside and there were no delays going downstairs and the cab
didn't have to contend with lots of traffic and lights. Then he'd
be some twenty to thirty blocks away, somewhat farther than
two subway stops, going someplace, where, though, well that's
the question.

   She, though—she's home, their apartment, now hers. That's
what they agreed on: he'd go, she'd stay. Not so much "agreed
on." Last thing she shouted was that she wanted nothing more

in life right now than for him to be gone for good and he shouted back just before he left: "You bet, same here, you ugly bitch: for good, for good." It was his apartment when they met. She gave up hers to move into it and they've been living here for several years, married for more than two of them, have no child or pet. She's pregnant, though, but he doesn't know it. Right now she's thinking there are two possibilities regarding this: should she have the child or abort it? That's easy enough to answer: have the child. She'll tell him she's had it only after it's born and maybe, if she can get away with it, not even then. But that's no good since he's sure to learn she's pregnant from one of their friends or a neighbor in her building or colleague at work or even one of her own relatives or if he just happens to bump into her on the street or comes to see her. If he does find out and says he wants to come back to be with her during her pregnancy and then stay with her to be with his child, what will she do? That's not so easy to answer. For she's sure he will want to come back and be with her for both of those. He's always wanted to be a father. By "always" she means since he was a grown man, or that's what he's told her and other people, and she knows from what he's said since almost the first day she's known him that he's wanted to have a child and even two or three. They've tried to have one for years and had just about given up and were talking of adopting one—several months ago, before they started arguing so much—so what will she say to him when he says he wants to come back? She'll say he can come back if he behaves better, works out his temper and all his other faults or most of them or at least makes a serious effort to, that is definitely the case and there can be no other way. Another question should be—well, it is, here: why would she think to let him back so soon after she told him to get lost for good? That one's tougher to admit than explain. Because she also thinks it'll be too difficult and maybe even expensive having the child by herself and bringing it up alone. And a child should have its father around unless the problems between the parents when they live together make it worse for the child than having the father live somewhere else. And she was the one who kicked him out and told him never to come back, and then later, if she did this, told him he couldn't come back when he heard she was pregnant or had the child and wanted to return, and that could be used in court against her if she wanted him to pay part of her rent and half the expenses of the child and other things, though she thinks no matter what he'd have to pay half the expenses of the child if not more. But she really thinks that things could get better between them with a child. Does she really believe that? She thinks: "Be honest with yourself for once. Hey, I've been honest with myself so far. Then just be honest: do you truly believe things will get better between you two with a child?" Yes, she does, she honestly does. A child will mellow him, for how can it not mellow almost anyone? And maybe even start the process of helping him get rid of his faults by awakening or reawakening things in him he's never thought of about himself or hasn't thought of for thirty years, more or less. Though the idea of sleeping with him, if she let him back, making love is what she's saying, having sex is more like it, letting him do it to her with her only doing the most necessary things to him to get it over with quick as she can, is what she's really saying, is the most horrible prospect she can think of right now. No, there could be worse. A madman entering her apartment through a window, let's say—just getting in here some way and sticking a knife to her throat and tearing off her clothes and raping her and stealing everything she owns and raping her again and sodomizing her from behind and making her do everything he wants and continuing this for a day, two days, and cutting her with the knife, slicing her, beating her, torturing her, raping her repeatedly every which way, that would be so much worse it's impossible to compare the two, the madman doing all that and her husband having sex with her first time after he returns if she let him back. Or a fire, that would be worse. Where she's burned and the apartment destroyed and all her favorite things gone: painting, prints, furniture she's inherited; that would be worse. Certainly getting burns over twenty to thirty percent of her body would be much worse. Having a small fire, though, one she could put out herself, a few things lost—one painting, a couple of prints, an old chair she loved and where she only got minor burns—that wouldn't be worse. They'd be even, having sex with her husband and that kind of fire. Losing an eye would be worse. Losing both eyes incomparably worse and maybe as bad as getting forty to fifty percent of her body burned. Getting a disease, one that would incapacitate her, make her incontinent, feeble, feeling sickly and weak every hour of the day, dependent on others for getting around, confined to a wheelchair—strapped into one—that would be infinitely worse than sex with her husband that first time if she let him back and all the times after that. Just having a minor illness—stomach flu that passes in several days or even a week, even that would be worse than having sex with her husband if the sex wasn't prolonged and she didn't have to participate in it much. But a stomach flu of one day, even one where she throws up a lot and has some agonizing pains: they'd be even, or having sex with him might not be as bad as the flu. For in having sex she could just lie back, not enjoy it, ignore it best as she can, let him do it quickly, tell him to, pretend it isn't even him, get into the most comfortable position for her where she doesn't have to do anything and can almost even fall asleep. If he said "Move a little, why don't you," she might move. If he said to touch it with her hand, she might do that a little too. Still, compared to a really bad one-day flu, one where you feel for a while you're going to die: even. But a cold—well, don't get silly. Losing the child, though, even at this early stage, that would be much worse than having sex with him numerous times that first day and maybe even as bad as losing an eye or a fire where she's severely burned, say ten to twenty percent of her body, even

STEPHEN DIXON / SLEEP

that twenty to thirty percent, plus all her possessions gone in it, she wouldn't care. For it took so long for her to get pregnant with this one—this is her first time ever—and she doesn't know if another one will come.

He's on the subway heading downtown. He doesn't know where he's going. Just wanted to get out and far away from her as fast as he could. Where should he go? It's Saturday, not a work day. Should he get a hotel room for the night? What's he talking of? For several nights, for a week, a month. Though he also has to go back to the apartment to get his things. Not today but some day soon—tomorrow at the latest, maybe the day after—and that'll mean he'll have to see her again. He doesn't know which would be worse, seeing her again after this tremendous fight that ended their marriage—and that's what it was: their marriage is ended for good and all time—or spending hundreds of dollars on clothes he already has. Seeing her again, maybe, but he's not so sure. Or he can call and say he'd like to come by for some essential things of his, shouldn't take more than an hour, could even be forty minutes—clothes, a few important papers, his favorite books—and he'd like her not to be there. If she says okay, she'll stay away for a few hours, or even "You bet, for who the hell wants to see you?" he'd go right over. If she says she wants to be there when he comes since she's afraid he'll take things that aren't his and that he may even try destroying some of her things—her family's old ugly table and ratty padded chairs and these antique paintings and prints he hates—he'd still go over. He wouldn't look at her, just go about his business, filling this, packing that, and if she said something to him he'd pretend not to hear. If she tried goading him into another argument, he still wouldn't answer or even look at her. In other words, he'd put up with another tirade or anything from her, except maybe if she started using her fists, just because he needs his clothes. For let's face it, buying a whole new outfit or two for work, and other things—toilet articles, his extra pair of glasses, boots—would put him back much further than he can afford, not to mention his two very good fountain pens and special night table reading lamp and his grandfather's pocket-watch his mother gave him which can't be replaced and is valuable enough to buy, if he ever sold it, which he wouldn't unless he was absolutely strapped for cash, six new suits and pairs of shoes. It would be nice, though—this is impossible but it still would be nice, people are allowed fantasies, aren't they? so this one's his for now—to meet an old girlfriend— "woman friend"?—just "girlfriend," everyone knows what that means no matter what the man's and woman's age—this minute on the subway. One who says to him clear out of the blue "Mitchell?" and he turns, since there couldn't be many Mitchells riding one not-too-crowded subway car, and she says "Mitchell Shanks, am I wrong?" and he says "No, right— Julia Ricklau?" He'd like it to be she, the girl he perhaps— "woman" 's more like it—loved most in the world, or his adult world, he'll say, before he met Theresa, the woman he hates most right now out of anybody in the world—his wife, of course, Theresa his hated wife. That's what he should call her when he calls her: "Hello, is this Theresa my hated and hateful wife?" But she'd probably say something like "Let me guess. This is Mitchell, my despicable and despised prize-winning harebrained husband," and then hang up on him and he wouldn't be able to come by for his things. So what good would it do calling her that? He could hardly ever get the bet-ter of her. She knows how to dish it out. She dished it, all right, just before he left. It was her words that drove him out and made him say the things he said to her before he left, though he's sure if someone asked her she'd say his words drove her to say what she did "and he's a pathological liar if he says the reverse." Anyway, where was he? Fantasy. Julia Ricklau in this subway car and he says "This is amazing," and she says "I also can't believe it, for it's been how many years?" He'd supply the number. They'd ride on the subway, chattering about old times and friends and things and what they've been doing since, gets off at her stop, she'd say "You sure this is your stop too?" and he'd say "I have no stop. I just split up with my wife and I was actually about to start looking for a hotel to spend the night or even the week, the month." She could say . . . Well, on and on, conversation never stops, laughs, yuks, pleasure, happiness, marriage, children, a long life together of love and contentment and fun and of course setbacks and resentments and sadness and spats. After all . . . well, don't get philosophical, but all because he left Theresa, and if he had to choose which of the two women he had loved most? Well, don't get comparative or competitive or whatever the word for it is either—and he met her for no reason except that he had to get away from his wife fast, took a subway downtown—downtown, because uptown it can get pretty rough—and, and . . . Well, that's life, what could happen, stranger things have. Just for a lark, or on a whim—both, even—he looks around the car to see if she's there and then peers through the door window leading to the next car and of course she isn't there either. Just thought, for who knows? He gets off at the next stop, goes upstairs to the street, at a hotel he asks how much a room is for the night or by the week. Too expensive. Tries another hotel. Also expensive. He hasn't got that kind of money and had no idea an ordinary to even a kind of run-down hotel in this city cost so much. Maybe she'd let him sleep in the living room for the night. What, did he hear right? Yeah, sure, why not? since what he'd like even less than being in the same apartment and in a way have to come back groveling to her is paying a fortune for a hotel or spending the night in a fleabag of one or sleeping at some friend's place and begging them for another blanket or a second pillow and such and their kids running around early next morning and watching their kiddy TV and especially being beholden to other people, really, and telling them what happened with Theresa and how he got himself into this spot. Besides . . . besides

STEPHEN DIXON / SLEEP

what? The whole thing's out of his system now or almost, isn't it? "Most hated" becomes "not so hated anymore." Just "somewhat hated, semihated." They've had fights like this before. He ran out of the house, cursing and screaming at her, she at him, went for a long walk or to a movie or bar—though they never cursed and screamed so hard where each of them said "Good, marriage is over," but that doesn't mean things built up to that now; it could mean the exchange did, that's all. Anyway, left the movie or bar, came back and everything became relatively normal again after awhile. They didn't talk to each other for a day, maybe two, except "I'm leaving for work," "So long." Or even for three days, but big deal, things became hunky-dory and even better than that soon after and the first time they screwed, once they did work things out, was usually better than any time since they last fought that hard and eventually worked it out. He's sure the psychologists could give the reasons. His is they just became very emotional being back together and clearing the air of everything that was disturbing them about each other and that hit the physical some way or touched upon something deep within them both or just unleashed things from inside. In other words, a connection combined with some kind of freeing. Oh, he's okay with books in explaining what goes on inside them but was always a dud in figuring or just articulating the real-life things out. So he calls and she says she was expecting his call and he says "You were, today? What did you think I'd say?" and she says "I thought you'd apologize and want to come back," and he says "I do, and I'm sorry for all the awful things I said," and she says "So am I, so come back." "You mean it? I'd sleep on the couch if you want. To be honest, that's where I was going to ask to stay," and she says "What are you talking about? Sleep with me in bed, if that's what you'd want," and he says "Only if it's also what you want. But this is extraordinary. For to be honest, fifteen minutes ago I hated you," and she says "And fifteen minutes ago—ten minutes—make that five, I hated you

STEPHEN DIXON / SLEEP

too." "So what happened?" he says. "What happened with you?" she says. "I went to a few hotels and they were all too expensive. And then, I don't know, I thought I'd ask you if I could sleep on the couch, since sleeping anyplace else—at a friend's, for instance, with screaming TV and brats—" "Oh, children don't all have to be brats." "Okay, then screaming kids—" and she says "They don't all have to be screamers either or not all the time or at once." "Right. But I just thought better with you than anywhere else, like at a flophouse I could afford, because I sort of got—not 'sort of,' *got*—the whole thing out of my system by ranting like an idiot at you. And I thought—well, I just thought this now, to be even more honest with you . . . and I'm not calling you an idiot by any means. In fact, one of the things I thought before, and this also is the most absolute honest truth, was how I never get the better of you ever—but that maybe you got it out of your system and everything was all right and forgiven and so on from your side too." "It is. I have. To me it's a bygone, though it took a little toll. And I neglected to tell you, long as you say you're being so honest with me, I'm pregnant." "You are?" "I am. I took one of those early pregnancy home-kit tests yesterday, which are as reliable as you can get and maybe even more so than the old rabbit tests, some people say, and you don't have to kill off the little dearies either. But I was mad at you yesterday also, though not as much as today, so didn't want to tell you yet— it would have given you too much pleasure," and he says "You're right, but what were you mad at me for yesterday?" and she says "If you don't remember the reason it's not worth going into," and he says "Maybe it is best you don't, at least not when I'm feeling so great about the good news." "So come back then," she says. "Pick up some stuff for salad on the way, we have none," and he says "Why don't we go out for dinner, celebrate our return and the kid's beginning, so to speak; have wine, a good meal, no dishes to wash or table to set and clean up. Mexican, I've wanted to go to the Mexican Gardens for months now and we saved money by my not taking a hotel room and, I was also planning to do, buying a whole new outfit for work just so I wouldn't have to see you again so soon," and she says "Think how much the baby's going to cost even with the medical insurance. A half dozen of your out-fits, and every year after that a dozen or two dozen more." "I forgot that. Okay, salad, anything else?" and she says "Some beer if you want. Pregnant women are supposed to take dark beer, so make some of it dark. No, I think that's for nursing mothers. Anything, nothing, just come home," and he says "I'm on my way."

Why'd she do that? she thinks after she hangs up. For she doesn't want him here. But talking to him, she felt better. But now that she's talked to him she almost feels worse. No, she still feels a little better than before she talked to him, calmer, relieved that their row's over, but he's going to expect to sleep with her tonight, especially after the things she said, and she knows how she feels about that. Maybe the moment he gets here or soon after, with these stupid eyes over dinner, and she's repulsed by him. He's a clown. He's a rat, he's a fool. But she wants the baby and doesn't want to have it alone. But she could have met someone else in the three or four months before it begins to show. Maybe. Even after it shows; some men might like moving in and taking care of her. She's attractive, men like her, and she might even become more attractive for two or three months after she shows. Some new sparkle in her face, her breasts will probably get fuller, and some of those mater-nity dresses can make any woman look like a doll. At work she's always getting propositioned. Or sometimes, or often. If it happens once a week or even every other, what would that be, often, always, sometimes? Propositions aren't proposals, she knows, and there's something stinking about them too, and some of them were really just the beginning of one or a sign of some kind of attention or amorous intent if she didn't have a husband. Anyway, there could have been a chance for someone else and now she's never going to find that person. One phone call from him maybe an hour after they said they were through and she suggests they get back in bed, he didn't. She could have said, "No, stay away," or "Yes, but only on the couch for one night," but sleeping on the couch, which he said he wanted, is sort of a way out of saying he wants to sleep in his old bed. And one thing leads to another even if she started to make up the couch for him or just threw him the bedding and told him to make it up himself. Men get pushy if they're feeling it and if you're in the same room with them it's even worse and if it's your husband you're dealing with he thinks it's the most natural thing he deserves. But he's not that bad. Compared to other men she's known and most of the ones that make propositions, he's okay. And he's good-looking, he can be very nice. He was nice on the phone. So consider the worst part's over and he's here and that's it. But the things he said, can she forget that? What was it he said tonight, forget yesterday's argument? He said . . . he said . . . something about her mother. No, his mother compared to her. No, that was yesterday's. He said . . . God, how can she forget? She'll ask him. No, don't. It's done with, so don't bring it up unless he asks. You've the baby to think of now. And it won't be so bad sleeping with him now that the row's over and you see things differently. And maybe they should go out. He'll say "But I went through the trouble of getting all that salad stuff." She can say "We'll use it tomorrow, it won't go to waste. Tonight let's go to your Mexican Gardens." He'll say "But the money it'll cost for the baby." So she'll say "What's that in comparison to what two dinners with double-x beer will cost. Peanuts. Nothing. A thousand to one. At least a hundred to one, but closer to three hundred. So one night we can splurge, maybe the last till long after the baby comes. Because that's my point: we have something to splurge on and toast about. The baby coming, which compared to anything we've ever done in our lives, together or alone, is the best thing by far by a

STEPHEN DIXON / SLEEP

hundred times a hundred percent." He'll agree, or it won't take much convincing. And she'll have a couple of tequila cocktails at the restaurant—sunrises or Margaritas. That's a nice name for a girl too, or Marguerite. And for a boy? Too soon. But come on, for a boy? Manuel, maybe. She likes that, it's real and not snobby and sort of goes with their last name, at least the sound. Will Mitchell? She can say "You can choose the boy's name, so long as I like it, and I can choose the girl's under the same terms." And with two Margaritas and a beer or two, she'll feel fine for making love. No, hold off on the alcohol. Little Mr. or Ms. Small Somebody might get hurt. She doesn't want to lose it, ever. So just a beer, nothing dark, which can be stomach-upsetting, or hard. And she can get into it if she wants. Hell, she will. Just close her eyes—well, they're normally closed during it—but think that the two of them, like this, created the greatest single thing in the world.

So what changed her mind? he thinks on the subway going home. Whatever, a baby. He can't believe it. You try so hard, you just about give up and screw for the sheer pleasure of it from then on, and it comes. Maybe that's how to do it, but how can that be? He wants to shout it out though: "Fellow riders and potential muggers, I'm gonna have a baby and it's great." And heck with the salad and whatever, before the argument, she had planned to make tonight: they're going to Mexican Gardens. Who cares what it'll cost. Can't cost that much anyway: thirty, forty bucks? A hotel would have set him back sixty, before the taxes and tips, so almost seventy-five, plus what he'd have to pay to drink and eat out. And think what the salad stuff would have cost and maybe a few good beers and bottle of wine at home, or at least subtract that from the total figure the restaurant bill. They'll be coming out way ahead and a dinner there will renew them in a way. Margaritas for a first round—one of those will put them in even a better mood. And just talking about the baby over beer or another Margarita and food and what hospital she thinks she'll have it

STEPHEN DIXON / SLEEP

at and when she'll first see a pediatrician and what to name
the baby and all will keep the conversation flowing freely and
with no end. But maybe she isn't pregnant. She couldn't be
lying for some reason, could she? Certainly not to get him
back. No, compared to every woman he's gone out with awhile
or had some kind of deep attachment to or relationship or
whatever it was but where it got very close, she's never lied to
him once, he's just about sure. When she says something it's it
and if it's wrong or far from the way the thing is it's only
because she didn't think right or gauge it well. And here he
thought she hated him and was telling himself he hated her.
How'd they get into the argument today anyway? He said
something or she did and it got out of hand. Which one started
it or at least kept it up when the other one might have wanted
to end it or tone it down? Maybe it goes back to the previous
day's argument she spoke of and that one might have been
unresolved and so resumed because of something one of them
said or did today, but who started that one he doesn't remember either or how it ended if it did or even that there was one
as he told her and of course what it was about. His memory's
certainly taken a slide since he was a boy and then a young
man and from year to year had the best spelling mind and
brain for other memory things in his entire class if not the
whole grade. Anyway, what's more important is what today's
argument led to. But no more leadings-to like that. He should
think before he shrieks. Treat her civilly and gently and let her
win a few too. He does, she'll treat him the same way. And he's
almost sure that gentler and more civil he treats her and where
he puts some kind of stranglehold on his rage, better things
will be in bed. Oh, this is going to be good. Home, a little kiss,
or a big one at the door, talk, maybe the longest juiciest kiss in
their lives since they were wed, and then some tears maybe on
her part and even a bit on his, happiness about her being pregnant and their being back together like this, jokes about her
body slowly blowing up and breasts swelling and things like

that, then the restaurant and getting a little high on Margaritas and such, and—something that just came to him but lots of times those are the best things that come—should he tell her he likes that name for a girl if it's a girl and if it's a boy he'd like it to be Vincent or Paul? The girl's he's never thought of but those two for a boy he's always felt were the strongest for a male without seeming fancy or unusual to the point where someone might think them better for a phony actor or a girl. No, jumping the gun too much. Then, after dinner, home, holding her hand most of the way, getting into bed and waiting for her, or undressing her soon after they close the front door. She likes to be undressed if he doesn't tear her clothing or stretch them. Start making love on the floor, even, or the couch, for he hates it on a hard floor and with all the dirt there and a possible rug burn, and maybe a joke about the irony of the couch. Pick her up, though he's not that strong anymore. But it would show how hot he is or ardent and be fun so he'll give it a shot and all the alcohol in him should help in lifting her. But she hates that kind of thing. Too beefy, she'll say: just trying to impress her with his strength or prove something to himself that needn't be proved. He doesn't much like it either, especially if he can't lift her or he suddenly feels he might drop her if he has lifted her or the effort of holding her up starts to show. Just go to bed and do it, that's all, no lifting or couch or floor. No, best, when he gets back to the apartment now and sees her first time since their argument, to say hello and look contrite and kiss her hand, give her another hand-kiss and maybe take both hands and start kissing them and after that go for the lips and kiss those a few times and if she'll let him the last one with open mouth and tongue and then say "Please, I can't wait, let's go straight to bed; later we'll go out for Mexican and talk and talk and talk." Okay, settled. And it's his station and he gets off.

She's looking out the bedroom window and sees him on the sidewalk heading in this direction and thinks it shouldn't be

STEPHEN DIXON / SLEEP

too bad. Everything will be all right, in fact, she's almost sure of it. No, really, from now on everything's going to be wonderful, or better than normal, or much better than it's been for years. At least better than the last few months have been with him, that's for sure. Now he's in the building. He didn't look up at the window when he crossed the street or just before he went in, something she expected him to do. If he had and seen her he would have waved and she would have waved back and then let the curtain drop, signifying—they've done this before—she's rushing to the front door to buzz him in so don't even bother taking your keys out, if he doesn't already have them out—he usually does, and sometimes all the way from the subway stop. It could mean he was too in a rush to get in and upstairs to her to look up or didn't think of it this time or he was saying something to her, if he did see her in the window from a distance—that he's intentionally ignoring her, isn't thinking of her, putting her on the defense, himself in front. Something, but she shouldn't waste her time thinking what. It'll take him a minute more to get upstairs. If he runs, half a minute; drags along, maybe even two minutes. If he had a quick drink to build his courage to call her and maybe another one to see her, he may have to stop on one of the landings and take some deep breaths. He may take them anyway, to think what he's first going to say to her and look like if he hasn't already done that. She goes to the door. Is she anxious about seeing him? Sure she is and to get the first fumbling uncomfortable moves and words out of the way. Brushes her hair back with her hands at the mirror by the door. Don't smile too much or at all when she first sees him and she shouldn't instinctively put out her lips and move her face toward his if he makes some sign he's going to kiss her. All that later, maybe much later. For now let him suffer some more. She doesn't like being so premeditative but this is how she thinks she has to be for now. Let him know she's still conscious of what happened before and that she wants fights like that to be a thing of the past. That today's and yesterday's and last week's and the big one last month and so on are the last ones. Spiffs and spats and such are to be taken for granted from time to time, but none of the other kind where they act like they want to shed blood. Say to him, before they do anything, "Let's sit down, have some coffee, and talk." His key's in the door and she lets him open it. "Hello," he says and she says hello.

other way

Driving on Falls Road I see to the right what looks like a body lying curled up between two bushes with its feet toward me. Should I stop to see if it is a body? Could be someone passed out or dying of something or dead. Probably it's nothing, bag or two of garbage, what looked like feet I don't know what. Half mile later I think maybe I should go back. Could be a person, dying, someone who just keeled over, heart attack or stroke, and can't get up. Nah, I'm imagining it, it's garbage, bags, or just clumps of it, or just something like clothing, thrown from a car or left there by a pedestrian, but like that. Driving up the hill to my house I think I really should go back. Probably isn't anything but I'll never feel sure about it till I find out.

I make a U-turn in front of my house. "Dada," my daughter yells from the porch and then turns to the door and yells through the screen "Mama, Dada's home." "I'll be right back, sweetheart—fifteen minutes; tell Mommy I forgot something," and I drive off. My wife's already at the living room window, must have been sitting reading right under it, looking first across the street where I normally park and then up and down it, and I wave to her as I go and maybe she saw me.

STEPHEN DIXON / SLEEP

I drive back. Halfway there on Falls Road I think this is crazy, it can't be anything, I'm wasting my time, turn around. It might not even have been anything like a bag or two of garbage, or clothing. Could have been a shadow, or tall grass, or there was nothing, not even a shadow, I was just seeing things. I stop, wait for incoming cars to pass, make a U and head home. Smartest thing, best. Almost to the street that takes me up the hill and home I think why'd I turn around? I could have been at the bushes already. Just passing them I would have seen it was nothing and then I could have made the U and driven home. Now I want to go back there to make sure. No, don't be silly, just forget it, and I continue home. But at the stop sign a street from my house I think I'll never be satisfied till I know one way or the other and I should remember that if I suddenly get second thoughts again about seeing what's there, and I make a U and go down the hill and then back on Falls Road. A minute later I think it can't be anything there. Really, I should stop thinking there can be. It looked more like garbage bags than a body when I first saw it and that's what it probably was—big black filled garbage bags, three of them, maybe even four. Anyway, if it was anything like a body—if it was a body, period—someone would have seen it by now, or several drivers would have and even a pedestrian or two, though hardly anyone walks along that road, and one of them—maybe a few—would have called the police. So I turn around at the light about a mile from the bushes and get all the way home, park, and get out of the car. My daughter's in front of the house, looking at something in the walk—she's interested in insects, ants and spiders especially, so maybe that's it—and I say "Hiya, honey," and she looks up, waves, yells to the house "Mama, Dada's home again," and I hug her and say "How was school today?" and she says "The same, okay," and I say "Do your homework yet?" and she says "All of it, nothing for after dinner," and I say "Good girl," and rub her head and think no, I really made a mistake not seeing what was back there and knew I'd feel this way so why'd I come back without taking a look? Dumb, real dumb of me and if I don't see what it is now and then I find out in tomorrow's paper or the next day's it was a body, I'll always think I could have perhaps helped that body before it died—done something, even if it was only to keep it alive a few more hours, unless the newspaper article says the person died instantly from whatever it was, but even there I'll have my doubts of the accuracy of the article, that perhaps that "instant" death came after I saw the body: the killer, if it was that, could have been waiting behind the bushes when I passed and then came out and clubbed or knifed this already keeled-over or just sitting person—that's far-fetched and a long way from what I thought I originally saw but something like that may end up being the case. This time go back and don't stop till you're there and keep telling yourself don't stop and then see for sure what it is. If there's absolutely nothing there when you drive past, go right home. If something's there, get out, even if it looks like garbage bags, to make sure it is that or whatever you think it looks like.

I go up to the porch and don't see my wife through the windows and door and yell "Janie—you here?" and she says yes, from the kitchen, and then comes to the kitchen door and says "Hi, where were you?" and I say "Listen, it's not that I forgot something again this time, if Marion told you that before, it's that I've got to go back for something. Believe me, I'll be back in fifteen minutes—around there," and she says "What is it you forgot?" and I say "No, you didn't hear—I didn't forget anything, this time or the last, and I haven't time to explain, I'm sorry," and I go down the porch steps and my daughter says "Can I come with you?" and I say "Sure, why not—no, stay here," because I just remember it could be a body, slight chance but it could, which is the whole point of my going back.

I get in the car, go down the hill and get on Falls Road and drive for about three miles till I'm around the area where I thought I saw something between two bushes. But there are lots of bushes on that side of the road, about a half-mile straight of them, no houses behind, just trees, and behind the trees a mesh fence and behind that, which I remember from driving past hundreds of times when it was light out but can't see now and really only probably noticed a few times, the golf course of a country club where no one could be playing now. Getting too dark for that—is too dark: way past dusk, which was what was settling in when I first drove past here and thought I saw a body. I drive slowly and see bush after bush or what looks like them but no place with two bushes and a space big enough for some garbage bags between them, and then the bushes end and it's a couple of service stations back to back and then a fast-food place and across the road on my side a high school and after it a cut-off entrance to the beltway.

I turn around at the light at the big crossroad that also goes to the beltway and head back, driving even slower than before so I can really look at the bushes. A car flashes its lights behind me and I think "What the heck?" and then realize my own lights are off and the driver was probably signaling that and I turn them on and hold up my hand, not that he can see it but just maybe in case he can, and wave thanks and the driver flashes his lights again and I think "What's he doing—signaling 'You're welcome' to me?" But then he flashes again and I think "What's he want, me to pull over more to the right? I'm in the slow lane already—go around me," and I signal with my hand out the window for him to go past, him or her or them, I don't know who it is, but he stays behind me and flashes his lights again and I say to myself aloud "What's bugging you?— go around, there's plenty of room to," and I flash my lights a few times, which may not mean anything to him and he probably can barely see them flashing, and then he signals left and I say "Finally," and move to the right to give him even more room and he gets in the passing lane and I look at the car as it passes, I'm always curious as to who's doing these things, what they look like I mean, and it's a woman jabbing her finger at me. I hunch my shoulders and make a face at her asking why? and still holding onto the wheel with one hand she jabs even harder at me and says something very angrily, she practically spits it at me—her windows are closed and I can't hear her and she probably has the air conditioner on besides, why else would all her windows be up? but from her mouth movements she seems to be saying "Stay in your own lane, jerk, stay in your fucking lane," so maybe I was straddling the lanes a little, I've done that a few times without realizing it, but I don't see where it warrants that kind of anger. Then she shoots off and by this time I'm past the bushes—it's just a few houses and parked cars along the road now—and I think "Should I?—yes, go on," and make a U and go back slowly in the right lane. I don't see anything, no space between bushes the size of the one I thought I saw, and I turn around at the first service station and drive back slowly but staying close to the curb. It's too dark now to see the bushes clearly. I continue till I'm past them, think "Now I should go home—no, a little legwork and then I'll have done everything I could to find out if anything was there." I make a right at the first street past the bushes, park, think of locking up but then think I won't be gone that long and if there is some reason I have to get back to the car fast, like someone needing help or even threatening me, I at least won't have to fumble with the keys.

There's a lane of grass wide enough above the curb to walk on like a sidewalk, so I do that instead of climbing over the bushes or walking in the street. Walking, I think what will I do if there is a body? Depends if it's live or dead. I'll be too scared or something to touch it to see if it is alive, if it doesn't immediately show it is with just my looking at or hearing it. If I get to the service station without seeing anything, then I've done what I came back for and I'll probably then just jog to the car. Which isn't to say there couldn't have been a body between the bushes before. It might have been asleep, drunk or something, and in the half hour or so since I saw it it might have got up and walked away. Or if it was knifed or shot or bludgeoned or whatever might have happened to it like that, it could have stopped a car to take it to a hospital. Or if it was dead it could have been taken away by a hospital ambulance or some kind of city van—no, that takes time—reports and such—so couldn't have happened without my seeing it. Or even dragged away by someone or two or three guys, maybe dumped behind a tree here or over the fence, though this, just looking for it between bushes, is all the looking I'm going to do for it and I wouldn't feel bad or much of anything except interest if I later read in the paper a body was found behind the trees here or just over the fence or even way off in the golf course. I can only do so much, not that I think there is a body here.

I walk and walk. Endless bushes, none more than three feet high, so I'm able to look over them to see if anything's behind. Then a break in the bushes wide enough to fit a few garbage bags side by side, so I think "Well that's that, go on home now, this is probably the spot you saw from the car, it had to be and was probably just shadows you saw. Or whoever was here, if someone was, picked himself up and left or even maybe a city garbage truck came and picked the garbage up if that was it. It's possible they work this late collecting trash in public places, which I think this is on this side of the fence." But then I think "Oh just go to the end of the bushes or almost to it," since if I remember right it was still a ways farther where I saw what I thought I did. So I continue walking and looking and about a minute later I see, maybe thirty feet from me, a person coming my way. He or she's going to think it strange someone's coming his or her way. Maybe not "strange" but no doubt he or she's already alert to it. But he or she will also probably think, if he or she's up to no mischief—just *he* for now—that the person coming toward him is probably already alert or just alarmed—I think that's the word I want—somewhat alarmed that someone's coming his way. So we're both in the same boat, if this

STEPHEN DIXON / SLEEP

person means no trouble. If he does, what then? Jump into the road at the slightest hint of it and if no cars are coming, run across and farther on across again to the service station where I can call the police. Or give the person whatever he wants if he pulls out a weapon that makes it that kind of matter. So I concentrate on the walker, who's just a few feet from me now, though I'm not looking tough or ready for an attack or anything, just regular with really no expression. It's an older man, and I say "Good evening, sir," and he steps into the road to get by me just as I was about to do to get by him and we laugh, I'm sure both of us at that and maybe out of relief also, I know I feel it, and I let him use the road and I continue on the grass and then he's past me and back on the grass. I walk a little farther and turn around and he's looking back at me. "Nice sort of cool night," he says, stopping, and I say, walking, "That's okay by me after the sweltering weather we've been having." "What?" and I say "It is, after the crazy sticky heat we've been having for this time of the year the last week," and he says "You said it," and resumes walking. I keep going, looking at the bushes and a few times over them and turning around once to the man who I now can't even almost see he's so far from me. I get to about fifty feet from the first service station, so about thirty feet from the last bush, and think "I'm sure I don't have to go any farther—ah, but see it through as you said you would, unnecessary as it is," and I go to the bush before the last and turn around. So that's it then, except for the twenty to thirty feet or so when I just stared at the man coming toward me and then for about fifteen feet when he was past me and stopped to talk and I kept walking, but I'll catch those spots on the way back. I won't jog though since I'm a little tired and I also don't want to catch up with the man, if he's still around, and startle him in any way. What could I say to him: "I was looking for something in the bushes"?—it just wouldn't work.

I walk back looking at the bushes a little but mostly at the road. Then, maybe three-quarters-way to the car, I see almost right underneath me a pair of feet sticking out between the two bushes I first stopped at. I jump back and yell "Hey, what?" and think "Good God, are they dead—the body to it is?" but then the feet start moving. "Hello—someone there?" stepping back a few more feet and a man says "Yes, it's me again, how are ya?"—the one from before; I can only tell from his voice since all I see of him still is the end of his pants and his socks and shoes. "Are you following me, young man?" and I say "Not at all—what are you talking about? I was in my car before"—I get close so I can see him; he's sitting up, maybe before was lying down— "and thought I saw something, two big black bags of garbage or a body between a couple of these bushes, and I drove back to make sure it wasn't a body and then decided to walk along here to definitely make sure. You weren't sitting or lying in the same place about a half hour ago—maybe more than that—were you?" and he says "I only started to rest now, was nowhere near here before." A car drives past on our side of the road, driver looking at us and I wonder what he's thinking: two guys up to no good? One guy up to it—me—and about to clobber the other? Or maybe he thought I did clobber the other guy and was about to take his money. Or it's possible he couldn't even see that much of us, thought we were two women, one man and a woman, just as I couldn't see much when I drove past. Garbage bags? No, that he couldn't have thought we were, since we were moving, or just that I was standing. But then who knows? Maybe his eyes at long distance are much worse than mine. Hundred feet away or so the car slows, brake lights flash, it starts backing up, then accelerates forward and keeps going.

"You sure you weren't here before?" I say and he looks at me as if he doesn't understand and I say "I mean, that half hour ago or more that I said: right here, the bushes." "Positive. I'm walking back from work, like I do almost every nice week-day after work, and most times I take a break in this same patch for a few minutes. It's a long walk, the feet get tired. But that was very nice of you, coming back to see if anyone was hurt I suppose is what it was." "Or if it was garbage. Meaning, to make sure it wasn't but not a body too. It's obsessive, fanatic, or I don't know what it is—compulsive, but I don't think it's what you said was good. Anyway, okay, I'm satisfied, and again good-night," and I continue to the car.

I get in, think "Should I make a complete turn or just back out?—back out, no cars are coming," and I do and drive toward home. I haven't gone two hundred feet on Falls when I see coming toward me very slowly in the nearest opposite lane that same car from before. I just know it is: white, new and shiny, with the convertible top up, and when it passes, all the windows closed and the same driver it seems: tie, white or light gray hair or even blond, who's looking at my side of the road and when we pass, very briefly at me. Probably looking or starting to for the same thing I was before, or out of the same reason: to see if something wasn't going wrong between the man and me by the bushes. Through the rearview I see the car still driving slowly, or looks that way—it isn't shooting out of view as fast as I think a car going even a normal speed would. He'll probably slow down even more when he reaches the bushes and maybe stop and get out and see about what he saw or at least drive past once or several times before he's satisfied as he'll ever be that nothing's wrong. If he sees the man sitting, what'll he think? If the man's sitting still or lying down, he could think from the car that the man's unconscious or dead. But if the man's sitting and moving around—scratching his nose, his head, like that—if his sight's good he could think the man's okay or maybe that the man's the killer or mugger and the body he killed or mugged is behind the bushes or off to the side someplace. He could think that and other things. I should go back. No, don't be silly. No, I should go back and if I see his car's stopped and he's out of it or still inside, I should stop and tell him it was nothing between the other man and me and about an hour ago I had some of the same thoughts I think he did and I'm now trying to save him from the consequences of them. "Everything's okay, nothing's wrong, don't bother your head about them," I could say. If he doesn't believe me, I could then lead him with my car or personally by foot to the sitting man and tell him to ask the man himself what happened before. The man I hope would say he and I were just talking. If he lied and said something different, like something that would put me in a bad spot, I'd just give up and walk away. But if the man's continuing his walk home from work? If that was a true story? Because he could have been the man I first thought I saw between the bushes and it could also be he only said he was walking home from work because he didn't want to be suspected of loitering. Or maybe he's unbalanced—he seemed so somewhat just by the way he couldn't understand things I said and calling himself, at least hinting, an old man when he's really no more than ten years older than me if that. Or maybe he's up to no good at all but thought he'd do his no-good on a woman or a much smaller and older man than I. If he's loitering for that—if I knew it for sure—I'd stop at the next pay phone and call the police. If the car man stops after he first didn't see anything when he drove past or nothing that satisfied him, and walks along the bushes as I did looking for a body or he doesn't know what, he could get mugged by the sitting man if the sitting man's like that. He might even be hiding behind the bushes now waiting for someone and the man in the car seemed much older than I from a distance so he'd be a better target. But don't go back. Or just drive back once to make sure nothing's wrong. Anything bad going on you could probably see from the car. If you see the car man outside his car talking to the man outside, or sitting in it but talking to the man outside, then maybe you could turn around, slow down when you get to them again and yell out the window "Everything okay?" Stop, really, if nobody's behind you, but motor going, and yell it out. It might seem odd to the sitting man, who knows you, and if nothing's wrong, but if the car man says something like "No, not at all, thank you," or just "Why you ask?" but doesn't look as if anything's wrong, just say "Good," or wave or something and go home.

I turn around and drive back and don't see the white car or anyone by the bushes the whole way and turn around at the second service station this time, not wanting to draw any more attention to me than I probably already have in the first, and drive back and keep my eyes jumping between the opposite lanes for the white car coming toward me and the bushes for the men or man and car parked alongside and see about halfway along the bushes what seem like a few big bags of garbage piled up on the grass, though I don't think it's the same place I saw the sitting man before. I stop, no car's behind me, back up and stop near where I think are the bags, turn my emergency lights and ceiling light on, and with those and the streetlight from about fifty feet in front on my side and even a little moonlight, or starlight, nightlight, whatever kind it is, since the moon doesn't seem to be up yet or at least not where I can see it from the car, I see what I thought were garbage bags is a tree-top shadow from some nearby tree made by one of those high-intensity antiburglar lights on top of a tall pole on the golf course fence. There seems to be one every few hundred feet or so—at least from what I can see between the trees—something I didn't notice before, or maybe they weren't on before. If they were, a shadow like that could be what I thought were bags or a body the first time, but it can't be since it wasn't dark enough then for those kind of shadows and I don't even think it was that much of dusk either. I forget by now. So nothing, nobody, so just go straight home, don't even look at the bushes again when you pass them.

I drive away, occasionally looking at the bushes. Even if I see someone lying between them and am even certain of it, I'm not going to stop. I've taken too long. It could be two men copulating, doing whatever two men like that like to do—not my two men, I don't think, but two others. It could be any number of things. I just want to get home. I'm starving. I want a drink, vodka and grapefruit juice with seltzer and ice or just scotch over rocks. My family's got to be worried about me a little, at least my wife. And also holding up dinner for me. All those might be things just to get me away from here, rationalizations—though I am hungry, I would like a drink—but so what? I don't want to carry my good Samaritan feelings to the point of craziness, do I?

I'm past the bushes and getting close to where I turn off Falls to the street that takes me to my street when a car coming toward me flashes its brights twice. "What's wrong?" I think. "Does he mean me, or someone behind me?" but in my rearview I see nobody's behind. Maybe just testing out his lights. A few cars later a car beeps its horn at me, or that's what it seems like, and the one after it flashes its brights. Then I realize. My emergency and ceiling lights are still on, and I turn them off.

the stranded man

Lying on my back, nothing to do, another day just like the rest. Not quite like the rest but almost. Similar. In a hammock. Not quite a hammock. Nothing like one. On some dried grass, in a hut. Something like a hut, more like a lean-to. Listening to the radio. No radio. Saying to my wife "Would you refill this glass but this time not with so much ice?" No ice, no wife. No woman or refill. All alone. No hut or lean-to. Nothing. No newspapers. Just sand, grass, trees, and sky. Of course no newspapers. Blue sky, black sky, sky lit up with stars, sometimes only a few stars. Moon, no moon, quarter moon and so on. All kinds, or all the kinds there are, day and otherwise. No animals that I've ever found or seen tracks of. On the island I'm on I mean, since plenty of porpoises and fish around it. Sometimes I pretend to listen to the radio, read the daily paper day it comes out. I lie down and read, like I'm lying down now. On a bed of grass but not much of a bed and the only writing I read is what I scratch out on wood and in sand. With some branches, dried grass, and leaves, I've set up something like a roof. When it rains, which isn't often and never much, except for a few days to a couple of weeks, I stay under a thick tree and wait the rain out. The radio program I'm now listening to says I've been found. A ship passed, saw me waving my shirt, came nearer to the island, saw me contine to wave my shirt, sent a small boat to pick me up. I've a long beard and no clothes. Except for the ragged shirt, which I save solely to wave. Clothes got worn, some of them just fell off, I've been here for years, some got torn off when I walked through this or that, one part of my clothes I tore off and then to shreds when I got mad at something, I forget what. I still play with myself from time to time. I walk the island often, across and back, round and around, sometimes climb a tree to look for passing ships, but in my long time here I haven't seen what seemed like a sign of one. I forget how I got here. Let me think. I forget. Truth is, I'm not here, or where I say I am, though I sometimes would like to be. I'm in my bed, no bed of grass. A real bed, sort of comfortable, orthopedic mattress, two pillows per person, queen-size, plump comforter, my wife's in the bathroom and just now comes out. "Honey," I say, "can you put a little more ice in this?" "In what?" "This glass," and she says "And what glass is that?" "Only kidding," closing my empty hand. "I was just thinking," and she says, walking around the room sorting, putting away, tidying up, "Thinking what?" "Thinking how would I be able to get myself to a small remote island, many thousands of miles from here and miles from anywhere, and then be on that island for years or at least a couple of years without being found? A deserted uninhabited island, maybe never inhabited till I got there so never deserted. No visible animals on it, maybe an occasional bird flying over it, and where I don't even once sight a passing ship or boat or even an abandoned or deserted raft or canoe. What's the word again when something like that's cast off but not intentionally? Drifts away, de-beached, premarooned?" "I don't know. I'm not a sailor or beachcomber and I've never, except summers when I flubbered around the ocean as a kid, been interested in the sea." "An island with some wild berries and fruit and maybe even grass I can eat and freshwater but not enough

STEPHEN DIXON / SLEEP

food—at least that I can find or where I know it's edible for humans or even food—to stop me from gradually wasting away. An island where I can make some kind of roof for myself out of branches and leaves and where from time to time I'm able to catch a fish with my bare hands or gib it, I think the word is, with a pointed stick. But where I've no way of making fire so I can't cook it and in fact the second fish I catch like that, if it's with my bare hands, I throw back or keep for a week in some hollowed-out receptacle I find or make. So an island where I catch fish just for the sport of it and maybe finally to make one or two my pet till I think it might die if it's not tossed back. But an island where I'm completely alone, is what I'm saying. No humans or animals, not even birds that stay. For you see, I don't want anyone to die just to place me on the island alone. So I don't want to say I landed on it with a number of people, even one other adult person, and that person or those people died and I buried him or her or them and spent the next couple of or few or even ten or so years on the island alone. If I came with other people or even one other person I might be able to think up some way how I got to this island. A large boat, even a ship that sunk and we were its sole survivors and then ended up on the island and then I was the only survivor after a while. Meaning, with more people in the lifeboat, let's say, we'd have a better chance of getting it to the island. So the question is, how could I get to this island alone?" "Why not in a boat to it alone?" she says. "You could jump into it off the sinking ship with other people, be in the water with no or few provisions and such for weeks, all the rest die, you survive, and while you're dying in the boat alone, too weak to steer or paddle anymore, it drifts to the island, you find yourself beached and you climb out and fall asleep on the sand, and the boat does or doesn't drift back into the ocean. That way you can lose your boat and get to eat it too, if you know what I mean." "Too familiar and I just don't see it happening. I'm the only survivor—oh sure. Besides, I told you I don't want anyone to die just to get me to the island." "Then swim to it," she says. "A long-distance swim, from one island to another, but you get lost and wind up on a third island, an uninhabited one." "I don't swim that well," I say. "Certainly not long distance. And I want this to be within the realm of reality. Meaning, realistic. It has to be believed by me, otherwise, it's no fun imagining it, for I'll keep seeing the holes. And if I didn't end up on the island I was swimming to—if I could even swim the distances you say. For I've never done more than half a mile at a time and that was always a lot if almost too much for me—they'd come to this island I landed on, looking for me. The people who run the long-distance swim, I mean." "Why would there have to be other people—organizers and things? You could do it all on your own. You've been living on this island a few months, there for some research or for us to get away, we'll say. And you've been building yourself up—running a lot, swimming a lot—for there aren't many other things to do there but eat, sleep, read, and drink. And you suddenly want to swim to another island. To test yourself—your endurance and strength—and one you can see from the inhabited island we're or just you're on." "That'd mean the islands would have to be somewhat close to each other—a mile, two, three. Ten miles away from each other, if I really built myself up for such a swim. Twenty, even, though that'd be, no matter how much I built myself up and trained, much too far for me. Anyway, the point is that these islands would be close enough to each other that boats and ships would pass. Pleasure craft, even. But the island I've imagined myself on, no boat or ship passed. It's five hundred, possibly even a thousand or two thousand miles from the nearest piece of land—island or archipelago and whatever they call Australia, a continent. Okay, not two thousand, but a thousand or so—around that. Maybe one boat or ship passed while I'm asleep. Maybe two. But in years, during the day, even at night with the lights of this boat or ship, I would have on the island you describe seen a boat or ship—lots of them, hundreds. And waved, built a fire, sent up smoke—something—and would have been found by one of them at least." "Then you were in a plane and it crashed," she says. "That's better. Crashed on the island or in the water? But since I don't fly a plane myself, and never expect to, there'd have to be another person—a pilot, and again, the possibility of someone having to die to get me there is one I don't want. And it's really not me, you understand, just someone I'm imagining." "If it's not you, then he can pilot his own plane." "He's like me, is what I mean, but isn't me. It's confusing, I know. But take my word this is—not the confusion but the situation—the way it is." "Then I've run out of suggestions," she says, "and I'm tired and going to bed." "While you're up," I say, not holding up my hand, "could you put more scotch and ice in this?" "What are you talking about? You have a glass under the covers? And since when do you drink in bed before you go to sleep?" "Just kidding. This is what my stranded man says. He's not hallucinating, he's imagining. Or maybe there is some hallucination involved. He's been wasting away slowly, as I said, hasn't seen anyone for years, so of course is talking to himself a little and imagining other people there. Though how to find a good original, meaning plausible way to get him on the island is something I'll have to figure out myself, I guess. But he's imagining he's on a soft bed of grass and under a well-made thatched roof. A cool breeze is in the air. Well, where else would it be? The weather's—temperature's—comfortable, as is the humidity, and the sky's clear. His beautiful wife or native girl-lover or something like that—she's young, anyway, barely out of her teens, maybe just into them, though probably the word teens isn't in her language. Anyway, the person he got stranded on the island with is the one he's saying this to about the ice and drink." "But you said he was alone," she says. "He is. He's just imagining all this. Even the bed of grass and thatched roof. The real ground under him is hard or at least lumpy and the roof is primitively made out of branches and twigs and leaves, and leaks." "I forgot. I wasn't paying attention." She gets in bed, pulls the covers over her shoulders, says good-night, turns over with her back to me and starts to fall asleep. At least that's her intention, it seems. "As I was saying," I say. "I know, I know, dear, but I'm really very tired." "Right," and I kiss her shoulder through the covers, hear some lip-smacking sounds as if that's supposed to mean she's kissing me back. I turn off my night table light, hers is already off, and lie back. "I'll have another drink, if there's no problem your getting it," I'll have my stranded man say. Meaning me: I'll say it; I'm saying it. "About an inch and a half of scotch and only two ice cubes. Oh, why get complicated? Forget the half; just make it two inches. Then I want you to sit near me." "Anything you want, my love," she says. Or she says it in sign language, or part her language, part mine, part sign. She gets the drink. She has no clothes on either. I watch her get it, watch her bend, straighten up, walk back to me, get on her knees at my side, give me the drink. It could be in half a coconut shell, or some receptacle like that. That shouldn't be hard to make with tools I could find on the island or make out of rocks or wood or shells. A shell for a receptacle, even. I drink, she sits there. I say "How did I get here—do you remember, or did I ever tell you?" "You came by plane, my love," she says in the language we've made up. "I couldn't have. I'm not a pilot. And there would have had to be one to crash-land a plane here, and I don't want anyone to die because of me." "You came down by parachute," she says, "and the plane continued on." "Then it would have come back for me, or sent a special rescue team to, because it would have known where I landed. Anyway, too fantastic, landing by parachute, and what do I know about using one? Come lie beside me please." She does. I hold her shoulders, kiss them, kiss her lips, other parts, we make love. She falls asleep with her head on my chest. I lie back and think about how I could have got here, remember how I did. I was

STEPHEN DIXON / SLEEP

on a ship with my wife, a cruise one, we'd taken a trip to the South Seas. We got into an argument, one of many arguments —years of arguments and battles—and I went to the rear of the ship, got a life preserver there, said to myself "I'm just going to end up where I'm going to end up even if it's at the bottom of the ocean," and jumped off. Obviously I was very depressed. I am no longer, or not as much. Nobody saw me, I think, or heard my yells. The yells because I suddenly felt I'd made the wrong decision, once I was in the water; actually, while I was heading for it. Maybe my wife saw or heard me but let me go. I'd jumped from only about fifty feet on deck where we'd had the argument, and my last glance of her, when I got to the rear of the ship, she was still looking at me. And she'd often said "Why don't you die, why don't I die then?—we'd be much better off without the other; why in hell do we stay together, put up with the crap we give each other?" The cruise was supposed to heal all that. A last-ditch reconciliation of differences, a renewal of love if it was possible. Maybe she did tell one of the crew I was overboard and for the ship to turn around, but the last I saw, before the waves and something to do with the horizon obscured the ship, it was still going the opposite way from me. I treaded water for hours, didn't see any land or boats or ships around to swim to. The water was warm. A plank passed just about the time I didn't think I could tread water any longer. I grabbed it, held onto it for a night and a day, fought off sharks by screaming at them not to come nearer or I'll punch their noses, and I shook my fist at them. I swear that last part's true—well, the whole of it is but particularly the last part, because I know it sounds hard to believe— and that they always kept about twenty feet away from me. Then an old lifeboat passed. There was no sign of anyone having been in it. It must have broken loose and fallen off a ship. It was up-side down and I could never turn it over. There were no oars attached to it and except for a can of water I found in one of its compartments, the provisions were spoiled

STEPHEN DIXON / SLEEP

or useless. I went to sleep lying across it, saw an island several days later and paddled with my hands to it. The wind also took me in that direction. I stayed there a couple of years. Many years. The boat was taken out to sea a week after I got there even though I'd kept it beached about fifty feet above the high-water mark. I knew that much. But a big storm came and when it was over I saw the high-water mark had risen another hundred feet or so. The boat was in the water, upside down again but too far out to swim to—the water was very rough that day—and by the time the surf had calmed down, the boat was gone. Enough about the boat. The native woman. How do I account for her being there? There was no woman. There was a woman. My wife turns over. I'd make love to her now if she were awake and willing or I could get her that way. I feel like it. Thoughts of the naked young native did it. I touch her breasts. She stays asleep. I rub her nipples, touch her bottom and crotch. She stays asleep. There was a woman. She came about two years after I got to the island. I saw her one day in something like a canoe. First the canoe, then when I swam to it, the woman inside. She was tied up and gagged. It seemed— I learned this after a while through the language we developed—that her husband or boyfriend of father or brother—I never got it quite clear—her uncle, even—had bound and gagged her and put her into the canoe, with some other men carried it around their island a few times, and then while some of them banged shells and sticks together and blew through cut-off birds' beaks to make some kind of processional or send-off music, shoved the canoe out to sea. She'd done something wrong. "Very very wrong," she kept saying in the language, but I could never find out what. "Something about a penis and vagina?" I said, pointing and touching. "No," she said or maybe she misinterpreted what I'd said. "Something religious?" I said, pointing to the sky, the sun, cupping my hands in prayer. "No," she said. Anyway, there she was. I was soon eating better because she knew how to live on the island and found things to eat I hadn't known were there. We had two children. She taught me how to help her give birth. The canoe rotted. She instructed me how to build a rainproof lean-to. We probably could have built a new canoe or some kind of vessel and gone out into the ocean looking for any inhabited island not her own, but she said it was too dangerous, especially with the children. "Best to wait till we're found," she said. There was no woman. I'm all alone. I listen to the radio. Try as I do to rainproof it, my lean-to leaks. The radio's in my head. I've taken to sun-drying the fish I catch and making that my staple, and I'm doing pretty well on it. The radio says it's been five years since I was discovered missing. It says nothing of the sort. I'm not someone a radio would bother about except perhaps for my initial disappearance and maybe if I were found. I listen to music. Serious music. I lie back on the bed of grass I've made for myself and imagine a native woman lying naked beside me. I grab my penis and shake it. I'd love to snuggle up to my wife if she were the native woman. I snuggle up to the native woman, rest my hand on her crotch and then start moving my fingers in, she takes my hand away and squeezes it and continues to hold it while she falls asleep. My children sleep. Ours: Ditty and Dino. Dilly and Dansky. I can hear them in the lean-to we built for them about ten feet away. I get up, look in on them, they're sleeping soundly. I run down to the ocean, jump in, swim, come back and stand till I'm dry, then lie down beside my woman again and fall asleep. It all makes sense now, how I got here, what I did. Then we're discovered. A boat, a ship, a plane. I take my island family back to this country, my wife's remarried or just doesn't want to have anything to do with me anymore. I get a job, an apartment, move in with my sister and her family first, then get a job and later an apartment, save money, we buy a cottage along the ocean and move there, I grow old, retire, our children move out, my new wife doesn't seem to age. I die in my sleep with her lying beside me holding me tight. No, we go back to the islands when I'm fairly old, find a remote one with some people on it. Our children stay behind and go to college, work, marry and have children and every now and then one of them with her or his family comes to visit us for a few weeks. I die beside her with her arms around me soon after I finished the scotch-over-ice drink she made for me, made love, and fell asleep.

STEPHEN DIXON / SLEEP

give and take

A man stands at a street corner. Man stands on a street corner. I'm that man. Or I stand on a street corner or just on the sidewalk someplace, people walking past. Big city, busy sidewalk, lots of people, I'm alone, it's a nice day, not too hot, not too cool, very little humidity, why didn't I just say mild day? sun out, nice breeze in the air, where else would the breeze be if I'm standing outside? no noxious or offensive city smells like car exhaust and garbage and dog feces, people continually passing, it's a well-traveled sidewalk, something that by now needn't have been said. It's afternoon, I've just had lunch, neglected to have lunch, didn't lunch because I didn't want to, didn't even think of having it, lunch. It's midafternoon. A woman passes. I recognize her. I've been waiting for her. I knew this woman would pass. It was more than a hunch, I'm saying, something I also needn't have said. I say hello. She says hello back. She continues walking. I say "Don't you recognize me?" She continues walking. I say "Don't you recognize me?" She could then say "Don't you have anything else to say?" I could then say "So I'll word it differently and say 'Don't you know me?' or 'So I'll say again "Don't you recognize me?"'" She says nothing. Continues walking, I follow her. If I don't, she won't be able to hear what I say. I'll also lose her, in the crowd I mean, till the next day when I'm almost a hundred-percent sure she'll be walking this way, on the same sidewalk—maybe to avoid seeing me, on the sidewalk across the street, which might make it more difficult to see her if I'm not on that side-walk but I'll see her if not as quickly as I did today—at almost the exact same time, since tomorrow's also a workday. She's coming back from lunch; now she is. She always leaves her office at the same time, give or take a few minutes, takes an hour outside for lunch, give or take—outside meaning outside her office building; her office building of course meaning the one she works in but doesn't own; well, some people do own the buildings they work in and some even some very big ones—skyscrapers—but she doesn't—and then comes back at one. It's almost one now, so not "midafternoon" but early afternoon, since noon starts, well, I don't want to say the exact moment noon starts since everyone knows when that is, or almost everyone. But she's walking. I follow, walking, hurry-ing because she's hurrying, meaning walking faster than nor-mal, than people normally do—just "walking fast" I should have said, and I say to her while we're walking this way "Don't you recognize me or rather don't you know me or rather, if just 'Don't you recognize me?' sounds too familiar or repetitive— has become too repetitive—and 'Don't you know me?' is too close to it—'I'm saying and have been saying, if in different ways, don't you recognize or know me for god's sake?'" She says nothing, doesn't look at me, dodges in and around people walking and hurrying in the same direction or toward us, I do too, though always keeping my eye on her. I was going to have her say something, not just nothing, but then she says "Yes, I recognize you. I've seen you around a lot. I once saw you a lot too, in the going-out-with-each-other sense. You were once my suitor, then my boyfriend. I was once quite fond of you, might even have done a bit of chasing after you if you hadn't done it first, and for a while I was in love with you. For a brief while very much in love with you. I would say that for a week or two when I knew you I would have sunk into a deep depression if you had suddenly said 'We're through and I'm leaving you.' I forget when that was but it's true. In other words, we were once close and for a while very close. We lived together for a while before we got married. We had children after we got married and before we got divorced. Now you've taken to pestering me almost every workday after I have lunch. I don't know why you chose to start doing this more than a year after we were officially divorced and I'm not sure you do either. I also don't know why you choose lunchtime to pester me but I assume it's because you know it's when I'm out. I'm a little surer why I don't stay in for lunch to avoid your pestering; because I like to get out during my workday, even in lousy weather, and I'm not going to let you stop me. I'll also say I don't know why you pester me when I return for lunch rather than when I go out for it, but I suspect it's because—well, I was about to say because you think I've less time to argue with you then, but that doesn't make much sense. Or that I'm in a better mood after lunch, which makes only a little more sense, so forget it." She continues walking at a normal speed—while she was talking we'd stopped, she first, or she stopped just before she started talking, and people had to go around us, a few people even bumped into us but not hard, just jarred, but one bumped into her so hard she bumped into me—and same with me walking beside or a step behind her: I continue. "And then what?" I say over her shoulder and she says "And then what what?" without turning to me and continuing to walk at a normal speed and I say "About forgetting it, you or I, or both of us, what you were saying before—was there something else?" and she says "There wasn't but there will be if you insist on it," and I say "Who's insisting, when do I ever insist?—I'm just asking." She stops, so quickly that when I stop as quickly to avoid walking into her, someone walking quickly behind me can't stop in time and bumps me into her.

STEPHEN DIXON / SLEEP

I say excuse me to her and then to this man and she says "Okay, here it is. I always—listen to me now, look at me," since I'm looking at the man walking away making spiraling motions with his finger to his head and then pointing his thumb back at me, and I turn to her and she says "I always tell you it's hopeless—not you or I but with the two of us. I also always tell you that we're finished for good, for this lifetime and the next, or have said it enough for the point to have sunk in. And that if you continue pestering me—and if you don't understand it said that way, then 'That if you continue to pester me'—I'll get a court order to keep you from pestering me and, in addition, I'll I don't know what." I was going to have her say "I'll also get a court order or police decree or whatever legal document it is prohibiting you from seeing our children on weekends and for the month by law you have with them every summer." "Yes, so what else do you have to say?" I say and she says "What else? This else, mister-who-never-insists-on-it. You're making it extremely tough for me. I'm involved with someone else now. We've been divorced—you and I, get that? you and I—for two years now. I have no feelings for you now but commiserative ones, have had none for the past year and, well, I've said enough so I don't want to say it." "Say it," I say and she shakes her head. "Say it, say it, go on and say it for christsake," but she continues shaking her head. I was going to have her say "I also can't stand to look at you anymore." "You also can't stand to look at me anymore, was that what you were going to say?" and she says "Not at all. It's—nah, it's hopeless and I'm sorry for going on as long as I have, so nothing, please, I don't want to talk about it anymore, okay?" I was going to have her say "Oh gosh, why am I saying all this, can you tell me? Because maybe I'm all wrong. Maybe I was too quick in dumping you and after that too quick in starting up with this new guy. Maybe you've changed as you say and maybe my feelings about you aren't at all what I've just said. Maybe we should remarry, first live together again with the kids, starting tonight, starting right now, soon as we can I'm saying, what do you say?" "So what were you going to say?" I say to her and she says "Do you want me to call a cop? That wasn't what I was about to say before, but I could call them, I will. Isn't it enough that all our old friends know what a fool you're acting like to me? Now does this whole street—the whole city—have to know? Because most of our friends have also told you to leave me alone. My lawyer has a dozen times also and a judge soon will. Because there's no reason for you to act like this. For a while we were happily divorced, weren't we?" Did she say that? She didn't. It's too stupid and common a remark, completely unlike her. Common meaning something a bad comedian might say over and over again. It's been said, often in different words or a different context, on stage and TV, in the movies and gossip columns, and probably other places. A famous bandleader, maybe famous because of all his marriages to beautiful famous women, most of them famous because of their beauty, was maybe the first to say it or to get attention saying it, and he said it in comments after each of his latter marriages ended and in numerous interviews and in a book he wrote about his life—I think it was even used in a shortened version for the book's title and many of those interviews were for this book—which I read maybe twenty-thirty years ago, or maybe I just read the title: *Eight Happy Divorces,* though what he originally said was "I've had eight terrible marriages and eight happy divorces." Or was it nine, or was it ten, and was it "terrible" and "happy"? The others who said it seemed to claim it as their own remark or didn't attribute it to the bandleader, who maybe didn't attribute it to the person who first said it, if someone had and he knew of it, or at least where he first heard or read it if he didn't originate it. But she wouldn't say it. Nothing so common and unoriginal. She also couldn't have said it in the way I said she did because she isn't on the street with me today and wasn't yesterday or the days and weeks and months before in

New York. She lives in Boise, I live in New York. Our kids live with her. If I want to see them I can always go to Boise. That's what our divorce settlement says: I can come see them when I want so long as I give her a week's notice and don't take them out of school while I'm there, besides my month alone with them every summer anywhere I want so long as she agrees it's a safe place. That's an expensive trip, going to Boise by plane, or a long one by car or train, but worth it to see my kids. We never had kids, though she does now live in Boise. I wanted them and she wanted to wait. Once we were married she felt maybe I wouldn't be as good a husband as she'd thought. Something happened. Pressures of my work. She didn't change, I did. I was actually pretty much the same; I just got more pathetic. Did I say that? Another thing a bad comedian might say, one who loves lacerating himself for laughs. Oh the l's. Bad, good, mediocre or ho-hum, but one who's self-lacerating. I'm not that. Like that. Am not a comedian. I can be funny but I'm no professional one or even one socially most of the time. Though I did say the line and want it stricken out. Out damn line. There's another. In this jungle of words: Shakespeare I presume. Or assume. Which is it? And that one too. Just awful stuff. So where was I? Is, am, for I'm on the street waiting for her. It's crazy, waiting, since she really does now live out West, though Vancouver, not Boise. Boise because it sounded better—oh the b's—and chance she'll come walking down this New York street is about as good as one she'll get back with me. So we can have kids. Time's getting short. I have to pick my kids up at school in six minutes. That means I've six minutes to finish this—five, really, since it'll take a minute to get upstairs from my basement desk, slip into my sandals, get out of the house, snatch the car keys off the front door hook along the way, into the car parked in the wrong direction on the street, meaning it's facing the opposite direction from their school down the street, so I'll have to back up, turn around at the cross street, back into that street is what I mean and then go forward and make a left on our street and drive a quarter mile down to the bottom of the hill where the school is to pick up my kids. All that will take about a minute. Just as explaining all that took about a minute. So I now have, if my watch is correct, and I set it to radio time just before I came down here an hour ago, four minutes to finish this and five minutes to pick them up. But good things are often rushed. It's happened with me a lot. Pressured or pushed, suddenly the mind works briskly, actively, quickly, sharply, automatically rejecting the wordy, discursive, repetitive, and superfluous. Though nothing's coming right now other than fake words and thoughts and also wrong ones. So where was I before I went into all that, just to get me away from it? On the street. I am on the street. The woman was my wife. My wife left me with my kids. Our kids. She left. I wanted her to stay but she felt strangled by me and a little by our kids. I love my kids. Sometimes I feel strangled by them too but nowhere near enough to ever think of leaving them, even if she had stayed with me, and I'm sure they sometimes feel strangled by me. If I was given the choice between my wife and kids, even when things were great between her and me, well, I was going to say I'd take the kids, and I would take them, but I want them both, want them all, wife and kids, I want us to be a family again, good, bad, or mediocre, for things can always change. I call her almost every night these days. Meaning I've recently taken to calling her almost every night. I want to say "Come back, all's forgiven, let's start where we left off but better, nothing's forgiven for nothing needs to be, I'm not making much sense here, probably because my wanting you to come back so much has totally confused me, I love you more than I ever have, the kids of course love and miss you too if not tremendously." Things like that. I always reach her answering machine. She got it—three minutes, give or take—even though she always hated those machines—and I'm sure if I got one and she reached it, she'd use my having it to pillory me—because I kept calling her, so getting one was her way of screening me out, avoiding even saying hello before she found out it was I and hung up. And why would I want her back? Sensible question. Or just good, good. Because I'm lonely too, meaning I am in addition to other things like a need for warmth and companionship and some sexual excitement now and then; to be fulfilled by a woman that way which I'm now not—I haven't done well at pursuing them since she left, and I'm also not doing well in the clutch here. Maybe things shouldn't be done this way after all. Pushing and pressuring myself like this—less than two and a half minutes left. I could have saved time by saying "almost two minutes." I could've saved time by not saying that, or this, etcetera, or just etc., or skip the "just," just the etc. But wife, kids, car. I've so little time, tho if I'm late a coupla minutes it's okay too. They wait, 2 boys. One in kindergarten—what a long word when one's rushed—other in 4th grade. Younger one waits by the entrance, or exit, since he's leaving, for the older one who always gets out last—usually. I pick them up at the door. They're always happy to see me—usually. I'm always happy to see them. I am, always, and always kiss them when I pick them up and take them for a treat after—often. So what's all this got to do with what came before it? Something I'm sure. I can do all that, pick them up—this isn't an answer to the last q—take care of them way I do, meaning giv them all this time, because I've a job where I work 8:30–2:30. Then I rush to school to get them at 2:45. Today I faked sickness and got off 2 hrs earlier. I thought I'd come home & write, go or come. Almost 1 minute. Nothing will come of this, shorthand won't help. I'll try not to call my wif tonight. Its better for us both. How wil I? I was going to say—I meant to—how wil I liv without the kids this summer when she has them a month? Did it last sumer so again itll be tuf the 1st few days but then ill be all rt. But how wil i be able to see my wif for just the hr or so it takes to hand them over to her, tho befor she said to send them on the plane on their own. ill do that of cours. that

STEPHEN DIXON / SLEEP

way i wont see my wif, ex-wif, wel, shes not my exwif yet, just acts like it, but i wont c . . . my wif just yeled from upstairs "its past 2:45, arent u going to pik up the kids?" so mayb my watch is wrong by a few minuts or her clock is. anyway, "im going," i said, and i go.

many janes

Give me a line. One night when I was sleeping a dream appeared to me. Wrong. A line. I woke up, got my socks on,
shorts, put on my watch, strode down the hall, went to the toilet, had breakfast, dressed, or dressed and had breakfast, read
a book first, made love to my wife, it's night, before I woke,
I'm in bed, wife comes to bed, wife's about to come to bed,
"Come to bed, wife," she does, love, sleep, wake up, toilet,
dressed, breakfast, work. Forgot my watch. I call home and she
says "It's right here where you left it," and I say "Where?" and
she says "On the night table by your side of the bed where you
always leave it when you go to sleep," and I say, I say what? I
don't say "Ship it," since I'm only ten minutes away by car, I
say "Please, I have tremendous difficulty without my watch, so
imagine it on my wrist and I bet it'll be there," and she says
"That's ridiculous," and I say "Hold it in your palm, close your
eyes and imagine it on my left wrist, please," and she says "All
right, little to lose," and next thing I know, thirty seconds at
least, it's not on my wrist. I jump out of bed, toilet, dress, don't
forget to shave, shave, downstairs, wake the kids, wake them,
prepare their breakfast, no wife, just me and the kids, no
woman, from downstairs "Kids, come on, I don't hear any

rustling, get up, school, breakfast, I mean breakfast and then school, don't forget to wash your face and brush your teeth and hair, in whatever order you wish but the brushing with the two different kinds of brushes," still don't hear anything, "Kids, please, I don't want you to be late again, it's embarrassing to me and also makes me late for work," no reply or movement, I call their names, listen, go upstairs, door's open because I opened it when I woke them before, they're sleeping or pretending to or one's doing one and other the other, I let up the shade, should have done that when I first woke them, kiss their foreheads which I did before, muss their hair, rub their shoulders, except for the kissing I can do each of these at the same time since there's little space between their beds, room's very small and really only for one person but since their mother died two years ago they want to sleep in the same room, they stir, I say "School, up, face, teeth, hair, breakfast, long-sleeved shirts today, feels a bit chilly out," and my older child, whose bed I'm sitting on now, says "I don't want to go to school," and I say "Heard that one before," and younger one says "I don't want to either," and I say "Come on, don't make me raise my you-know-what," and she says "What?" and I say "Long-sleeved shirts, bit chilly out," look in four of the five dresser drawers, two for pants, two for shirts, top mutual one's for their underclothes, pajamas, tights and socks, find two matching shirts and pants, put them on their beds, "Fresh socks and underclothes today, now up and out, you've five minutes to do everything I said to and get downstairs, starting now," and I look at my watch, or rather my wrist for my watch isn't on it, go into my room and look where I always put it when I go to sleep, night table on the right side of the bed, side Jane slept on and where I mostly sleep now, not there, yell out "Either of you kids see my watch?" no answer, go into their room, "Anyone see my watch?" blank stares, they're dressing now, look sleepy, both have their momma's long thick thighs and full tushy. "Don't forget to brush your teeth." "Brushed them when I went to sleep," older one says, and younger one "I did too." "Bad breath in the morning, even I smell it, so you want to make your mouth fresh. Do it for me, for yourselves, for your teachers and friends. But my watch, I can't leave here without it." "Maybe you left it downstairs by the record player, I see it there a lot," older one says. I go downstairs, it's there, I put it in my wallet, my pocket, what did I mean "my wallet" and why not just put it on my wrist?—no time—put water on for coffee, bring their food to the table, make and pack their lunch, mix juice up and fill their thermoses and stick all this into their schoolbags. It'd be nice if I had a wife and she was pregnant—always wanted three—but not so pregnant where she couldn't help me get the kids off to school, just someone else around here, much as I love them, and for of course other reasons, phone rings, who can it be so early? I think. It's my second wife, at the airport, decided to take the red-eye special rather than leave this morning, "If there's not too much traffic I should be home in an hour." "I'll wait for you but in the meantime take the kids to school. —Jane will be here in an hour," I say to them. "Good," both say, and younger one "She have her baby yet?" "If she had don't you think you would have heard about it? No, let me rephrase that and also apologize to you, since it wasn't nicely said. You would have known if she had the baby, sweetheart, since you two will be the first to know after me." "And the doctors and nurses of course," and I say "Of course," and take them to school, come home, Jane's there, we make love, Jane's there, we kiss, she's having coffee, Jane's there, I say "Hi, hello, you look exhausted, I missed you, I'm so horny for you, let's go upstairs or do it right here on the chair," "I'm ready," she says, Jane's there, she says when I say some of that "I'm feeling a little nauseous, maybe from all the traveling, so possibly tonight?" Jane's there, a photograph of her, on my night table, dead now five years, one of her nursing the younger child with the older one standing beside her chair holding her hand, she was in the car of a friend when it ran off the road and hit a rock, on a train that hit a train and several people in her car died, flying home from an academic convention I'd told her it was futile going to since with the new baby and the one we wanted to have a year from now she wouldn't be able to work for a couple of years, drowned while swimming, I swam out but couldn't reach her in time, in a boat that capsized, kids had life jackets on but were struggling in the water hysterically and seemed to be drowning, "Save the girls," she said, "I'll try to swim to shore," "You can do it?" because she was seven months pregnant, eight, weeks from delivery, "You really think it smart for me to get in this boat?" she'd said, "Just save the girls, I'll make it," I grabbed the girls, one in each arm, and started swimming to shore on my back, "Jane, are you near, are you swimming?" I yelled as I swam, "The girls, I'll be okay," got them to shore, looked quickly at the lake and saw little waves but not Jane, made sure the girls were breathing, said "Stay here, I'm going for Mom," looked for her, screamed her name, no one was around, no houses, cars, plane overhead, "Jane, Jane," jumped in the water and swam to where I think I last saw her, "Yes, dear, what is it? you must be having a bad dream," we're in bed, kids in the next room in theirs, "Should I turn on the light?" "Turn it on," I say, she does, "I'm all right now, don't worry, turn it off, the light's blinding," she does, I feel for her body in bed, it's not there, of course it's not, she died a year ago, longer, I hear my youngest daughter snoring in the next room, something to do with the adenoids, year ago doctor said she should have them removed, then Jane got very sick very quickly, weeks after she was diagnosed she died, baby she was carrying with her, nothing's been done about the girls' health except their semiannual teeth and annual eye examinations, both wear glasses, I wear them, Jane wore them, the baby in a few years probably would have worn them, it's morning, I wake up alone, it's an apartment, no kids, I go to the bathroom and wash up, do a few

exercises, in front of the bathroom mirror and on the bedroom
floor, shower, shave, brush my hair, I should get a haircut I
think, I'll get one during lunch, put my watch on, dress, put
my wallet and keys in my pants pockets, tie on but don't tie it
tight at the neck, kitchen, breakfast, get the newspaper from
in front of the front door first and read it while drinking coffee
and eating toast, news is awful today, or maybe I'm not in the
right mood for hard news, turn to the arts section, book by a
beautiful young woman, or at least her photo makes her beautiful, hand sweeping back or holding in place her long dark
hair, I fantasize getting up with her in the morning, her name's
Jane, previous night our first time in bed, review's a good one,
"witty, warm and wise," which is what they seem to say about
most of these first novels by young women, I take the subway
to work, she's on the subway reading the paper with one hand
and other hand clutching the pole, I think should or shouldn't
I? Absolutely don't pass the chance up, I push through some
people between us and say "This is amazing—I mean, excuse
me, Miss, but you are Jane so and so—I either forgot or didn't
catch your last name so no offense meant with that 'so and
so'—the writer, in this same paper, the book review today?"
and she says "That's right," "Well, congratulations, a terrific
review," and she says "Thank you, and my stop's coming up,"
making a move for the door as the train pulls into the station,
and I say "Mine too, and that's the truth—a coincidence rather
than a ruse," and she says "I believe you, why wouldn't I?"
and we get off and I say as we leave the station "Do you have
to work too because the writing doesn't pay sufficiently, or
maybe you have an early appointment with an agent or editor,
or is that too personal a question and assumption, which if it
is I'm sorry," and she says "No, it's not, and yes, I work,"
"Where, at what?" and she tells, we're on the street now and
she says "Well, it's been nice talking but I'm a little late," and
I say "You going this way?—me too, and again, coincidence,
no ruse, Galaxy Imports, Hundred-eight Water," and after

STEPHEN DIXON / SLEEP

several seconds of silence while we walk—I've looked her over, she's sweet-looking rather than beautiful, nice shape and gait too—and when I don't know if I should say this, but what the hell, do, for lots to gain but not much to lose, "You have children, married, leave someone at home, or is it just you, or are all those again too personal as questions and assumptions?" and she says "Just me," and I say "Just me too," and then "How long it take to write the book?"—I've always been curi-ous about that and the intricacies of it, and this time I won't wait till a book comes to the library or out in paperback before I get it, something I probably would never do despite the good review unless I had met you, I don't know why, money per-haps, laziness I presume," and she says "Maybe fiction isn't one of your main interests," and I say "But it is, reviews of them the first thing I turn to in the paper if the front page news isn't an event," tell her what I'm presently reading and have recently read, she tells me what she thinks of these books, more questions, answers and assumptions from both of us till we're in front of my office building and I say "Maybe you won't want to, I'm sure short time we've spoken you don't see much reason why you should, but would you like to meet for lunch today?—I was going to get a haircut but I can do that after work," "Sure, where?" we meet, have dinner the next day, make love the following week, I move into her apartment and sublet mine, hers is much nicer and she preferred it that way, marry, two girls, she dies, I meet and marry another woman named Jane, I don't look for them with that name, just the only kind I seem to find, she dies, another woman named Jane, Jane Jane Jane, my three Janes, I have four daughters altogether with them, the fourth is named Janine but after her mother dies I call her Jane, they grow up, move out, I retire from work, buy the cabin we always rented summers for a month and winterize it and move in there, the town's librar-ian's named Jane, I say "That's a coincidence, and this is no ruse, really, and of course it's one of the more common names, but my three wives were all named Jane," and tell her they all died of natural causes only and that I loved dearly each one, she's much younger than I, I'm attracted to her and now maybe even her name and like the selection of new books the library gets and go to it almost every day it's open, she invites me to her house for dinner, I invite her out to a movie, we hike up the one monadnock in the area and picnic there, make love, marry, I don't want another child but she does for she never had one so we try, it's a girl, I wake up, put my watch on, take it off, exercise, jog in the park a couple of miles, shower, coffee, dress, leave for school, leave for the office, leave for work, subway, bus or car, when I get there I see my watch is gone, must have come unclasped and slipped off without my knowing it, I buy a new one at lunchtime when I'd planned to get a haircut, same cheap kind, runs on time, come home from work, make several calls, none of the women I speak to seem interested in going out or staying in or really doing anything with me and this time each of them, perhaps because I'm so eager to see someone I persist in trying to persuade them, says it, wonder how I'm going to meet one for I'm getting close to middle age and might even be in it, since I'm not sure when it starts, and want to marry and have children or a child, maybe if I took an evening course at a continuing ed school, one that lots of relatively young women attend or at least hang around the school's bookshop or cafeteria, or one during my lunch hour: writing, painting—maybe the model, a painter or writer earning a few extra bucks, she's wearing only a bathrobe, walks around the room during her break looking at the students' work of her, says something to me about mine, "I have breasts as big and fat as that?—boy, are you fantasizing," or "It's quite good," or "I'd go easy on the shadowing and multilayers of paint if I were you, but I should mind my own business," and I say "Thanks," or "No, thanks, do you paint?" she says yes, or no, is an actress, "Can't you tell by how well I do the modeling part? and can't get work right now and have to pay the bills and got bored sick with those temp jobs," and I say "But this doesn't pay as well, does it?" "Pays enough and gives me plenty of time to think and memorize scripts—what do you do?" and just as I'm about to say, art instructor calls out "Five minutes are up, model," she poses, alternates looking at the clock and me as she does, returns to talk during the next break, bathrobe now fastened at the top, so I can't as I want see in, which she might have caught me doing last time, I tell her what I do, she compliments me for not just having lunch on my lunch hour—"I admire people, no matter how old, who are always extending themselves, trying out new things and not getting stale, you know?" I say "Thanks, and you might think this presumptuous—after all, we've only spoken for two short breaks," and I pause, say "No, it's silly, besides wrong," and she says "What is?—go on, I might be so sweaty and smelly next break you might not want to continue this conversation, which I find a nice relief from the silent stony posing," and I ask if she'd like to have coffee after class, she says she has another class right after, "so another time maybe?" "When?" I say, she tells me when she'll be free, I say I'll still be working then, she says "Then when do you get off and I can probably meet you in front of your office building if it's not too late, though for something as long as dinner I'm not really interested in," I say, we meet, coffee, she has tea, go out, stay in, out, in, make love, her name's Jane, when she told me I said "That's remarkable," she asked why and I said "Oh, it's just that I guessed it moment I saw you there on the modeling platform," I call her J for short, move in, marry, children, bed, watch, getting them up, years, city, country, sickness, death, exercise, shower, shave, newspaper, no news, old news, turn to the reviews, my kids whom I kiss good-night every night, when they're awake and later when they're sleeping.

survivors

He died or at least we think he did. We haven't heard anything of him for a long time. My friend Maurice and I were
talking about him and what his work and Albert, meaning the
way Albert conducted his work life, meant to us years ago
and Maurice said "Why don't you check? If he's dead we
should know it, shouldn't we?" "Why so?" I said and he said
"Because if someone asks if we've heard from Albert, or what's
the latest on Albert, or do we know anyone who's seen anything on him and his work lately, or do we know if he's even
alive? —those kinds of things, and just our own curiosity
about him, we can say he died." "Suppose he hasn't died, and
we're certainly hoping he hasn't, right?" and he said "You have
to ask me that? Of course, what do you think? Like you, I've
nothing against the guy personally, so I can only hope he lives
a long and happy and fruitful life for years to come. Forever, if
it's possible. So if he's alive, we know it and that makes us feel
better than just sitting here thinking he's more than likely
dead. And if he's alive and still producing, even better, for we
feel good the guy never gave up no matter what rewards never
came his way. But I'm only assuming he has died because he's
around that age when lots of people do. Like ourselves, let's

face it, but unlike us he never let himself stay healthy after he was a relatively young man and he worked himself so hard for years and years you'd think by now there wouldn't be much left of him. And also, and this maybe more than all of it, that we haven't heard a whisper about him or seen anything of his or any mention of it for around ten years, and I've kept pretty much in touch on those things and I know so have you. So go on and do what you can in finding out about him and let me know right away if you come up with anything."

So I call around and nobody I know who knew of Albert or who even knew him a little way back when has heard anything about him or seen anything of his or about it for more than ten years, and a couple of them say fifteen, maybe twenty. But I tell them both I know for a fact there was something of his, though granted not so prominently displayed, some twelve years ago or even less. I'm about to give up finding out anything about him when on a hunch I call his phone number in the city he was living in last time I knew him, New York, and which I still have in my little address book and for some reason haven't scratched out. I guess I always thought I'd contact him at it some day, even if the last time I tried—or last times, for I tried for a month without anyone answering the phone—was maybe eight years ago, though what I wanted to speak to him about then I forget. I figure that this time I'll get a no-longer-in-service recorded message, or at the very best a message with his new phone number, or get someone or this person's answering machine who'd been assigned the number once the phone company took it out of service for about six months or however long they take it out before giving another customer the number. Anyway, I for sure didn't expect to reach Albert at it. I was just, now out of ways to contact him, covering the last of my bases, so to speak. But, surprisingly enough, I get a nephew of his who I only learn is the nephew when he says "No, Albert Rampskin isn't in, I'm his nephew Nelson, may I help you any?" "Yeah, a lot. I'm looking for your uncle, or just would like to know what's become of him. I'm a former contemporary in the same field, you can say, and I—" but he cuts me off with "Oh, he died, sir, years ago. Five, six? Something like that. I'm here with his old number because I inherited the whole works from him, phone, furniture—the apartment, is what I'm saying: books, linen, kitchen utensils, even a couple dozen cans of food in his cupboards. It wasn't easy either. Getting the inherited apartment, I'm saying, and it wasn't an inheritance so much as a turning over to me from him. As for his death and how easy it was—well, certainly not for me, being a guy who kind of liked him a great deal; as for Uncle Al and how easy it was going, isn't for me to say for him." "I'm very sorry to hear of it, very. And about the apartment, I'd say you were lucky to get it, if you just continued the lease with a little increase when the renewal for it came up and didn't have to pay the landlord through the nose to keep it. I've been there, several times. Though it's only a one bedroom, the rooms are spacious and all of them facing the river, including the bathroom. So if the trees across the drive haven't grown up past your floor by now and sprouted, you got one of the great views in the city and probably breezes in the summer even." "Rarely, breezes. It's got one exposure, so the heat stays for days inside once the rest of the city's cooled off. But the view's as beautiful as you say, if you like lots of river and ugly forty-story apartment complexes across it on the Palisades, and it's cheaper and cleaner and a lot more convenient than my former place. As for acquiring it, the landlord wanted me out of here if I wasn't immediate kin like parent or child, since he figured that after he'd splash a little paint on the walls and got a new flushometer for the toilet he'd get fair market value for it, which would mean three times what Uncle Al was paying, so I had to go to court. You see, to head off all this, since nobody knew the city mind like Uncle Al, he'd signed a paper and got it notarized saying I'd taken care of him like a nurse the last three years and made this place my first residence, when all I really did was bring him a bagel and coffee once a week or so and spend a night on the couch here every month if it was too late and dangerous to go home by subway to my room in Brooklyn. As for closer relatives by blood, he had a daughter and there's also my father, but they wanted nothing of the place since they lived a thousand miles from here and thought New York to be Satan in a bottle. But that paper and our same last name and that no one checked out his more immediate kin convinced the judge I deserved the apartment." "Tell me," I say, "and not so much to change the subject and if you don't mind my asking, but how'd he die?" and he says "Not from overeating." "Excuse me, what are you saying, he was too sick to hold down food? Or just too poor to buy any and keep his apartment at the same time and didn't know he could probably get assistance from friends or people who'd respected him in his work or just some big institutions in his field?" and he says "Hey, where you going? No, he didn't eat intentionally, is what I mean. He just got tired of living for several reasons, he told me, so he thought starving to death was the best way to go, painless for everybody, no carcass lying around with blood all over it to clean up, and the lighter he was, easier it'd be for the death squad, as he called it, to stick him in a body bag and cart him away." "You know, this doesn't have that ring of truth to it, I'll say. It'd seem because of the unusualness of his death, as you described it, somebody like myself would have heard it from other people or at least from the newspaper which I read every day, since you'd think with all Albert had produced over thirty years he'd have rated a minor obituary in the *Times,* with picture or without, but something instead of the kind you pay for. But starved himself to death? How does one even do that except not to eat, and how do you do that?" and Nelson says "That's it, what I've been telling you. Not a thing to eat or drink for eleven days. He laid here for the first ten of them and then the landlord came in and sent him to a hospital but he already had something signed that said no means to keep him alive should be taken, or something to that effect—you know the phrase, what I mean, right?" and I say "Yes, but didn't they put him on intravenous feeding there, even with this no-means thing he signed?" and he says "They did, a little, but it was too late. And he also kept pulling the tubes out till they strapped down his arms, but by then he was finished, probably also from years of semistarving himself before that only because he lost interest in most foods." "I still don't see someone killing himself that way. And why in the world why? Things weren't going well with him? Okay, that's never been unusual with any of us, but he was terminal with something?" and he says "Terminal with life, is the way Uncle Al put it. Just didn't see any reason anymore to live. He'd produced, the word you used, a ton of stuff and no one much took it with seriousness, even when it was out there for everyone to get if they made a first step to. He was also exhausted by it all and couldn't do anymore or wouldn't because of that reason of not much interest I gave, plus his daughter and my dad couldn't take him because he was such a critic of their materialism and no-culture ways and so forth, so he lost them too. And listen, a guy's in his fairly right mind and wants to go, who's to legitimately stop him, is the way I see it. If you knew Uncle Al as you say then you remember nothing could really please him in his later days. And his friends—well, let's say you were one of them, but they got to the point where because he was so angry over almost everything after awhile but especially the stinking way people received his work that they couldn't take him either, even the ones who said they admired it so much. Like you, one would call once every five to ten years, he said, to see if he was still around, but certainly not come over to see him or make a lunch date-like, and you probably would have done the same if he was alive today when you called. You would have said 'So, good talking to you, pal, just checking in with you, seeing you're okay,' and that would've been it till another five to ten years." "I don't know about that," I say and he says "Well, no harm meant in that remark, as I got to admit he was kind of a tough bird to get along with at times and his work, whatever the big minds might say about it, was a bit too pretzel-like and in the serious vein for my tastes, besides dark. But now that you know what's happened to him, tell who else might want to know about my Uncle Al so they wouldn't be calling me every five to ten years here to find out."

"Sure, will do," and I hang up and call my friend and tell him what I learned about Albert and he says "Too bad, he was an all-right guy, didn't you think? Tough to get along with as his nephew said but smart and occasionally friendly enough and not mean-spirited that I could see, or more than anyone else, and a heck of a talent—a hell of one. So, a terrific loss to the field even if he hasn't done anything in it the last ten years or from what I've seen and heard, but his works will stand out, even if they're mostly forgotten now, sometime in the future I bet," and I say "Probably not. Once you don't get a name after working so long you never get a name, or not, for sure, after you're dead. Or maybe not except by some rare fluke or if you do something like jump off the Empire State Building with your work strapped to your sides, but they'd probably put you down as another crazy dying for attention. I didn't mean that 'dying' there, by the way—it was an error, unintended, not made for laughs in any way or form. But that'd be it for you, a funny story to people who heard it—an anecdote of despera- tion that didn't succeed. Anyhow, nothing like that's going to happen to Albert because his stuff is so, well you know, like the nephew said—dark and highly serious and just off- putting to most folk and in a way inaccessible to the degree that nobody's about to make a fuss over it in the future. And especially when I think just the opposite's what people will be making fusses over in the future under the same set of circumstances—serious, dark, not easy, and so on—the way things are going with culture. What you got to credit the guy for is working hard at what he liked doing—this alone will get you nowhere, you understand I'm saying—and then having the sense to give up on it after thirty or so years once he found it almost impossible to get his work around except for a little. And then snuffing himself without any fuss and no bother to anyone, really, except the most minimal—I didn't ask and wasn't told but I bet he requested to be cremated and his ashes kicked to the winds—besides leaving his place to his nephew instead of the landlord, who as the kid said would have looked at his exit as just another way to make big bucks with little investment. So I say here's to Albert. I personally didn't care for him much as lots of others might have but I did think his work was of a pretty good caliber as well as being honest and direct, and I admire him even more now for going so easily and considerately and with no to-do."

"Here's to Albert," my friend says, "and when I get off the phone I'll actually drink a drink to him in his honor. May he R.I.P. and all that stuff. So, see any sign of Tim Phickerson lately?" and I say "No. In fact it's been so long since I've seen his name or heard even a peep about him that I'll lay odds he's gone too." "Why don't you phone around to find out?" and I say "This time you do it, that last one took me hours. We haven't spoken about him for a while but he was right up there in our estimation, am I wrong?" and he says "As much as anyone among the not-so-knowns except Albert, perhaps, in the category of their conviction against the odds and stick-to-itiveness. Especially when it became clear after more than thirty years that his work would never sell much or really get around. All right, I'll call, or do what I can to sniff some info out about him, and let you know what I come up with."

He calls two days later and says "I'm not going to suggest you won't believe this but Phickerson walked into the ocean at Honolulu four years ago and was never found. Did it intentionally, is what I'm saying, with the last person to see him saying he saw a man traipsing calmly into the water with these iron weights hanging around his neck and thought he was doing some new kind of exercise. Now that took guts, I'd say, which in his work we both knew he always had. The ranks are thinning, my dear pal, wouldn't you say?" and I say "You never know a man's dead till you find the body unless you saw him fall without a parachute from a plane, that's what I learned from bad dick novels when I was a kid, so don't count the guy out yet. He had imagination, humor, sense of adventure and an irreverent way of not going by the rules, in his work and out, if I remember correctly, so who knows if he won't turn up someday and say to us all 'Fooled ya.' What else they say he do, leave his clothes and a note on the beach, because that'd be in the tradition," and he says "His clothes, piled precisely, shoes and socks first and so on, but no note, though it could have blown away, did you think of that?" "Who'd you finally hear it all from?" and he says "For this one, once I couldn't uncover anything about him from people, I had to push some computer buttons and keys in the reference room of the main library—the local ones had the tools but nothing on him. Actually, I had a librarian do it for me, as I'll never be able to figure out those things even though the instructions are given in clear elementary English right on the screen. After that I went to the Honolulu newspaper with the correct death date, almost ruining my eyes trying to read the articles on this new kind of microfilm machine." "Any new works by him in the last ten years?" and he says "Nothing the computer and microfilm thing know of." "So," I say, "another one, if it's no hoax, who we'll have to assume did himself in because he got too discouraged about his work, or the reception to it, for that guy was such a hard worker and inventive that I'm sure he was thinking of something new while even walking into the ocean. That is, if it wasn't because of a serious illness or even at that late stage in his life a romance that backfired. But you really couldn't reach anyone who might have known something about his last years, or you just got lazy at the last minute or cheap with the telephone?" and he says "All my queries came up blank. And since I knew you'd complain if I wasn't absolutely thorough about this or as much as I could be, I phoned people in Paris and London and all over whom I knew he once knew. Nothing. Even the old places that used to take his work were either under themselves—and you get the reference there, don't you, that 'under' in relation to him? and I think it's accurate all the way as a comparison too," and I say "Yes, it's good, or was till you started explaining it—I mean, what do you think my mind's been doing the last thirty years?" and he says "Or the people still working at the places still in business that once took him said they haven't heard or seen a thing from him since they don't know how long and because he never made their companies any money from his work or boosted their reputations much by their having him, they weren't about to seek him out for more. How about Hy Solowitz?" and I say "Boy, that's a name from the past—what about him?" and he says "Long as we're sort of doing a little survey of old-timers, let's see if he's still around. Though if he went the way the last two did, and with the three of them born around the same decade and going into the same field at about the same age and staying in it for a similar number of years and facing almost the same things in it, that would be something to mull over, wouldn't you say? But with Solowitz, seeing how we've been alternating these, you do the calling and finding out," and I say "Fair enough," and phone around and learn that Solowitz, who was maybe as good at what he did as Albert and even a little better known years ago, which means we're talking about two hundred people in this world who knew of his work compared to a hundred-fifty for Albert's, and who was more than just a little better known than Phickerson— here it could be two hundred compared to a hundred— crashed his car into a wall seven years ago, and the police and medical reports on it couldn't determine if it was an accident or self-done though sort of leaned to the latter.

STEPHEN DIXON / SLEEP

I call my friend but his line's busy. When he hears the news about Solowitz I wonder what he'll say about the third one we talked about ending up as a more-than-probable. Maybe, knowing him, that it was a good thing the two of us didn't have as much talent as any one of that threesome but more important that we eventually got to realize it and pulled out before we really began deluding ourselves that we were better than we were and would become more known than we'd been and that real worth always wins out in the end and also that with lots of hard work, perseverance and sacrifice and so on we'd get to be as good if not better than the others, which could be true—you never know, though look where being so good at it and working so hard and giving up so much got them—but those kinds of things. I call again and his line's still busy. Maybe I'll fool him and say "Listen to this: Solowitz is not only alive and still plugging away at it but he hit it big critically and monetarily a year ago," and see what he has to say. But he'd probably tell me "If he did hit it big I definitely would have heard about it, since isn't that what we've been getting with these calls and inquiries all along?" Nah, I'll just tell him the truth and if he brings up some other guy's name from the past and wants me to do the calling and stuff, or even volunteers to do it himself, I'll say "Really, three's always been enough. If you haven't had your fill or learned what you had to learn from that many examples, then something's got to be wrong."

•

the elevator

I'm in the lobby waiting at the elevator door for the elevator when a man behind me says "Did you by chance catch Pinker's new story?" "No," a woman says, "is one out?" "Sure, in *Moments,* just hit the stands, though I got my copy at the office yesterday." "Is it a good one?" and he says "You be the judge, I'll pretend I'm impartial. This is the story. I shouldn't have said that; you'll know what I mean. But this, right now what I'm going to quote to you. 'Here is the story, this is the story, that was the story, and that's it, the story.'" "So?" she says and he says "So, what? I told you, that's the story, all of it. I'd show it to you if I didn't leave my copy in the office. —Where is this elevator? It's been stuck on the eleventh for the last three minutes." "Someone's probably loading things in it—going on a trip, a vacation, or perhaps only lots of laundry to be done in the basement." "Let them use the service elevator if they have so much to take down." "Oh, and that's so easy? It's not a self-service elevator." "It's simple. You ring Julio in the basement, on that intercom thing we have in the kitchen, and if he's not there then you phone the super. One of them's always around in the day till about 10 P.M., or that other handyman who takes over for Julio. I think it's part of the city building code or something, when you have an elevator building this size. But this elevator's strictly for regular passengers, up and down, up and down; all the tenants should know there's only one elevator here for that purpose, and if they have someone visiting or working for them they should let them know." "I'm sure everyone knows and I'm almost sure it won't be long, unless it's nothing to do with a passenger and is just stuck." "If it's stuck," the man says, "we ought to do something, like get the super to look into it. He can take the service elevator to the eleventh. Think I should ring his bell?" "Give it another couple of minutes. So, what about the Pinker story?" and he says "What do you mean? What I quoted was what it was, read by I'm sure a hundred thousand people already and ready to be read by several hundreds of thousands more." "But that couldn't have been all of it. If it was, then it wasn't a story." "Who's to say? We live in a modern age and it seems anything can be anything if you have the authority to say it is. Anyway, certainly nobody like the likes of you and me can declare what is and isn't a story. The petty pedestrian? No way, my dear. The man in the red bowler? I'll say." "What man in a red bowler?" "An expression," he says, "meaning, well, meaning . . . since people don't normally wear red bowlers, except to costume benefits perhaps. Or bowlers of any sort in ordinary company, then I suppose it means the unusual rare but insignificant man . . . no, that's not it. Or maybe it means the everyman—bowler, you know, once a common hat fifty years ago or so. I don't know. I got the expression from somewhere, I think when I was a kid, and it always seemed appropriate for certain examples of things till you just challenged me and I had to really think of it. I've never used it to you before where it made sense? For maybe, if you remember, you can tell me what I meant." "This is a first. That you've spoken it. And what I said was hardly a challenge. But Pinker's story—it was actually in a magazine and presented as a serious piece and not like some skit? And same

STEPHEN DIXON / SLEEP

with the length—that was it?" "Not only in the current *Moments* but listed on the cover—billed, you can say. 'Avery Pinker's new story,' or new story by him, and then his name and the story's title in the table of contents inside, and by now you can probably guess what the title is." "What?" she says. "Guess. You'd have to come close." " 'The Shortest Story'? 'This is the Story, My Friend'? Really, I'm not good at guessing; what?" " 'Story.' Just 'Story,' but without the 'just.' In other words, 'Story,' 'Story,' but just one of them. When you think of it, it was pretty adventurous for that rather dry or dull . . . well, you know, staid magazine, to publish it. I guess they think they're juicing it up a bit with one of his works—a work like that, I mean, and that title." "True," she says, "it doesn't seem like the typical *Moments* story, but then some haven't been, which I suppose means there is no typical *Moments* story. And because it can be such a staid magazine, as you say, I have to admit I only read about half their issues, and when I do, less than half the magazine, but usually the stories, if they're not too long, though I've never seen anything as short as that one. But repeat it again for me, would you? Maybe I didn't quite get it the first time and there's more to it than meets the eye, or ear, in this case." " 'This is the story, that's the story,' or rather, 'This is the story, here's the story' . . . Oh, I've already told you it. Once, and I say this out of complete impartiality again, isn't enough? But what about the elevator? It still hasn't moved. I'm going to do something I don't normally do. Forgive me, but like *Moments* I'm going to be adventurous for the moment though I think with more of a point behind it." He bangs on the elevator door and stares at the ceiling right above the door and bangs some more and yells "Hello, up there. Eleventh floor, can you hear me? Send the elevator down. We've been waiting in the lobby almost ten minutes already, so send it down now."

A man comes out of an apartment a few feet from the elevator. "What is it," he says, "elevator stuck again?" "It might be. In fact I was going to ring your bell right after I yelled up to the elevator. We've been here—" "I know, I heard; I was inside; you should've knocked instead of yelling. I would've come that way sooner." "What my husband's saying, Elio, is that someone might be filling it with belongings, for a trip of some kind, or laundry for the basement machines. But it seems it's been on the eleventh floor for so long that no one could have that much laundry to wash or be able to pack a small elevator full with that many possessions, even if he was—" "I should go upstairs then," Elio says. "We were hoping you would," the woman says. "You didn't ring for the handyman to do it?" and the man says "No, we thought you'd want to. "Why would I? First the handyman, then the super for that. That's how it goes unless for major jobs. Trouble, always trouble in an old building like this. Today I spent five hours with the plumbers when the main hot water pipe burst between the twelfth and thirteenth floors on the B line." "That's not our line, thank God," the woman says. "Five hours, maybe six. You can't just not watch them or they'll be there for three days, and my handymen don't know what to watch for. All right, I'll go." The service elevator, across the lobby, is open and he gets in it and shuts the door. "Wait . . . Elio," the man says, running over. "You can take us to the tenth long as you're going up," but the elevator takes off. "Mr. Muniz?" the man yells. "Elio? Can you take us to the tenth, or even the eleventh and we'll walk down one?" He comes back to the passenger elevator. "Why didn't I think of it sooner?" "He still could have done it," the woman says. "He heard you before he started up. What an SOB. You want to try walking?" and he says "Ten flights?" "Nine, but good exercise. Okay. And if this elevator's broken the super will quickly get the handyman to run the service elevator till the passenger one's fixed. Isn't that what they usually do, with someone manning the elevator all night?" "I suppose," he says.

A man enters the building through the revolving door. "Alain, how are you?" the man says. "Phil, hello. You know my

wife, Evelyn . . . " "Of course," Phil says and Evelyn and he
shake hands. "We're waiting for the elevator," Alain says. "It
seems to be stuck on the eleventh floor." "Seems?" Evelyn
says. "Is stuck, or more than likely," Alain says. "Oh damn. Is
anyone running the service elevator?" Phil says and Alain says
"The super's in it but he just went up to check on the passenger elevator. The whole thing only just started." "Oh damn, I
have to take a leak bad. I think I better go up the block to do
it in a restaurant or bar. This may take more time than I have
before there's a minor accident. Excuse me," and he goes. "Do
you know who that was?" Alain says. "Phil Sifkin. You just
introduced us for about the fifth time in the last three months."
"I have? I forget. But do you know what he does? It's amazing
but he's an editor at *Moments*. It's because of him that I get a
free subscription to the magazine at my office. I mentioned to
him once, how wouldn't it be nice to get a subscription—I
meant that I wanted to take out one, and I said it more to show
respect for what he does than anything else—and he just put
my name in and place of business, as if I were some big deal in
the field, and it's never stopped coming for a year." "How
come I didn't know that's how you got it?" and he says "I don't
know; it wasn't something I'd hide." "Because I've wondered
why you get it there and then have to schlepp it home. Though
most of the time you don't, which is probably why I've only
seen half the issues." "I'd like to ask him about that Pinker
story. What the heck he thinks of it and all that and if he was
instrumental in buying it for the magazine. And to tell you the
truth, if they paid their normal rates for it. If they did, because
theirs are just about the highest, I'm telling you, I'm going into
the story-writing business. Because you're a hundred percent
right. No one can call that piece of mischief a story—am I
being impartial enough now? I don't care who wrote it, what
the writer's international rep is, and what serious publication,
known for its quality fiction, published it. Nor what the most
esteemed literary muck-a-mucks of our day say about it, if

STEPHEN DIXON / SLEEP

they do speak well of it, which I'm sure some will do with this slight . . . well, this—"

Phil comes back. "So fast?" Alain says and Phil says "I got halfway up the block when I decided I didn't have to go as badly as I thought. I also felt the elevator would be here by now, but I see I was wrong." "How do you feel now?" and Phil says "You mean my little problem? Listen, less we talk of it, better off I am. Out of mind, out of bladder, or something. No, not 'out of bladder.' Oh please not out, not now, at least. Excuse me, I'm being silly." "Phil," Alain says, "I got *Moments* at the office this week, which I again want to thank you for, by the way, but I wondered about the Pinker story in it." "What story?" and Alain says "It's *the* story in the issue. The one that goes, and this is it in its entirety, and you have it bannered across the cover also—" "Not I. I've left *Moments* and gone to Nappy Publications, editing its two boat magazines." "I didn't know that." "Thought I told you the last time we bumped into each other down here or in the elevator." "The elevator," Evelyn says. "Good God, I wish it would come." "I doubt it ever will, and we will have to walk up nine flights." "About that story you mentioned of Pinker's?" Phil says and Alain says "Doesn't matter now. I thought you had a hand in it." "Was it any good? Should I read it, as I've never much cared for the guy?" "Only if you've lots of time on your hands." "It's that long? They'd do that every so often," and Alain says "I was joking; it's about three short sentences long. Actually, one not-so-long sentence, but three to four short clauses." "And that's all of it," Evelyn says, "according to Alain." "I'll take a look at it, sounds interesting for them. I never saw anything literary there that short except a poem." "If I were you," Alain says, "I'd tell myself not to bother. In fact I'll recite the whole story and save you the trouble of looking at it. It's titled, clever clever, 'Story'; see? 'Story.' One word, 'Story.' With my short-term memory receding a bit further every day, I was still able to memorize it, story and, if you can believe it, title as well."

STEPHEN DIXON / SLEEP

"That suggests it has some enduring power," Evelyn says. "Sure it does, sure. Though I will admit it might be better read on paper than heard. Most stories, I've found out, are. Anyway, 'Story,' by Avery Pinker. Ahem. 'This is the story, here is the story, that was the story, and that's it, the story.' Unahem. You get the 'unahem,' right?" "Yes," Phil says, "good. But that's the story?" "That's the story, folks, unless the printers and proofreaders goofed up and left half of it out, let's say, though from what I've heard, they never do. No errors." "That mag has the best there is in both categories, I'll vouch for that," Phil says. "Look," Evelyn says, "the elevator floor signal's gone from eleven to nine. Now on eight. Now heading to seven. Elio must have fixed it. Or he told whoever was holding it up to release the door." "The point is, it's descending," Phil says. "Now watch my urinary system move into action. It always does when I have an inclination to go and the conveyance that'll take me to my deliverance spot . . . anyway, it becomes a second-to-second battle of wills, the physical and my—" "Spare me," Evelyn says. "You're right. I'm sorry. I apologize. Too personal and also so silly of me again."

The elevator door opens. "So," Elio says from inside, "it was stuck and I did something with my hands and got it to work again. It'll be fine now, no more problems, but I'm getting the elevator service to look at it tomorrow. I want no more repeats. It was the eleventh floor door, not the car that was the trouble, but I fixed it with a little jiggle." "One can do that," Alain says, all of us stepping inside, "fix a door with a little jiggle?" "I straightened a bottom part that was keeping it open." "Thanks," Phil says, "you don't know how much. You're not getting out?" "I have to get the service elevator. What I should've done is sent this one down to you without me and taken the service one myself, but I thought you would want to know why the elevator got stuck." "Thank you," Alain says, and presses three floor buttons—I suppose his, Phil's, and eleven—and the door closes and elevator goes up. "What floor?" he says to me, his finger by the button panel and I say "Jesus, I forgot. I'm going to Rutter." "No Rutter in this building," Elio says. "She's subletting someone's apartment for a few months—name that starts with an s, I think." "Lots of s's. Salaman?" "No." "Slaza?" "I'd know it if I saw the tenant roster. There was one in the lobby." "I don't know a Rutter sublet. Could be it's an illegal or through management without my knowing, but they don't do that." "I'm sure she did it legally," I say. "There is someone new I've noticed the last few months," Phil says. "Small pretty-young woman, usually a long braid in back?" "No, short hair," I say, "and she's almost my height." "Very slim?" Evelyn says. "No, she's kind of, you know, heavyset, and around forty." "Hey, what happened to my floor?" Phil says. "I know I pressed it," Alain says, pressing ten and eleven. The elevator passes ten and stops at eleven. "What in the world's happening?" Alain says and Elio says "You see? It only wants to take me." The door opens, he gets out and holds the door in with his hand. "Something could be wrong in the panel box if you pressed it right and the car didn't stop. I'll have the service inspect it, but try your floors again going downstairs. Could be it wasn't this door after all." "We should get off here and walk down the flight," Alain says to Evelyn. "Oh, let's stop at ten. I'm sure it'll stop there, and it'll be another adventure if it doesn't," indicating with head shakes and her eyes she doesn't want to get off with Elio. "And about your friend," Elio says to me, still holding in the door, which is making these back-and-forth motions it wants to close, "tell her to see me. She can't occupy without management giving written permission and its getting the rent increase the city lets them for sublets for no matter how short time." "I'll do that," I say and he releases the door. "Not Steinberg, 4A?" he says and I say no and the door closes.

The elevator goes up. "Now where?" Phil says and Alain says "Possibly someone on one of the top floors pressed it." "Excuse me," I say to him, "but about that Pinker story. I'm sorry if this sounds like eavesdropping, but he's one of my favorite writers and what you said doesn't sound like one of his." "Which is what I've been saying," and Evelyn says "Not quite." "Are you sure," I say, "and I know you covered this, that that wasn't the opening of the story—a tease by the magazine, so to speak? You checked?" The car stops at PH, door opens, no one's waiting there, Alain says "Yes" to me, keeps his finger on the PH button, sticks his head out and looks to both sides, presses buttons 10 and 8 and the door closes and elevator starts down. "I knew we should have gotten off on eleven," Alain says and Evelyn says "I simply didn't want to be with that man. He's crude, he's rude, he talks too much and always finds fault with everything and I felt we were next." "Would it be possible, and I know I can get the magazine myself, but to quickly quote it again?" I say to Alain. "I just have a feeling something's been missed." "Believe me, nothing has," Alain says, as the car stops at ten. "I'll do it, I love reciting," Phil says. "You mind?" to Alain, keeping his finger on the 10 button and Alain says "About keeping us here, now that we're here, and so long as you don't let the door close, no." "I meant the Pinker piece," and Evelyn says "I wouldn't mind hearing a different voice doing it. It's possible it's all in the recital," and Alain says "The mike's yours, Phil." " 'This is the story, that's the story, here it is, there it was, that's it, the story, story.' " "You've changed it considerably," Evelyn says and Phil says "How? First story in my life I thought I was able to memorize perfectly in its entirety—first of anything literary, poem or story—and without even having read it. Where'd I go wrong?" "I think you used a past tense for a present, introduced a couple of 'storys,' besides mangling other things." "Say, what's the difference?" and she says "If the man wrote it for a purpose and the story's so brief, I'm sure there's plenty of difference, not to get into a big argument over it, though that might be exciting—not since college." "Do you really believe he racked his brain over every single word and verb and comma and so forth?" Phil says and I say "Probably; of course he did. I mean, this guy's no hack." "Phil, don't you have to do something important?" Alain says and he says "Now that you mentioned it, unfortunately, I do. And the more I think of that story the more I agree with you that *Moments* must have had its nuttiest if not most drunken weekly editors' conference in thirty years to accept such a sham." "Good-night, all," Alain says and Evelyn nods to Phil and me and they leave.

Phil releases the button and the door closes and elevator starts down. He looks at the indicator light above the door. "Nine . . . eight . . . and it's stopping," as the elevator slows, "what do you know." The door opens and he says "Well," looking at me and I say "Yes, nice talking to you," and he steps out. "But I have to tell you. I actually liked that Pinker story, as a joke, hoax, sham, credo, everything all in one and nothing at all, or something. Not that, the last thing I said, but I—" and he says "Come on now, sir," and I say "No, I mean it. I heard it at least three times, in slightly different versions, admittedly, from you and that man, Alain, and I think I just about got it all—I was able to put it together, is what I'm saying—and I'm not sure why but it says something about story-making." "What not to do, perhaps." The door starts closing and he presses the "Open" button and it opens. "No, really," I say. "When so many stories these days go on too long, his is extra short, and so on. Most today are also too lifelike and clear . . . not his. You can interpret it—I like that—and it's not only tricky but funny. Maybe the magazine shouldn't have bannered it so big on the cover, as Alain said it did. But to me, this might be why they did it; it reads like the last story Pinker's ever going to write." "I wouldn't—the door starts closing and he presses the "Open" button again—"I wouldn't, if I were that kind of writer, want to go out with that one." "Anyway, I'm going to get it and give it a good read, or at least do it a few times at the magazine stand," and he says "Good. Make your

STEPHEN DIXON / SLEEP

own assessments of stuff, don't listen to ours. I will say that if it's in there it means that more than one person on the staff liked it—those editorial meetings are serious and often quarrelsome and partisan. For certain, they didn't buy it for his name. Good-night," and I say "See ya."

"Hey, everything okay up there," Elio yells from somewhere downstairs, probably the lobby, "or is the car stuck again?" "No, everything's okay," I yell. "I forgot to press the button to the lobby." "It's pressed, it's pressed, people are waiting, so just let the damn thing go." The door closes without my touching a button and the elevator starts down.

to tom

I don't know. Last night four young people streaked down the block with all their clothes off and then back up it with both times I'm watching and none of them even trying to hide their genital parts or the girl her breasts. And three days ago I'm walking past this avenue bar down the block where suddenly there's a shoot-out inside and someone yells duck and I do and a man staggers to the street with blood spouting out of his head and falls over me and my groceries lying by my side. And today some old lady I know gets shot in front of her building not ten buildings away from me here when she refused to give these two nice-looking young men her purse. Oh moma, I wish I'd be given back our language and your old country, because this city's no place for me to live anymore and there's no where else I can go.

Maybe if I went into these three incidents more thoroughly instead of getting so sentimental over it all I'd be able to make some heads and tails out of them and also spend part of my day. The shoot-out there isn't much more to speak about as it was in a bar where there are known pushers and prostitutes to the rest of the neighborhood, so it was their business and part a gang feud I heard and fortunately nobody not connected with them criminally got hurt or killed. But the four streakers were these three young men and the young lady while I was in my parked car. I had nothing to do last night as I don't most and sometimes I just like to sit in the front seat watching the people going in and out or walking their dogs, catching sight of way down several streets above the Hudson and New Jersey the sun setting when it looks red-hot or every now and then a plane or helicopter twinkling by, in other words just something to do. When suddenly they ran past and I rubbed my eyes thinking I'm seeing things and look and it's four backsides I see and I get out of my car when just then a neighbor from upstairs is leaving our building and I say "Buddy, listen, you're not going to believe this, but I just saw four young streakers streaking past me here to Columbus without a stitch on, that's what they're called." He said "Four of them? Streaking down this street? I thought that fad was over. Any a girl?"

"One was, though I didn't see her front and she was skinny, but she was a girl all right, though young. I could tell by her rear end and waist, the way the curves go, which weren't like a young man's or older woman's and certainly no boy."

"A girl streaker? Tough luck that I missed it. Oh, old unadult joke. Didn't know I was so horny, right? But in this cold? That's a first for this block in any weather so far as I know."

And then we see coming back up the street on the same sidewalk we're on these same four youngsters streaking and running past and the girl free as a bird saying to the young man holding her hand as they ran when I look at her more than the others "I don't care. Let him get it off if he wants to, but I bet it's the first time in thirty years."

"Little do you know, missy," Buddy yelled after her. "Fresh kid," he said to me, "but she's got plenty of guts."

They ducked down the basement stairs of the Central Park West building up the street and both Buddy and I thought they maybe lived there or one of them did and would take the service elevator up but were gone for good. But two minutes later, after Buddy and I told Bella with her big white poodle and who's the landlord next door and she's saying "No, that's really incredible, Robert. Have you ever seen it before, Buddy? Something not to tell my emulatory daughters but my future grandchildren if I had seen it and adds a little dash to this drab street, don't you think so, Buddy? Robert?" they run out of the basement stairs with their clothes on at just the moment a new Mercedes sedan pulls up, jump into it and there they are plus about five others all laughing when the car with the young woman driver drives past and the girl streaker squashed in back but still managing to roll down her window and stick up her middle finger at me or us all.

"Till we meet again, toots," Buddy yelled, bowing with his navy watchman's cap in his hand, "and may it be real soon with all your friends."

Bella said "That's the one? She's kind of cute. You think so, Buddy? Ah, just take a look at him, I'm sure you do. But she didn't seem like more than a well-developed thirteen."

The shooting incident came about when these two as I said nice-looking young men in good clothes stopped a woman who was walking out of her building and asked for all the money in her purse. She wouldn't give it, someone who watering her window plants saw it all and told me later, and became hysterical and started screaming without stop and one of the men said "Shut up" while the other tried grabbing her purse away and then the one who told her to shut up put a gun to her voice box and said "I said shut up or I'll kill you," and she screamed even louder and he backed off and his friend said "Let's go," but he shot her in the leg. Or he was aiming elsewhere but got her in the leg. Then they grabbed her purse. But just then two policemen who were walking the beat on Columbus must have heard the shot and knew it was no backfire as I thought it was because they ran up the block to the men and from quite a distance yelled for them to freeze. The men did. That's when I was walking down the street. I didn't see the men or lady but only the policemen running up toward me on the same sidewalk and I looked behind me to see if it was from behind me they were running toward and then looked in front at them still running at me I thought and I pointed to myself and said "Me? Freeze?" They didn't answer but darted left down two steps into her building's areaway where for the first time I saw the woman on the ground holding her leg and the two men with their arms raised. The policemen turned them around, frisked them, got the gun, dropped it, the one who didn't drop it picked it up and laughed, handcuffed them from behind and kept them turned around facing the brownstone wall like that till several police cars from both directions and some in tandem screamed to the scene I can almost say they came so soon after the shooting and so loud and fast. The woman was bandaged. I already had recognized her. Mrs. Greene, a kind of acquaintance of mine over the last twenty years, where we've had coffee once or twice together when we met by accident in diners and also met many times in markets, the library, and on the street of course and once during intermission at a Broadway musical. She was helped to the police car by two policemen. As they passed I said "Mrs. Greene, how do you feel? What happened?" She shook her head. I said "Excuse me for asking. You must be in terrific pain." She nodded and got in the front seat. They drove her to Roosevelt Hospital. The muggers were questioned for a short while and put in the caged back seat of a police car together and driven away. They were so young. At the most, middle twenties. When I described them later to a man who asked "What's the fuss? Someone mugged?" I said "What could they have expected to get from her? She was retired, an executive secretary, and couldn't have had enough cash to pay for their shoes or socks, they were that well-dressed. One with long wavy brown hair and the other curly blond and both looking like male fashion models with the very latest styles in looks and clothes."

STEPHEN DIXON / SLEEP

"One was blond?" he said. "You mean dyed?"

"No, I don't know, it seemed his real hair. An almost dirty blond, which doesn't seem the color someone would dye it."

"He was white?"

"Both were white. The victim too."

"They were white? White men did that? Why white? I don't get it. Maybe they were Cubans."

"They weren't foreigners. Or if they were, then born there just a few years before they came here, because I heard them speak. The curly blond one said he didn't know the other and was innocent and the other said that was a lie. They spoke English extremely well. Better than me or you. As if schooled."

"Look," he said, pointing to the areaway where Mrs. Greene had been and now were many spattered drops of blood and blobs on the flagstones there and a few against the wall and where they had stopped running down the glass door. "White," he said. "I still don't get it."

At that moment someone yelled down from a window in Mrs. Greene's same building "Hey, what's happening down there?" From four floors up, a young woman, in pin curlers and bathrobe. She must have been asleep or more likely in the shower and just looked down and seen the different groups talking. The man with me yelled back "A shooting."

"Someone from around here?" she said and he looked at me and I yelled up to her "The elderly lady who lives on your first floor. 1-R."

"No, I don't know her. Was she hurt bad?"

"Taken to the hospital."

"What was she, knifed?"

"I already said," the man yelled to her, "hit over the head."

"That's right, shot. They didn't get them of course."

The police put an orange tape between the two stair railings leading down to the areaway. On it it said nobody allowed past tape till police search is done. Several policemen with flashlights were searching the vestibule floor and walls and ground floor hallway behind, though there seemed to be plenty of natural electric light. I stayed around talking about the mugging and the continuing increase in city crime and lowering of public morality and rise of private indecency as one couple called it till all the groups broke up and there were only a few isolated people left and I went back home and to try and get some meaning out of it all and also for something to pursue, started to write this.

No, I didn't explain it well. Just gave details, accounts of what I and other people said and thought they saw and their personal prejudices. I know it was just something to do but still, do it right I was always told as a boy, I still sometimes think of myself and say. Why, I want to know, did the streakers streak and muggers mug and even that shoot-out, though try and find out too much about that incident and I might get myself hurt too. Something sociological no doubt. Psychological and economical and probably climatological besides. But I'd like to get it from the mouths themselves and just not assume or generalize from me.

So that evening I go to that bar for a drink. Be careful in what you say, I tell myself going in. "Beer," I tell the bartender, sitting on a bar stool. It's a dark place. Long wooden bar. Clean it seems. Kitchen and a few empty tables in back, though I can hardly see. Three other single men separated by single stools at the bar, all watching TV. One man at the window, sipping from a shot glass while staring out. A girl walks in, sits with a customer, seems to know him, puts her arm around his shoulder, they talk. Tight white boots and a wig and skirt up so high on her thighs in this nippy weather and also her look, I figure her for a prostitute. I get my beer. Cold and in a frosted glass, like I think beer should be. Given my second beer I say "Heard you had a little excitement here the other afternoon."

"That?" the bartender says. "Was nothing."

"Five people get killed or hurt is nothing?"

"That how many? What can I say."

STEPHEN DIXON / SLEEP

"How'd it start if I can ask."

"Fight between friends that got out of hand, I suppose, though I wasn't here."

"Anybody here who was?"

"I think it's something everyone wants to forget."

"Well I'm glad you didn't lose your license at least."

"Oh, they're still gonna close us for a week, reexamine our license and then open us again when they find it was only some dopes from the outside. That's the law of the beast, or whatever the slogan is."

That's all. Nothing I didn't know. He avoids my talk about the predicted heavy snowfall this year when I ask for another beer and I avoid pushing it. So I drink up and leave. The girl and man leave at the same time and outside in front flag down a cab. I go for the morning newspaper and a frank and papaya drink.

Next afternoon after three I go to the local Blimpie Base a couple blocks away where a lot of the younger people around those streakers' age hang out. Sure enough, the young lady from that night and two of the boys who were with her are there. I get a Coke and go over to them and say "Excuse me, but I think I saw you three plus another one streaking two nights ago on my street and I want to ask you a couple questions about it if you don't mind."

"What about, pop?" one of the boys says.

"Why'd you do it for instance?"

"Because we wanted to," the girl says.

"That's the only reason?"

"Because we felt like it," the other boy says.

"No other reason?"

"Fun, games . . . you know," the girl says. "And also to give you old codgers your cookies and kicks for a change."

"Really?"

"I saw your look that night," she says.

"Sure, I looked. It's natural perhaps. I might be eighty—"

"You're eighty?" she says.

"Doesn't look it."

"Looks sixty the most," the other boy says.

"Eighty, but my point's what's your point in streaking, not that I'm saying it's wrong or any holier-than-thou attitude. Is it a form of protest like I've read? Or just for fun as you said? For you see, I'm doing what you could call a personal study and maybe even an article for myself on it and other such things that's been going on a bit oddly lately in the city, so I'd just like to know."

"Because we wanted to," the girl says.

"That's the only reason?"

"Because we felt like it," one of the boys says.

"No other reason?"

No, I imagined that conversation of course. I did go to the Blimpie Base, but didn't see them from the window outside. Didn't think I would. Don't think I would have gone in if I had. And I really don't know how close to the truth I might have gotten with any of the above I wrote if I had spoken to those three or four or anyone else their age about the subject. But I did get a little excited seeing that girl. Have to admit. In my imagination she was right: my cookies and kicks. Got them. All that hair. Lot for a little girl it seemed, or maybe I've forgot. Lot for one so young I mean, and then the few of the nude magazines I've seen I don't think I can trust, for they all look like professional models and showgirls with their hair down there snipped and preened to what maybe it's the publishers who think should be the right height and amount. But nice shape. Glad I was on the street that night. Stocky legs. Hippity-hoppity movements on her behind. Haven't seen it for a time. Lucky boys. For twenty, thirty years I'll wage. But I'll be finished with them for good now, as there's obviously nothing new I can say about the subject, and go on to the muggers and my acquaintance friend.

Night of my Blimpie Base day excursion, I go see Mrs. Greene in the hospital. This is the truth, not imagined. Short trip by bus, after I had my two Manhattans at Steak and Brew. It's a pretty big room. Cheerful and pale blue. Five other women in it. One wrapped almost head to toe like a mummy it seems. Skiing in Central Park I'm told, and I don't question it as a week ago we did have a few inches of snow. "Nice of you to come," Mrs. Greene says. I brought her afterbath cologne. She unwraps it. "Just what I can use," the patient in the next bed says. From her own bed Mrs. Greene sprays it around the room. "Delightful," the mummy says, "spray some more over my way, Lena." I ask Mrs. Greene how long she's going to be in here and why she thinks it happened.

"What, that I got shot? It happens every day. Not to me, naturally, as I'd have to make my home here, but always did, always will. It didn't happen as much when you and I were kids? Then you weren't born here then."

"I've lived here all my life. East Side and West, except for the time at Navy boot camp and ports and ships."

"Then you should know. Money. Stick 'em up, Joe. Always money. Bang bang yuh dead, Moe. This is why it happened and took place. I was coming out of my building with my bag waving and two men came up. One stayed on the sidewalk and the second walked down to me and said 'Give me all your money in your bag and keep your mouth shut.' I screamed. I don't know why. I only remember that that was my one and only reaction. If I was in my right mind then, which I was till the man demanded my money, I would have given him it quick as a second and done anything he said. But me, I screamed. The sidewalk man said 'Let's split.' The man down below with me said 'Stop screaming and hand over your money now.' Do I stop screaming and consent? Next thing I know there's a gun to my head. 'Money,' he's shouting, 'money, your damn money, your money,' though I don't really know if I didn't just dream that up. Next thing I know both of them are down there below with me pulling the bag from my arm and I'm pulling it back but still screaming like a drunk band. Then I'm shot in the leg and think I'm dying or dead and next thing I know I'm being helped into a police car and see you."

"But how could he have shot you?"

"Why not? I was screaming and so a prison threat."

"Why didn't he just hit you over the head with the gun?"

"I'm glad he didn't. I could have been made crazy for life or dead."

"You ever see those two guys before?"

"Sure, in a men's store ad for Macy's and right up there on the stage and screen. They were handsome as actors."

"That's what I told people, which is what I really can't understand. They absolutely didn't look like muggers."

"Why? Actors get out of work also, maybe even more."

"But you don't look like a person who could be carrying much. Or at least what it seemed they'd need for just a not-too-fancy dinner date."

"But they knew. I was. I had two-forty in my bag which I was walking across the street with a receipt slip to pay the landlord his rent."

"He gets that much?"

"Yours is still rent control?"

"When you get out of here we'll go out for dinner. My treat."

"That will be very nice. I'll need it by then."

"Chow not so hot?"

"Look, lucky to be alive I say, so I'm not going to be so stupid to complain about the food."

Then she had to go to the ladies' room, as she put it, though I know from what she's already told me that she'll be confined to using a potty on this bed for another two weeks. So I say, "Well, good time to leave, I guess, though I'll come again real soon."

"Please do," the woman in the next bed says, "as Lena hasn't got one visitor before you and she's nice enough where she should."

"All my friends live too far away or work and don't want to come here nighttimes," Mrs. Greene says, "but they call."

STEPHEN DIXON / SLEEP

"That's what I meant before," I say. "That more and more people and especially women are staying indoors because they don't feel safe on the streets night or day," and she says "No, around here that's always been the case and is even improving. And it didn't seem to stop you, but really, Robert, I have to go," and she rings for the nurse.

"Me? I've nothing to lose—it's others," and we shake hands and I leave, take the stairway down rather than wait with these sickly wheelchaired patients for the elevator, bus back to my neighborhood and have a frank and this time a piña colada at the papaya drink stand. I get the earlybird edition of the newspaper, think about reading it in a nearby bar with a beer, but all the old good ones of just five years ago that aren't for whores or rummies have been take over by patios and kids. Then I sit in my parked car in front of my building, where I am now writing this down, not knowing anything much more about those three incidents and what as a whole the total significance of them might be than when I first started writing this only thing I ever wrote down like this before, except maybe why I began and still continue to write it and also that it's not what happens to me I'm really afraid of so much and maybe also why I sit so much in this parked car. For I don't go anywhere much in it anymore except from one side to the other every day twenty minutes before the alternate side of the street parking is up, and also along the river drives during the summer a few times for the breeze and every half-year to my nephew's house in Connecticut for dinner with his wife and kids, and sometimes when my building's ice cold, just to sit here with the motor running for the heat.

Oh, this is terrible. Something just written as I've said and said, to waste time for myself spent worse in other ways but not to be read. Anyway, I'll end it now and when I go inside I'll leave it in my top dresser drawer where all my personal belongings are and which my nephew has been told has all my so-called important papers when I die. And when he does look

through that drawer, which he has instructions and the keys
to, he can find this and read it if he likes and which he'll certainly have to be somewhat curious about, and then throw it
away. If he gets as far to this part or got here by beginning ass
backwards from the last page first, he'll maybe know something more about me than I ever answered to him before or
always till now told lies about or denied. Maybe it will just
prove the opinion he already has of me and my fairly alone life
for so long. But anyway, though I didn't say much in here if at
all, I do think I at least came close to saying more about myself
than I have to anyone for the last thirty years.

So, my dear nephew, if that way of addressing you doesn't
embarrass you, thank you for your nice dinners and also your
wife for the wonderful way she prepared them and your kids,
which I can tell you I looked forward to more than you'd ever
believe. And my last words to you are do what you want with
the little money and things I ended up leaving you and which
we both know won't be much, and lots of luck and years of
happiness and if my car, this kind old buddy of mine's still
around in front of the building or on the block on one side of
the street or the other if not by now towed away, sell or just
junk it too, and good-bye.

No, I don't have to tell you about the car, as you're a sharp
guy all right and will know what to do with it, and good-bye.

heat

Someone's ringing my downstairs bell. It's 7 A.M. I'm in bed. Ringing continues as I grab my pants off the chair. The old pants, bought in a thrift store, wrong pants to put on in a hurry, as sometimes the zipper gets stuck, but the pants nearest the bed, other pants in the closet on a hook. Ringing continues without letup. Then a few seconds letup. Probably so the ringer can switch fingers or give the hand a rest. I have the pants on but the zipper won't go up. Shouldn't have suggested it. I pull at it gently. I tug. I hold the cloth back below the zipper teeth where it's stuck while I try pulling the sliding piece up. Ringing continues again without letup. Could be important. A fire? Not likely as I don't hear anyone ringing the apartment next door or any noise near the stairs. Ringing stops, resumes. I look for my shirt. Thought I threw it on the easy chair last night just before I jumped into bed. "Screw it. No shirt, I won't die." Zipper still isn't working no matter what tactic I use to pull it up. Never stayed stuck so long. Screw it. Ringing without letup. Has to be important or a mistake. Nobody's ever come near to ringing my bell so urgently or for such a long time before.

I leave the apartment with my fly open and no shirt or shoes or socks on and round the first of the four flights to the ground floor. "Yes yes, I'm coming," I yell. My door's open, so behind me I still hear my bell ringing. "I said I'm coming." It's cold. No heat this morning or yesterday from around early evening on. But the building's hallways are always warmer than my apartment when there hasn't been heat for a day, and longer we haven't heat, colder in comparison to these halls my apartment seems to get. Maybe because there are no windows in the halls and that's where most of the cold's supposed to come through, next through the exterior brick walls. Though with no radiators or risers in the halls and the building's front door opening all the time, I'd think that would sort of balance things out. I reach the ground floor and see through the vestibule door a tenant from the next building. Mr. Whittle, eighty years old a couple of weeks ago he said on this birthday. I bought him a bottle of wine same day he told me that. "You trying to kill me?" he said then. "For how you think I lived this long and both kept my health?" I apologized and took the wine from him. I grab my fly at the top and open the door.

"Same thing's happened again," he says. "I told her two days ago she was running out of oil and to call in for a new load. She wouldn't. Next day I slipped a note under her door saying she needs at least four inches of fresh oil over the six inches of sludge she's got in the tank and so she has to order right away. She didn't. Now we've run out. Even if she gets oil today or the next few days, the sludge will clog the pump and feeder pipe and so the boiler might start up all right if she gets someone to relight it, but in two minutes won't work. And you know that affects both our buildings; she's got one huge boiler for the two of them and so it services all our hot water and heat."

"I knew something was wrong. Damn place is an icebox."

"Knew? Hell, you should've done something about it. Both you people and she expect me to do it all. But since my last birthday I'm retired from everything but looking after myself. Even still I did my best, since it's in my interest too. I like showers. Running dishwater. I'm clean, despite what kind of kennel she

STEPHEN DIXON / SLEEP

keeps. Fifteen-watt bulbs in the public hallways. Illegal. I went down there two days ago like I always do when I feel we're running low and witnessed it on the petrometer and warned her. Now last time we had no heat and hot water for a week, right?"

"Nine days."

"Nine. Eleven. In this weather, what's the difference? Three. Four. All of them beginning with two we begin freezing to death. Most of us move out by the end of five or six. Building gets like a desert. Deserted. Not warm as one. Hello, I sometimes shout up the stairs, thinking I hear someone. But last time after a week nobody but she and me in her building next door and both of us on the first floor. Thought maybe because hot air rises and then realized it'd be the reverse. But with our low ceilings and ovens on full blast and good electric heaters from the old days, that's why it must be better for us than you people upstairs and why she can hold out long as she does. You're on the top floor, so it must get pretty cold up there, even with your heater and oven going. Or maybe because you are that high up it's the reverse from what it'd be for she and me downstairs if our ceilings weren't the building's original basement, and yours are high, right?"

"Only my stove burners work. But because the kitchen's off from the rest of the apartment and too small to sleep in and with the burners going, too dangerous, it does me no good. And the heaters I've tried always blow a fuse."

"Because her wiring's fifty years old. Twenty years ago I told her to replace it. Nothing. Well this time it's going to be the same thing for us and we're even deeper in winter. And you're the one who put all those signs up last time and got us heat, so you've got to act again."

"It was a few of us. And last time it wasn't even winter. And time before that was early November and before that, October, but both times quite cold."

"That's what I'm saying. But I'm retired. Not that I'm sick or tired or anything, just that I want to keep it that way. Seems I've fought that woman half a lifetime, but now I have to stop. I'll still bring in the trash cans and replace the fuses and bulbs on the first floor because she's older than me and not as healthy and I feel sorry for her, rich as she is. That woman is wealthy. Took out a forty thousand second mortgage last year and put it right back in the same bank as savings for the interest, not listening to me that the bank was bettering her on the deal by one and a half percent. I do all that as a favor because I know her for years. I check the boiler. When I see the oil's only six to ten inches above the red line, I tell her. Sometimes she does something. Summers she usually doesn't and nobody much minds with the small rents and so hot outside people even prefer cold showers and most are away. But today it's twenty-five. Call the city. Don't stop. That special heating complaint number. And the mayor, call and call. And see that Democratic club on Seventy-Second Street. As for me, I'm paying only half my rent this month. Put that on my money order. Half the rent for no oil quarter of a month, I wrote, and no exterminator for thirty years and also for my hospital bill where a spider bit me on the foot. Limped for two weeks but wouldn't tell anyone an insect bit me. Said it was a dog in the park. It crawled up the stairs and under the basement door and past my own, as I'm right next door. Once a month we're to get service—a city law. I put all that down on the money order so everyone could see when she deposited it and it passed through both our banks, for I checked. Silverfish, spiders, ants, roaches, sometimes rats and mice through the walls, I wrote, and the other things and no heat or janitor and the roof leaks and the rest. But you do that. The political help. City pricks up its ears when congressmen call. Organize. You got to organize this house. No seven to nine days wait. Get all the tenants here to sign a statement to all these facts and then come to my building and get them too. Then you go down with me to the Rent Administration and you show your signatures and I'll talk to them and we'll get her good. The city will take over her buildings. We might pay a little more rent after that but we'll be warm."

STEPHEN DIXON / SLEEP

"Excuse me, Mr. Whittle, but I have water on for coffee. I don't want to burn the place down."

"That's another thing. She nearly blew us all up the other week by turning the basement's automatic heat control switch to manual. Always fooling around with that thing like a ship's engineer to keep the temperature low, though the control box is fixed by boiler men to do it all for her. But this time she left it on manual. I heard something sissing through my floor and rushed down there and saw the boiler spurting water and switched the control switch back to automatic. Told her and she smiles. She doesn't care. Buckets of sludge from the generator filter have been piling up for years for the whole basement to go up in blazes and she just laughs but won't get a man to take them away. Place is a firetrap. You got to put all that down too."

"Look, I'm very cold. I ran down in a hurry because of your rings, so didn't put on a shirt. And I've got to see about that boiling water."

"That's right. Water from the boiler spurting all over the place and ready to explode. Called me crazy when I adjusted it. I got mad then. And a liar. Me? I said. But she's crazy. Senile. That's old. Outside of a painful disease, the worst. But she's been senile for years and has no respect for her age."

"Okay, I'll take care of it," and I run upstairs.

"Organize," he says. "Don't just try. Each time she likes to make the agony longer for us, so this one could go on for weeks. And nobody pay their rent, you hear?"

I change to my warmest pants and put two shirts and two pairs of socks on and run in place till I sweat and make tea and get under the covers and read till half past eight when I go to the corner newspaper store and call the landlady. Didn't want to disturb her till now. She's probably in, but doesn't answer. Never does when the heat goes, but thought I'd try. Locks herself in her single room all day and won't answer her vestibule bell or door knocks or ground floor window raps or inquiries or threats through her door. I call the city's heat complaints number.

STEPHEN DIXON / SLEEP

"Three-eight-hundred."

"Heat complaints office?"

"Yes?"

"Good. Usually your line's busy. I want to make a complaint about no heat or hot water in my building. My name is Jan White. Address is 5 West 75th. I have no phone. Landlord's name is Mrs. Alba Long. She lives in the next building, number 31. That's 5 West 75th. That building shares the same boiler as mine, so they also have no heat or hot water. Mrs. Long's phone is unlisted, but it's UR 8-0216. There are twelve tenants in my building, eight in the one next door, plus Mrs. Long. I phoned in an identical complaint to you a month ago and one about a month before that when both times we didn't have heat or hot water for several days. Last time reached nine days. This time I wanted to contact you right from the start of the problem so we can get an inspector today."

"Call back at nine. I'm only here to man the all-night complaints phone till when the real people who take them come in."

My apartment seems colder. I turn on the four stove burners and work on my book about the history of city planning for this city, which begins with what's known of the Ice Age cave dwellers and ends with the slaughtered open-space Indians and fortified colonial settlements. It's a scholarly work, first of two volumes. A few hundred pounds of my notes and reference materials and other writers' books on the subject or the same or similar subjects but for different cities and encampments are scattered in a fairly systematic way throughout the apartment, which is why I can't stuff it all in boxes along with my enormous typewriter and go work someplace else for the time being. Sleeping in the cold doesn't bother me much once I put on my flannel nightshirt and get under the down comforter I bought during our first landlord-caused heat crisis last year.

I return to the store and call Mrs. Long. I'd be very nice to her, try to get her to understand the situation a little more, suggest several ways she can solve the heat problem and stop the rising tenant militancy almost immediately, be concerned about her health and how the cold and the dry air from her oven and stove burners must be affecting her respiration negatively, and she'd call me a liar and crook, tell me to mind my own business or move out of the building and then begin gossiping about some of the tenants now and from forty years ago, talk about totally irrelevant things such as the broken dumbwaiter cord and tripling in price of locks and doorstops and probably shriek and scream some more at me before hanging up. But she doesn't answer. I call the heat complaints office.

"Three-eight-hundred."

"I want to make a heating complaint. Is it time yet?"

"Yes, go on, what is it? Though first let me remind you we're very understaffed here and have hundreds of complaints coming in every hour, so be specific and brief."

"Heat and hot water complaint. We've neither." I give my name, address, apartment, no phone, number of tenants in my building, landlord's name, address, apartment, phone. "Both buildings use the same boiler, so her building with its eight tenants also has no heat and hot water."

"I'm only concerned with your building, nobody else's there. One of them wants to call in a complaint, that's their privilege, but not you for them. Now how many days without heat and hot water for your address?"

"Since early yesterday afternoon."

"That's not very long. Maybe the boiler broke down and your landlord's already called her emergency repair service."

"She has no service. She waits till the oil runs out. Then the tenants of both buildings threaten her through her door with no rent for that month and stick ugly notes in her mailbox that they're going to deface the hallway walls or call the city's agencies against her, and after a couple of days of this tension she calls the oil company for a delivery. That takes a day or two to come, but then the boiler won't start up because of the sludge in the tank, so it takes another three to five days of threats before she phones for a mechanic. Last time we gave her a little leeway before we called your office, and we still didn't get heat for another five days."

"Last time doesn't count for now. Forget the sludge—you sure there's no oil or it isn't a boiler break? What's your landlord say? Because the building inspectors aren't exactly overstaffed either. So though they have to check in to every complaint we process here, we're also told about being careful not to process every wild-goose chase."

"My landlady won't answer her phone or door. If I was even so lucky to see her on the street and try to speak rationally with her about what she's doing about the heat, she'd swing her pocketbook at me. I tell you this every time we have this crisis and this is abut the sixth time in a year. The tenants of both buildings, or let's just say of my building, have sort of elected me their representative for these calls. That's because I'm the one reasonably lucid tenant who also lives and works in his apartment and so is always here in case an inspector does come when we still haven't had heat instead of two weeks later to tell us the boiler's working fine so what's the complaint?"

"Look, you read the papers. There's layoffs. City job attritions. So the inspectors are probably very busy."

"And look, we're freezing and in another day are going to need a bath. All we're asking is to have an inspector come in the next two days. That way we might get heat in a week. We don't want to drag the landlady to court. She's eighty-four and as someone else here said, selectively senile, and the judge would laugh or scorn us away. We just want to put a little scare in her that the city's looking after our interests a little. Maybe from then on she'll take care of the heating problem when it arises and not when most of us have moved out till it's over and the rest of us are hacking away from throat and chest infections and haven't the energy anymore to complain."

STEPHEN DIXON / SLEEP

"You know, I'm not required to tell you this, but I will. Each inspector has a full case load every day and proceeds with his inspections in his assigned district in the time order these calls come in. So I have your complaint, Mr. White, and it will be processed as soon as we get off the phone." She hangs up.

I call Mrs. Long. No answer. I go home and write a note which says "Dear Mrs. Long: I understand there is no oil again. This is not a criticism. I in no way want you to think I have any bad feelings to you. I am in fact very concerned about your health during this cold spell and hope you are feeling well. If you are not feeling well, please let me know and I will do what I can to assist you. As for the oil, if you had regular service, the oil wouldn't run out. And if the oil didn't run out, then the oil burner wouldn't go off and we would always have heat when the weather called for it. When the weather didn't call for it, then of course we wouldn't deserve heat. Please call an oil company today for oil. And then please call a heating company to relight the boiler. If you don't, I am afraid most of the tenants will hold back their rents this month. That would amount to about $2,000, which is far more than an oil delivery and boiler mechanic would cost you. You could avoid all these problems in the future by engaging on a regular basis an oil company that both delivers oil and provides repair service. The company would automatically deliver oil before the tank runs out and give routine boiler checkups and cleanings and emergency service whenever you needed it. Believe me, Mrs. Long, all the tenants respect you a lot and don't wish to make you feel we are ganging up on you or trying to run your building for you and we only wish now for hot water and heat. Listed below, as I did last month in a similar note, are the names and phone number of three oil companies that both give oil and service. I got the names from landlords on the block who told me they never had a complaint against these companies, and some after forty years of continued service. Thank you." I sign it and list the companies.

STEPHEN DIXON / SLEEP

I also write two identical notes informing the tenants what's been done to get hot water and heat. "Fellow survivors," I end, "stay well, have heart, eat plenty of oranges, make sure your ovens and burners are off when you leave your apartments and keep the city busy with your own irate citizen calls." I tape the notes up in each building's vestibule and stick Mrs. Long's note into her mailbox. She once told me that "because of my exceptional aural sense, which physicians have tried to write scientific articles about," she can hear through her wall everything that goes on in her building's vestibule including the faintest foot shuffling and heavy breathing, and also see "because I have eyes and when I'm looking, of course" from behind her window curtains everyone who walks into both buildings. I'm sure by the time I'm upstairs she'll have grabbed my note and torn the other two off the walls and slipped back into her apartment with them.

My apartment seems colder. I put on another pair of socks and a sweater. Steam comes out of my mouth. My teeth chatter and fingers freeze when I wash a celery stick under the water tap. I leave my door open to let in the warmer hallway air and occasionally hear a tenant saying to himself something like "Please please, may there be heat" as he climbs the stairs and then curse out Mrs. Long when he enters his apartment. I work a little, get under the covers and read. Later, I go outside to get warm. My note to her is gone and all that remains of the tenant notes are a couple of cellophane tape ends. I write the same tenant notes in very large letters this time and tape them above the mailboxes as high as I can reach. Mrs. Long isn't very tall and will have to get a chair or use a broom to get these two down.

Around six, someone shouts into my apartment that the tenants of both buildings are meeting now in 2B. We sit around in coats, mufflers and hats. Some brought toddies and thermoses of tea and coffee and blankets to wrap around their chests and legs. We first vote that the chairman should be called the chairperson and next that the chairperson should be me. Someone suggests that one of us phone Mrs. Long's heating oil company and in her voice ask for an immediate delivery. The motion is carried. Several people volunteer. Of those, the person who comes closest to sounding like Mrs. Long is a young operatic tenor from the South with a natural high girlish speaking voice. He practices impersonating Mrs. Long by saying "Revenge, that's what I'm doing it for—revenge, revenge, revenge," which is what she yelled through her window to a few of us conferring on the sidewalk last time, five days after the oil ran out. Then he dials the oil company and says "Emergency service? This is Mrs. Alba Long of 3 West 75th Street. I'd like an oil delivery tonight if you can mange it, and this time could you give me as much oil as you can? . . . The account number? . . . No, dear, I've entirely misplaced it in my head—so many numerals . . . I'm calling from the druggist two city blocks away because my telephone's temporarily out of order. . . . You see, I'm going to be either eighty-three or -four in a month, so now you know why I don't want to be making so many moves from store to home to store and home again to phone you with the account number. . . . Then why not make the delivery and I'll give it to the driver when he's done? . . . Can't do that? . . . This one time? . . . No matter how grateful I'd be and nice I say please? . . . I understand, dear. Life is short, one mustn't take chances. I'll find the number by tomorrow and get back to you. Bye now." He hangs up and says "I know that's not how she talks. But I thought anything more in character would so rile him no matter what her age that he would have told her to kiss off."

"You don't understand her," another man says. "She knows she gets things done because she does act so crazy and brusque. People give in because they don't want to deal with her. Now what we should do is look for an oil truck making a delivery in the neighborhood, grab the driver, knock him out or threaten to inject him with a deadly narcotic if he resists, roll the hose back in the truck, drive it here and pump in a full tank. Then we'll all take full responsibility for it, pay for the oil out of our rents for the next month, yell murder to the media about the callous inaction the city gives to tenants of low rents and no heat and even go to jail for the night if we have to. I was in the army. I'll lead you if you want. All I need are three more of you to hold down the driver, as those guys can be awfully big and tough."

We all admire his courage but tell him his suggestion is too radical.

"Then let's slip the driver a hundred bucks to deliver us some oil."

"We don't want to be inducing an innocent man into bribery for our own personal gain," I say, but he insists it's a good idea and that we vote on it, and the motion by a slight margin is denied.

We finally vote to write a note to Mrs. Long telling her we're going to withhold our rents for the next month unless she provides heat and hot water by the end of the next day. We sign it, the radical's signature three times as large as the rest of ours and with an underline that tears the page, and stand in front of her door and knock on it and then ring her bell. No answer.

"She's in," Mr. Whittle says. "Let's break the door down and force her to call the oil company."

I stick the note under her door. Next day there's a note in Mrs. Long's handwriting taped above the mailbox in our vestibule. It says "Exxonman. Ring super's bell in 3 W. 75 for a NO. 5 type oil delivery of no more than 1,100 gals." The super's bell is Mrs. Long's. Unless this is a delaying maneuver on her part, we'll at least have oil.

The oil's delivered that afternoon. I ask the driver if he would turn the burner on and he says that's not his job. By evening we still haven't heat. I call Mrs. Long, stick notes in her mailbox. "I see we have oil," I write. "Thank you. Please get a mechanic to light the oil burner today. Otherwise, what's the

sense?" By the next afternoon there's still no heat. I call a tenants meeting that night. Only eight people show up as most of
the tenants have moved out till the heat's returned. We decide
to call in our own mechanic. We phone a few of the supers on
the block and one of them says his cousin knows everything
there is about boilers and he'll send him by early tomorrow.

Next morning the mechanic rings my bell. He parks his bike
by the basement door and we go downstairs. He carries a
knapsack, is Italian, wears a folded-up paper bag for a cap.
"Only America for three months," he says. "But know. I know
furnaces and boilers well." He gets right to work. Takes tools
out of his sack, unscrews this, tightens that, dismantles, rein-
stalls, lights the boiler generator, "Niente," he says, "but I
think, soon." Lights the generator fifty times, cleans the filter
a dozen times, cleans the feeder pipe from pump to filter, filter
to generator, tank to pump, everything he fixes he wipes clean
with a cloth, asks me to get "light without electric . . . long
strong wire for shoulders that bends . . . rags to clean . . . can
of gasoline . . . hard paper, but not paper paper, like box paper
to make gasoline go in tank pipe." Every so often he throws
one of his tools to the floor and shouts in Italian. After four
hours he gives up. "You need boiler man, big boiler company.
My tools no good. Good, but not enough. Need machine.
Snakes. Pipes too dirty. Pump no work. Boiler machine to get
oil not go back and to, back and to, like pump pump, pump
pump, like that." I say "How much do I owe you?" and he says
"Nothing."

"Come on, you have to take something. Twenty dollars. Ten.
You've been here for four hours without a break."

"I no fix, can no take money."

"I don't understand you," I say and he shrugs. We shake
hands and go upstairs.

That night there are notes from Mrs. Long above both
buildings' mailboxes. "Boiler now repaired. There will be heat.
In turn, please pay your rent on time from now on and not

when I have to write begging letters to you and think about selling the buildings or go into bank debt."

There isn't heat or hot water by the end of the day. She must have seen me with the mechanic and assumed the burner was fixed. Or else her notes are just another stall or something else she has in mind that I can't figure out.

Next morning I call the heats complaints office. "It's been five days," I say. "My windows are totally iced outside and in. All my plants have died. I can't even get moderately warm no matter how many layers of clothes and covers I pile on. All the tenants have left except for an elderly couple in my building who say they have no place to go. And an eighty-year-old man in the next building who to spite the landlady will stay here and freeze to death even though he has family down the street."

"Once a tenant's complaint has been processed, another complaint can't be taken till the next time you haven't hot water or heat or anything like that like an elevator broken down."

"Then when's the inspector coming over? I want the inspector today. If not I'm calling the mayor's office and the police and all the local political clubs. That nice couple on the third floor, forty-three years together, you want them to die?"

"We never see the inspectors here or know who they are or their routes. They're in another office, maybe another building or borough. You'll just have to be patient and wait."

"Let me speak to your supervisor."

"She's on another phone."

"Then put me on hold for her or give me her extension."

"She's on another floor and we're not allowed to transfer to her or give her phone number out."

"Then what building she in? Her name and address. All this cold and no heat has kept me from my work, so I'm free to go wherever she is anytime."

"It's also something we can't give out."

"Then what department she in? Housing? Buildings? Rent Administration? Which one? All I see in the phone book here is your heat complaints number among the city's listing of the most frequently made emergency calls."

"Can't give you that either. You don't know, but there are cranks."

I call the mayor's office. The man who answers says "Five days is a long time in this weather and we'll do all we can. But you have to realize that as important and immediate in need your situation sounds, it's not the most urgent call we get in any one day."

"I understand that if a landlord continues to ignore a building complaint such as no heat, the city will send over an oil truck or mechanic from a private company and bill the landlord. So what about sending a mechanic to turn the heat on? None of the companies I've called will do it without my landlady's permission and she can't give it because she won't answer her door or phone."

"I don't know where you heard about the city doing that."

"Then it's not true?"

"I don't know."

"Could you find out?"

"What do your heat complaints people say?"

Five more days pass. Many calls to the city, visits to political clubs, city departments, the police. Even the fire department about the potential disaster from the other tenants' lit ovens and burners going all day. "It could be a hazard," the fire marshal says, "but is out of our jurisdiction. Both her buildings get fire inspections once a year and they either come out clean or she clears up her violations in a week. Call Health." The other city departments always tell me they're working on it and then add something like "But you can't demand an inspector make a special case out of your complaint when there are fifty just as hysterical cases that came in before. This is a democracy. Rich or poor, whatever your color or race, nobody comes ahead of the other guy because of who he knows or what's his political connection or fancy address."

Mr. Whittle visits me every day. I stay under the covers in my clothes, he sits in the easy chair encased in my sleeping bag. Tonight he says "I'm moving out. She beat me, you see. Older as she is, I can't take it anymore, and it turned out both her room and mine aren't any warmer than the next. I'm retired, didn't come here to get frostbit or put up useless fights. Couldn't stand looking out my window and seeing people across the alley walking around in their underwear and taking baths. I'm not going to my nephew's down the street. He brings in whores, drinks all night. There's the Edison—not a bad cheap hotel. Pimps and thieves there though, but call me when she gives back the heat. Here's my key to feed the fishies and sleep there if you want. At least my electric heater and blanket don't blow fuses and the oven works well enough to warm the feet."

I stay in his room that night and the next. I'm the only tenant in his building, so the place is very quiet, nobody even running up or down stairs. Around 2 A.M. the second night I'm there I hear a door shut on the floor and locks set in place and the squeaking of wheels. Couldn't be anyone but Mrs. Long. Her apartment's next door and nobody's heard of her letting visitors past her door for thirty years. I'm in bed, but all I have to do is grab my hat. I rush out of the building and see her walking down the block. In her old cloche hat, stockings that hang around her ankles, well-kept brown cloth coat with its fox collar of the twenties or thirties, pulling a shopping cart. Maybe she thinks now is the only time she can shop without bumping into one of her tenants. I catch up with her.

"Mrs. Long," I say. "Why are you doing all this? You want to be responsible for my deteriorating composure, and Mr. Whittle's and everybody else's hotel bills and the deaths of the Scowcrofts in 3C?"

"Oh you, the troublemaker, Mr. White. Not running around jogging today? You know how they cure TB?"

"No, why?"

"You wouldn't know. You were too young then. But the greatest percentage of deaths in this country once came from TB, but now from cancer and heart diseases and attacks. Did you know that?"

"No. Though what's that got to do with no heat for twelve days?"

"Well, they put those people in tall buildings on high hills without any artificial heat in the cold. Heat makes the bacteria grow."

"Are you saying you have tuberculosis or you think you do or that one or both of the Scowcrofts may have it and that's why you kept the buildings cold."

"No. Only that that particular cure was proven successful over many years and is a fact. But my sister died last week."

"I'm sorry to hear that. Of TB?"

"She did have it when she was a girl but we sent her to a mountain—a special sanatorium. She was given no heat there and only the best of fresh air and good foods and exercise and was cured. The last of the Dukenays—that was her married name. Somewhere in Indiana—I didn't even know her address. For years she wanted me to visit her and sell my buildings and live with her for life. I refused. Those buildings are my life. Who wants to live in the woods and get water from a well? A postman came the other day. That's how I found out."

"Somebody sent you a telegram or wrote you about her death?"

"He came with a box, rang my bell. I wasn't home. Two weeks ago. So he left a postal form in my letter box telling me my package is on the table at the ground floor rear of my building where you now stay. I went back there, thinking it was something for me by mistake or for one of the tenants with my name in care of for them above the address. It was a package. No bigger than if it contained a small hatbox. Square, wrapped in string. Not heavy. I could hold it in my palm. On it was my name and address and many dollars worth of stamps and a company's return address in Anderson, Indiana and the word 'Cremation.' Just that, which is how I found out."

"That's awful. I'm really sorry. You sure you should be out so late, Mrs. Long?"

"My hours have changed. There's an all-night market on Broadway that's open this hour with the same bargains and overpriced goods you can get there during the day. But the next morning I went to our post office on 68th Street and said to the postmaster 'You shouldn't send such a package to someone like that. That word was a warning to you. I would have come to receive it in a special room.' I haven't seen my sister in more than thirty-five years. She was the last relative I had."

"You were absolutely right to complain. It must have been an awful experience. How do you feel now, though—okay? And if you're not heading back to your building, I guess I'll say good-night."

Next morning there's still no heat. I call several friends and finally one says he'll put me up but at the most for three days. I go back to my apartment and pack some of my things. Then I hear a clinking sound from the radiator which always meant heat is on the way. I open the front door and smell oil. That means the burner's been lit and is working after it's been off for more than a day. I put my hand over the first two pipes of the radiator which are warm and then get hot as the next two pipes get warm. I stick my hands on the third and fourth pipes till they get too hot. I put my cheeks above the pipes till my face feels burnt. Then the fifth and sixth and seventh pipes get hot. I run to the corner store and call Mr. Whittle and several tenants at work and in hotels and say "Heat, we got heat, it's coming up right now." They say things like "Fantastic . . . Thank heavens . . . Jesus, it's been a drudge . . . That witch . . . That bitch . . . She's not going to get my next two months' rent, maybe three." I try to explain "But she's old, recently went through a lot, her only sister died and she learned of it in the most terrible way." They all say "That's a lot of bull" or "She deserves everything she gets" or "Tough."

My apartment's almost warm now. I peel off the first layer of clothes, then the second and third. I let the water run till it gets warm and I wash the pans and greasy dishes and when the water gets hot I wash my hair under the shower and then take a bath.

By nighttime most of the tenants have returned. They throw a party in my honor and I try and tell them I had nothing much to do with getting the heat and hot water back. "Anyway, enjoy them while you can. Because who knows if in a month from now we won't be going through the same thing."

Two days later an inspector rings my bell. "Too late again," I say. "But tell me, how do we stop her from not keeping a minimum amount of oil in her tank so the burner doesn't die? And if we can't, then how do we avoid these long periods of no heat the next time she lets the oil run dry?"

He's writing something under my name on the top sheet of a thick casebook, turns to the next page and says "Would you know if 57 West 66th is between Central Park West and Columbus or Columbus and Broadway?"

the hairpiece

Arnold wondered whether he should wear his hairpiece to Maxwell Craft's funeral. It was different when his partner Hank Rabin died two months ago. Hank was buried as an Orthodox Jew, so all Arnold had to do to conceal his baldness was abide by their religious custom and wear his wide-brim hat throughout the services. But Craft, never affiliated with any religious group as far as Arnold knew, had recently converted to Catholicism, which for one thing meant that Arnold couldn't wear his hat during the funeral services. Arnold had also been picked as one of the six pallbearers. He figured that since Craft had been a well-known play director and notorious ladies man in his day, a few news photographers would be at the church and cemetery. He knew that the shot of several established theater personalities lugging the coffin of one of their more famous colleagues out of a church was too much of a natural for any photographer to pass up—an image which particularly upset him when he envisioned his own face looking ten years older than he felt plastered across the front pages of the city's afternoon dailies, besides the chance that many of his West Coast friends would see distorted wirephoto copies of these photos in their own papers, making him look even worse. Maybe he should just put the hairpiece on, rather than work up a headache over it, and hope for a series of blurred unrecognizable photos.

He took out a pair of black nylon socks from a dresser, stood on one foot while holding on to the back of a chair, and slipped the sock on. Switching positions, he rolled the second sock up past his other ankle. Then he put on his shirt, pants and tie, making sure the color and style of each was appropriately funereal, and stepped into a pair of tasseled loafers. He was completely dressed, except for a jacket and the hairpiece.

He peered into the dresser mirror. His gray wiry hair, not the most adaptable kind for a toupee he was told when he first inquired about buying one a year ago, hadn't been trimmed for two weeks and had grown into thick kinky curls at the sideburns, neck, and above the ears. He flattened back most of the side hairs with a brush, patted down the thin strands on top, and removed the hairpiece from the night table drawer where he kept most of his personal belongings. He dabbed the inside edges of the hairpiece with a special type of scalp glue and set it on the dresser hair-down to let the glue get gummier.

He touched the glue a half-minute later, then very carefully placed the triangular mat of gray hair on his head. He smoothed down the top, combed out the sides till the natural and unnatural hairs blended into one hairline, and fingered the fake widow's peak till two curls flopped over the right temple. He felt this made him look younger, his hair almost brazenly windblown, and also covered one of the two more obvious pasty edges. And if he furrowed his forehead by raising his eyebrows as high as he could, his hairline would seem unreal only to the most wary observers, and maybe to those petty stupid people who went around searching for such weakness in others.

Arnold stepped out of the elevator and signaled the doorman to get him a cab.

STEPHEN DIXON / SLEEP

"Certainly, Mr. Fields," Jimmy said, tipping his hat. Arnold opened the *Times* to the theater section, always the first thing he turned to in the morning newspaper.

"Cab for you, sir," Jimmy yelled from the street. Arnold was sitting on a marble bench in the building's vestibule, engrossed in a critic's panning of a Broadway show that opened last night.

"Excuse me, Jimmy?"

"I said your cab—it's here." Jimmy opened the back door and leaned in to speak to the driver. The cabby seemed about to laugh, then shrugged and turned forward and grabbed the wheel, waiting for his passenger to get inside so he could drive off.

"My God, just look at me this morning," Arnold said. "Must've been dreaming or something not hearing you there, eh?" He lifted his foot into the cab, froze in that stance till Jimmy buoyed him up by the elbow and gave him a push inside, where he plopped back into the seat. "Thanks, Jimmy."

The cab roared down Central Park West, but quickly pulled to a stop when the light changed at the corner. At one point during the trip across the park Arnold saw the driver staring at him through the rearview mirror. He wondered what could be so damn interesting, since anyone else with brains would have turned away long ago when the passenger caught him staring at him like that. Maybe it was the hairpiece, and he touched it to see if it was on straight and the curls still dangled over his temple. Or else Jimmy might have told him that Arnold was a play producer who once had three hits running concurrently on Broadway and the driver was trying to see if he recognized him. Arnold nervously lit a cigarette, inhaled though his doctor had warned him not to if he had to smoke at all, and started reading a theater news article. He looked up only once more during the ride to see if the cabby's eyes were on him. At that moment the cabby threw up his hand and started cursing a row of double-parked cars and delivery trucks that lined the avenue.

STEPHEN DIXON / SLEEP

The cab pulled up in front of a limestone church off Park Avenue. Arnold climbed the steps, stood in front of the iron doors on top and looked at four elderly women sitting and gabbing on a brownstone stoop directly across the street and then stared up at a third-floor window in the same building, where he saw a thin middle-aged woman putting on a blue dress. No, she wasn't putting it on but holding it up to a mirror, as he saw her bra strap when she twirled to the side. And she wasn't middle-aged but young, no more than twenty, and laughing it seemed and spinning and one time even going into some kind of ballroom dance, the dress—her partner—easily dipping her, when some people climbing the church steps caught his eye. One woman had separated from the group and was approaching him, waving an arm laden with noisy chains. He squinted at her, not knowing who she was but hoping that neither she nor any of her friends has seen him looking into the window, then put on his glasses and waved back at her, though she was almost on top of him now. He was smoothing down his hairpiece as she reached him.

"So how are you, Arnold?" she said, giving him her hand.

"Cynthia," he said. He squeezed her gloved fingertips and tried to recall her last name and if she was married or not in case he had to introduce her to anyone later on. He repeated her first name over to himself, remembering now that she'd once had a small role in one of his flops a few years back, though which one and whether she was a good actress or not he had forgotten also.

"You're looking well," she said. "Really excellent."

"And you too. Still as pretty as a young girl."

She smiled, and pointed to the church. "You're going to the funeral?"

"Me? I'm one of the pallbearers."

"Really? I'd say that's quite an honor."

"It was something the family asked me to do. Otherwise, I'd've shied away from it for sure. These things are just too depressing for me."

STEPHEN DIXON / SLEEP

"It must have been terrible when you heard of it—the passing, I mean."

"To tell you honestly, Cynthia, something like Max's illness I, he, his whole family knew long ago what it'd bring."

"It was just a matter of time with him then, that it?"

"That's the word: just a matter of time. To Max, even, and I know because just one week ago I spoke to him as close as I'm speaking to you now. But business he carried on as usual like nothing was eating away inside him. He was a real wonder."

"He really was. But tell me, how are things going with you lately?"

"If you mean business, it couldn't be worse."

"I was actually thinking of your health, but do you mean the theater's really in that bad a shape?"

"Worse than that. Just ten minutes ago, even, I'm coming over here in a cab and reading about another flop last night. You know: *The Inner World*—that satirical thing from London? It's a dead season. And with production costs shooting up like sky-rockets every year, it can't get anything but worse."

Cynthia shook her head back and forth. Arnold stared at the steps, wondering how much time they had before the service began. He looked at his watch.

"You want to go in now?" she said.

"Were you with those people there?" He pointed to the door where some people had been waiting for her and had just now entered the church.

"Just some fancy friends of Craft who picked me up on the way. You didn't know I'm living in Queens now, did you?"

"No, but it sounds nice. Some parts of it can be very attractive."

"Not my area. But when the city tore down my place to build another high school, I had no choice. What a blow it was. I'll never be able to forgive the city—never." The thought disgusted her so much that she turned away, looked at the elderly women across the street and then at the sky. "Nice day in a manner of speaking, isn't it." She took a deep breath, asked if he was ready to go in, and started for the door. He followed her a few steps, then dropped back to see that his hairpiece was in place and to glance at the building across the street. The girl was still in her bra, pointy and full, leaning forward on the windowsill and looking at the church steps. She waved at him when she saw him staring at her, and he immediately swiveled around and went inside the church.

A funeral official rushed up to greet Arnold, just as Cynthia grabbed his arm and was trying to urge him into one of the back pews. Arnold apologized to her—she smiled and said she'd forgotten he had a duty to perform—and walked after the man to one of the front pews where the other pallbearers sat. He shook hands with two of them, fluttered two fingers at another he recognized at the far end of the bench and sat back in his aisle seat, his hands folded over his lap.

The organ, which had been humming a plaintive melody since he entered the church, boomed two resonant chords and then resumed its droning. The organist was perched on a narrow balcony at the rear of the church, his face reflective and grieved and lost in the music as he opened his eyes to turn a page. Abut a hundred fifty people were present, Arnold figured, and among them were some of the more prominent and prosperous members of the theater profession, so at least in this way Craft was getting a fine send-off. Most of the wives of these theater people sported expensive dark dresses and subdued jewelry and fresh hairdos and were talking lightly to one another, a few constantly undraping and redraping their shoulders with their fur coats and wraps. Yet he failed to see this as pretentious and comical as this has-been old playwright next to him had just pointed out, as there really was an occasional draft in the room which for a moment even made his own body shiver. Then the Mass began, just as Arnold was waving to a midget ticketbroker friend he had only now noticed sitting two rows behind him.

STEPHEN DIXON / SLEEP

It wasn't an especially sad ceremony, Arnold thought—certainly nothing like his friend's reformed Jewish one six months ago, which used a ten-man choir that brought nearly everyone to tears. At times he did hear a sniffle or faint cry, and one woman sitting across the aisle in this shabby green coat and black veil, broke down when the service was a few minutes old. The ingenue-type blonde beside her rubbed away her own tears and then quieted the bawling woman by throwing her arms around her shoulders and burrowing her head into the woman's chest. Most of the congregation turned to stare at them. It seemed that they too couldn't place the weeping couple, as just about everyone in the first ten rows was at least vaguely familiar to one another.

"I think the older one's a former maid of his," the playwright said.

"Two-to-one she's that waitress he knocked up in Iowa on one of his tours," another pallbearer said, "and the kid's his."

"You think so?" Arnold said, not knowing who to believe.

For a while the only sound in the room was the combined sobbing of these two women. Even the organist had stopped playing, but only because he was having trouble turning a page. Once he resumed his somber passage and the priest, who seemed to be fighting off a bad head cold, faked two coughs and crackled a page in the prayer book he held, the audience turned to the front.

What bothered Arnold most during the service was the continuous chattering going on between two women behind him. They remained silent when the priest reminisced about Craft's early days in Berlin and Hollywood and his vast contribution to the theater and more recently to this church, but resumed their chattering when he spoke in Latin again or paused to wipe his runny nose. Arnold wanted to turn around and politely tell the women off. After all, no matter how indifferent he felt about the Mass or even Craft's death in a way, this was still a house of worship and there were some real mourners present. But why risk offending two people he didn't even know —possibly even giving them a chance to make a fool out of him while he was doing it? He was never much for words, especially the tit-for-tat kind, till the argument was long over, so he just sat back, hoping the Mass would end before his temper really exploded.

With one thunderous organ blast the service was concluded. All the pallbearers were directed to rise, and Arnold, while he was stroking his hairpiece, was asked by the head usher to lead the pallbearers' march to the coffin. When the organist began another mournful hymn and the head usher signaled them with a flick of his finger, each pallbearer grabbed a bronze latch on the side of the coffin, lifted the coffin off the stand and walked up the aisle after the priest, who was now reading from a book and murmuring in Latin. Arnold couldn't remember the last time he'd walked so slow. Two of the more obvious reasons were the languid pace of the priest and the weight of the coffin—for Craft, though withering away rapidly the last two months, still weighed a boastful two hundred twenty the last time Arnold saw him. But the main reason for the slow march was Craft's elder brother Emmanuel, who held the first latch on the right side and was about seventy-five years old and looked too weak and exhausted to crawl out of the church empty-handed. As they carried the coffin through the door, Arnold saw Cynthia and another bit actress standing together behind a braided rope. He nodded to them after they both mouthed a choked-up hello.

A swarm of news photographers were waiting for the funeral entourage at the bottom of the church steps. The priest raised his hand, pleaded something about courtesy for the bereaved and respect for the dead, but the photographers still took pictures of the men carrying the coffin and the numbed veiled widow walking behind them. Arnold quickly felt his hairpiece with his free hand, arched his eyebrows taut and managed to put on his horn-rimmed glasses, since he felt they

STEPHEN DIXON / SLEEP

took a lot of attention away from his scalp and focused it on the center of his face.

"Now enough's enough, gentlemen," the priest said as the photographers continued to dart around getting angle and overhead and floor shots of the coffin, pallbearers and relatives, all now four steps nearer the sidewalk. "I've got to ask you to call a halt to this right now—do you hear?"

One photographer apologized to the priest, saying he was a good Catholic himself and had taken his quota of photos anyway. He also tried persuading the others to quit, but they pushed him aside, one of them shouting he hadn't gotten the shots his magazine wanted. Emmanuel, his face twitching on one side, swung wildly at this photographer and without realizing it let his end of the coffin drop to within inches of the ground. He cried out and pointed to his loose end and grabbed the latch with both hands and tried sticking his knee under the coffin while each of the other pallbearers was clumsily trying to level the different shifting weights to his own side, but the load was still too much for him and he yelped as he let go of the latch, and fell on his hands and knees. Two men rushed to Emmanuel's position, grabbed hold of the loose latch which had been flapping against the coffin like a doorknocker, and lifted the front end till the balance was restored all around. Emmanuel got up and turned a complete circle as he scanned the gaping crowd. Seeing the photographers—who along with the man who said he'd taken enough had even more frenziedly snapped pictures of Emmanuel's wild swing and fall and the pallbearers' ungainly dance with the coffin—he shook his fist at them and screamed that they should all swallow a six-inch fishbone at their next meal. Then he grabbed his latch and led the coffin to the hearse.

Arnold, who for several seconds had pictured the coffin crashing open and Craft rolling all the way to the gutter with the back half of his tux missing, now breathed regularly again as he walked with the others to the hearse. As he helped slide the coffin into the rear of the van he saw that Emmanuel was examining a cut on his palm.

"Can I help you there?" Arnold said.

"I don't need no help, thanks."

"Maybe something to tie around that," and he pulled out the silk handkerchief from his breast pocket and offered it.

"I already told you *no*." Emmanuel wiped his hand on his pants, walked to the lead limousine and sat straight in the front seat without saying another word to anyone. Arnold was amazed at the guy's composure and courage. If the same thing had happened to him he was sure he'd have sought help to get off the ground and away from the stares into the limousine. And once in the car—the back seat and preferably between two close friends or relatives—he would have had the shades pulled down and ridden that way till they were at least on the bridge leaving the city.

It took an hour just to get to Nassau County. Most of the talk among the four other pallbearers in the limousine centered around this year's Broadway flops and hits and their own plans for next season—a subject Arnold never tired of himself. What silenced him throughout the trip and made his stomach woozy was that one of the men had asked that the car windows stay shut because he felt a cold coming on, and two of the others and the chauffeur smoked long smelly cigars that some theater owner had handed them through the car window just before the cars left.

At the burial service, Hank Richardson, a matinee idol in his day and who still got good feature parts on TV, had been flown in from Hollywood by a local theatrical club to make a twenty-minute eulogy in front of the grave. It broke up the widow and most of the guests standing around the pit, but Arnold wished for its quick conclusion. Not that the delivery was bad. Richardson was an effective actor with a rich articulate voice that with the microphone he used must have been heard all over the cemetery. It was just that Arnold's stomach still ached from the ride, and then a pebble had got under the ball of his foot while he was carrying the coffin along the graveled path to the gravesite, and he felt it'd be rude to remove it till everyone was returning to the cars.

The drive back to the city was much more comfortable. He let the limousine leave without him and got a ride in the empty back seat of a private car, where he dropped off for brief naps. The driver, Craft's neurosurgeon, never said a word to Arnold or to his own wife till he quietly mentioned they had reached the 34th Street side of the Midtown Tunnel. Arnold came out of his half-sleep and thanked the two profusely. She said nothing, just sat erect and looked straight ahead till Arnold was out of the car, then bent forward and began powdering her face. The doctor mumbled something, seemed very sad, and drove away. Arnold walked a block for a cab. Once home he'd finish the morning paper, take an hour's nap, and go to the office. If anything, he was glad it was going to be a short working day.

He had been in the apartment an hour and was completing a *Variety* article on this year's sagging theater attendance, when the phone rang.

"Hello, that you, Arnold?" the woman said before he could answer.

"Cynthia?"

"That's right. How do you feel?"

"Fine, just fine, I guess—why?" puzzled why she had called.

"I phoned you at the office before. When they said you weren't in I got worried. You looked a little sick or something at the cemetery."

"Just a little stomach upset, but it's fine now. I took a Bromo."

"I'm glad to hear it's only that, though I know how painful it could be at times. By the way, wasn't that something out there today?"

"I'm sorry: what was?"

"You know: those obnoxious pests with the cameras. And then Craft's brother—what's his name?"

"Emmanuel?"

"That poor man: thrashing his fists like he's going to brain them one and going through what he did. I'll tell you something. People who invade one's privacy like that—and especially that of a devoted brother at a funeral, and to a widow who perhaps hadn't been that devoted—well they ought to be thrown in jail or even worse."

"There's still the freedom of the press, I suppose, though you might have a point." Cynthia's reminder of the church scuffle prompted him to touch the top of his head. Good God, he thought, he still had his hairpiece on, though when he was alone he always took it off first thing when he returned to his apartment. He fingered very gently the coarse edges along the temple. They felt sticky, somewhat out of place, and he wondered if the hairpiece had been unfastened from the paste when he was struggling with the toppling coffin and had been askew like that for everyone to see including the photographers up until the time he got back here. He started sweating, his stomach was aching again, and he wanted to run to the bathroom to see what horrible shape the hairpiece was in.

"Maybe you think I'm being too harsh with those men, is that it?"

"I don't know, Cynthia, I just don't know."

"Then what do you really think, Arnold? I'm saying, for the protection of us all: should we just expect such goings-on in our profession and accept them?"

"Maybe we have to. I just don't have any thoughts on the subject right now. Listen, would it be all right if you excused me now? I'm not trying to give you the rush act or anything, but the funeral sort of cut into a lot of important things I've got to take care of."

"Important?"

"Just some theater business."

"I'm glad to hear that, I really am. I mean, if it's a play or some-thing—like that—then an awful lot of good can come from it."

"That's true."

"Because Broadway can really use a good hit. The whole prestige of the theater can be raised with one great show. And then who knows? There might be even a little something in it for me—I'm saying, if there was such a role. Though that's not why I called. I want to make that clear, Arnold."

"If there was something for you, you know I'd call first thing."

"Oh, I don't mean now exactly. I already assumed you were referring to something else—simpler plans in the making, nothing definite."

"I was."

"There, you see? I was right. And look, Arnold, I want you to know I don't expect any special favors from you just because I got some pretty excellent notices in a role for you once and got to know you a little better than the next actress might. But some people seem to think I should take more advantage out of all my good contacts. That I should kind of push myself. You think that's so wrong?"

He outlined the hairpiece with his middle finger, trying to determine what position it was in. When Cynthia again asked if he thought she was approaching him and her other producer friends too openly—"Too broadly, which is so unlike me, but then I've had so many bad breaks and unfair rejections lately that I don't know what's the right way to look for a part any-more"—he said "Why no, not in the least. After all, what are friends supposed to be for like you say, right?"

She thanked him and hoped she hadn't been too much of a bother, gave her new phone number just in case he hadn't received her photo composite and he might be hearing of some replacement jobs for her this season. Then saying how encour-aged she felt after speaking to him now, she hung up. Arnold slammed down the receiver. He kicked off his loafers, peeled down to his undershorts and went to the bathroom, where he stood squinting in front of the mirror, trying to adjust his eyes to the two vertical fluorescent tubes on either side of the medicine chest. These lights also irritated him because they cut too deeply through whatever real hair remained on top, making him look even balder than he was.

The widow's peak of the hairpiece now pointed to the uppermost tip of his left ear. He never imagined himself looking anything as bad that. How long had it been that way? In front of the church? At the cemetery? Even if it was only during the car ride back and when he walked into the building and Jimmy saluted him and the elevator man rode him up.

He pulled the hairpiece off his head and tried to tear it in half, but it wouldn't rip. They make these things too damn well, he thought. For three hundred dollars they make them indestructible. He opened the bathroom window, squeezed his body out till his waist rested on the sill, and threw the hairpiece as far as he could. He lived on the sixteenth floor and the wind, much stronger up there, picked up the hairpiece and carried it over Central Park West into the park. And the hairpiece was still flying, looking like a graceful gray bird—a pigeon heading toward the lake on an even course till Arnold could hardly see it anymore, when he realized how far out he was heading and edged back into the room. A man could catch one hell of a cold out there, he thought. Could even lose his balance and get himself killed.

the tellers

Two men come into the bank. One has long hair reaching his shoulders and is carrying a shopping bag. The other has a big beard like a lumberjack and a coat on that practically touches the floor. Both of them I've never seen before, and in this town you get to recognize almost everyone after a while. We have no guard. To reduce payroll costs the bank had a television system installed—three cameras with signs all around saying the cameras are linked up to a private protection service, though two are dummies. The dummies focus on the manager's office and anteroom and on the steps leading to the downstairs vault and time-lock safe. The live camera focuses on the main floor and two teller booths, and I hope the person monitoring the screen now is keeping a close eye on these men.

I knock on the glass separating the two booths. Jane, the other teller, waves for me to hold it a minute till she finishes counting a stack of fives. The bearded man is writing on one of the bank slips at the customer's desk. The other man sits on a bench near the door reading a book. I knock on the glass much harder. "What?" Jane says angrily without my hearing her. Because the booths are totally enclosed with bulletproof glass, Jane and I communicate by exaggerating our lips, face and hand movements without making any sounds.

"You recognize those two men?" I say.

"No."

"Don't they look suspicious to you?"

"No," and she wraps a rubber band around the fives and puts the stack in the drawer.

The bearded man is finished writing. The other man turns a page of his book and then flips back to it as if to reread the bottom lines. There are no other customers on the main floor. Past the low gate to my left is the anteroom where Pati and Darlene, our two secretaries, work. Past them is the office of our manager, who's talking with a woman I've only seen in the bank once.

The bearded man is standing before my window. Jane's busy counting out tens. He points to a withdrawal slip and passbook. The book's one of ours, so I don't know what's been going on in my head about these two men. Maybe I'd recognize him without his beard, or else I wasn't around the time he opened his account. I unhook the disc over the speaker's hole and say through the screen "May I help you, sir?"

"How much can I withdraw from my savings account?"

"As much as you got in it."

"Well this is my bankbook and a withdrawal check for ten thousand."

I switch the revolving tray to his side of the window. "May I see them, please?"

"You'll see them all right—of course you will. But not yet. But you see my friend reading by the door?"

"You came in with him."

"That's right. We're good friends—very close. But my problem is I haven't the ten thousand in my savings I made the check out for."

"Then it's something you'd want to be talking about with the bank manager, Mr. Bayer."

"Mr. Bayer. Good idea. But one more thing. I don't want you to look alarmed. But I have two grenades in my pockets. So I want you to do exactly as I say without showing any emotion, or they go off."

"I thought so. But don't worry. I'll do like you say. But maybe you more than me who can get hurt, as this booth's built to take the concussion of a bomb."

"Your foot's not near the alarm, is it?"

"No."

"Well you're right—I could get hurt. But those office girls will get hurt much worse than you and me put together if the grenades go, and the manager and lady with him too. You see, I'm willing to take the chance. That's because I'm involved with this absolutely insane political group that needs money fast to buy arms. I'm telling you all this so you'll nod and smile back at me. That's right. No, don't overdo it. Fine. Now the only way to get arms is by stealing or buying them. And we've decided, after weighing the risks of both thefts, that there's more chance of getting caught and killed robbing a guarded armory or police station than a small bank patrolled by television set. So continue to look natural. Step back two steps. And in the order I now give you, tell the girl next door not to look alarmed at what you're going to tell her, to step back two steps, and that the bearded man here and the long-hair at the door are well-armed and robbing this bank."

I knock on the glass. Jane, counting twenties, says "What?"

In our silent language I start telling her what the man told me to say.

"Don't mess about," he says. The other man stands and stretches. "Speak so I can hear."

"But she can't hear me from in there. Even my loud knocks sound like taps to her. For her to hear me her speaker hold would have to be open and I'd have to yell out my lungs through mine." Jane knocks on the glass and says "What do you mean don't get alarmed?"

STEPHEN DIXON / SLEEP

"Joe," the bearded man says.

Joe walks behind the main floor camera, pulls a bench under it, stands on the bench and unsticks a strip of masking tape from his jacket lining and sticks it over the lens. He jumps down, locks the front door, lets down the venetian blinds on the window and door and takes out a grenade and pistol from the shopping bag. Pati and Darlene are still typing. Mr. Bayer reaches over his desk to the woman, who has pushed her chair back and clasped both hands over her mouth. The bearded man tells Jane and I to raise our arms high and Jane to step back two steps. Joe tells Pati and Darlene to can their typing. He opens the office door and orders Mr. Bayer and the woman out and everybody to the middle of the main room.

"Should we get on the floor on our bellies?" Pati says.

"Yes," Joe says, sliding the bench away. "Everyone on the floor on their bellies."

They all get on the floor. The woman is crying hysterically, but stops when Joe tells her to shut up. The bearded man climbs over the gate, goes left along the corridor to my door, and not finding a knob on it, tries pushing it in. I yell to him that I can't open the door without first getting a tick-back from the manager's office.

"What?" he says.

"A tick-back, a tick-back."

Jane is trying to explain to him also. He tries to push in her door.

"Give them everything, Gus and Jane," Mr. Bayer yells from the floor. "For all our sakes—don't be reckless."

I point to the place where in regular doors the knob would be, then to the manager's office. I curl up my left second finger and press my right second finger into the knuckle as if I'm pressing a buzzer.

The bearded man takes a grenade out of his pocket, sticks a second finger through the pin ring and makes jerking movements with his arms to show he's ready to pull the pin.

STEPHEN DIXON / SLEEP

"Come around," I say, waving him to go around to my window so he can hear me. Joe, keeping his gun pointed at the people on the floor, comes up to my window and says "What's with this stupid tick-back?"

I motion the man at my door to stay there and I'll tell Joe what's wrong.

"What we do when we want out is buzz Mr. Bayer's office," I tell Joe. "Then he ticks back, which electronically releases the door lock. They're on the top right of his desk—top one mine and one below that Jane's."

Joe waves to his friend that everything's all right. He tells the people on the floor to stay put or a live grenade will be rolling their way. He runs to the office and ticks back both our booths. The doors open. The bearded man pulls out two folded shopping bags from his coat and empties my till into one of the bags. Jane comes into the booth and drops the twenties she's been holding into the other bag. He empties both counter drawers of all bills and express checks, tells us to stand in the corridor with our arms raised and goes into Jane's booth. He empties her till and drawers and comes out and takes my wallet and tells us to go round to the front with him and get on the floor with the others. Jane and I lie on the floor next to one another.

"The phone wires," Joe says. He hands the bearded man his grenade, pulls a pair of cutters from his back pocket and runs into the anteroom and manager's office.

The bearded man listens to Mr. Bayer explain why it's impossible for anyone to open the time-lock safe without blowing it up. Someone knocks on the door. The bearded man looks through a slit in the window blinds and opens the door. Mr. Heim, a grocer, walks in and says to the bearded man "How come they closed?"

"On the floor on your face with the others," he says and locks the door. Mr. Heim gets down like the rest of us. Jane says in our silent language "I don't see how they expect to get away with this. They're taking too long."

STEPHEN DIXON / SLEEP

"Just hope they get caught outside and not in," I say.

"Remember that book which said if a bank isn't robbed within two minutes, the robbers mostly get caught before they leave. That figure was more than nine cases in ten."

"The one with the beard said it's a political cause they're doing it for."

"Political? What's he ever mean?"

"Now be smart and listen to me, folks," the bearded man says. "I've fixed one of the teller alarms with an explosive. So if the alarm's set off, the whole bank goes up. We also have a third man who'll be guarding outside after we're gone, so nobody gets up, nobody leaves. After five minutes he takes off and then you can do what you please."

They tuck some rags into the tops of the shopping bag and leave the bank and lock the door with Mr. Bayer's keys.

"What do we do now, Mr. Bayer?" I say.

"Breathe."

"With a bomb ready to go off in one of the teller booths?" Pati says.

"That was just a con story so we wouldn't set it off," I say. "I was watching the bearded guy filling the shopping bags, and he definitely didn't wire any explosive to the alarms."

"*Fixed* is what he said he did," Pati says.

"Fixed, wired, or anything."

"Oh, you know all about bombs now?" Jane says.

"You saw him. All he did was empty our drawers and tills."

"You still couldn't get me to ring it no matter what you say," Pati says. "And nobody else should either."

"Absolutely," Mr. Bayer says.

The woman customer resumes her hysterical crying.

"Will you please stop that, Miss Frost?" Mr. Bayer says.

She begins weeping quietly.

"This ever happen here before?" Darlene says.

"Never," Mr. Bayer says.

"And what about that great protection service you got rid of the guard for, and their calling the police? Some protection. I bet the one who watches the screen is drunk. Or so dumb he thought we turned the camera off."

"They know there we can't turn it off," Mr. Bayer says.

"Then he thought our electricity went. But something."

"I think it'd be safe getting up now," I say. "After all, there really can't be any third man outside. And if I checked out the alarms and found nothing wrong with them—"

"You stay away from them," Jane says.

"She's right, Gus," Mr. Bayer says. "Let's play it safe and believe everything those men said."

"Listen to your boss," Mr. Heim says.

"But he didn't have time to fix either alarm, I'm telling you. I was standing next to him or watching him from the hall all the time he was in Jane's booth, and he never got near enough to reach the buttons or wires. Now you know I wouldn't be kidding you on that matter."

"Old Hawkeye Gus," Pati says. "Never misses a thing. Okay, so you didn't see him touch it. But I'm still not getting up."

"The police could probably still catch the men if we rang it," Darlene says.

"Are you crazy?" Pati says.

"Nobody gets up or steps on any alarms," Mr. Bayer says. "Now that's an order."

"Good," Jane says.

"Does anyone know how many minutes we've been lying here?" Mr. Heim says.

"Not five," Mr. Bayer says.

"What I'd like to know is how many minutes those men were in here," Jane says.

"Ten I'd say," Mr. Bayer says.

"More like fifteen," Pati says. "Where do they get the nerve? Not the nerve like it's something wrong they did, which goes without saying. But the physical nerve. Fifteen minutes. By all rightful means more than one person should have been wanting to get in the bank in that time."

"Someone else did knock," Mr. Bayer says. "A couple of minutes after Mr. Heim."

"I didn't hear it," Pati says.

"I did," Darlene says.

"I was on my way to make a safe deposit," Mr. Heim says. "Lucky they didn't take it off me."

"They got my wallet," I say.

"Mine too," Mr. Bayer says. "And my car and home and bank keys."

"My wallet was sitting right on the door shelf," Jane says, "and he didn't touch it. I have more than fifty dollars in it too. I was going to buy a coat after work."

"He didn't get any of Darlene's or my money either," Pati says.

"I'm getting awfully tired in this position," Mr. Heim says.

"Imagine how we feel," Pati says. "We've been lying like this five minutes more than you."

"But my stomach's too big to lie on so long. I'm getting up."

"Please wait the full five minutes," Mr. Bayer says. "Otherwise you'll be jeopardizing the lives of us all."

"I'll turn over then." He turns over.

"Why didn't I think of that?" Pati says. She turns over. So does Darlene, Miss Frost and Jane and I. Mr. Bayer stays on his stomach. The door opens.

"Oh my god," Darlene says.

"We've decided to take a hostage," the bearded man says. "An idea we suddenly got, just so we can get out of the area if we're trapped. You," he says to Mr. Bayer.

"Too much of a squeeze with him," Joe says. "Take one of the girls."

"Not the weepy one," he says. "She'll drive me crazy with those tears."

"All women weep. Take the teller. He's thin enough and he really used his head before."

"Up you go, teller. Everybody else turn over the way we told you. And no stepping on alarms or the bank goes. No getting up for another five minutes or our third friend barges in. No even turning over on your backs again. And when the police come, tell them who we got and not to follow us because your teller here—what's your name?"

"Gus Millis."

"Millis gets killed if they force us into a chase."

"I'll tell them your words," Mr. Bayer says.

We leave. Joe locks the door. We get in a sports car in front of the bank. Mr. Bayer never would have fit. The bearded man sits behind the wheel, Joe in the other bucket seat. I sit between them, my shoulders and thighs touching theirs and the hand brake between my legs.

"Comfortable?" Joe says to me.

"I'll manage."

"Take more of my seat. I still have some room at the door."

We drive out of town, onto the connecting road that leads to the turnpike. Past the junior and high schools I graduated from, the cemetery my parents are buried in, the beer and burger place I've met so many girls at. The bearded man never drives more than five miles over the posted speed limit. A police car is heading toward us in the next lane and Joe tells me "Look natural. Turn your head to me now and when he passes us say 'How is the weather, Joe?'"

I turn to him and say "How is the weather, Joe?" as the police car passes. Through the rearview mirror I see the car continue down the road and out of sight. We get on the turnpike on-ramp going south.

"Where we going? I say.

"A ways," Joe says. "Don't worry."

"You really going to do something to me if the police give chase?"

"How do we answer that?" Joe says.

"My answer to him is don't try and find out," the bearded man says.

"I won't be any trouble. I'll in fact do everything you want me to to help you escape. And if it does all go right for you, could you later give my wallet back?"

"You'll get it," Joe says. He has a mirror in his lap and is snipping off large chunks of hair with some scissors.

"You don't want to use the wire cutters?" the bearded man says.

"You use them," Joe says.

"And Mr. Bayer's wallet and keys? They're very important to him and the bank."

"Look what he's worried about," Joe says.

"You don't remember those days?" the bearded man says. "Yes sir, no sir, always sucking up to the boss. You're going to go far in the bank business, Gus. Very."

"I only thought," I say. "It's not important."

"You don't have to tell us."

"And that alarm system. You didn't really fix it with an explosive."

"Oh yes I did."

"But you couldn't have. I told them it wasn't."

"Now what the hell you do that for?"

"Because I was watching you in both booths. You never had the time. All you were doing was shoving money in the bags."

"I bent, dumbo. For what do you think—to tie my shoes? I had a gum hold. A miniature E-Z-4. But why am I talking to you like you know what I'm saying? But in the girl's booth. Right after I cleaned out her bottom tray. All I had to do was stick it to the wire and the moment the alarm's touched and vibes start, the bank blows."

"Paul became an expert in explosives in the service," Joe says, still cutting his hair.

"That'll be enough," Paul says.

"I didn't say which service. Not even which country."

"You've said more than enough."

"His names's not Paul," Joe says, throwing his hair out the window. "It doesn't even start with a P."

"All right, Joe. And you, Gus. Let's hope they all know you for the big blowhard you are and my warning sunk in."

"I'm sure they do. I'm sure it did." I pray it did. And that Mr. Bayer's inborn cautious nature and last order about nobody touching the alarm, had swayed the group. The police would find the explosive and know what to do with it after that.

We leave the turnpike twenty miles after we got on it and park behind a new station wagon on a deserted road. Joe, his hair crewcut short, finishes shaving the back of his neck with a dry safety razor and says to me "How do I look? No, really, Gus, how do I?" He gives the razor scissors and mirror to the man he called Paul. He dumps the shopping bags of money into a valise and sticks the valise into the rear of the wagon where there are boxes of food and beer and ten-gallon cans of gas. We get in the wagon. Joe at the wheel, me in the middle again, and drive north on the turnpike past the same places we passed some minutes ago. Paul begins cutting his hair.

"You think we cleared ten thousand?" Joe asks me.

"More like twelve."

"Twelve? What about trying for fourteen, twenty-four, even four hundred thou?"

"No, twelve. There were no big withdrawals or deposits today. And Jane and I usually have about six thousand apiece."

The radio still hasn't mentioned the robbery. Joe says it's because the police don't want to tip us off as to how much they know or don't know. Paul shaved his face clean and now trims his hair. They both look completely different, maybe ten years younger. They're also now wearing conservative sports jackets and white shirts and clip-on ties, though they didn't change their soiled blue jeans.

I awake during the night. Paul's at the wheel. The radio's still on. "There it is," Joe says, turning the volume up when the newscaster leads off the headlines of his report with the explosion bank robbery in my town.

"Oh no," I say.

"Shhh." We stay silent through a minute of commercials before the newscaster returns with the details. Two people were killed, four hurt, one seriously. That's all of them. Twelve thousand stolen, a bank hostage taken, the entire first floor of the bank destroyed. The robbers got away in a red sports car hardtop, no license plate reported and were last seen driving south. They carried shopping bags. My name is given. The robbers are described. The long-haired man was referred to as Joe. The bearded man was called Hank and Frank. His name on the withdrawal check and bankbook was a profanity and apparently a fake. A third might be involved. All are considered highly dangerous and heavily armed. Then another commercial and the next story about the war.

"Twelve thousand," Paul says, whistling. "You hit it on the nose, Gus."

I start crying.

"Look, I don't feel too good about it either. But I warned you about the alarm. You should listen when someone warns you on something like that."

"Maybe it wasn't your friends who got hurt," Joe says. "Maybe it was two police or army men from a defusing squad. It was that complicated a little device."

"No, it was my friends."

"There you go again," Paul says. "Always so sure of yourself. You saw the trouble it got you in before."

Around midnight we reach a national forest reserve. We keep on its narrow rising road a mile till it ends at a twenty-foot high snow drift where the plows must have stopped. We park, keep the motor running, have sandwiches and beer. Joe climbs over the seat to get my wallet out of the valise. Paul runs the radio up and down the band till he picks up the one clear station. A news report comes on. The victims were Jane and the woman customer. I've known Jane since we were kids. We went to school together, both elementary and high. Her age is given as 22, though she's three years older than that. The seriously injured person is Darlene. Darlene is a roomer in the same rooming house as mine. We dated regularly for a few weeks till a month ago when Mr. Bayer got wind of it through an anonymous letter and told us to stop dating or lose our jobs. He was afraid the bank would lose its contract with the agency that bonded us. The newscaster gives my correct age and says federal and state officers are now convinced an accomplice in another car took part in the theft.

"Which ones were Jane Stight and Anna Frost?" Paul says. I tell him and he says "Pity about the teller girl. She seemed like a nice sweet thing and showed lots of courage. The woman with the tears though I think the world's better off without."

"I feel bad about them both," I say.

"Hear, hear," Joe says.

"Of course. So do I. That was an insensitive remark I made about Miss Frost."

"Well, we got to be leaving you," Joe says, handing me my wallet, a blanket, sandwiches, and beer. "There's a hiker's lean-to left past that pine tree. Curl up in the corner of it and you'll survive the night. Then tomorrow early, follow the tracks back to the logging road and go any direction on it and you'll find civilization by the end of day. Oh yeah," and he gives me Mr. Bayer's wallet and keys.

"Won't be needing them as I'm not going back. There's nothing for me there now but a worn-out car, beat-up clothes, and a good chance of a negligence or accessory to murder charge that'll land me in jail for years. I'm going to change my name, grow a mustache, and settle somewhere else. Another kind of job shouldn't be too hard to come by, so long as the hirer doesn't know the damage I caused."

"You'll feel different about it in the morning," Joe says, and they drive off.

STEPHEN DIXON / SLEEP

But my feeling hasn't changed when I wake up. Back home, if I did get off without being arrested, I'd still always be afraid of running into Jane's family or that woman's, if she has one. And most of all, Darlene's violent alcoholic folks, if she dies. The people there would never let me forget the part I played in destroying the town's only bank and ending those lives. I'd never be able to find a job or get back any of the respect or just plain indifference they once showed me. I'd be known as a fool and murderer for the rest of my life.

I start downhill. At the logging road I go in the opposite direction of where my town lies. After a few hours of walking without seeing anyone, I hear a car approaching from behind. I stick out my thumb. It's a new foreign model, long as a limousine. Inside are Joe and Paul.

"We need your help bad," Joe says.

"Our political movement turned out to be as corrupted as the government we were supposed to overthrow and replace. They were serious enough about buying and using the arms before we robbed the bank. But once they saw the cash, all they could talk about were the cars and dope they were going to buy, the trips and movies they were going to make. They wanted to split it halvsies with us, but it wasn't for their pleasures we'd snitched it for. We tried some associate cells in other cites, but it was the same ride three times around. So, no place to go. Stuck with a wad we've no use for. We're now going to try and avoid a stiff prison rap and possible death trap by turning the money and ourselves in, exposing the hypocrisy and whereabouts of the various groups, and making sure the police know there never would have been any explosion or deaths if you hadn't told your coworkers to ignore our warnings about the alarm. Hop in."

"I already told you: I can't go back."

They chase me down the road, run out and drag me into the car. Except for gas stops, we make it straight through to my town. My legs and arms bound, they carry me up the police stairs and turn the money and car keys and themselves and me in.

That same day, with the information and addresses Joe and Paul give, many of their organization's headquarters and cells are raided. The attorney general calls it the most successful roundup of political terrorists in the nation's history. He says an attempted armed revolution has been averted that could have cost the country hundreds of lives and millions in property damage. The press and government leaders hail Joe and Paul as reformed anarchists. All charges against them are dismissed.

I'm booked on two charges of manslaughter. But federal officials persuade the state to drop its case against me as it doesn't want to embarrass the country and its new nationally acclaimed patriots—unpunished kidnappers, who would have to be two of the main witnesses against me.

I'm released and go to my rooming house for the night. A note from my landlady is on my bed. "I expected this'd be the first place you'd come running to, which is why I'm staying the night safe with armed friends. Poor Darlene will live, no thanks to you. Though her doctors told me personally she'll be pitiably scarred in the face and mind for life. Your past living here has brought this house sufficient disgrace. Please be gone tomorrow no later than the regular check-out hour—11 A.M."

Next morning I drive through town to the road that leads to the turnpike, the same road I was on with Joe and Paul four days ago. After a mile I get bogged down behind a funeral procession. There are hundreds of cars, all with their lights on it seems and driving very slowly, some with black crepe and cloth tied around their fenders and aerials. Jane, besides being extremely well-liked, once brought fame to our town by winning the state's beauty contest and almost the country's—in front of network television cameras she strutted and sang and came in third.

The opposite lane looks clear all the way to the end of the procession. I get into it and drive past the creeping cars and limousines. Just as I pass the flower cars and hearse, I see a state trooper standing in the middle of the two-lane road signaling me down. I stop. The hearse catches up with my car and makes a left between the trooper and me to enter the cemetery. The flower cars follow and then the lead limousine. Inside are Jane's parents, worn from weeping and shaking their heads sympathetically at me as their car crosses the road and passes through the cemetery gates. Jane's brothers are in the next limousine, enraged, all four of them at the windows shaking their fists at me. And then the rest of the limousines and private cars filled with relatives, neighbors, friends, teachers, bank customers, civic and state officials, people who did business with her dad, young men and women we both went to school with, the man she was going to marry next month, Pati, Mr. Bayer, Mr. Heim, my landlady sitting between Darlene's bawling parents, most either shaking their fists or umbrellas or sticking their fingers up or screaming behind windows or opening the windows and spitting on my car hood or in the direction of my car and yelling obscenities at me and my future children and grandchildren and the memory of my folks who are buried inside. I close my windows and press down all the locks. Finally the last cars pass—people I don't know and who don't recognize me. Then the state trooper turns sideways and waves me on.

tails

I'll start where I began. I'll even start before then. Before I was born, before my parents were born. Before their parents and the parents of their parents and their parents' parents' parents' and their parents were born. Before then. But when was then? Long and very long ago. The last century, century before the last. The century before the one before this one perhaps. Perhaps even before that. And where were they born? Some here and some overseas. Some just somewhere here and somewhere overseas. Most just many places here and overseas and many of those over many seas overseas and many other places other than that. But could there be any other birthplaces other than that? On and below and above the seas, but I'll be more exact. I was born here. My parents were born here. Their parents were born overseas. The parents of my parents' parents were born overseas, but my parents' parents' parents' parents and their parents were born somewhere here. But that wasn't where it began. The parents of my parents' parents' parents' parents' parents were born overseas also, though not the same or even the adjoining continent overseas their parents and parents' parents or my parents' parents and parents' parents' parents were born. Most of us have died. That's a relief. I live. My mother died. I've a sister who lives, or was alive, but my father died. My father's father and his father are dead too. I don't have to say that the parents of my parents' parents died or any of our ancestors before that. They're, or course, dead. Because they're, of course, dead, why did I then say it? "You repeat too much and too much of what you repeat is the obvious," someone recently said to me, or let me just say someone said. And that's where I'll begin or would begin if I hadn't begun with what I've begun with so far.

She was sitting in her rocking chair. I was sitting on the bed opposite her, the only two sitting places in the room other than on the desk and floor. No, they're not the room's only two sit- ting places, which I want to make more of but won't. "Don't," she also said. "You too often go too circuitously and deeply and completely and in the long run drearisomely into where people are and what they're sitting on or leaning against or on or stand- ing in or against or on, etcetera." But where was I? "You've done too much of that too, saying 'Where am I' 'Where was he?' You forget or intentionally forget or like to make people think you forget or forgot or have forgotten you forget or forget you've forgotten you like to forget, etcetera, too much," she said. Who said? "That too," she said, "as if people don't have names till you ask who's done or said what you've just said they've done or said, etcetera. But you know what I mean."

What did she mean? What do I mean?

"You've done too much of that too," she said. "Just begin. But you say you've begun. So just get on with it, into it, end it, retype it and photocopy it, if you haven't carbon-copied it or if you now like to both carbon-copy and photocopy it, and send out the original, keep the copy or copies in your desk drawer or wherever you now keep your copies if you're still making copies or sending out originals or sending out or retyping or ending or getting into or on with what you've begun. And don't now say you'll call or consider calling this piece *The Piece,* since you called the piece before this piece *The*

Piece. Call it *The Second Piece* or *The Piece after the Piece* or even *The Peace after the Piece* or vice versa, though not *Vice Versa* or *Piece Number Two* or *Piece* roman or arabic number two, meaning either one of those symbols for cardinal number two. Call it whatever you want, and don't now say it'll make little to no sense to call it *Whatever You Want,* as you've done too much of that thing too."

But where was I?

"Aha," she said.

I forgot.

"Or forgot how much I know you like to forget, etcetera," she said.

When? Who?

"You see?"

Her. Dana.

"Is that her real name?"

No, only for this piece. Her real name is Dita.

"Really her real name?"

No. And I won't say "Where was I?" But I've just said "Where was I?"

"You've done that device to death too," she said.

So I'm nowhere in this piece. I haven't got anywhere in this piece. I'm not far along to be more exact. I'm about sixty-five sentences along to be even more exact, and now, if that was sixty-five, sixty-six sentences along to be just as exact, though sixty-six, and now sixty-seven if that was sixty-six, of my manuscript sentences, if this is a manuscript, since if this were in or is in a magazine, newspaper, pamphlet or book, it wouldn't be a manuscript and would be more or less or the same number of sentences along as in my manuscript form.

"Is anyone really interested?"

Is anyone interested if anyone's really interested?

"That too. Because why bother, since people don't read fiction anymore," Dana, Dita, her real name, said. I said "You read fiction." I actually said that. She said "Only your fiction, if this is fiction, and not just the word 'fiction,' though now I'm starting to do what you like to do, not making fiction, and I'm still doing it, I mean I don't make fiction as you do if you still do make fiction, but I'm still doing it, so I'll stop." I said "I read fiction, and not just my fiction." She said "That's true, you do. I suppose then some people still read fiction. We do, or just you do, if yours isn't fiction anymore and the other fiction you read is. So if people don't read fiction, at least one person does." She gets out of the chair. The chair she was rocking in and hates for me to speak about. The old chair, almost an ancient chair, certainly an antique chair, "The chair my mother's grandmother bought used at a used furniture store more than a hundred years ago," Dana, Dita, some other name, Dora said.

She gets out of bed. She has no clothes on. I usually love to see her walking away from me naked to the bathroom. Or just out of the room to any room or just away from me if we have no other room. Her boy, her girl, one of those, neither of those, sleeps or doesn't sleep or can't sleep or can't be sleeping, etcetera, in the next room or this room or one of the other rooms if we have no other room or rooms or have more than two.

She gets off the couch. She's warmly dressed. Almost overdressed. She has on a jacket over a sweater over her turtleneck jersey over a T-shirt and heavy woolen pants over her tights which are over her underpants and over the two pairs of socks she has on are a pair of pile-lined boots. That would be both warmly and overdressed in a well-heated home. Ours is not. We have little heat. It's too expensive. Fuel shortage, they say. The thermostat is down. Down? The thermostat is on the wall, at her eye level but down from mine. The thermostat's down to around sixty-five. "In some homes," Dora, etcetera, said, "sixty-five is the temperature they turn the heat down to when they go to bed." Now it's early afternoon. We usually go to bed at night. Ours is a very hot home when we're hot, when we're home, and sometimes in the summer when we're not. Now it's fall.

STEPHEN DIXON / SLEEP

She gets off the floor. I get out of her rocking chair. A new rocking chair, fairly new rocking char, old rocking chair that looks new. The rocking chair I bought yesterday, found today, was given, gave to her, took from her, stole from the next door neighbor's porch and painted or stained another color and filed the serial numbers off. I get out of bed and walk naked away from nobody in the cold, hot or mild room to somebody in another room or to no other room or around many rooms. I walk around this room. I stay in the room and walk around the bed. I stay in bed and walk around on it. Nobody sleeps in the next room. There is no next room. It's a one-room house. A one-room apartment. I have to go to a friend's room, house, or apartment to make number two. I piss in my sink. There is no sink. I have no friend. I do make number two. There is no bed. I sleep on the floor. I only try to sleep. There is a window and door. There is no window. I sleep in the closet. I can't sleep. I stand. There is no door. I was sealed up inside that closet. It isn't a closet. It's a space in the middle of the room. I was forced at gunpoint or at some point by some point to stand in this space which then isn't a space but is still in the middle of the room. To stand on a spot in some part of the room while a wall was built out of bricks all around me till it reached the ceiling, sealing me in. There is no room to move. There is no room, I cannot move. I'm not in a room. I'm outside. The wall wasn't built out of bricks but poured over me as cement. It's not a wall. It is cement. It's an impression of me that can only be seen from the outside. I can only feel it from the inside. There are no holes in it for me to breathe. I die.

I get off the floor. I've been reading the newspaper, my head on a bed pillow on the couch, my back against the couch's side. Something like that. She still sits on the chair. She sits still in an old dentist or dental chair. Which is it? Look it up. Why all of a sudden don't I know? Will it turn out to be one or the other or some other kind of medical or professional chair? I get off the toilet. I don't flush the toilet because there's

nothing in the toilet or there is but there's no water in the toilet tank or bowl. Or what's in the toilet bowl doesn't need to
be flushed or it does but the toilet can't be flushed or it can but
someone said it shouldn't be flushed or it's the last time it can
or will be flushed or I don't like flushing it simply because I
don't like to or I don't like what's on the toilet bowl handle or
I have no hands to work the handle or any body parts that can
jiggle the handle or lift the tank part and work the flusher or
there is no flusher or no toilet or many things, an infinite
number of things, "You're doing those permutation things
again," Dana, Dita, some other name, Dina, Dona, says, might
say, would, could, can't or doesn't say, said, never said, thinks,
writes, winks, types, "You're doing these things again and
again plus that rhyming thing you said in some other thing
you wouldn't or never would again," she said.

I go into the house. I'm in the house. I'm alone. I'm with
someone. She's here. Or he. Another man or boy. Or me. I'm he.
Just I'm here. I talk, I walk. I can't talk, I can't walk. I crawl on
my belly like a reptile, as she said. I won't say "I won't say
'Who said?'" But I just said "I won't say 'Who said?'" I'm some
place. It's dark, it's light. Or it is dark, it's light. Or it's dark, it
is light. Or it is dark, it is light. That's about the extent of it
minus its transpositions and different punctuations. Or that is
about the extent of it minus, etcetera, or etc. The room's bright-
ly lit. Or the room is, it isn't. I hold my hands over my eyes, I
don't. I'm blind, I'm not. I hold my hand over my eyes because
they hurt, my hands hurt, not my eyes hurt, and not from the
light, which I can't see, so I am blind, but if I am, how do I
know the light's on? I heard a click. Someone announced the
light's on over a loudspeaker in or outside the room. Someone
across the way who can see into my room phoned to say the
light's on. Someone yelled from the sidewalk or the building
across the way or someone with binoculars from faraway
phoned from nearby or faraway to say "Hey, your light's on or
is on or lights are on or at least when I last saw it or them." But

STEPHEN DIXON / SLEEP

I should move on. I'm sitting in the chair, lying on it, huddled up in it, one foot off the ground, other foot on. But no feet. I have none. He doesn't. No arms either. Sitting there like that. Yes. He sits. I do. On his buttocks. But not buttocks. I sit on one buttock. Sits now but was set there before? Could he have climbed there? No. Yeah. I climbed up with his chin. I've over the years trained and developed his body to lift me on to the chair by his shoulders, neck, chest, and chin. Somehow. And then I just lie chest-down in the chair, or he sits in it. Sits in it if he can hook my chin on the chair arm, and then, with this technique I've developed and the strength in his chest and my buttock and his neck, I flip myself around so he can sit on my one buttock. Where he sit. But if he can't that day flip me around or even get his chin over the chair arm, I just lies there chest-down in the chair. Like a buttock but not on my buttock. Like a sandbag but not a sandbag. Like a torso but a torso and head. He am both. That's what I is.

She comes through the door. "It's cold out," she says. Cold out? I think. "Cold, considerably cold out," she says. Ah, so you want to speak about the weather, I think. Well whether or not I could speak about the weather or whether or not I could even speak about whether or not I could speak about the weather or even speak it doesn't matter, since I can't speak, I think. But you say it's cold out. "Very cold," she says. "I'm cold. You must be cold. Let me feel your lips. Usually your lips are cold if it's cold out. Your lips are cold. Very cold. So it must be cold out. Very cold. I like the cold. I'm going out." She goes out.

She comes through the window. "You said the door was locked," she says. Who said the door was locked? Who said you said the door was locked? Who said you said the door was locked, she says? Who's saying who's saying who said who said you said the door was locked, she says? "And you didn't open it when I knocked," she says. "How could I have when I'm nothing but a torso and head in a chair?" I could have said if that's all I was or wanted to pretend that's all I was and I

STEPHEN DIXON / SLEEP

could speak. But I've limbs. Mouth to boot. Two arms and legs to be exact and quite healthy in fact. I do calisthenics every morning. Run an average of two miles every weekday and weekends I average four. Not four runs on weekdays or two miles every weekend day. But four miles every weekend day. That averages out to how many miles a week? Per month? The thirty or thirty-one kind or either one of those February months and starting on what day of the week?

She comes down the chimney. "Surprise," Dora, Dona, none of the D's, Effie, Essie, Ellen says. "And I'm surprised there are no windows or doors in this place. No way to get in but down the chimney. How come?"

"Glad you could come and could ask me that," I write on a piece of paper, my only known affliction being that I can't speak and maybe the minor complication that I can write or just that I've paper. "But why'd you come at all?"

"To ask why you've no windows or doors or just a window or door or really any entrance to this place besides down the chimney, which isn't an entrance but an exit, for smoke, not for people, though I suppose it could be for both and both an entrance and exit for both and even for one of those, if it's necessary, just as it was, if it was necessary, an entrance for me. But get on with it."

I'm on the floor, in a chair, on the toilet, in bed, in a bath, I haven't been in a bath yet, hot and cold water running concurrently out of two spigots, mixed through one spigot, too hot, too cold, no hot, just cold, no water, can't bathe, no toilet or sink, can't wash or drink, no bathroom, in a tub in the kitchen, no kitchen, in a pail in the living room, no room and pail, I'm in a barrel on the porch, no roof, I bathe when it rains hard, no plug, can't bathe, no porch, I'm in a barrel in the great outdoors, not great, just the outdoors, not just, the outdoors, no barrel, I'm lying without any clothes on the grass, no grass, on the earth, no earth, in a hole, no hole, but in a hole, don't know anything about this hole, can't see or feel this hole, can't see or feel, can't smell or even taste this hole, can't do either of those, what is the other sense I can't do if I can't do it? I can think, but that isn't a sense, maybe a sixth sense, but how can it be my sixth when I haven't got from four to five of my other senses, I don't know, could not knowing be a sixth sense, for if thinking can't be maybe not knowing can, I don't know, let me think, I don't know, all I know is I'm still in a hole, this hole, don't know how or when I got in this hole, if I haven't always been in this hole, if I can't see because this hole has always been black or at least black while I've been in this hole and I've always been in this hole, not for a while whole and while whole a while in this hole, so I'm still in this hole, here in this hole I'm still in this hole, that I still am, still I am, that I am, here in this hole I am, here I am I. "But get on," she says.

She gets out of the tub. "Aren't there any dry towels left?" she says. I say I'll look. I open the closet. "Lots of dry towels left in the linen closet," I say. "Any clean dry towels left in the linen closet?" she says "No, only dry dirty towels. The dry clean towels are right in the linen closet." "And the dirty dry towels aren't right in the linen closet?" "No, all the dry dirty towels are hanging off the closet's shelves and dragging out on the closet floor and preventing me from shutting the closet door." "Get me a clean dry towel before you try shutting the closet door," she says. "Lots of clean dry towels left," I say, "but who cleans them?" "Don't start," she says. "Who is she who says don't start?" I say. "Don't continue," she says. I go back to the bathroom and see her standing on the bath mat. "I don't recognize you. What's your name?" I say. "Give me the towel," she says. "But what's your name?" I say. She says "You're such a card." "A card?" I say. "A joker, a kidder. You're always kidding around." "Kidding around?" I say. "Teasing. You're always teasing me and teasing Rachel. In fact, Rachel says you tease her too much. No child likes to be teased so much." "Child?" "Rachel's hardly a grown-up yet, even if she is beginning to mature." "Mature?" "Don't tell me you haven't noticed. I've

STEPHEN DIXON / SLEEP

seen you looking between her legs at her developing hairs there when she changes into her pajamas." "Developing hairs there? Pajamas?" "Just because you haven't got a pair, don't pretend nobody else does." "Pair of developing hairs there? Pajamas?" "Either then, if that's what you prefer." "Either? Prefer?" "Yes, prefer. You know damn well what I mean." "Mean?" "Yes, mean." "What do you mean yes mean?" "And what do you mean what do I mean or you mean yes mean? You see, anyone can do it. It's not hard." "You're right. And I know who cleans the towels. I do. And I know your name and who Rachel is. You're Ellen and she's your daughter." "She's my cat." "She's a cat with a pair of developing hairs there and pajamas?" "Yes," she says, "though Rachel is my daughter. But forget it. I'm dry. The air dried me. I don't need your towel now—dry, dragged or cleaned. I could still get a cold though, so I'm going to get dressed. I am getting dressed. I'm dressed. Now I'm going downstairs. I am going downstairs. I'm downstairs. Now I pick up a book. Now I open the book and read 'Now I open the book and read "You see, anyone can do it. It's not hard."'" Now I take my clothes off. I mean, now I put the book down and take my clothes off. Now I walk upstairs, begin to fill up the tub, get in the tub, wash myself, rinse myself, get out of the tub, say to you aren't there any dry towels left?"

The phone rings. I pick it up. The phone continues ringing. I picked up the phone, not the receiver. I put the phone down and only pick up the receiver. The phone isn't ringing anymore and nobody answers when I say hello. Nobody's there or else somebody's there and didn't hear my hello or else nobody or somebody's there but didn't hear my hello because I only mouthed the word hello because I can't say hello because I can't speak or even groan so I don't groan into the phone but only tap my nose on the mouthpiece because fixed to the tip of my nose like a nose warmer is a plastic disk to tap out messages on the phone to the person who calls. I tap three times for hello.

"Hello, John," the caller says, "how goes it today?"

I tap three times, though this second time I tap three times means I'm fine.

"Then everything's not too hot with you, eh, John?"

I tap three times, which means "No, you got that message wrong, everything's fine, just great." Then I tap three more times, which means good-bye, and this caller, who calls every day though not always at the same time, hangs up.

Only once on this phone did I get a call from someone else. A long time ago. Years to be exact. The phone rang. I picked up the receiver and tapped three times for hello. The person said "Hal, this is Harriet, why you tapping like that, anything wrong?" I continued tapping all kinds of taps: four taps, five taps, twenty taps. The person said "Hal, you have to tell me what's the matter. Is this a wrong number I reached or what can I do to help?" I continued tapping, though much more elaborate tapping than before: some fast, some slow, some mixed up together like four fast and three slow and then a long pause followed by a tap and a short pause followed by three fast taps and four slow. She said "Don't worry, Hal. Wrong number or not, I'm coming right over and will call someone to phone you to try to find out what's wrong with you even before I get there," and she hung up. That was also the only time anyone offered his or her name to me since the first day I was brought to this place, put in this chair by the phone with a pipe nearby to suck food from and another pipe next to it when I wanted water to drink or to rinse my mouth with or to drip down my chin, and two more pipes connected to me below when I wanted to excrete or just excreted, and that's all. Right after I was put in this chair and the person who put me there left the room, the phone rang. I picked up the receiver and the voice said "I will tell you this only once: when I phone you once every day after today, pick up the receiver and give three taps for hello on the mouthpiece with your nose, which if you feel it, has a nose tapper fixed to it, and if you can't feel it, take my word there's a plastic disk about the size of a nose warmer on your nose for you to tap out messages to the person who calls. After you tap hello, I'll say 'Hello, John, how goes it today?' You'll tap three times, which means you're fine, but I'll say 'Then everything's not too hot with you, eh, John?' You'll tap three more times, which means 'No, you got the message wrong, everything's fine, just great.' If you tap two times that third time, which means 'Yes, you're right, everything's not too hot with me,' I won't come over. Nobody will. And no one else will call you that day, and you can't call anyone as your phone's only wired for incoming calls. So you might as well tap three times that third time as you might as well think everything's fine and great. Then tap three times again, which means good-bye, for it really will be good-bye till the next time I call the next day at around the same hour and every day after that unless I can't call. If I can't, someone will call in my place and you'll tap hello and he or she will ask the same two questions which you should tap the same answers to and then tap good-bye, though it makes no difference if you don't. If I die or for whatever reason leave this job, someone will take over for me and ask the same questions and never say good-bye. That person will have a substitute if he or she can't call and a replacement if that person leaves or dies who will also ask those two questions and never say good-bye, and that replacement will have his or her substitute and replacement and, if necessary, all the substitutes and replacements will have their substitutes and replacements too. So this is the last time I or anyone else except for the possibility of a wrong number every year or two will ever say anything different to you or good-bye, unless the system changes. Good-bye."

She comes into the room. She's with her daughter and she says "Say good-night and go to bed." "Good-night and go to bed," Rachel and I say. Or only I say it. Rachel isn't there. Ellen says "That was always an old joke." Rachel must have gone to bed. Ellen's hanging her pants up in our clothes closet. She looks at me and says. She can't speak. Rachel isn't there and

Ellen can't speak. Ellen isn't there and Rachel never was. There is a closet though with both our clothes. But no women's clothes. There's no room in the closet for her clothes. No closet in the room for clothes. No room in the house for a closet. No house. No room. I have no clothes. I can't speak. Ellen, I say in my head. But no head. Rachel, my dear Rachel. No use. I'm just a body with a brain inside my chest. But no chest. Just a brain in a box or some container like that. How do I know? I heard. Before I was cut out of my head I heard. A voice that said "While you're under anesthesia we're going to excise your brain whole and put it in a plastic box or some transparent container here and we'll continue to nourish your brain while we watch and record its development, decline, and eventual end. So you're now being put to sleep. We only tell you these blunt details so we know your brain knew what went on till the end of its body's natural life and its own excision. What it hears from now," but then I must have gone asleep. Those were his last words. The last words I ever heard. "What it hears from now." And hearing, I now see, was my fifth sense. And seeing, I of course knew, was one of my five senses. And thinking or not knowing, I once thought or said, might be considered my sixth sense. Though I don't think I ever said or thought that thinking or not knowing could be considered my seventh sense if the one that isn't my seventh is my sixth. Now does that make any sense? How would I know. Ellen, I wanted to speak about our sex.

STEPHEN DIXON / SLEEP

the dat

I've a cat on loan. He belongs to woman I lived with, and a week after we split up she said "Will you take Cosy for a few months? I want to see if I'll stop sneezing and getting rashes when I'm not around his long hair. I only chose you because you seemed to like him when you lived with us."

I did like him and do now. He's an agreeable cat, stays out of my way most times, comes to me when I want companionship, and doesn't cost much to keep. Recently though I've had trouble selling my magazine illustrations, so I've been trying to scrimp on a lot of things, like the phone bill and my food and the cat's. It's easier scrimping on mine, which comes in many edible kinds and different prices and because I can use self-control. But the cat food, for all the variety the pet food companies offer, seems to go for the same amount: two four-ounce cans of wet food for seventy-nine cents and a twenty-two-ounce box of dried food for ninety-five cents, and then I can't expect Cosy to exercise self-control.

Finally I phone Cosy's owner to tell her that I'm spending more on Cosy's food than I am on mine and she'll have to help me out with his. I get her on her answering machine. "I've gone to Spain to make a film," Rina says, "and won't be back for two months."

"Really, a lot you care for your cat," I say to her machine, "leaving him without a word and no food money like that," and hang up.

I go to several supermarkets and look around again for cheaper cat food, but they're all the same high price. A man's stocking pet food on the shelves of the last market I'm in and I say to him "Would you know if I could give my cat dog food to eat?"

"Why when it's a cat?"

"To save money. By weight the dog food in both the boxes and cans is about half the price of cat food and in its ingredients and nutrition and things seems to be the same in every way except for the shape of some dog food: meal bones for instance. I doubt my cat would like those, though he might if they were shaped like birds and mice, though then the dog wouldn't I suppose."

"Cats are fussier eaters than dogs. But after a couple days without eating the dog food put in front of it, and the store's told me never to tell a customer this, but you look like a guy desperate to save a buck, your cat will come around to eating the dog food rather than starve. After a few more days of this diet your cat will like it as much as he did his cat food and not lose any of his energy and health by it too."

"He never much liked his cat food."

"Then like it as much as he did, whatever that was. Believe me, I'm not trying to sell you anything, since we sell both kinds of pet foods and obviously earn more from the cat's."

I buy some dried and wet dog food and that night mix a little of these two in his bowl as I used to do with his cat food, but he won't touch it. "Come on, boy, come on," but he walks out of the room. I don't give in though and twice a day I mix up a new batch of dog food for him. He ignores it for two days, then takes a bite, chews and spits it out and walks out of the room.

The next morning he swallows the one bite he takes and from then on bites and swallows more and more of the dog

STEPHEN DIXON / SLEEP

food till after a week he's eating as much of it as he used to eat of his cat food.

I find that I save enough from feeding him dog food to eat a little better myself. I'm still almost broke, with no new commissions for work coming in, but I gain back a couple pounds in a week.

So does Cosy it seems, or else he's just gotten hairier. And though he's five years old, in the month since he started eating dog food he's gotten taller too. I can tell he's taller because whenever I mix his dog food now, which also happened when I mixed cat food, he stands on his back feet and stretches up as far as he can reach and scratches the refrigerator door with his front paws. In his first month of living here and eating cat food, he left scratch marks on the door in the same place. After a month of only eating dog food the scratch marks were two inches above the old marks and now a month later they're almost four inches higher. He's either growing from eating dog food or else Rina, his owner, has his age all wrong: he's not five years old but maybe only one and he's now going through something like his final growth spurt, not that I know that much about cats.

Four months after I get Cosy, which is about three months since he started eating dog food, I get a letter from Rina saying she was stricken with a terrible illness and will be laid up in a Spanish hospital for a long time. "This is not even me writing, I'm so weak," she says, "but a professional letter writer who charges by the word, so I'm going to keep this letter short. Please take good care of Cosy and ever my thanks."

So I continue to take care of Cosy, giving him what love and attention I'm capable of and plenty of dog food. I get a little work illustrating but I'm just as broke as I was two months ago because of how much more it's costing me now to feed him. He's eating twice and then three times as much as he did when I first got him and has almost tripled his size. I've a big refrigerator and he can make scratch marks almost two-thirds the way up it. One day I say to him "That's enough. No more dog food. You're getting way too big from it. Back to cat food for you, because I spent half as much for your food then even though it was twice the price per ounce of your dog food today. Maybe you'll stop growing by eating cat food again and even reduce yourself somewhat to a more normal cat size."

I go to a supermarket and buy the cheapest cat food, which is now eight cents more per box and can for the same amount than it was several months ago. That night I give him a bowl of cat food. He wolfs it down in two bites, then scratches the refrigerator door. I give him a second bowl of cat food. He wolfs this one down also and scratches the refrigerator, but so hard this time that his claws put quarter-inch deep holes in the door.

I say "No, that's it for tonight. Twice as much in fact than I gave you when you were eating cat food months ago," and I go into the bedroom. He follows me in with the bowl between his teeth, something he never did before.

"Okay, just a little more, but that's all, okay?" and he rubs his head against my leg.

I give him a third bowl of cat food. He gobbles it up, then scratches the refrigerator for some more. I lock him in the bathroom, leave the apartment, and walk around the neighborhood for an hour. When I get back I find the place a mess. Cosy got out of the bathroom and turned over a table and lamp, tore at the couch and rug with his paws, knocked my paints and brushes off the shelves and made all over the floor when before he was always so clean about himself and only did it in his litter box.

I slap his behind. He yelps and runs behind a chair. I clean up the apartment, lock my bedroom door, and go to sleep. An hour later I hear noises behind the door that almost sound like barking. I think "What do I have here now, a dog?" though his appearance hasn't changed, only his size. I yell "Cosy, shut up, go to sleep," and he stops barking and begins whimpering and sniffing like a dog.

STEPHEN DIXON / SLEEP

I can't sleep because of these noises and after awhile give him another bowl of cat food. He still scratches for more, I haven't any left, so I go to an all-night market and buy some. When I get home I mix a fifth bowlful for him, which is equivalent to the amount of dog food I gave him all of yesterday, and he wolfs this batch down too. Till tonight though he nibbled and picked at his food like a cat, even when he ate dog food, and always left a little over for when he'd be hungry later.

He continues to grow larger. Since he eats even more cat food now than he did dog food, I decide it'd be cheaper feeding him dog food again. So I buy only dog food for him and he continues to grow, barks more than he meows now and his ears turn from being pointy to somewhat floppy like some dog's. He also stays by the front door half the day wanting to go outside, which he never used to do, and makes on the rug and floor more often than he does in his litter box.

I send Rina a telegram saying "Get well and hurry back soon, as Cosy's eating me out of home and everything else I have and his character, body, and personal hygiene have also turned into something resembling a dog's."

Next day I get a telegram from her saying "Would you please be a dear and take care of Cosy a while more? I'm well now, thank heavens, but fell in love with the doctor who saved me and he's treating me to a post-convalescent wine and food tour of Europe. Write me care of American Express, Paris. I'll be there in three months, no doubt with spots on my liver and grossly overweight. Incidentally: what is this strange and so far unfunny joke of yours about Cosy resembling a dog?"

I take Cosy to a vet. I have to walk him on a leash to the cab, since there isn't a cat transporter big enough to fit him and I'd feel funny putting him in a dog's.

The vet examines Cosy and then to get some sound out of him, pulls his tail. Cosy barks and whimpers and only once meows.

"Something's definitely the matter with him," the vet says, "though he most assuredly isn't turning into a dog as you suspect. That's not only biologically and medically impossible but just impossible per se. He appears healthy, though is abnormally large for a cat, but that's probably related to the same hormonal trouble that's causing his voice to change. For four hundred dollars I can operate on his thorax and glands and I'm sure cure him."

"I haven't thirty dollars."

"How much do you have?" and I tell her "Maybe twenty-five dollars to my name." She says "That'll be just enough for today's examination," and takes my money and I start for the door.

"By the way," I say, "you think I should continue to feed him dog food?"

"For a cat that big and with his appetite, I'd feed it the cheapest of whatever kind of food I could find."

Eventually I have to walk Cosy on the street twice a day. He's outgrown his litter box and has also gotten so large for my small apartment that he needs outdoor exercise.

He's also begun to look so much like a dog that very few people stop me anymore to say what an enormous cat I have. Most people seem frightened by his size and looks, but when I am stopped the usual question is "What kind of dog is that?" Mostly I say "A dat." The most common response to that is "What's a dat?" and I pretend to joke the second question away by saying "Dat's a dat—him, an extremely rare breed," and then walk off with Cosy either sniffing at the sidewalk or trash cans twenty feet in front or behind me or striding beside me on a leash.

In a few more weeks Cosy gets to be such a financial and physical drain on me that I try to give him to one of Rina's friends till she returns. A couple of people will take Cosy if I provide the money to feed him in advance, but I tell them I'm too broke for that. When I still can't contact Rina in Europe, I bring Cosy to a pet adoption service and say "Will you please take this animal off my hands?"

STEPHEN DIXON / SLEEP

The man in charge there says "If that's a cat you got there, nobody's going to adopt one that big."

"It's a dat, not a cat, which is a cat that became a dog from eating too much dog food because its temporary owner couldn't afford to pay for all the cat food it wanted to eat."

"Well, we only take birds, dogs, cats, monkeys, an occasional ocelot and horse, but certainly no animal we haven't a zoological classification for."

I leave the adoption service and think the heck with staying broke and my globe-trotting ex-lover who if she really cared for her cat wouldn't spend so much time away and relying on another person to take care of it and would come home sooner. I remove Cosy's collar and leash and say "Take a walk, friend. Maybe you'll find someone real nice to adopt you and you can eat him out of house and home," and I get on a bus and from the back seat wave to Cosy looking forlornly at me.

He's waiting for me in front of my building when I get home. I try and get rid of him other ways: leaving him on a dock and another time putting him alone in a rented rowboat and pushing it out into the park lake, but he always finds his way home.

Since I can't seem to get rid of him, maybe if I put him on a crash diet for a week his stomach will shrink. After his fast I could probably afford to keep him because he'd be eating much less.

I don't feed him for three days. The next morning, when I'm out of the apartment, he destroys most of the furniture, turns over my easel and with I suppose paint tubes in his mouth smears up all the walls.

I feed him immediately and give him food twice a day from then on. He continues to eat and grow till I find myself so destitute from having to feed him that I hardly have money to feed myself.

But the next day Rina calls and I say "God, am I glad you're back. Could you come right over and take Cosy and reimburse me for all the money I spent on him these past months?"

"That's what I phoned to tell you. It turns out I wasn't allergic to Cosy's long hair after all. My doctor friend, the one who took me through Europe, also put me through a series of allergy tests and found that what was making me sneeze and break out was only my new pair of uncured leather shoes."

She comes over and Cosy's so happy to see her that he leaps at her when she walks into the apartment and knocks her down.

After I help her up she says "You telling me this beast has been in the same apartment with Cosy all the time I was gone?"

"That is Cosy—you can't tell?"

"No more jokes now. I'm mad as hell and your foul animal ruined my raincoat. Now where's my cat? I want to get out of here before I'm attacked again."

"It's a complicated story, Rina, which if you'll just sit calmly for a few minutes, I'll tell."

"If you don't produce Cosy in fifteen seconds, I'm getting out of here and going to the police and suggesting to them that this beast of yours killed him."

"For the last time—"

She leaves without listening to me and a few days later I get a lawyer's letter saying that if I don't return Cosy to Rina or give a suitable explanation why I can't plus $250 for lawyer's fees and the purchase of a new cat of a similar breed, I'll be charged with animal murder and theft and also sued for the emotional damages to his client and the cost of the cat.

I tear up the letter, as my main problem right now is finding something to eat. I've lost five pounds in the past few days from trying to stretch the last of my money as far as it could go and as a result sort of starving myself. I look in the refrigerator. There's nothing there but a bottle of ice water and an opened can of Cosy's dog food. "Liver and Turkey Platter," it says, two of my favorite dishes though not in this particular form. But I'm so hungry that I hold my breath, grab a fork, and eat the food right out of the can.

STEPHEN DIXON / SLEEP

It doesn't taste half as bad as I thought. And I'm still very hungry, so I get a dog food can of "Ranch Style Dinner" out of the cupboard, as another one of the dishes I really enjoy is a combination of chicken, veal, and beef ribs. I open the can and start eating it when Cosy barks at me.

"Oh yeah, sorry, I forgot," I say, "and what a slob I've become, right?" and I empty half the can into his bowl, put my half on a plate, mix both with a little dog chow, sprinkle salt on mine, and eat. It turns out I like this food better without adding salt. Then I slap my head and say "Stupid, stupid," when I think of how much money I could've saved myself since I got Cosy if I'd begun eating dog food then.

That day, with what money I've left, I go to the supermarket and see it has a terrific sale on dog food. I buy a case of it for Cosy and me and later give Cosy his food in a bowl and serve mine on a plate. A couple days later the plate somehow seems unaesthetic to eat off of and I put my food in a bowl. A few days after that the table doesn't seem the right place to eat on and I put my bowl on the floor next to Cosy's, get on my knees and lean forward and eat like him.

By the next day I'm serving all our meals the same way: two different food bowls on the floor for Cosy and me, though we share the same bowl of water. Occasionally, just out of fun, he nuzzles me away from the water bowl and I might do the same to him. But if he thinks I'm hogging the water, he growls at me. If I think he's hogging it or trying to steal food from my bowl, I yell at him. Still, I become much friendlier with Cosy the more we eat together, and after breakfast and dinner every day we usually roll around the floor wrestling for a while and then go for long walks.

A few days later, the same day I get a summons to appear in court to answer charges brought by Rina against me, I open our last can of dog food. It's rotten and I go to the supermarket with Cosy to exchange it. A guard stops us at the door and says to another shopper: "Whose dogs are these? Can't the owner read the sign: No animals allowed. Out, out," and he boots us both

STEPHEN DIXON / SLEEP

in the behind. I stand up to take a swing at him, but he grabs me by the back of the neck and throws me outside.

"Now what're we going to do?" I say to Cosy, or bark it really. "We're all out of food, the cops will soon be after me, and if I get thrown in jail you'll be tossed in a pound and maybe in a week put away."

"Just for now," he says, "I'd like to know how we're going to get back in our apartment so I could go to sleep."

"With my keys of course," and he says "Oh sure, but try using them when we get there," and we run back to the building. I stick my hand in my pocket but can't get a firm grip on my keys. My hands are still hands but clutch at the keys like paws and I drop them every time.

"We'll think of something," I say and we hang out in front of the building to think. I can't think of anything. A couple of hours later I say "I don't know about you but I'm starved."

"Let's just scavenge. I used to do it as an alley cat before Rina found me. I'll teach you." With his front paws he flips over the cover of a garbage can, stands on his hind legs and sniffs the contents on top.

"Something meaty in here but much deeper in," he says. "Help me knock the can over."

I stand up against the can just like he's doing and with our combined weight we push it over.

"Hey, you goddamn mutts, scat!" someone yells from a window and we run around the corner, wait, and come back and go through the mess we made on the sidewalk. There are some pretty good things people have thrown out: bones, half a chicken wing, an uncooked innard. I see some of my own trash in there, though just packaging, nothing edible.

We get enough from the can for several tasty bites. Then we go to the next building and knock over a couple of its garbage cans. After an hour of this we both feel filled and run to the park, find a safe hiding place behind a bush, lie real close together to keep warm, and go to sleep.

STEPHEN DIXON / SLEEP

the knife

On her way home from work she bought two bagels, a package of cream cheese, and a quart of milk. At home she turned on the radio, let the shower run so she could get some warm water in fifteen minutes, took a knife out of the dish rack and rinsed it, because when she was out the roaches took over her kitchen, and started slicing through one of the bagels. The knife didn't cut that well. It never did. It cut apples and solid chunks of hard cheese all right, but things like bagels, unsliced bread loaves, and any kind of unground meat, it never cut well. "I'm going to buy a better knife," she said. "Yeah. Tomorrow. Some day soon. No, tomorrow. On my way home. One with a serrated blade. Those cut bagels and loaves and meat and maybe even solid chunks of cheese the best." She knew. Who was it? Maggie. And she cut with Maggie's serrated knife when she ate over at her place the other week and maybe it didn't cut the meat that well, which was tough to begin with and got tougher the longer it cooked, but it really flew through that bread loaf. Zip. And bread from loaves she cut every morning. And every night a bagel or two. This knife might spread cream cheese and butter better than any knife with a serrated blade, but it couldn't cut bagels for hell.

STEPHEN DIXON / SLEEP

She sliced the bagel in two, practically had to rip through it with the knife, and put it on top of one of the stove burners to toast, because the toaster always blew a fuse and the oven part of the stove hadn't worked in a year and wasn't about to be fixed. She ate the bagel with cream cheese and a glass of milk. Then she took a shower, got in pajamas, cut and toasted the second bagel and spread it with cream cheese, listened to the radio while finishing the morning newspaper and beginning a new library book, threw the book against the footboard as she was bored in general and this one wasn't holding her interest or making her sleepy, drank a glass of sweet wine and went to bed.

Next morning she went to work. What she did all day was type type type. At lunch with a few coworkers she spoke about wanting to buy a knife and one of them said "Honey, what you need it for I'm sure a serrated's definitely the best."

After work she subwayed to her stop, bought two bagels, cream cheese, and other groceries and went to the local five-and-dime. She chose a cutting knife the size of her regular silver dinner knife, but with a plastic handle and serrated blade. She paid. The salesgirl spread out a sheet of newspaper on the counter and put the knife at one end of it. It was the front page headline she was rolling up the knife in and it said RUNAWAY TRUCK KILLS 3, INJURES 12; DIPLOMAT VICTIM.

"Don't bother with the bag," the woman said. "Paper shortage. I'll put it in with my food."

"I have to bag it. Store regulations. There might be a shortage but I don't want it costing me my job." She stapled the bag on top with the receipt showing and the woman left the store.

At home she turned the radio and shower on, read the headline the knife had come in and thought was the diplomat one of the injured or dead? The paper was several days old. The story was on page 5. It was an afternoon paper and she hadn't seen the same story in her morning one. The photo beneath the headline showed six of the victims, injured or dead, two with blankets over them though with their heads exposed, maybe one was the diplomat, all lying in a line on the sidewalk where they were struck, the truck's rear end sticking out of a discount furniture store. All the caption added to what she already knew was that three of the fifteen people run over were hovering near death.

She squashed the newspaper sheet into the garbage bag, flattened and folded up the knife bag and put it in a shopping bag filled with folded-up smaller bags, and held the knife up by its handle. It was a good-looking knife. She sliced one of the bagels in half. The bagel was fresher than most she got this late in the day and so ordinarily more difficult to cut, but the knife zipped right through. She toasted the bagel and spread cream cheese on. The knife didn't spread as well as it cut, but she didn't see herself using one knife to cut and a second to spread. She wondered if she was really that much further ahead with this knife. It cut more than twice as fast as the other one but only spread half as well. She figured she was ahead but not by much.

She ate the bagel, cleaned the knife, and held up its blade. The blade had STAINLESS etched in it. She hadn't seen that before. Did that mean stainless steel? If it did then the blade was a lot better than its handle, which not only was plastic that wasn't even made out to look like wood but wasn't riveted on that well. It already felt loose. If she cut something much harder than a bagel would the blade slip away from its handle and jab into her hand? She didn't want to wait and find out when she wasn't thinking about it. As a test she got a frozen piece of beef liver from the freezer compartment and tried cutting it with the knife. If it was a strong knife like Maggie's then it would, with a little pressure, cut the meat into inch-wide slices, which was how she liked her liver cooked. It wouldn't. She used more pressure on the handle and one of the rivets got even looser. Why had she been so stupid before? Cheap's more the word. As long as she'd waited this long to buy a serrated knife, why hadn't she bought one with a wood handle riveted in tight? Maybe she still would. It'd be an investment, both in safety and having a useful knife. The small loss of money with this cheap knife could be justified in her once and for all proving to herself that a serrated blade cut much better than the straight kind. If it wasn't too expensive the next knife she bought would have a handle that wouldn't break if she dropped it, become undone when she forced it, and which would last, if she didn't lose it, the rest of her life.

She cooked the liver without cutting it, sliced the second bagel in half with the knife she used to use, toasted and ate it with the cooked liver. Then she took a shower and did most of the things she usually did at night before going to bed.

Next day during her lunch hour she went to a cutlery store and selected a knife the same size but three times the price of yesterday's knife and which the salesman said was unconditionally guaranteed for five years by a company in business since the Civil War. On the knife's handle it said ROSEWOOD HANDLE. She didn't know this wood and wondered if it was actually from the trunk of the common rosebush. The serrated blade also had STAINLESS etched in it followed by the company's name and USA, neither of which yesterday's knife had.

After work she subwayed home, bought two bagels and other groceries, and right after she turned her shower and radio on, tried out the new knife. It cut through the bagel as well as yesterday's knife and spread cream cheese just as badly, but the handle felt much better to grip. She tried the knife on some frozen hamburger meat, and with a little forcing but no rivet-slipping, it cut through. She'd keep the knife. She put yesterday's knife in the silverware tray, but during her shower she thought what for? She or some visitor might one day take the knife out of the tray to try to use it, forgetting, or for her visitor, not knowing the handle wasn't riveted tight, and the blade might slip loose and go in a hand or fall out of the handle entirely and go through one of their feet or shoes. She could give it to that organization that has handicapped people who fix broken things and sell them, but this knife was the only thing she had to give away except for maybe a couple of clothes. It wasn't worth bringing over so few things. Or keeping the knife around till she'd accumulated enough things to give away and possibly using it by mistake during that time and having an accident. The best thing was just to dump the knife in the garbage bag.

Next morning when she went to work she dropped her garbage bag in one of the cans in front of her building. It was around the same time a man was beginning his scavenging trip at the other end of the block. He did this every weekday and on Sunday if he'd had a very poor week or two or more of the previous days had so much rain and snow to keep him from work. He started this block around 8:30, when most of the tenants had left for work and dumped their garbage. A lot of garbage was also dumped the previous night, but the cans themselves weren't put on the street till around 7 A.M. He usually did this side of the block in twenty minutes and then worked down the other side in half an hour, as it had more renovated brownstones on it and so more apartments to the building, cans to the street, and higher-paying tenants who threw out more and better salvageable garbage. He was generally finished a few minutes before the sanitation truck entered the block and the sanitation men began collecting garbage. He was always at least ten to twenty minutes ahead of the truck though, as he finished his last can at the opposite end of the block the truck began at. After that he'd go to another block nearby that had proved to have good pickings and which he knew the sanitation truck wouldn't have gotten to yet.

He made his way up the block. So far today he'd found an old sweater and hat, a pair of ladies pants with a broken zipper, pencil case, sunglasses, new screwdriver someone must have thrown out by mistake, a toy, pair of men's shoes with good heels and laces, cup, plate, two college economic books. All these things were in the large shopping cart he dragged behind him. The cart had four double-bagged shopping bags in it, three geared for goods to different kinds of junk and thrift shops and the fourth filled with a variety of things he hadn't been able to sell yet. Occasionally he came across something more valuable that he might be able to sell to one of the local antique stores. What he didn't sell in a month that wasn't what he thought valuable, he dumped in one of these garbage cans.

He removed the lid of the first garbage can in front of the woman's building and gave it a quick look. No good, this one. Nothing but plaster on top. Can very heavy. It was probably filled down to the bottom with part of someone's former wall. He put the lid back on and opened the next can. This one was also filled with plaster but had a pile of newspaper on top. Two of the magazines were unsoiled, men's, nudie shots inside, recent issues, so worth a nickel apiece to one store: he put them in the magazine sack that hung off the back of the cart. He opened the third can. It had a few paper and plastic garbage bags and parts of newspapers. Other scavengers have said that most times instinct told them when a can was going to be good and then they'd give more time to it. He never felt that. He relied on giving the inside of the can a quick first look, and unless it obviously wasn't worth his time like that broken plaster before or was just too grubby to go through, he poked around and felt most of the bags with his gloved hand.

Something metal, he thought, and a bottle or jar. He turned the bag over in the can and out came food scraps, package wrapping, a wine bottle, milk carton, cream cheese package, knife with a serrated blade. Not a bad knife. He could get a dime for it, maybe fifteen cents. He put it in the houseware shopping bag. People who threw out still useful things like the knife were liable to junk almost anything fairly good. He began emptying all the other bags into this can and the next one. He never made a mess. When he put a lid back on a can it never looked as if it'd been picked at and he often even cleaned up the garbage other people had dropped around the can, just so the super and landlords wouldn't think he was the one who dirtied their sidewalk. If they did they'd get mad at him for causing them extra work and would then try and keep him off the block. He was putting a glass doorknob into the cart's hardware bag when two men walked by.

"Look at your father," one of them said.

"Hey. My old man never got so low as that," the other one said.

"You kidding? These creeps always got a wad pinned to their inside clothes. Watch." He tapped the scavenger's shoulder.

The scavenger look up and said "What, what, what do you want? Leave me alone. I'm harmless, not bothering anybody, get away, I didn't do anything. I clean up my mess, don't worry. What's the problem? What trouble I'm causing? I understand nothing, nothing. Don't bother me. Please. I haven't time. I got lots of runs today. Blocks and blocks. Lots of neighborhoods to cover, junk shops to get rid of my crap. I'm a poor man. Why the look? You see my rags. You're not so good off yourself. Who are you? Let me in peace. You want a license, I got none. I'm doing nothing but taking what's been thrown out and useless, so go."

"Listen to the mouth on him," the man said. "What you got under your coat, ragman? In the lining here." He began feeling inside the scavenger's coat. "There's something."

"There's nothing."

"You got money. Give it."

"I said I got nothing. Go away. I'm broke, just scraps. B.O. I got in there."

"Come on. We know you bums. Thousands socked away. But still getting your greasy nails greasier by digging for more."

"Nothing."

He ripped open the scavenger's coat. Buttons and safety pins dropped to the ground. The scavenger fell on his knees to pick them up.

"Get up," the man said.

"Let him off," the other man said. "He's crazy."

"But he's got something. Can't you tell? Better than any dude."

The scavenger put the pins in the houseware bag and pulled out the knife he found in the garbage can before and jumped up and said "I got this, I got this. Now go. I told you to leave me alone. Nobody takes from me what's mine. No money. Not a screw."

The second man reached into his own pocket for something.

"No gun," the scavenger said and lunged at the man as he was about to say something and stuck the knife in his chest. The man sort of froze, everything: eyes, opened mouth, hand in his pocket, everything but his legs, which went out from under him. The scavenger let go of the knife as the man fell. The other man pulled the knife out of his friend's chest and said "Why'd you do that? He had no gun. We don't carry anything. That was my best friend, my cousin. My best cousin." The scavenger turned to run and tripped over his cart. The man put the knife into his back. A woman walking a dog in the street was screaming. People in apartment buildings on both sides of the street looked out their windows, ran from their windows, one man opened his window and yelled out "Hey you guys, what gives? Lady, what's the trouble down there?"

The man ran up the block. The police were called and the man was identified by the woman with the dog and several people from the windows. He had red pants on, a yellow hat. Ambulances came. The police drove around the neighborhood. Five blocks away they saw a man in red pants and no hat walking toward the subway entrance. They yelled from their cars for him to stop. He didn't. They drew their guns and ran down the subway entrance. The man leapt over the turnstile and ran along the uptown platform. The police followed. When the man reached the end of the platform and couldn't go anywhere except out the other subway exit which had two

STEPHEN DIXON / SLEEP

policemen coming down the steps, he jumped onto the tracks.
He ran along the tracks farther downtown. Got to watch out
for the third rail, he thought. Which is the goddamn third rail?
A train was coming. Was it on his side or the express? Third
rail really that hot? "Rotten creep! Goddamn luck." No room
on my right. That might be the third rail on my left. He heard
the train's whistle, saw its flashing beam of light. Heard the
wheels screeching. Jump on your face and pray for dear life.
He jumped into the well between the rails. The train clipped
him before he hit the ground, and when he finished bouncing,
ran over his legs. He died a few minutes after he reached the
hospital. The scavenger died on his way to the hospital. The
cousin died on the sidewalk. The woman bought two bagels
and some other groceries on her way home from work that
night. She cut one of the bagels with her new knife, toasted it
and spread cream cheese on with the same knife and said
"Forget it. I might as well spread the cheese on with the handle for what good the blade does. For spreading I'll just have
to go back to the old knife."

Next days she was off from work and she read the newspaper with her morning coffee and eggs. One of the stories she
read was about two men stabbed to death on the north side of
her block near the park the previous day with a kitchen knife.
A knife, the newspaper said, that the scavenger had probably
found during one of his many quests for clothes and house-
hold goods he sold to junk shops over the past dozen years,
and which he probably had concealed under his coats to protect himself from a possible mugging.

She called her friend Maggie and told her about the story
she'd just read. "Right near my building. Yesterday. Right after
I left for work. It had to be right after because it said just
before nine and when I left for work quarter of nine there
weren't any police cars or commotion on the street. For all I
know it could've been my building and the same knife I threw
out that morning in my garbage bag. It wasn't that knife, as the

newspaper said he probably had it hidden for years in his clothes to protect himself against muggers. But next time I throw out a knife I'm not going to throw it out whole. Too dangerous for everyone concerned. I'll break it in two and if I can't, I'll bury it in an out-of-the-way place in the park. I suppose it's like a refrigerator that you throw out. To prevent little children from getting locked in them and suffocating to death, you either have to take off the door or put the refrigerator out with either the door part flat on its front on the ground or turned around while standing flush up against a wall."

STEPHEN DIXON / SLEEP

game

A man is let loose. We are given the signal and chase him. He's fast and hardy but two of us are faster and hardier. They catch him. We catch up to the three of them. They're holding him from behind. I say "Why'd you run away?"

He says "Why shouldn't I run away? You let me loose."

"Oh, me?"

"Not you specifically, but your kind. Maybe one of you or maybe someone still back there. I know your game. You lock me up. You keep me locked up till you know that what I want most is to get out of there. Then you unlock my door and the main gate and let me run away. Then you wait a little while and begin chasing me. Gives you a bit of a rise, eh? Catching up with me. Holding me here and then bringing me back and locking me up so you can let me loose in a couple of weeks to chase me again. You couldn't have caught me if I'd been in better shape. But your food stinks and is barely nourishable and my room was too small and damp to exercise and sleep in the way I have to to get in the best shape I can. Next time, put me in a room where I can exercise more and give me the same food you get and keep the room at the same temperature yours are and then let me go after a few weeks and see if you can catch me."

STEPHEN DIXON / SLEEP

"We would," I say.

"You might, but it would take you longer."

"Longer, perhaps, but in time we would," someone says.

"A couple of you might drop dead by the time you caught me, and that would give me satisfaction, I'll tell you. I'd almost say it would be worth being locked up for weeks and then being let go and caught again, just to have a couple of you drop dead. And if each time after you caught me you put me in an even larger room and continued giving me the same food and room temperature you people have been getting, I'd exercise more strenuously and longer and so each time I'd be in better and better shape. So each time it would take you longer to catch me than the previous time, and maybe each time a couple more of you would get a heart attack from the chase and die. In time, I'd outlast you all."

"We could exercise too," I say.

"Sure. But because you don't have to get away, I don't think you'd exercise as much as me."

"Why you telling us all this? Because you know if we believe you, we'll never go along with your game."

"I feel I've more to gain by your becoming interested and maybe challenged by my game than by not telling you anything and having the old game and conditions and results continue the same."

"He makes too much sense with his game," one of us says. "I think this time we should put him in an even smaller room than the last one and give him less food and heat than before."

"The same size room and conditions should do," I say.

"If it's the same room, then let's keep him there longer before we let him loose."

"No, shorter," someone else says. "Because then he wouldn't have exercised as much and his will to get away won't be as strong."

STEPHEN DIXON / SLEEP

"What about the largest room we have for just a couple of days?" I say. "And the same food and heat we get and maybe as comfortable a bed."

"I say take away the board he has now and let him sleep on the floor."

"And the blanket too," someone else says.

"Does he have a pillow?" someone says.

"No pillow. He has a rock to put his head on, or is it a log?"

"Either one. Let him keep it, as they probably hinder his sleep as much as they help."

"What about keeping a light on in his room all the time?" someone says.

"Good suggestion."

"Bad suggestion."

"Look, we're getting nowhere," I say, "and meanwhile he's getting all this restful fresh air, and we don't know how potentially beneficial or harmful it is. First of all, we don't want to make his living conditions that bad where he ends up too weak to run away from his room. Let's just decide what kind of room we should put him in now and for how long and what room temperature and sleeping arrangements and food."

"No room or food at all," he says. "Just let me loose and don't chase me."

"But if we do, you might in your own home and under your own conditions build yourself up even better than you could in our largest room. Then it might be impossible to catch up with you if we decided we wanted to lock you up so we could eventually let you loose and chase you again. The game would be too one-sided, in other words, and we might all get heart attacks finding that out. And you also might get across the border somehow. Even the very same day, if you only asked to be let loose for a day. Then we couldn't chase you no matter what good or bad physical shape any of us were in. No, we have to lock you up now."

STEPHEN DIXON / SLEEP

"But I promise I won't build myself up or try and get across the border. Just let me get away without chasing me and then, anytime you want, come around for me and I'll be there and go back calmly with you, or if you want, I'll run as hard as I can away from you till you catch me."

"No," I say. "Even if he's telling the truth, what assurances can we have that what he's proposing will turn out as he says? To be safe, I say that we settle on giving him exactly what he had before."

"Then I won't exercise or eat at all this time and I'll sleep as little as I can. And when you next let me loose, I won't run or even crawl out of the room. I'll just stay there and die."

"Fine with us," someone says. "There are others besides you."

"All right. I'll exercise and eat. But put me in a room a little larger than the last one and for the same length of time, and with my living conditions only slightly improved. Then when you open my door, I'll run. I'll run as hard as I can to get away from you, and I swear one or two of you is going to get a heart attack from that chase and die."

"I don't think his new conditions can change the situation very much," I say. "And maybe to give him an even slightly larger edge over us than the last time, we reduce our own exercising a little and eat and sleep just a bit more."

"Then agreed?" someone says.

"Agreed," we all say.

"Don't forget," he says. "Last time I was in my room for three weeks."

"Three weeks," someone says. "Right. Get that down on paper."

"It's already in my head," I say. "Three weeks. No more or less."

Two cars pull up. We all get in them and drive back to the building. We put the man in a room that's a couple inches wider and an inch higher than the one he had before. On his door I tack up a notice which says "To be let loose on March

STEPHEN DIXON / SLEEP

6th, 2 P.M., same food as before though three ounces more per entire serving, and to be allowed to exercise at will." The man gets down on the floor and begins doing push-ups. I turn up the thermostat a degree and lock his door. When two of us bring him his food a few hours later, they find him running in place.

my life up till now

My oldest brother went to the war and died. I was two at the time and only heard about it years later: that I was actually one of seven children instead of six.

The second oldest child in my family is now a grown woman living in an institution for people who can't cope with life on the outside. That's the way it was put to me this year. I've never seen her. She went away when I was very young. But I was always told she was my oldest sister and that one day she would come home and live with us again. But I've heard, when my parents or relatives didn't know I was listening, that she would never come home. That she was "incurable," they said. There are no pictures of her in the house or clothes of hers in the closets or drawers. I sometimes imagine what she looks like. I see a sad, tired, thin figure, sitting on the floor in the corner of a room which doesn't have much furniture except a single bed, white walls all around her, her hands over her eyes or wrapped around her raised knees. Sometimes at night when I think of her I feel so sorry for her that I have to tell myself to get her out of my head. It always works. All I have to do is open and then quickly shut my eyes again and something always replaces the thought of my sister in that place.

STEPHEN DIXON / SLEEP

The third oldest child in my family ran away from home when he was around fourteen and hasn't been seen or heard from since. He's about twenty-five now. He ran away around the time I was born. My parents say they got into a fierce argument with him one night. He'd stolen a car and held up a service station with a real gun. He was convicted, served only thirty days because it was a first offense, and was then put in the custody of my folks. About two days after he came home he got into that fierce argument with my folks and ran away. Since that night he's never sent a letter home or tried to get in touch with anyone in the family. One day my folks expect him to show up in the house. Every year on his birthday they put an ad in the newspaper asking him to come home. I don't think he will. I think he's gone for good too.

The middle child in my family is at graduate school a few thousand miles away from us. He's already been a newspaper reporter and I suppose is studying to become a super journalist. He's always gotten great grades, my folks say, and was always very nice to me and my other brother and sister and to my folks. I only knew him for a year or two before he went off to college the first time, so I don't know him that well, since he doesn't visit us much. But what memories I have of him are good. He's tall and broad. He liked sports and reading a lot, I understand. He got along with everyone. He stole nothing, never did anything to disgrace the family, my father's said. He's already married and has a child. I know, as much as I don't like to admit it, that he'll never come home to live with us again, since he has his own family to live with and help support.

The third youngest child in my family drowned when she was twelve. I was with her at the time. I was in a way responsible for her drowning, something that I think has affected my whole life in a bad way. We were in a rowboat together. She was rowing. I was twiddling with the water at the back of the boat, making my own waves, when I suddenly fell overboard. I was five. She held an oar out for me but I couldn't hold onto it. I was too panicky, and I had swallowed too much water. So she dove into the water, swam to me, pulled me back to the boat by my hair, and pushed me out of the water into the boat. Just when she was about to get back into the boat herself, she got these severe stomach cramps. She fell back into the water and the boat went one way and she the other. She called out to me to help. I wanted to jump into the water and save her as she did to me. But I knew I couldn't. I was too full of water. I was also too exhausted, sick and scared and small and I didn't know how to swim that well. Now I think why didn't I throw over the oars for her to hold onto till somebody from shore saw us or another boat came along? I feel guilty about my sister sometimes. I miss her a lot and I know my parents, when they talk about her, usually look at me and quickly turn away as if they wanted to say to me "You're the cause of Molly's death." But they never say that. And maybe I'm just imagining they think that. Later on in life, in a few years, I'm going to ask them if they do think I'm responsible for Molly's death, and why.

The child in my family closest in age to me is only a couple of minutes older. We're twins of course. But he's not at all like me. We came from different eggs, my mother's said. He beats up on me and he can do it successfully because he's much bigger and stronger than I. He doesn't look at all like me either. His hair is lighter than mine and his eyes are gray to my brown. Our noses, chins, ears, everything is different. He has long arms and legs, while all my limbs are thin and short. I don't like being his brother. If he weren't my brother I wouldn't like him to be my friend. If I had my choice I would never speak to him. But he sits at the same dinner and breakfast table with me every night and our bedrooms are right next to each other and we take the same bus to and from school. He does the most rotten things to me sometimes and there doesn't seem to be anything I can do about it or anyone I can see to make him stop. He tears up the homework I've done and pulls chairs out from under me when I sit down. My parents have warned him to stop and a couple of times have beaten his fanny or sent him to his room for doing these things to me. But he never stops, except for a few hours to a day, and I don't think he ever will. I don't know why he resents me so much. I've thought about it a lot and have concluded that maybe he thinks I'm smarter than he is and is jealous of that or maybe it's just in his genes. I asked my mother. "Was Henry born like that—so nasty and mean?"

She said he was born like every baby: "Cute, cuddly, and nice."

"When did he change?" I asked my father.

"Oh, he isn't that bad," my father said. "He's just a rough kid, like lots of kids are, and maybe not as sensitive as you, but give him time. Just don't get him so angry so much over whatever it is that goes on between you two."

"What have I done to make him act like he hates my guts?" I said.

"You tell me," my father said. "I can't see everything that goes on."

"I've done nothing," I said.

"It has to be something. Brothers are supposed to get along. Maybe in your own way you needle him, but I don't know."

"How can we be sure what goes on here when you two are alone?" my mother said. "Henry claims you bait him, and who's to say it isn't the truth? It's your word against his. Since you're both my sons, when I don't see what's happening in front of my eyes, I have to take both your words. Anyway, in time both of you will change and become the closest of brothers."

"I doubt it," I said. "I'm in fact positive that we'll have nothing to do with each other in the future—not even speaking over the phone once a year as Dad does with his brother who he hates so much."

That's my family. My folks I didn't really go into, but I now will. My father's a carpenter and makes a pretty good living at it. A lot more, he's said, than carpenters used to make in comparison with other workers when he was first starting out. He also designs small homes for people and then builds them with a three-man crew, so he has a couple of skills that take up most of his time. The only time I ever really see him, or almost, is the half-hour at the dinner table when he comes home and sits right down and starts eating, and then maybe for an hour after dinner before he's so tired that he goes to bed. Even on weekends he spends most of his time in his studio going over figures or designing homes.

My mother also works. She's a secretary in a law office four days a week. Four is the most she can put in, she's said, because she does have work at home to do and also sees my sister in the institution once a week. My mother also paints and once a week in the summer she goes away to some painting school. That's when my only aunt comes in and takes care of us and tries to change our eating habits and things in a single week.

We also have a bird and cat. The poor bird stays in its cage all the time and the cat's always under once piece of furniture or another, so I hardly ever see it. Even when I put out its food it doesn't come out from wherever it's hiding until I leave the room. When I have caught it, it scratches me, so I've learned to respect its wishes to be left alone.

We are not a happy family, I think. Maybe my parents get satisfaction in their work, but I don't think they get it at home. They fight a lot and mostly at the dinner table or in their bedroom when they're going to sleep. Whenever they have a really bad fight, I think they're going to break up for good and that one will take Hank and the other will take me. I think this would be the best thing for us all. But I've overheard them say to one another that bad as their living with each other is, they're going to stick together till Hank and I are in college.

I sometimes think that our family has had too much tragedy and sadness over the years to be a happy family. I think my parents work as hard as they do at their jobs and taking care of the house, just to avoid thinking of what's happened to their

STEPHEN DIXON / SLEEP

children and maybe their marriage. Occasionally when they talk about the two who have died and the other who's been institutionalized, they start to cry. I sometimes think they should have stopped having children before they had my twin brother and me. We don't offer much to the family but a running feud. And if it wasn't for me, my sister wouldn't have died. My twin brother will probably end up like my brother who held up that service station and ran away, or at least that's my opinion. He's already stealing things, which I don't understand. For one thing my parents have been very generous with, if it hasn't been affection or attention, is money. In the kitchen is an old peanut butter jar with lots of change in it that we can use whenever we like, within reason. But Hank prefers stealing from my mother's pocketbook or my father's pants or from kids at school and of course from me. He's threatened to beat me up if I ever tell on him. Because he seems to be especially serious in that threat, I keep my mouth shut.

There is a couple who lives on the same street as us who I'd like to be a son to. They have no children but do have a friendly dog and cat. They say nice things to me every day if they see me pass their house. They're interested in me more than they are in any young person in the neighborhood. They always want to know what my grades are and what I'm studying lately and what's my favorite food or sport or movie or hobby and all about what I'm involved in and things like that. They were both schoolteachers. They're retired now but tutor me in the subjects I'm not too good at, and everything they've tutored me in I've managed to better my grades and understanding of the subject by a lot. They don't eat sweets themselves, but always have a container of ice cream in their freezer for me whenever I want. They also give me presents on my birthday and Christmas, and for the last three summers have taken me camping with them for a few days. I would love to live with them for good and have told them so. They said that that's the nicest thing anyone has ever said to them and that it makes them extremely happy. "If your parents ever consented to it," they said, "you can live with us till you become an adult."

"Are you serious?" I said.

"Sure we're serious," Mr. Pitowski said, "even if it's impossible, since your parents love you so much more than we do that they'd never want you to leave their house."

"It isn't true about them loving me more," I said.

"Sure it's true," Mrs. Pitowski said, though I call her Kay. "But let's change the subject and see if I can't find the leash for you to take the dog for a walk after you finish this new peach ice cream."

A few evenings later I tell my parents at the dinner table that I want to speak to them alone before I go to bed.

"What is it?" Hank says. "You want to tell them how you spilled water all over my bed last night so I couldn't sleep? He did it intentionally."

"I did not," I say to them, "intentionally or any other way."

"He did too. You can see how tired my eyes are from no sleep."

"You're a liar," I say. "You're always trying to get me in trouble."

"That's enough," my father says.

"It's not enough. Do something. Tell Hank to stop lying."

"Shut up. Don't talk back to me that way."

"There," I say, "you see? He's already gotten me into trouble with his lies."

"How do we know who's lying?" my mother says. "Nobody checks your beds every morning and Hank does look tired, though that could come from other things. Just tell us what it is you want to say."

"After supper when Hank's not around."

"Why can't you two get along better?" she says.

"You don't know by now?" I say.

STEPHEN DIXON / SLEEP

"Because he's a liar, a thief, a sneak, because he's filthy and tells horrible stories about me and is mean," Hank says.

"I give up," I say, because I don't know anyone our age who can make a lie seem more like a truth than Hank.

After dinner, when Hank isn't around, I tell my parents that I want to live with the Pitowskis. "They really want me to and it's what I want most too. I don't want to live here with Hank anymore. I want to disown him if that's possible. I love the Pitowskis like I love you two, but I think I even love them more. I'm sorry, but that's how I feel and I think this new living arrangement would be better for us all."

My parents are very sad and upset at first. They ask me "What did we do wrong to make you feel this way about us?"

I tell them that I don't really know. "Maybe it's just in our family—that things never seem to go for the best or something, so I figure with one less member in it you'll be better off. But more than you it's Hank, who I just can't stand to live with anymore.

Anyway, they say no. But the next night they say they're still thinking about it and the following night my father calls Mr. Pitowski. Apparently things are arranged between them. I go to live with the Pitowskis on an experimental basis, it's called. Hank is overjoyed. Eventually I'm adopted by the Pitowskis and about a year after that, my parents and Hank move out of town. I get to be much happier living with the Pitowskis. They help me and are always very nice and understanding to me and in time I have a lot of friends and things like that. I am glad to be away from Hank. I miss my folks a little, but after awhile I see how much better it is to live where I am now. I grow up and eventually go off to college and do very well there and meet a woman I love very much and begin living with her in the same apartment when we both go to graduate school.

—

That's how I would have liked it to be, but it doesn't turn out like that. I did speak to my parents after supper about my going to live with the Pitowskis and they said "Nothing doing. You crazy? What kind of request is that for a child to make? You are our son and Hank's brother and here's where you'll stay till you're old enough to move out on your own, and we don't want to hear another word about it."

"Why not?" I said. "I'm telling you how I feel and what I want and I'm being honest with you, so what's wrong with that?"

"Because it hurts your mother," my father said.

"Just as it hurts your father," my mother said. "And it would hurt Hank too, no matter how much he might try not to show it."

"It doesn't hurt me that much," Hank said, coming in from the other room where he'd been listening to us. "He wants to leave, let him. He's a big pain in the you-know-what anyway, and you think I like living in the same house with him any better than he does with me? He makes my life miserable. He's practically turned all my schoolmates against me and besides that, he killed my favorite sister. I want him to go."

My father called Mr. Pitowski that night and said "Stop encouraging Sam to come live with you. Just don't give him any ideas like that—it's causing family dissension."

From what I could make out, Mr. Pitowski said something like "We were only joking around with Sam about him coming to live with us and thought he understood that. Not that we don't think he's one of the greatest boys in the world and wouldn't have loved having a son just like him."

Maybe they were joking around about my living with them and I didn't understand them. But I still feel they were serious and it was their way of feeling out my folks and me to see how we'd go for the idea.

Anyway, I go through the next year unhappier than most boys and girls my age. Hank continues to torment me, but even worse than before. Some nights I have to stay awake just to make sure he suddenly doesn't sneak into my room and pounce on me when I'm asleep or throw something hard at my head. Or at least that's what he threatens to do to me some nights, and by this time, in something like that, I take Hank at his word.

As for my parents, they practically ignore us, which means more than they ever did before. Maybe they've given up on Hank and me and our fighting and his cruel nature and my unhappy one and my outspokenness to them. Or maybe they've given up on having any luck with any but one of their children and are just trying, for the most part, to pretend their two youngest sons aren't there.

To move out of this house, I write my brother in graduate school and ask if I could come live with him for a few years. I figure that my parents might go along with my living with a brother a lot better than my living with an older couple on the block.

My brother writes back saying, "Tina and I haven't enough money or room here for our own baby boy and you, much as we'd like you to be with us, just as we'd like Hank to be with us too."

I write back saying, "Hank I don't think you'd want to live with you, if only for the safety of your baby. I was speaking only for myself to live with you, if that makes any difference in our decision about it," but I get no answer back.

One of the things I don't understand about my life is how most of my schoolmates and the kids in the neighborhood around my age prefer Hank to me. I know I wouldn't. Maybe because Hank bullies them and is so big and strong that they have to like him. Or maybe it's because I'm not the happiest kid in the world and they pick up on that and try to avoid me. Or maybe they see something in Hank that I don't. For instance, Hank might act much better and nicer and kinder with them than he ever does with me, and especially when I'm not around. I think the last could be the reason and that he also might have convinced almost everyone we know who's our age not to hang out with me. I could be wrong though about all of that. But one thing for sure is that Hank isn't doing anything to help me have friends.

So most of the time I play by myself. I invent friends and games and new brothers and sisters and parents. I know that must sound sad. But sometimes playing by myself can be fun and then I don't suppose it will last for very many more years. I also go over to the Pitowski's house a lot. And with their help, I do even better in school than I did before, even if Hank ruins my homework a quarter of the time and says awful things about me to the teachers. The reason I work so hard at school and get such good marks is because I want to get out of Hank's grade and graduate earlier and go to college faster than usual and on a scholarship, just in case the time comes when my parents might not be able to afford to send me to an out-of-town college away from them and Hank.

The few friends I do make, or maybe I should call them acquaintances, Hank scares away from the house. So I have to play at their houses after school and on weekends. These friends usually live too far for me to go to by bus every day or for my parents to take the time to drive me by car there and pick me up. So I don't really see these few friends or acquaintances very much, except during school.

One of the unhappiest days of my life is when the Pitowskis move. They're getting old, they say, and want to live farther south where it's warmer and maybe even healthier for them and where they don't have to spend so much of their retirement money trying to get through the long cold winters we have here.

I tell them "You two have been the closest and most considerate people I've known outside of my sister, who died, and I wish you could take me with you."

They say "We'd like to, but it's impossible, so don't even mention it to your parents, as your dad might blow his stack

STEPHEN DIXON / SLEEP

at us again." They give me their new address and phone number and say to call collect anytime I want, and to write and they'll also write me and maybe I could come down to visit them this summer for a few weeks on the beach.

A couple of weeks later, after a real bad argument with my parents over Hank, I decide to hitch south to see the Pitowskis, and I pack a bag with some clothes and food. I figure that if I get there, maybe they'll change their minds about my not living with them a few years and that maybe my folks will also see how serious I am about living away from home and will change their minds too.

I walk to the outskirts of town and put my thumb out for a ride. The first person to pick me up is a policewoman in civilian clothes on her day off. When she finds out what I'm up to, she drives me straight home.

The Pitowskis and I correspond for more than half a year and then they stop and my last two letters to them are returned to me unopened. I call them collect a couple of times and nobody answers their phone. I later learn from my parents, who got the news from a neighbor of ours, that the Pitowskis died in a car crash.

After I heard this, I cried and also couldn't eat for a week. I felt that everyone good who's been attached to me just somehow up and dies in an accident or goes off to somewhere and never comes back. I got sick because of it and was out of school for a month. The doctor called it "an acute state of depression, which can lay a person out as badly as the worst case of pneumonia can." My parents were unusually attentive to me during this period, but Hank showed no sympathy for me or the Pitowskis. He said "They were always so cold to me and too old. Besides, they liked you way more than they did me and didn't do anything to hide their feelings either, which made me like them and you both even less."

STEPHEN DIXON / SLEEP

I know this is a sad story so far, but sometimes a kid's life isn't all that great. Maybe my family just happened to have more difficulties than other families, though I'm sure there are some families and kids my age who have suffered even worse things than us. I do have good moments though—make no mistake about that. And sometimes, days in a row go just great for me. I like to get out by myself on fairly windy days and fly kites. I love to run as hard and as fast as I can or just cut grass till I practically drop. I like sitting up in bed late Friday or Saturday (especially when Hank's sleeping over at a friend's house for the night) and sipping soda and nibbling cheese crackers while reading my favorite books till I just about fall asleep. But what I love most of all is collecting this country's coins and going around to the various coin stores to see what they got that's new or what I might not have yet to complete a coin set. I've even made some money out of collecting: selling several of my coins to dealers and individual collectors for a lot more than I bought them for a year ago or so or discovered in my own or my mother's pile of change.

Anyway, this is my life up till now. I covered about three years of it, besides the flashbacks, and since I began with the family, I think I'll end with them too.

My sister in the institution has been taking a new experimental drug for the last year. The doctors say it's doing wonders for her and might balance out whatever's wrong with her brain enough for her to communicate with people again and come home and even get a part-time job and lead a halfway normal life.

My oldest living brother, who robbed that service station years ago and then ran away from home, sent my folks a letter saying he's a successful fashion designer now, living under an assumed name in a foreign country and that he's also married and has children. He said that for his own reasons he would never see my folks or any of his brothers and sisters again, but he did want us to know he was happy, wealthy, and alive. He

STEPHEN DIXON / SLEEP

ended his letter by saying it would be mailed from a different country than he lived in and that none of us would ever hear from him again.

As for my journalist brother, he's doing very well also, writing television news. I've given up on trying to live with him. It's become more and more obvious to me that he doesn't want any of us around. My feeling is that he thinks we're all bad luck for him or something, or just not respectable enough for him or something, both of which could be why he never visits us anymore or wants us to visit him.

Hank's at least thirty pounds heavier and six inches taller than me. He's also meaner and tougher than he ever was and finally got put away in a children's home for a year for beating up a girl so severely that she had to be hospitalized. He wanted to steal her ten-speed bike, even if he already had one that he stole from someone else, though my folks thought he bought the first one with his own money. When the girl fought back, he hit her over the head with her tire pump. I wasn't surprised, but my mother gave the impression she was.

As for my parents, my father met a woman half his age when he was constructing a beach house for her, and they're now living together in another town. They already had a baby boy this year and she's pregnant again, though my mother's still going through the last stages of her divorce from him for deserting us and non-support.

My mother seems much happier and friendlier and more relaxed without my dad and Hank around. We've become like two close friends and she recently said she never really appreciated me as much as she should have until now. She's jokingly told me not to rob a service station, go off to war, or put on airs or beat up on anyone or even go crazy or drown for the next few years, as she's going to need me to help her with Hank and my sister after they come home.

So things aren't too bad anymore, not that they always were or that I was really complaining before. I've friends playing around the house with me again. And since I hardly ever saw my father when he lived here, I don't miss him too much now that he's gone and never comes around. And in a few years I'll be going, extra early for someone my age, to an out-of-town university. Because of my aptitude and glowing grades so far, everyone assumes I'll be there for four to eight years on a full scholarship.

As for the cat, who's really also part of the family, he still stays under the furniture most of the time and hates as much as ever to be picked up or even touched.

never ends

"Okay. That's it. We're done. No more. Now out, out—out the door."

That's what I'll tell him. I sit in a chair, read a book, but mostly wait.

The boys come home first. "Hi, mom."

"Hi. How was school?"

"Great."

The other: "Awful."

They have a snack and go out.

I read but mostly wait. I hear a key in the lock. I put the book down. I don't want to give any false show. The door opens. I go over to it.

"I have something to say to you."

"Hello," he says.

"Hello."

He starts taking off his coat.

"All right, take off your coat."

"Can I take off my hat and scarf too?"

"Take them off too. All right. But I've something to tell you."

"Thanks for letting me take off my scarf but especially my hat. I only live here, you know."

STEPHEN DIXON / SLEEP

"I know. And that's what I want to speak about with you. Not speak about."

"You want to send me a letter about whatever it is?"

"I want to say to you. I don't want to talk with you. I want to tell you and for the last time."

"Let me get my boots off too. That was some snow today."

"I don't want to talk about the snow."

"You don't? That's too bad. I like talking about snow. How it covers everything and makes the city look like a big winter fairyland. You know—though I'm not so good with words—but you don't want to talk about it."

"Neither do you. You hate snow. You say people don't buy your sneakers when it snows."

"I should make boots too. Then I wouldn't complain about the snow. Maybe then I'd really mean it when I say it makes the city look like a fairyland."

"You got everything off you want now?"

"Everything. Now I'd like a drink."

"I want to tell you what I have to tell you before you have that drink."

"Well, I want that drink now. It snowed. I'm cold. My feet got wet through those lousy boots. Maybe that's also why I should make boots. So I can have a good pair."

"You could buy a good pair. You happened to buy a cheap pair."

"You know my pair so well to say they're cheap?"

"Yes. When I was looking for my boots once, I picked up yours, not to put them on but to look at them. They're not rubber, they're plastic."

"Plastic's not snowproof?"

"Snowproof, yes, but not as durable as rubber. That's why yours probably leaked. Because they probably cracked someplace, so the snow went in."

"If ever I manufacture boots and need an advisor or even a designer, I'll call you."

STEPHEN DIXON / SLEEP

"Good. And I hope from your own apartment. Because that's what I have to talk to you about."

"My drink first."

"Get your goddamn drink."

"You don't want me to drink? You think it's a bad habit?"

"I didn't say that."

"Because you drink."

"Not as much as you. Not a tenth as much."

"What do you do, walk around with a ruler when I drink? Believe me, a tenth as much you drink. Maybe half as much. And since you're about half my weight, you drink, pound for pound, as much as I do and maybe even more."

"This is getting ridiculous. Get your drink. Then come in the living room so we can talk. So I can talk."

"Got a Band-Aid?"

"You have a cut?"

"No, for over my lips. Because I'm not allowed to talk when I get to the living room, right?"

"What I mean is I don't want you sidetracking me when I tell you. After I tell you, talk all you want. I'll probably go into my room and slam the door on you anyway."

"Your room? Which room in this place is suddenly your room?"

"Starting tonight our room is my room and the living room is your room. Or one of the boys' rooms is your room tonight if you can get the boys to sleep in the same room. But that's up to you. But our room is my room which is one of the things I was going to tell you in the living room. You want to hear the rest?"

"Let me get my drink. You want one?"

"No."

I go into the living room, sit on the chair, pick up the book and think it stupid I picked it up because the last thing I want to do now or can do is read. I throw it across the room and yell "Damn, damn, damn."

He comes in. "What's wrong? Why you yelling?"

STEPHEN DIXON / SLEEP

"I'm yelling at you. You make me so damn mad. Why do I have to even tell you what I'm going to tell you? You know I'm going to say to you 'Out, out, I want you out of this damn house tonight but definitely by tomorrow night and for good.'"

"You want me out of here? How come?"

"Because I want a divorce from you—you know how come."

"How come you want a divorce?"

"Stop it. You know why."

"No, why?"

"Why do you think?"

"I asked you the question first."

"I've told you a dozen times—a dozen dozen times."

"You also carry around a pocket calculator and calculate how many times you tell me? Maybe a couple dozen times only you told me."

"So what about it?"

"What about what?"

"Will you stop acting stupid? Are you giving me the divorce or do I have to slap a summons on you to show cause why you're not?"

"You slap me, I'll slap you, but half as light."

"I'm not pretending. I don't want jokes. I gave you four months to get your own place. That was six months ago. Stop fighting it. We don't work. I hate you and you hate me."

"No I don't. I love you."

"You're full of it. You hate me. You have to. The link between us is absolutely and irresolvably cut. The whole relationship is worthless, useless, unfortunate, whatever. I don't care how bad it is for the boys or what your parents will think or your brothers or how much extra it will cost you to live somewhere else or anything—I want you out of here now. That's what I had to say. That and that if you don't leave tonight then find another room to sleep in. And if you aren't completely out by tomorrow night, you're going to get that summons served on you the day after tomorrow. First thing when you leave the building or in your office with your brothers looking on or any place after that where the server can slap it on you. Now is that clear?"

"I poured myself too short a drink. I'll be right back."

"Drink yourself silly, you moron—and cook your own damn meal tonight and for the boys, because I'm going out."

"Where?"

"Out, just out. Where is none of your business."

"I don't have the right to know?"

"You have the right to know why you're being so pigheaded and stupid but not where I'm going, no."

"Wisecracks and insults won't work on me—you know that."

"You're impossible," I shout.

"Shouting won't work either."

"I hate you," I shout. "I hate your guts. You're a masochist and sadist both. You want to destroy me while you destroy yourself. The hell with you then—I don't care what my deserting you and the boys cost me. I'm leaving here myself—not for an hour or the night but until you've cleared out, whether that takes you a day or a year."

"Do if you want to, but you don't have to."

I run to him and he shoots his hands up in front of his face. The drink goes over his shoulder. I slap at his face and hit his hand and knock the glass across the room. I hit him with my other hand but can only hit his hands. The rat used to box in college and still knows instantly after I swing at him how to stop my blows. I bring my knee up to his groin and catch him. He wasn't expecting that. That's not a blow they use in boxing. He should've wrestled in college. He grabs himself down there and falls. I jump to the floor and tear at his hair.

"Stop it," he says, "I hurt, I hurt."

"You miserable phony. Even if you do hurt, I still hate your guts. You're trying to drive me crazy with your calmness and the rest of it—your coolness, whatever that is you pretend to be, but you won't drive me crazy. I'm getting away from you for good."

I go to the bedroom, get a valise, throw a few things in it and from the bathroom, put on my coat, cap, and boots and start for the door. He's standing in front of it.

"The boys won't understand," he says. "They'll think I hit you or worse and forced you to leave. You have to stay to explain to them why you're going and that it isn't my fault, then you can go. They know to come back for supper, don't they?"

"Don't play dumb. And you explain to the boys. Now out of my way."

"What could I tell them?"

"Tell them I deserted you and them. Tell them anything. Tell them I'll call them later. Tell them I'm taking a room at a hotel for the night and then finding my own apartment because I can't live another second with you and that you and I haven't loved each other for years and that I can't stomach you and am fed up with your delays in leaving here and that what you like best in life and which in the end seriously damages the kids is to torture us both, which is the only reason you insist I stay—that and because you're too damn scared and cheap to get your own apartment and live alone, now move out of my way."

"Your explanation isn't enough. Take a seat in the living room, I'll get you a drink and when the boys come you can explain it to them properly."

"I'm going to give you three. The numbers three. One-two-three. If by the time I count those three numbers out you're still blocking the door, I'm going to do something drastic to you."

"Like what?"

"One."

"Smash the suitcase over my head? I'll stop it from hitting me. You know I'm good at that."

"Two."

STEPHEN DIXON / SLEEP

"Kick me in the groin like before? All that was a joke on my part. You didn't hurt me. Your hair-pulling did a little, but not the knee. You never even touched me there."

"Three."

"So what are you—"

I throw the suitcase at him. He knocks it down and it opens on the floor. I take a print off the wall and throw it at him. He ducks and it smashes against the door behind him. I start screaming "Help, murder, my husband's trying to kill me—help, please, someone, save me."

He puts his hand over my mouth from behind. I try biting his hand. He keeps his hand pressed over my lips in a way where I can't open my mouth and my gums hurt. I struggle to get out of his grip, try stepping on his shoes and punching him, but his feet keep jumping out of the way of mine and his body twists and turns so I can't really get a good punch or elbow in.

"Give up?"

"No," I muffle through his hand grip.

"Is that a no? Then I can't let you go."

"Yes," I say.

"Yes you will or yes you won't?"

"Yes I will."

"Yes you will what?"

"Please," I muffle through his grip. "Your hand hurts."

"Okay. One . . . two . . . What's after two? Three."

He releases me. I step back.

"Into the living room now, into the living room," pointing with his finger.

I start for the living room. I want to find something that will temporarily immobilize him. I have to get out of this place now. I turn around. He's putting my things back into the suitcase and closes it.

I can't find anything. I'm not looking for a knife or gun, just something that will temporarily but harmlessly immobilize him.

STEPHEN DIXON / SLEEP

But what could that be? Alcohol in the eyes maybe. Liquor, a strong gin. I don't know if alcohol in the eyes really does have that burning sensation for so long as it does in some movies on TV where it temporarily blinds someone, so I don't want to try and use it. Besides, he'd duck and the alcohol would go past him when I threw it. I look.

"You calmer now?" he says coming into the living room.

"Yes. Leave me alone please." I go into the bathroom, open the medicine chest and cabinet, find nothing. Body powder. That might do it. It's at the foot of the tub. If I throw it I know he can't avoid it and whenever I get even a little in my eyes it makes me blink so much before I wash it out that for a half minute or so I feel blind and in my lungs it makes me cough like I have the croup.

I take the whole box and leave the bathroom. He has a fresh drink in his hand. He says "Let's talk nicely this time, without the histrionics. What do you have there?"

"Powder. For my neck." I start powdering my neck.

"Funny time to be powdering."

"I need it to compose myself. You got me all in a sweat."

"Anything, if it works for you. Now about your leaving tonight. What I want you instead to do is sleep in our bed with me. Not to make love. I'm not that much of an unseeing dope, not that I wouldn't want to with you."

"Then why?"

"You really have to powder in here? I'm glad it's making you calmer, but it's getting over things. And don't come near me with it. I don't want it on my tie and pants."

"It'd spank out."

"Still, if you don't mind?"

"Sure. Now tell me why you and I in this bed thing tonight?"

"Thanks. —Why? Because it's good for the kids' heads and images to think that we don't dislike each other so much where we can't even sleep in the same bed together. It looks bad."

STEPHEN DIXON / SLEEP

"Why? It's the truth, isn't it?"

"Not for me it isn't and I don't want them thinking I was so weak where I couldn't at least convince you to continue sleeping with me. Or at least where I wasn't so much of the ogre you think I am and so forth. That's why, or something like that. That we were still nice and polite and even slightly affectionate to each other before we broke up."

"Excuse me, but they haven't been able to see for themselves how we've been at each other's throats for the past few years?"

"I want to change that image for them. I don't know why, but I'd like them to think that we feel a little all right together."

"Well I don't care what they think. And you just said we are breaking up?"

"I'm not, you are. I'm staying here forever, far as I can see, fighting the divorce but keeping the boys. You want to leave— that's desertion and of course I can't stop you eventually, though tonight I can."

"You'd stop me in front of the boys?"

"I don't think so. But you'd leave in front of them?"

"Why not, but I want to leave right now."

"So leave."

"You'll let me?"

"Go ahead if you want to," and he steps aside.

I walk toward the door. He steps in my way and says "You're not going to put your powder down first?" I feign turning my back to him to put the powder on the table and then throw the box at his face. He starts coughing and swinging his fists in the air but still hasn't moved away from the door. I try to get past him and one of his fists grazes my nose and I think breaks it. I heard a crack and the blow knocks me to the floor and I can feel blood on my face. He's yelling and cursing at me when I take another print off the wall and smash it over his head, glass part down intentionally. He couldn't see it coming. A gash opens up on his forehead. He swings at the place where I was and I duck down and around him and get my hand on the doorknob. He leaps at me, catches my coat and throws me against the door. At the other end of the door a key's being put in the lock. It's one of our boys, maybe both.

"Stop—the boys," I say.

He starts strangling me.

"Mom, Dad, what's going on in there?" Bruno says.

I try to scream but can't because his fingers press down on my voice box. The door unlocks but I'm against the door and Bruno can't get in. I slide down the door to the floor and Stan continues strangling me. I feel the air going out of me, like I'm going to die.

"Help, someone, my mother's getting mugged," Bruno shouts.

Doors open in the hallway. Plenty of people home by now. Our door's forced open by several people. Two men and a woman jump Stan and he fights them off for a while, but several other people from other floors join in getting him to the floor and holding him there.

"She forced me to it, she forced me," he yells while someone puts a towel to his gash.

I'm being taken care of by a couple of neighbors. One's a nurse and she breathes air into me from her mouth but I wave her off, indicating I'm not that dead where I'm not nauseated by her breath.

I'm given water and helped up and carried to the living room couch. Bruno sits beside me holding my hand. The blood from my nose has stopped. The police have already come.

"We're not encouraged to get into family disputes," one of them says, "but we have to ask you if you want to press charges. Your husband says he's going to press charges against you."

"For what? Throwing body powder at this face? He wouldn't let me leave the apartment, that's why. Yes, I'm pressing charges. He tried to kill me. I want him locked up for the night."

STEPHEN DIXON / SLEEP

"I don't know if we can lock him up but we can certainly take him to the station and book him. He'll probably be released on his own recognizance, but that should give him a few hours down there."

"Then I want him taken away now."

"Dolores," Stan says, "please, don't. I have to be at work tomorrow. This is going to cost me plenty as it is. Come on, drop it and I'll leave on my own tonight."

"Leave now and I won't press charges."

"I can't. I have to get cleaned up first, dressed, packed, have at least a little rest from this cut."

"Will you stay here till he goes?" I ask the policemen.

"We've other things to do, lady. You want to press charges for him strangling you, we can take him now. To wait till he goes on his own without you pressing charges, that we can't do."

"Then I'm pressing charges."

"All right, I'll go now on my own," Stan says, "mess as I am."

He ties a bandanna around his forehead, puts his coat on and says "I'll phone you later, Bruno, and tell Donny I love him too and it was all your mother's fault, all your mother's, that witch, that whore, that son of the worst thing that God ever brought on this earth—you bastard, you lousy rotten—" and he jumps at me.

The policemen step between us. Stan tries barreling through them. They grab him and he fights back. "Don't make us do anything to hurt you, sir," one of them says. He hits this policeman in the face with his fist. The other policeman clubs Stan across the head, and when Stan's on the ground, raises the club to hit him again, but I yell "Stop."

The policeman stops. "I'm sorry," he says, "but that idiot should've known better. Now what?"

"I think we should call an ambulance, Rick," the other policeman says. "Not for me—I'll be all right—but him."

Bruno's bawling and I just sit there with one hand over my lips and my other arm around Bruno's shoulder. The nurse puts a blanket over Stan and takes care of his head. His eyes are closed and he hasn't moved since he was clubbed. Several more neighbors come into the apartment. Donny comes home and screams "Dad—what's wrong?" and when told a policeman did it, shouts at a few policemen who just came in the apartment "Murderers . . . killers," and runs to his room.

Several reports are being written up at once now: a detective asking Rick how it happened, another one asking me and a third and fourth asking the policeman who Stan hit in the face and a few of our neighbors.

"He's still breathing," the nurse says. "Where's the damn ambulance? I think he really got hit too hard for a head, even if it was justified."

I continue to sit on the couch, both hands over my eyes, crying. If only he'd let me leave when I wanted to. Better yet, to have gone when I wanted him to. Gone four months ago, six months ago, when I practically begged him to. Now he's going. The ambulance has come and two men bring in a stretcher and a doctor squats beside Stan and checks his eyes and pulse.

"Get a respirator, this guy's getting cold," the doctor says, her ear on Stan's chest. "I think it affected his heart."

I let out a scream and stand and scream. Two neighbors grab my arm, take off my coat and scarf, move Bruno off the couch and sit me down on it, both of them sitting next to me and patting my hands.

"Maybe we should take her to her bedroom," one says.

"No, don't," I say, "I want to be here when he leaves."

"Then take it easy, Dee, okay? He'll be all right, so don't worry."

I think: maybe he will and maybe he won't. Either way I lose. If he dies I'll feel responsible always and the boys will hate me. If he lives he'll come home from the hospital after a while and I'll have to stay here till he recovers fully.

STEPHEN DIXON / SLEEP

"No," I shout.

"No, what?" the doctor says, taking out a bottle and syringe.

"No, I don't want to stay here, can't," and I get up and run for the front door. A man's wheeling in some medical equipment. I push past him and run down the hall and ring for the elevator.

"Mom, come back," Bruno says from the door.

"I can't. I meant it. I'll call later. Take care of yourselves tonight or get a neighbor. You don't understand or how sorry I am but I have to go, Bruno, I have to," and the elevator comes, I get in it and the door closes.

"What happened on your floor?" a woman says in the elevator.

"A couple had a bad fight."

"You know which one?"

"No, I was only visiting here."

"Visiting here? Mrs. Niton, I know you—you live in 8F, one floor right below me. Where are you going—getting your laundry from the basement?"

"No, outside."

"Without a coat? Honey, I don't know but it's ten to fifteen degrees above freezing out, and with the wind the way it is, I bet it's like the top of the Arctic with the temperature and snow."

"No, I'm going outside."

The door opens. I hurry through the lobby, outside, and walk through the snow. The woman's right behind me. "Len," she yells back at the doorman, "I think we better help this poor woman—something seems to be wrong."

hand

He puts his hand through a window. He puts his fist through a window. Slams his fist through it. He's forcing the window up because it's stuck when his right hand slips and goes through one of the small bottom panes. Wanted some air in his office. "Well, I got some," he jokes a few days later. He got mad at something and slammed his hand through the window. "If you're going to pick anybody, don't pick that polemical jerk, you stupid bastards," he said. "Damn, my hand," he says, looking at it. "Screw my hand," looking at it. With his left hand gets a handkerchief from his right pants pocket. Hanky out of his pants pocket. Wipes the blood away with it. Dabs the hand with the handkerchief and sees three gashes, two very deep ones on his pinky and second finger, one not so deep on the back of his hand. Three, oh crap, he thinks. Jesus, good thing it didn't cut the wrist, he thinks. Now the cuts are really bleeding. For the first half-minute or so it came slow. Maybe, if you don't hit a main blood vessel, that's the way it always is. Wraps his hand in the handkerchief, presses down on the cuts for about a minute, handkerchief's a navy blue railroadman's kind, so isn't easy to see if the cuts are bleeding through, takes it off. Bleeding just as much now, maybe more.

Wraps his hand again and goes downstairs to the campus bookstore in the basement and looks for adhesive bandages. Finds them, widest kind the store has but not the brand he thinks sticks the best, price seems okay for this overpricing store. Hanky feels soaked, opens it and looks at his hand. These bandages won't help, he thinks, nor pressing down on the cuts. Finger cuts look deep enough for sutures. Puts the hanky around his hand, sets the box of adhesive bandages on the checkout counter and says to the cashier "Excuse me, but is the student infirmary still by the old freshmen dorms? I was there about eight years ago for a bad cold, but with all the construction since I thought it could have moved." "You buying those strips?" she says. "I was but I don't think they'll do for what I want them for and you didn't seem to have any real bandages and surgical tape." "Sorry, this is our medical stuff except for Mercurochrome and if you think aspirins are that. Gosh, the box has blood on it, so we can't use it now either. But if you don't want it, I guess it's okay." "No, I did it, I'll pay, I don't mind. But the student infirmary?" "Infirmary?" "Heath clinic or services then. I don't know what you call it but it was called an infirmary when I was in college and maybe eight years ago here." "Why, your hand? Seems to be bleeding bad. You got a little on the case also, but not to worry, I got plenty of tissues," and takes one from behind the counter and wipes it. "And the clinic's on the left side of Freshman Dorm B on Henzel Quad—big sign above its private door, and a five-minute walk from here." He pays, puts the box in his back pocket, and going back upstairs, the hand hurting now, he thinks Oh damn, and my good hand. How am I going to work now or for the next week, maybe two? I got a ton of papers due and my own crap. Ah fuck, how stupid I was. He writes a note in his office with his left hand: "Conference people today, I cut my hand opening the window, hv gone to the health clinic. Sorry for the inconvenience. I shld be bk soon, so if you can, wait. It's now 12:35." Starts for the clinic, stops in his department's main office on the first floor because going downstairs he thought of something and didn't want to walk back up. "May I use your phone?" he asks the secretary. "Goodness, your hand, what happened? And you're dribbling blood all the way in here. I don't mean to sound insensitive, but tie something better around it." "I'm sorry. Cut it in my office and am on my way to the health clinic now. It's bleeding worse than I thought." "How'd you do it?" If I told her I did it by slamming my fist through the window, what would she say? he thinks. "Punching my fist through the window, actually," he says. "Goodness, what a temper you have," laughing, knowing he's kidding. "Here, quick," giving him several paper towels. He wraps his wrapped hand with them. "And let me dial for you. You use it and I won't want to touch my phone again today and I don't know who else will want to clean it till the janitor comes at five." "I only wanted to call Maintenance to tell them my window's broke. It's getting cold in there." "Oh, I can do that. Room four-twelve? And you know, when you're through at the clinic call Workmen's Compensation here. You can get all the medical bills paid for; you injured yourself on the job and in the line of work, right?" "But if I tell them I slammed my hand through the window because I was angry at the chairman, does that count?" "Don't tell them that. It'll hurt your chances. Don't even tell me that. I might think it the truth and worry for him." "It isn't the truth; don't worry. If I didn't like something he did, not that I have any complaints, I'd tell it to his face and spare my hand." He goes to the clinic. "Yes?" the receptionist says through the speaking hole in the window, and then "Oh, I can see. Is it an emergency emergency?" "If that's the difference between getting it treated now or an hour from now, yes. I mean, it's not an artery but it is bleeding badly and in three places." "Three. That should qualify. You work here?" "I'm a teacher." Well, Professor, we usually see people by appointment unless it is a dire emergency, but I'm sure someone can see you." She takes his name and department and tells him to sit and wait. They take him, treat the cuts, give him a tetanus shot because he can't remember if he had one in the last ten years and if he did, if he'd had a serious injury in the last five. Sutures, and while he's being bandaged he's asked how he cut his hand. "Didn't I tell you?" "That must have been the nurse who cleaned it." "I was opening my office window, wanted air, hand slipped, that's about it." Doesn't tell her he was angry at the time because he'd read in the paper early this morning that someone got an award he was up for and felt he deserved a lot more than she, though for all he knows, since he hadn't read their works, so might have the other three nominees. But her, her?—God, what a choice. It had to be politics, he thought, plus the writer's notoriety and her publisher's prestige. He'd been steaming ever since he read it, stomped around the house, threw the section with the article in it to the floor, snapped at his kids when they came downstairs for breakfast, snapped at his wife before he left the house for school, but didn't tell her why he was so angry. She would have talked about vanity, that it's enough just to have been nominated, which she'd say he never expected to be in the first place, that all contests like this are crapshoots and even being nominated is one. Later today—she probably already has—she'll see the article and know what set him off and then when he gets home she'll say all those things about vanity and crapshoots or lotteries—lottery is the word she'd use—or would say it if he hadn't cut himself so badly. He did read all that this morning and do all that snapping and stomping and throwing, but by the time he got to his office for student conferences he wasn't angry anymore. Or not much. Occasionally thought of the award and who won it and might have felt a little peeved but didn't flare up. He was opening the one window in the room. He wanted air. The heat was on through some central control system and there was no way for him to turn it down or off. The room was stifling, he was suffocating, he took his sweater off, rolled up his sleeves, but it was still too warm for him. So maybe the heat contributed to his anger or made him angry—something physiological that provoked it at least—but he suddenly thought of that lousy writer, that literary fake, really, and not just in that book but in the two others of hers he's read, and he yelled out "Goddamn idiots"—meaning the judges—and slammed his fist through the window. It was all so stupid. Window was stuck. He should have stopped trying to force it open after a while when it wouldn't budge. But he pushed and pushed and hand went through. "What can I say? It was dumb of me." "It was an accident," the nurse says, "pure and simple. Unfortunately, now you got to live with it a couple of weeks." He goes back to his office. Three students are waiting for him. "Hello, hello, how are you all? As you can see, and from the note, this happened," and holds the bandaged hand up. "Oops, that hurt too, just raising it, though I was told to try and keep it above my heart the whole day to stop it from bleeding," and unlocks his door with his left hand. Cardboard's covering the window. "Boy, they work fast, Maintenance. Come in, come in. Any of you carry around extra-strength pain relievers or just ordinary aspirins? Four of the regular aspirins should add up to two of the extra-strength. The infirmary—health clinic—didn't have any, can you believe it? Said they don't even get samples. I think they're saving them for the students, the professors can pay for their own." "How'd you hurt it?" a student says and he says "Accident." "Sure you didn't punch it through the glass?" another student says and he says "What do you mean?" "Just joking, sir, but you saw who won the Langston Prize you were nominated for, didn't you?" "No, was the announcement today? I thought tomorrow. Meaning, I mean, that the press release for it would be issued today but it'd be in the papers tomorrow. Anyway, I guess you're saying I didn't win, since if you're not then it'd be pretty bizarre to think I'd put my hand through a window because I'd won a prestigious award. Want to know the truth? Just being nominated was fine by me. Winning might have its own problems, though the extra award money would be nice, and who'd expect to win but a giant egohead?" "But Miriam Codona?" "It was she? Well good for her." "C'mon, 'good for her.' You or one of the other three guys should've won, because did you read her book?" and he says "No, is it that bad?" and the student says "Even worse. You would've had a good excuse to put your hand through a window on purpose—you and the other three guys nominated, though if I had my choice I would've punched the wall. But what really happened, you trip or something?" and he says "Sort of. Window got stuck and I lost my footing try-ing to force it up. Anyway, my friends, I'm sorry but I've got to get out of here. This thing is getting more painful by the second, and I have some good painkillers at home that I got for a tooth extraction a while back, so if you'll excuse me?" and they tell him they hope he feels better and he says "I'll be all right, and Wednesday, twelve till two for makeup conferences, okay?" He calls his wife. "How are things?" he says and she says "Fine. Nobody called, mail hasn't come yet," and he says "That's not why I called. Listen, I cut my hand pretty bad before—" and she says "Oh no," and he says "Don't worry. I got it fixed at the infirmary on campus, stitches and stuff, and I'm coming home now, canceled all my conferences." "How'd you do it, my poor dear?" and he says "I'll tell you it all later." "Just tell me how it happened now," and he says "I got mad at myself and punched it through the window—no, I was open-ing my office window and my hand slipped and went through a bottom pane. Cut it in three places, one of them right down to the bone, another pretty close." "Actually, your first expla-nation sounds more plausible—because this morning, I'll tell you . . ." and he says "No, please—hand killer? not me," and she says "But you were in some mood then. Anyway, can you drive with it—is it the left or right?" "Right," and she says "How can you drive then and use the floor shift?" and he says

"I can do it. No nerves were cut and I've three fingers that weren't touched and they're all in a row and I'll steer with my left hand. By the way, you see who won the Langston?" and she says "I did but I didn't want to bring it up. I was thinking, even before you phoned, that that was what made you so furious this morning, since from what you've said about her I don't think she deserved it. And now with this window incident—" and he says "Not a chance. If I had any illusions about winning, I would have been crazy. It was rewarding enough to be one of the nominees, I thought when someone here told me who won—I didn't see the paper, so save it. And the two thousand they give as the booby prize isn't so bad either. See you soon," and she says "Drive carefully." He writes a note with his left hand: "Office hrs canceled today, I'll be here Weds, 12–2," and takes the other note off the door and tapes this one on. Drops the old note into the trash can by his desk and sees the blood on the floor and then on the wall by the window and on a couple of window panes. Doesn't want to leave it there for his students to see or someone else to clean up, not that Mainten-ance will, or so soon—they usually mop the floor and polish the desk once a year during summer break when he's gone. Goes to the men's room down the hall, gets some paper towels and soaks them, goes back to his office and washing the wall with the towels thinks of the prize and the winner and his hand and how much work time he's going to lose and just that he now has to clean this goddamn mess and then thinks with the prize, mangled hand and all, it still would have been a good day. A great day, who's he kidding? Maybe the best of that kind in his life, since just being nominated—that phone call and for a while after—was just about the best of that kind he's ever had, or at least can remember. He throws the towels at the window. "Bastard, stupid idiots, chickenshits," he yells, then turns to the door—nobody's there and he doesn't hear anyone out-side—and closes it. "Moron, fools," he says lower. "Ah, hell with it," and gets his briefcase, fills it with what he has to, and leaves the office and kicks the door shut. Shouldn't have got mad today over it, he thinks, going downstairs. Scared the kids, horrified my wife, made a total ass of myself. Shouldn't expect anything, but it made me upset where I didn't know what I was doing. Was opening the window. Slammed my fist through the closed window. Forgot what I was doing. Forget it.

sleep

Several people wanted to see him to his car after the burial but
he said "No, I'd like to walk to it by myself, I don't know why,
do you mind? And everyone has a ride back? Good. Then
thanks for coming, and I guess I'll be seeing you." He was
thinking of sleep even then, during the short walk. How in
maybe an hour, or two to three, he'll be in bed, under or on
top of the covers, and if on top then with the extra blanket,
which is usually at the end of the bed, over him, phone off the
hook or in some way disconnected, curtains closed. Moments
after she died, or maybe a minute after, but anyway, almost the
first thing he thought once he realized she was dead was "Now
I can sleep better." Or was it "Now I can get some sleep"? Now
in the car he thinks "What'll be my procedure for today, and
one day at a time, after that?" He'll go home, park, pick up the
newspaper somewhere around the carport where it's always
delivered, go in the house, take off his shoes, the tie of course,
he won't get the mail, prepare a scotch on ice with his usual
splash of water—a big scotch, so a couple of splashes: he
wants to sleep—sit in his chair in the living room with it and
read the paper while sipping the drink, not let himself go to
pieces, maybe only one section, maybe the whole paper except

the business section. That one he never reads unless it has
something he's interested in continued from the first page.
He'll start with the arts, food, science, and home section, the
everything-but-news section, he calls it. It's usually light,
uncomplicated, plenty of photos and reviews and sort of time-
less articles, will be easy to read and maybe even distracting.
He won't read the obituary page. It's never in the everything-
but section, which may be why he thinks he'll only read that
one. Or maybe he will read it. Hers will be there, or should,
since he placed it yesterday and in plenty of time. "Hello," he
said on the phone soon after he got home from the hospital and
got the number out of the newspaper, "I'd like to place an obituary for one Wanda Monterra. Would you like me to spell it?"
"Eventually, yes," the woman said, "but first let me have yours
and how we should bill it." He started rambling on about
what he wanted to put in and how he'd like it worded. The
woman helped him. " 'Loving wife of Courtney Patton,' okay?"
"Fine," he said, "but the flowers." "Well, it could be 'in lieu of
flowers,' or just 'no flowers,' or something about contributions
to charities instead of flowers," and he said "Come to think of
it, none of that. I'd like to keep it short, only the essentials, and
not to save money; just that that's how I think an obit should
be: who it is, where and what day and time it is, and who sur-
vived, I don't know why. Meaning, I don't know why I think
an obit should be like this." But when she died, in his arms, in
the hospital, she was already dead. Of course she was dead if
she'd died, but he means he saw her in the bed looking dead,
rushed to her, held her in his arms, first lifted her up from the
waist, he means from under her arms till she was sitting up
straight from the waist and of course only with his support,
and then held her in his arms. She was cold, motionless, lifeless, she had no motion or life, her eyes were closed, body
seemed cold, she had that look he was told in a matter of days
to expect, her skin becoming what they also said to expect, he
thought "My darling"—thought this then—"now I can sleep

STEPHEN DIXON / SLEEP

better." Or "Now I can get some sleep." Both sound right but he only thought one of them. And did he say it rather than think it? He doesn't know, and could be he did both. And it wasn't a hard thought or remark, was it? Meaning, not a cold one, a deliberately self-centered thoughtless one, was it? One could even say that at the time he said or thought it he was in some kind of shock. Probably, but probably not. Meaning, one could say it, but he wasn't.

Now he's home, in the living room in his favorite chair, didn't get the paper, no, got the paper but not the mail. Way he sees it, won't get it for days. Phone disconnected?—forgets but thinks he did, drink in his hand, double scotch with a double splash, unopened newspaper in his lap. It was only yesterday, wasn't it? Knows it was only yesterday, and it wasn't a hard thought or remark, was it? and knows if he knows anything that he wasn't in any kind of shock. He'd taken care of her for months, so was prepared. Well, even then one could still not be, meaning that right up to the last minute and despite every kind of preparation for or against it, one still doesn't know. Meaning . . . well, he knows that. Took care of her for four years or more, five, six, at home, in the hospital, mostly at home but the last year or so each time a little more in the hospital, always by her side when she was home and sometimes in a bed beside hers in the hospital. He could have moved to another room at home. They had two bedrooms and a study that can be turned into one, but he continued to sleep with her. She made such noises at home. Not just snores and groans. He liked to joke about it with her if he thought she was in the right mood for it, though sometimes if he was feeling cross or exhausted because her noises had kept him up the previous night, he joked about it even when he knew her mood was sour or dark, but she never found it funny no matter how well he thought he'd gauged that her mood was good. "My hibernating Siberian bear—that's what you sounded like last night." "I'm not laughing," she said. Another time: "Really, you slept like a groveling warthog last night, and you rolled over like one too. You thrashed and spit and chomped as if you were eating bark or slop." "Screw you too," she said, "since it should be obvious I can't help it, and you think your blowing and snorting doesn't keep me up?" "Nothing like yours does, because nothing could be louder, and it just kept coming. I felt like leaving the room and sleeping in the guest room or on the couch." "So why didn't you? I only wish I could do that when you wheeze and grunt through half the night. But it'd mean struggling for an hour to get there if I didn't have your help. And if I fell down on the way and you didn't hear me because you were sleeping so soundly, I'd be there till morning." "You're just saying I make noises like that, or if I do, then saying I do it as much as you, to get back at me; but all right, I understand. But it's also that I get anxious every night I go to sleep, thinking I won't get any rest for the next day." "You get plenty; you sleep more than your fill. It's me who's starving for it and needs it much more than you. But as I said, sleep somewhere else if you don't like my moving around in bed and my sounds. And if you do want to sleep with me or just in this bed here, put up with it best you can. But not, which you like to do, wake me by jabbing or stabbing my back or yelling in my ear." "I only do that, and never that hard or loud, to stop you from making those noises; otherwise I'd never get any sleep." Another time: "It seemed like a whole barnyard of animals was sleeping on your side of the bed last night: mooing, whistling, growling, snarling, clicking, snapping, barking, and squalling, besides what seemed like blubbery bubbles popping out of your mouth and nose." "Thank you, oh thank you, but don't give me that crap you couldn't get any sleep again. I got up several times to go potty—I wish I didn't but my stupid body makes me—and you were dead asleep like a baby each time." "I was pretending," he said. "More lies." And he said "That's what you'd like to believe, and I'm not going to start contradicting you now. Last thing I want, after everything else, is another big argument and you crying away with real fat tears. For the next hour just forget I'm alive." She said something to that but he forgets what. Tonight he'll sleep. Hasn't slept much the last three weeks, but tonight he thinks he will only because he's so tired and what's there now to stop him? Four nights ago she was up all night, coughing, breathing hard, complaining of pain. Took her to the hospital the following morning. Next two nights he slept in the hospital, in a chair in her room or in the visitors' lounge on a chair or couch. They weren't really sleeps. Her noises were very loud when he tried sleeping in her room, and the lounge was cold, and the couch, which was more like a long board with thin plastic cushions on it, was uncomfortable, maybe not so much for sitting but definitely for sleeping on, which might have been what the hospital had in mind when they bought it.

"Do you want to mention surviving parents?" the newspaper obituary person said. "Or even grandparents or children, if there are any?" "Oh yes, her parents," and gave their names. "No grandparents or children, though. We couldn't have any—children, I mean." "I'm sorry," she said, and he said "Oh, it wasn't a problem for us, and I apologize if I said it in a way to make you feel it was, for we didn't mind no kids. Short as it was, we had a nice life together, thought of each other as soul mates till she got ill. Meaning, we had a nice life together till she got ill, and even after that it was okay, and we were for the most part soul mates till she got very ill. Then we were still pretty good to each other, but as you can imagine, it became very hard on us both." "I'm sorry," she said. Friends wanted to go home with him, and his wife's sister. He forgot to put her name in the obit but she'll understand, if she even sees it, since she should already be on the train home by now and she probably also, like most people, doesn't read newspapers from any city but her own. He said to all of them he wanted to be alone today. He'll sleep, have a drink, have a drink first and then sleep, have two or three drinks, but anyway he'll be all right, so don't worry, he said. Tomorrow too and for the days to come, if they don't mind, till he phones them, if he does, or contacts them in some way. "Oh, do," they said. "A letter, maybe," he said. "Whichever way you choose." And he said he would. "You know you can come to our house for dinner any night you want," one friend of theirs said. "Several nights a week even, and for as many weeks as you like. The invitation's open and open-ended." "I know," he said. His in-laws flew in from their city and were flying back soon after the funeral. Nice people. He said good-bye to them at the gravesite and while he was kissing their cheeks he thought "I'll probably never see them again." It must have been very tough on them the last few days. Of course, what's he saying? And of course for him too.

He sips his drink, opens the paper, starts to pull out the everything-but section, then thinks "Oh, go to the obits, you know you're curious." Curious? Well, something. He just wants to see, her name, his, together, his right after hers. "Just 'husband,'" he told the newspaper obit woman, "because 'loving' goes without saying, or should. And even if it didn't apply, though in my case it did, it had to have at the start or some part of anybody's marriage, wouldn't you say? And who am I trying to impress with that word anyway?" "That's not why people include it," and he said "Then why, can you tell me? I've always been interested, or have occasionally, when I've read obituaries, or maybe only one other time but today," and she said "Lots of reasons, too many to go into, for everyone seems to have his own." A little part of him also wants to see if the obit came out the way he wanted or if the woman didn't instinctively insert a few of those loving and adoring adjectives. No, they're pros, so they wouldn't do that, and they also know the customer pays by the word so might object to anything extra. And then to tear it out. Rather, fold it over in four places and then cut it at the seams carefully. That's what he really wants to do most and maybe even without reading it. For if he doesn't cut it out now he might forget for later and then he won't have it, the paper having gone out with the trash or, if he continues to do some of the same routines he did before she died, the biweekly paper pickup for recycling. And where should he put it after he cuts it out? Little things like that get quickly lost. In the intricately carved Indian wooden box on the fireplace mantel where he already has a pair of cuff links from when he was a teenager and a gold tiepin from then too with only his three initials on it and some marbles from when he was even younger that his mother found behind her stove twenty years ago when she had it replaced and a couple of his baby teeth, "two of your first three," she said, "though I can't say for sure if either of these is your very first," a metal token from a board game he had when he was around ten, the marriage announcement his in-laws placed in their local paper of his wife and him and her photo, and—who knows?—years from now, two, three, he'll see the obit folded up in the box and look at it as he did the marriage announcement a few days ago, though that one he did intentionally, and remember this day, the funeral, burial, walking from the grave to the car by himself, how he cut the obit out, what gave him the idea to do it—what did?—even him sitting here. So he opens the paper to the obituaries, finds hers, and reads. Everything got in right. The woman was a lot of help. Doesn't say anything about sleep or the need for it. For some reason he thought he put something about it in. He should have, for himself only, no matter how strange it would have seemed to anyone reading it. But why? Well, so years or a year from now when he takes it out of the box and reads it for the first time since today he'll recall his thoughts now about sleep. Not enough reason to risk seeming so senseless, and the newspaper obit woman would never have let him put it in if he'd wanted to and was willing to pay, let's say, even triple the charge. They have standards to maintain that money can't buy. They can't let oddballs and brooders and loonies and practical jokers horsing around or making light of or acting crazy on what should be a solemn page. Most people take the obits quite seriously, and there are many who read them every day, and some where it's the first thing they turn to in the paper. They've told him, at least one or two have, how it makes life for them seem more poignant, or meaningful, or fragile, or something along those lines. Especially the paid obits that say "surviving parents and grandparents," for that says something about the deceased's age. They should have had children. He means he wishes they had had them, his wife and he. Sure, it would have been sad for a child to see its mother die, but he would have had these kids or at least one to be with after. He might even be taking care of them this minute instead of sitting here thinking about them. Making them lunch, or taking them out for lunch, or lunch home and then going to the park with them perhaps, places they'd like to go, like the zoo or merry-go-round or both, and then to some place in the park for a snack, or nearby for dinner if it's around that time. Trying to distract them from their mother's death, is what he's saying, while at the same time using them to take his mind off it too, rather than him drinking here alone, paper in his lap, place quiet, shades down, windows shut, curtains closed, chair he's in lit by a floor lamp in a room usually flooded at this time with natural daylight. Oh, best he cut the obit out now, and he tears that page of the paper out, creases the part around the obit, then thinks "Too slow, it's going to tear anyway, or might, paper's so frail," and rips the obit out, tears off little pieces till the area around it is a square, and puts it on the side table next to him. No, he might spill his drink on it, or the next one, or almost certainly the one after that. Or it might be blown off the table when he just walks past it, or from the little breeze he makes when he stands, and then get lost under the couch or something and maybe when he next sees it in a month or two he'll have, without really looking at it, forgotten what it is, or he'll remember or read it but it'll be so covered with dustballs and

STEPHEN DIXON / SLEEP

stuff that he'll throw it away, though regret that he did later. "Put it in a safe spot now," he thinks, "and you'll know you have it," and he gets up and sticks it in the mantel box and then sits again in the same chair.

So where was he? Children he doesn't have. He'd see to them for sure. He'd do everything he could for them, try to be both parents, whatever that means. He would have been such a good father, he's almost sure of it. He'd probably cry a lot with them; over their mother, he means. They'd be crying, or inter-mittently, how could they not be? and he'd start in too when he saw them that way. He wouldn't be thinking of sleeping, he doesn't think. Or maybe just thinking of it but with no imme-diate plans to carry it out. He'd be too busy doing other things. He also wouldn't think of cutting out the obituary. Wouldn't want it around to remind them of their mother, if they found it. Well, instead he could put it in his wallet, to take out and look at when he wants, but it'd be in shreds in a couple of weeks. He's found that newspaper clippings don't last long there and magazine articles or pieces he's cut out of them do just a little better. He did think of sleeping when she died, though. Right after it, he means. Thought it right after. He held her in his arms. Picked her up, lifted her from behind. He was facing her, standing up but leaning over, and put his arms under her and held her back up as he lifted her toward him. He was standing, or sitting up on the end of the bed, he forgets which. At the edge of it, he means, and if there then he would have had to lower the side rail first and he doesn't remember doing that. The side rail was always up except when a nurse or aide was changing the bed. So, standing, most likely. Yes, standing, definitely; it makes sense and it's what he pictures too. "She's like a rag doll," he thought then, when he was holding her up. No, he thought that later. No, he thought it then but told a friend about it at the funeral home that night. "I picked her up." This was only last night. He can hardly believe it: just last night. "I picked her up. Lifted her away from the bed. I knew she was dead. Knew it beforehand, knew it now. She was like a rag doll in my arms. I know that isn't an original thought or comparison or whatever it is for what she was but it is what I thought." He didn't tell this friend that the first thing he thought or said aloud to himself after he looked at her and thought she was dead was "She's dead, now I can get some sleep." Or "Now I'll get some sleep." Or " I can sleep better now." Or "Now I can sleep better now that she's dead" or "I'll be able to." Or was it "Now that she's dead I'm going to get a lot of sleep"? Or "I'm so tired I'm going to bed right after the burial and sleep for I don't know how long. A day, I mean a whole one, or maybe two." He must have known he wouldn't sleep the night of the day she died. Wouldn't sleep that night, he means. There were still lots of things to do and so many things running around in his head, and where could he sleep, since he wouldn't be home or at least for sleep till the next day? Then he left the hospital room and went down the hall. Though first he rested her back on the bed, set her down with her back back on the bed, just put her back down same way she was before he lifted her. He let her down, that's all, meaning he put her down, or set her down, and right after that he kissed her lips. Wanted to do it then before things in her body really started changing. He was told to expect that too. Of course they were already changing, but weren't yet visible, or to him. Well, to no one so far, for he was the only one in the room. Do it now, he told himself. He definitely remembers saying that, and aloud. "Do it now, for you're going to do it sometime before you bury her." And then bent down and kissed her. He didn't press hard with his lips; he just let them rest on hers for a few seconds. He forgets what hers felt like, or never recorded the impression—the impression in his mind, he means—and he also probably closed his eyes—he always did when he kissed; hers had been closed for two days, at least every time he looked at them—and went outside her room— it was a private one—shut the door—he didn't want other

STEPHEN DIXON / SLEEP

people looking in—and went to the nurses' station and said "I think my wife died, Wanda Monterra, or Mrs. Patton, you might have her down as. In fact, I'm almost sure she's dead— I'm positive, really. She shows all the signs you told me, or some other nurses did, to look out for—room 823. Please see to her right away." He rushed back to the room. He doesn't know why he rushed. After all, she was dead; at the time he'd've staked everything on it. Maybe because she was alone and he didn't want to leave her that way; he didn't know why or whom it'd hurt, but something told him it was wrong. But he thinks he thought then "Maybe there'll be a miracle and she'll be alive when I get back, even beginning to recover. Maybe my kiss did it. That it was all she needed to pop out of it. What am I thinking of? She's dead, she's dead, so start getting used to it." He thinks he thought all that but maybe in different words or with some of the same. A couple of nurses, doctors, and aides—in other words, several people, maybe six or even —barged into the room a minute later, so it took them about two minutes to come from the time he told the nurse at the station. They quickly sent him out. Later, he went to a public pay phone on the floor and called his wife's parents and a funeral home. First he waited outside her room for the medical team to come out. A few minutes later two nurses came out and walked past him and he caught up with them down the hall and said "She's dead, my wife, in 823, isn't she?" and the nurse said "Sorry, I didn't see you. One of the doctors will speak to you when he's through in there. Just stop him." He went back to the door and opened it, wanted to see what they were doing, if they were trying to revive her, if they were only cleaning her up, and an aide standing by the door inside said "Something you want?" "I'm her husband," and the aide said "Oh; excuse me. We're not ready yet; soon." A doctor came out about five minutes later, went straight to him, and said "We thought it would be today, didn't we. We talked about it, you and I, I'm nearly sure I recall that. I knew, at least, it'd be soon:

STEPHEN DIXON / SLEEP

today, tomorrow, or the next day. I think that's what we said, so it's not like we're surprised she died today; the medical staff, I'm saying." He asked what he should do now and the doctor said "You can go in; everyone will leave. Then when you're done you can make your phone calls to people and to the funeral home you have in mind, but because we have some more work to do in here, from one of the phones down the hall. While you're doing that—phoning, I'm saying—your wife will be taken to another place downstairs, so don't be alarmed if you don't see her in here when you return. Though you might see her. Sometimes we don't get things done as fast as we want." He went into the room; bed had been remade, covers pulled up to her neck and tucked over, arms evenly by her sides. He lifted her hands and kissed them, said "Good-bye, my dear." Of course he cried, a little, a lot. In fact he thinks he broke down; yes, he broke down, so much so that if someone had been there he's sure he would have collapsed or fallen or done something like that into that person's arms. Because no one was there—well, of course someone was, but he knows what he means—he thinks he had to hold on to something to stop him from collapsing: the bed rail or head-board. He tries to picture himself then. He thinks he actually braced his hand against the wall to keep standing, then sat in the chair by her bed and looked at her and left. He went to the pay phone down the hall and called the funeral home. Then he called her parents in the hotel they were at, hoping they were in. He didn't want to leave a message and have to call again and again. They took it badly. He realizes now he should have called them first and doesn't know why he didn't. There was no rush for the funeral home to send a hearse over for the body. She first had to be examined and there were some documents he had to sign, the doctor had told him, and the hospital was also going to remove a couple of her parts. Her parents had been there that morning and left an hour before she died, telling him they were coming back with their daughter that evening. Their other daughter, he of course means. He hopes he didn't offend or hurt them when he said he'd just got through speaking to the funeral home, which they must have picked up meant he hadn't called them first. Anyway, that's the order he made his calls yesterday, next calling a few friends and coworkers of theirs to tell other friends and coworkers that her funeral will be tomorrow at the Clementz Funeral Home sometime around noon, look for the obituary in the paper for the exact time. He of course first told these people that his wife had died. Then he returned to her room, but the bed was empty and stripped and the linen was in a pile on the floor. He thinks "Did they remake her bed with fresh linen just for the short time I'd be in the room with her after the doctors and nurses left?" He means, did they remake it only for the time he'd be in there alone? He didn't ask anyone at the hospital if that was so, but if it was it was very considerate of them but probably unnecessary. But it's just linen, probably washed with a ton of other linen in a big vat somewhere in the hospital and not thrown out, so what's the difference? Then he went home, thought of having a scotch but made himself coffee, placed the obit in the paper, said he'd call back in an hour or so with the exact funeral time. Phone rang a number of times but he didn't answer. "Couldn't speak to anyone now," he thought, "just couldn't," and suppose it was someone who wanted a contribution of some sort or was trying to sell him something? A gravesite, for instance. They've called for that, maybe more calls for it than for anything else they're selling. "We don't plan to die," he used to tell them. "We're both very healthy, and besides I don't like these calls coming to my home." Then: "We got two graves that were part of a friend's plot, all we need, so no thank you, and I also have to tell you I don't at all like these calls coming to my home." Changed his clothes, brushed his teeth, thought about shaving but didn't see any reason to. Now he has almost a two-day growth, or is it three? and it doesn't feel itchy, so he'll shave sometime after he wakes up. He's certainly not going to grow a beard. She always wanted him to, or said she thought he might look good in one and only way to find out was to grow it. Went to the funeral home to choose a casket and see to some details of the funeral: flowers, officiator—he had none, so they said they'd get someone for him. She was there by now, and he waited in the lobby while they worked on her, called the newspaper with the exact time of the funeral and where the burial would be, and when the funeral people had her ready, he sat by her casket in the sitting room reserved for her. Some friends and her family came, sat beside him awhile, tried talking to him but he wasn't talking. He knew it was just as sad for them, but in different ways—after all, she was a loved woman and very close to her family—but nothing he could say could help them and they couldn't help him. Her mother asked if she could have the casket opened for a few minutes, and he nodded and left the room. Spent the night in the sitting room with the casket. Tried sleeping sitting up on the couch there but only got a half an hour in. He didn't sleep well, little there was of it. Of course she made no noises. Now that's a terrible joke. It's not a joke. He means, it wasn't meant as one and he doesn't know why he said it or what it is. It just came out. Out of his head, if that's possible. He said it seriously. Said it in his head, he's saying. He made noises, though. Not while he was sleeping, he means, though he could have. Things like "Oh my dear . . . My darling . . . Oh my gosh . . . " Not noises really. Just things he said aloud once everyone was gone. He didn't cry, though. Doesn't know why. He can't say he did all his crying in the hospital after she died or over the last two days or three. Memories flooded through him like crazy in the sitting room. He'd think some of these would have started his crying, but they didn't. So leave it at that, for who can explain such things and why does he think they need explaining anyway? And while he slept, that half an hour, he also saw her doing things she'd done before she got sick, so maybe he wasn't even sleeping then. Early next morning—meaning, this morning, morning of this day, which is still amazing to him; really, still—he went to a nearby restaurant for a coffee and a muffin. Then, back at the home, he asked one of the funeral directors if they provided toothbrushes and toothpaste. He suspected they did, for the people who stayed overnight, just as he suspected enough people stayed the night beside the caskets to warrant the home getting a large supply of toothbrushes and toothpaste, and he was right. He wanted his mouth to smell clean. He didn't want to make the funeral any worse for guests who had to go through what they felt they had to with him, kissing, hugging, getting their faces close. And he only had the muffin because his stomach was growling and he didn't want to make noises during the service. Then he went back to the sitting room, and after the casket was wheeled into the chapel, spoke a few minutes to the officiator about his wife: where and when she was born, names of her parents and sister, schools she attended and professions she had, facts like that, plus two or three things she used to do to entertain herself: books, classical music, cook—and at eleven or so . . . actually, the funeral was scheduled to start at 11:15 and it did, on the dot. He yawned through a lot of it, at one point during the officiator's long opening remarks, found himself falling asleep, but everyone must have known why or could guess.

Now he'll sleep though, for real. He's home, whole thing's over. House is his; paper's his also. He doesn't, he means, have to divide it up every morning as he used to do before she got very sick or read the everything-but section when she couldn't sit up in bed, nor from now on think of moving to another room because of the noises she makes. He'll buy half as much food now. Well, he's been doing that for months. "You've got to eat something," he used to say, "you've got to—please, if only for me. . . . Well, if you can't, you can't, what can we do?" Won't buy milk because he doesn't drink it; she did, at the end, by the spoonful, or tried to, so most of the quarts he bought went to waste. He won't buy lots of things, and he'll throw away lots too. All her clothes; he means he'll give them away. Her catalogs. She had a few hundred of them, and they'll be coming three a day maybe for the next year or two; maybe until he moves. He didn't want to tell the officiator that reading through catalogs was another of her great pleasures; it just wasn't something he wanted said. "In the end they paid off, didn't they?" she said. "It's much easier ordering by phone than trying to get me to a store." Made sense; he never argued it didn't. If he had any complaint it was she had several boxes of them in the bedroom in addition to all her medical things, so there was little space for him to maneuver around in the dark or anytime wheel her out of the room. A couple of chairs she liked and he didn't—out. Lamp he hated, some things on the walls, and of course all those medical supplies. He won't feed the birds the way she did, filling up feeders every third day and the last three months having him do it, so they'll go too but on their own. He also won't take care of her fruit trees and flower beds. He'll mow the grass only when it's absolutely necessary and water around a little if the grounds look particularly dry, but that's about it. Maybe in time he'll get rid of the house too: sell it. Move into a small apartment. But right now, or soon, sleep. He held her in his arms and said "Now I can sleep," or one of the others. Held her up, in a sitting position, as he said. He did what he could, took care of her fairly well, did his best, is what he's saying, and that's something—nobody could argue with that, not that anyone would, so why's he bringing it up? He cooked for her, dressed her, changed her bed every other day for months, sponge-bathed her daily, gave her shampoos the hard way, with her head lowered back into a basin, and sat behind her for thirty minutes holding the hair drier to her hair. "You know," he said, "if you cut your hair to just shoulder length, not that I want you to, it'd probably save me an hour's work a week." Took her out for air in her wheelchair. Took her to places, not just for strolls in the park or on the street—

STEPHEN DIXON / SLEEP

restaurants, coffee shops, public gardens, museums. Tried to make things interesting and normal for her. Got her books from libraries and bookstores, and when she could no longer read, books on tape. Who'll do their income taxes now? That'll be a problem when the time comes around for it, which is a month from now, since he has no head for figures and following written directions and he'd hate spending money on an accountant. Fed her when he had to be fed, made her fresh dishes every day though she ate very little of them, gave her injections, cleaned her up after each bowel movement, did a wash a day at least, sometimes pulled her in her wheelchair up ten steps, twenty, once to a party four flights up but thank goodness some of the guests helped him carry her in the chair downstairs. He did just about everything, he's saying, though he's not boasting, or doesn't think he is. Well, who's to boast to anyway? When he was at work he called her every hour. "How are things?" "Fine." "Feeling all right?" "Good as can be expected." "Anything wrong?" "No, I'm okay." "I shouldn't worry?" "Don't be silly." "You're feeling better then?" "Than what?" "I didn't mean that than, but the other one." "I'm feeling the same." "I'll leave here soon as I can." "Don't hurry for me." "But I want to." "So, good, I like having you home, and it does make things easier." "See ya, sweetheart." "Bye, dear." Oh, he's going to miss her. He won't be able to sleep. He shouldn't have cut out the obit. He should have kept the whole page with the date on top and then done something with it, not frame it, of course, then what? He should have gone to a friend's house for the night. How would that have helped? No, he wants to be here alone but he doesn't want to think of her, or as much as he's doing. "Go on, think of her, think of her, why not?" It's the drink. He shouldn't drink anymore today. It'll make him sad, it's making him sad, very sad, so be sad, what of it? Cry, bawl, pound the chair arms with his fists, he should do what he wants or just comes, so long as it isn't destructive. Destructive physically, is what he means. For he doesn't deserve it? The bawling and pounding, he's saying, and who's talking about "deserve"? And he doesn't need a drink. He's tired enough after almost no sleep for three days, and just because of the emotional thing of it he's gone through, to sleep straight for a day without drink. Drink will probably even get him up in a few hours with a stomach-ache or just to pee. And then keep him up when he want to sleep. He hasn't had enough to eat. It's okay, the drink feels good, paper on his lap feels good, he's not hungry—it all feels pretty good, in fact; suddenly he doesn't feel so sad. He did, but what's he going to do now? Sleep, what else? Long and hard, then wake up refreshed. It's going to be bad awhile, maybe a month, maybe half a year, maybe more—probably more. Well, that happens and should be expected. What's he mean by that? But start off right. Get to bed, out of your clothes, get under the covers, take the phone off the hook, and just sleep.

He goes into the bedroom. A long yawn—a good sign, the best. Undresses and gets under the covers. The curtains, and he gets up and closes them. Back in bed. "Close your eyes," he thinks. Why did he think that when he was holding her in the hospital, that thing about now he can sleep? There he was, sitting in the chair falling asleep, maybe he did fall asleep for a few minutes but what of it? and when he looked up she looked different. So, something abut her look. Wait a minute, he doesn't quite understand. He knew she'd died—that's it. Sensed it, rather—something about the frozenness of her face—and would have been surprised if he'd touched her and found she was alive. Went up to her. Felt her heart, temple, her wrist pulse. Pulled her eyelids back. She was dead, he thought, or maybe just in a deep coma. The deepest of comas, much deeper than the one she'd been in for the last day. The doctors had talked about a coma so deep it would seem to the layman's eyes she was dead. Did what they said for him to do if no doctor or nurse was in the room. Felt around her ankle where the pulse is. Her foot was cold. Other one, too. For the last half year they'd been cold, but now they were very cold.

STEPHEN DIXON / SLEEP

She was dead. No, there were other things to do, the doctors had said. Put his ear to her mouth, then to her nostrils. Felt her heart, temple, and wrist pulse again and also her neck's, he'd forgotten to feel her neck's. She was dead, that's all, he was sure of it, there was nothing about her that showed any life. The pin, he remembered one of the doctors saying, and he got it off her side table and pricked the bottom of her foot. No response. Other foot. Nothing. Several fingertips. Same thing. That was it. She was lifeless, dead, what else could she be? "Oh no," he said. Aloud, definitely, remembers it clearly. And lifted her up and held her to his chest, her chest against his, her face someplace and same with his, his arms around her, and he closed his eyes, he thinks, and thought "Now I can get to sleep." "Some sleep"? "Sleep better"? "Tonight I can"? Something like that. Not necessarily one of those. But how odd. Well, it's inexcusable—excusable, he means. For he didn't think "Good, she's dead, now I can sleep." In a way, though, he felt it, about her being dead. All she'd gone through. It was good she didn't suffer like some people with her illness do. Suffer at the end, he means. She just stopped breathing. In a coma for a day or so and then just went. And he thought something about his future sleep soon after. Is he a bastard for having thought that? Of course not. He did his best, as he said. Did what he could for her, and for years. And just think of his state of mind at that exact time. The poor dear—she. He could never sleep, never sleep, maybe never again. That's ridiculous, but he won't sleep well or at all for a while, that's for sure. The phone rings. Forgot to leave the receiver off the hook, or just pull the plug out of the jack. It rings and rings, and he gets up and goes to it and lifts the receiver. "Yes?" he says. "My darling, I'm here. Where have you been, why don't you come see me?" "It's you," he says. "This is wonderful, a miracle, everything I wanted, you can't believe how great I feel. I'll be right there wherever you are." She sounds so healthy too. But he knows he's already asleep.

STEPHEN DIXON / SLEEP